On Her Watch

ALSO IN THE DON'T TELL SERIES

In His Command

On Her Watch

RIE WARREN

A Don't Tell Novel

FOREVER
YOURS

New York Boston

Forever Yours

Hachette Book Group

237 Park Avenue, New York, NY 10017

Hachettebookgroup.com

Twitter.com/foreverromance

First ebook and print on demand edition: June 2014

Forever Yours is an imprint of Grand Central Publishing.

The Forever Yours name and logo are trademarks of Hachette Book Group, Inc.

The publisher is not responsible for websites (or their content) that are not owned by the publisher.

The Hachette Speakers Bureau provides a wide range of authors for speaking events. To find out more, go to www.hachettespeakersbureau.com or call (866) 376-6591.

ISBN 978-1-4555-7415-5 (ebook edition)

ISBN 978-1-4555-7517-6 (print on demand edition)

Acknowledgments

Many, many thanks to my readers and friends who fell in love with "Big Man" Cannon and "Blondie" in *In His Command*. I hope you enjoy Liz and Linc just as much! Much appreciation goes to my editor, Latoya Smith, for bringing all the different layers of this project together and for keeping me on point—sometimes I tend to get a little carried away.

As always, I must thank Gillian Littlehale. She's been with me through every novel from start to finish and long before that as my beta and friend. I have an incredible group of supporters and critique partners who rally around me through the good, bad, and of course, the crazy. Jenna Barton, Christine Cox, April Gasaway, Rowan Moon, and Tracey Porcher, y'all are the bomb! Special thanks to Ron McAuley for his help with weapons and military tactics.

I couldn't do this without the love of my husband, my beautiful daughters, and my parents. They put up with me when I stay up way too late writing and let me sleep in so I can start it all again the next day.

On Her Watch

Chapter One

"Liz Grant, are you the daughter of Robie Grant?"

I held the polished doorknob in my hand, straining to see the young trooper's eyes hidden beneath the low brim of his cap. I nodded, my heartbeat knocking around inside my chest.

"Your father, First Class Medical Officer and Chief Geneticist Robie Grant, is dead." He sped through the details of a gruesome killing at the hands of Nomads, speaking like an automaton, no emotion on his face, no inflection in his voice.

I stared at the badge on his chest until my vision swam and what was left of my heart sank to my knees, knees that buckled. The gleaming metal of his insignia winked when he turned toward the corridor. I stood in the open doorway, watching his retreat, tears spilling down my face.

"Lizbeth?" Mom called from behind me.

Bending in two, I retched, shoving an arm out to ward her off as her cautious footsteps came closer.

"Lizbeth?" She hurried forward, pulling my face around. "Lizbeth, what's happened?"

Vomit stained the carpet, curdled under my tongue. I spoke the words I never thought we'd hear. "Dad's gone."

"Your father's—" She was a tall woman with black hair, so elegant and refined she could sweet-talk any Company stuffed suit. Mom backed away from me, her hand shaking, her finger pointing. "Don't you dare say that."

"Mom?" I rose to my feet, and my stomach heaved again. "Mom!"

Stopping halfway down the hallway, she crumpled to the floor, wails breaking from her as she beat her head against the wall. "No, no, no, no. He said we'd be safe! He said he'd make sure. Rob told me not to worry."

I crawled to her, sliding her head into my lap, my world falling apart with each of her fragmented cries. "Mommy?"

February, 2071, Chitamauga Commune

Jesus and Christ! A litany of swears sped past my lips as I jumped off the bed, hefting one of my Desert Eagles in a shaky grip. The sensation of all-seeing eyes watching my every move didn't stop just because I was in the Freelanders' Chitamauga Commune, somewhat safe from immediate danger. Scanning the moon-saturated surrounds of the caravan and coming up clear, I put the safety on, rubbing the barrel against my cheek. My thin top clung to me, and perspiration slid in icy trickles between my breasts, brought on by the habitual nightmare of my dad's slaughter.

I was a hard-ass. The Revolution, the deaths I'd witnessed, and the kills I'd caused, not even the Company itself—with its aggressive worldwide lockdown on so-called aberrant sexual behaviors—could break me. The only thing that terrorized me each and every night was my dad's murder. The blame had been placed on a Wilderness Nomad tribe—people we'd been brainwashed to believe were bloodthirsty savages. I didn't buy that particular feed anymore either, not after I'd ended up in Chitamauga, where the people had proved themselves to be exactly what they purported: Freelanders, not vicious, ignorant Nomads.

I lay down on the bed, snuggling my pair of pistols under a pillow. They were the only nighttime comfort I had. I kept my hand on the butt of a gun instead of the sweet bottom of a petite blond spy who'd become my playful pastime and a fond friend far too quickly for my liking. The smile gathered from remembrances of Farrow was replaced by a grimace when I shut my eyes, thoughts of my father spinning back to me.

Sleep off the roster for a second night running, I tossed the pillow aside and lit one of the old-fashioned lanterns, its warm glow nothing like the cool halos powered by Territory electricity. I ripped several pages from some ledger Farrow had left behind and located a stilo-pen. After my dad's death, I'd ransacked the condo searching for his personal digi-diary, coming up empty. This was one connection I still had with him. Distilling my thoughts and fears into mere words on a page I'd later destroy meant I didn't have to truly face them. Some hard-ass I was, all right. I gave a dry laugh and set the pen to paper, scribbling quickly.

Heading up to Beta in a couple days. My mind hasn't been on straight since finding out about the cover-up on Dad. Eleven years and it feels like yesterday I answered that knock on the door in Beta. I expected a mandatory quarantine order because of the spread of the Gay Plague or another CO soiree invite for my folks. Judging from the sharpness of the knock, I should've known it was neither. The young trooper outside carried himself with an air of authority that belied his age. The cap he wore shaded his eyes from view until he pushed it up, revealing scathing snapdragon-blue irises.

Looking down at the paper clenched in my hand, I saw the wet blotch of a tear making an even bigger mess of my words. That my father had been sent into the field should've been my first tip-off something wasn't right with the bullshit palaver my mom and I had been force-fed. He was high ranking and a scientist, not a frontline medic. But I'd been only eighteen at the time, and watching my mom fall to pieces with the news hadn't left me with a whole lot of thinking space.

The Company, the CO—the Cunts—remain oppressive to the core. Pumping us with a dawn-to-dusk spin for the good of mankind during day-long doses of pro-CO promos filtered in on our handheld, government issued Data-Paks for two generations running. The thing is, I used to believe in them. It was how I'd been raised, all I'd had left. Now I feel sick about all I've done to keep them in power. This regime with their so-simple manifesto: Maintain order, recoup the InterNations population, and execute anyone who stands in the way of their brainless Breeder politics.

Maintain order; that's one thing I'm good at.

Too bad for the CO, a few million civilians teamed up with a massive wave of Freelanders from every InterNations Territory and the surrounding pockets of Wilderness to finally lay some beat-ass on their homophobic, hate-filled regime.

Too bad for them, but good for me, for us. I'd finally done the right thing, something I could be proud of, and I hoped my dad would've been, too. I'd dropped my first lieutenant rank and dropped out altogether from the Corps—the military branch of the CO. I'd skipped off their grid, joining up with the Revolution that had begun only seven months ago.

Blindly searching the bed where Farrow usually slept, I flattened my palm to nothing but a bunched-up pillow. She'd left two days ago, a spook for the Revolutionaries and the best babe around, care of her CO connections and the way she made me come, fingertips traipsing over my clit, her puckered lips slipping up and down my slit. My body pulsed with memories, far better memories than deaths dropped on my doorstep or bullet holes I'd plugged into possibly innocent tangos on both sides of the war. I should've been worried about Farrow, but she could take care of herself and so could I.

Shaking my head, I started writing again.

I've been taking care of myself since the minute that knock sounded on our door. Took care of myself in other ways, too, hardly lingering over a handful of infrequent lovers. All of them military men until Farrow. <u>Hitting It and Heading Out</u>: a little insider Corps motto, and we're not just talking about sorties.

Being with those men had been about the need for release. With Farrow I'd been looking for a connection, reaching for something I'd lost along the way. My first affair with a woman and probably my last, since I'd figured I was incomplete in a way even she hadn't satisfied. I'd never had the time or wherewithal to explore my femininity, my sexuality, and Farrow's nightlong erotic escapades hadn't filled that aching hole.

Jesus, if Cannon could see me now. I remember one afternoon in Alpha, the two of us sitting side by side on the pavement, tinkering with our motorcycles, spending silent hours on the endless maintenance he called "twat to tit." He popped me on the shoulder. "Beats journaling, right?" Because we'd never be caught dead doing that. I came back with, "Maybe, but not as good as getting laid." He turned so red, for a minute I thought he took my remark as a come-on. Nah, I was only digging for a little truth about the commander, even back then.

Ah, fuck this. Maybe I should blame my mental mastur-bation on him. Cannon's infected me with his lovefest. It's no joke he and Nate go at it like rabbits. I knew about his ille-gal activities long before he made a clean cut from the Corps, but I never let on until he gave me the send-off last September. Pulled from his duties as commander of the Elite Tactical Unit in Alpha, he was ordered to escort Nathaniel Rice, the Company head of technological acquisitions, to the Outpost. He didn't deny my suggestions then, but he didn't affirm them either.

I pressed the slim stilo against my temple as I had the barrel of my gun earlier. A grin tugged my lips. Cannon would murder me if he ever read this.

Nathaniel Rice, known to his lover as Blondie…I'm not even calling him Nate anymore, preferring "Cannon's Fuck Bunny." He's proven himself a worthy asset in the Revolution and the mastermind behind it. Cannon's love for Blondie makes sense. He never had any women around, just his boyfriend, the Fist. It doesn't matter to me which way he swings his club. But I wish they'd left their caravan—called the Love Hovel by Cannon, me, and everyone else within hearing distance—in its honeymoon position on the edge of the Chitamauga meadow, because Blondie the Fuck Bunny is a screamer.

Eyeing the pages in my hand, I placed the stilo on a stand beside the bed. The potbellied woodstove in the corner burped out faint gusts of smoke as fire ate through wood, warming the one-room caravan. The small door whined when I opened it, ash blazing blue. I shoved in the papers, waiting for the edges to curl and combust. I burned the evidence of my late-night weakness. Leave no trail behind.

My head slightly clearer, I returned to bed. I checked my rounds, hilled a few quilts to buffer my body, and closed my eyes. This lying-low-and-hiding-out gig had gotten old. It wasn't my style. I had some work to do, in the name of freedom…and for my father.

* * *

Leaving my caravan behind the next morning, I hastened through the snowy network of the wagoneer neighborhood. The caravan itself was another surprise I liked more than I cared to admit. Its brightly patterned fabrics put me in mind of the Alpha digs I'd filled with colorful, luxurious black-market finds—works of art, books that were banned. The feminine touches had been more than decorations to me. They'd been cherished treasures speaking to a side of myself I kept hidden from all others, except for that nosy son of a bitch Cannon.

Once freed of the forest, I crossed onto the commune's main street. Snow crunched beneath my high-laced boots as I secured my Corps cap to my head. I passed the mess hall, the trade stands, and the schoolhouse. Inside every silver-wooded structure, fires blazed and men, women, children, and animals milled about, working off the winter's cold in this thriving back-to-the-earth community.

The usual undaunted mutt hightailed it after me. His owner's gray, bleak face and growly voice was the same as his dog's when he snapped an order to the mongrel and a slightly less irate *G'mornin'* to me.

Brought up a Corps brat, I preferred the war room—aka the meeting hall—to the women's hour that took place every morning, noon, and night within the open-air kitchens. Stepping into the town hall proper, I was greeted by a round table filled by the usual group of down-home councilors, including Hills, Hatch, Darke, Eden, and Fuck Bunnies one and two.

Maps were splayed on the table, real paper things we could touch and handle. Before exploring the commune's well-maintained archives, I'd never seen a nondigital representation of the Territories, thanks to the CO destroying our history and replacing it with neat and tidy readouts easily digested from our D-Ps. Around the table, Hills and Eden carried on a murmured conversation while Nate winked at me and Cannon perfected his fear-inducing glare from deep brown eyes. It was one day before I was to depart for Beta Territory and he wasn't happy. Surprise.

Cannon's finger struck the green landmass at the upper-right quadrant of the InterNations map of the former United States, an area just outside Beta. Beta used to be the home of someplace called Wall Street; now it was just another walled Territory like all the rest.

He didn't even wait for me to take a seat before high-handing me. "Tell me what happened again."

Fuck. I mutely went about making myself a cup of coffee from the fixings in the center of the table, ignoring the hulking giant across from me.

"I won't stand for your insubordination, Grant." Cannon addressed me with a growl in his voice.

Holy hell. Clearly someone woke up on the wrong side of the caravan this morning.

"I don't think you have the brass to tell me what to do anymore, Caspar." Smiling sweetly, I took him down a notch by refusing to address him as *Commander*, *Cannon*, or *sir*. I loved Caspar Cannon like a brother, but sometimes he needed to be slapped, and Nate was probably too soft on him to do it.

Leader of the commune's well-organized militia, Darke matched Cannon's size kilo for kilo and came in a couple years older at an even thirty. From down the table, he didn't seem too fond of listening to us spar. "Now, I know you two don't need to fuck it out—pardon me, Miss Eden." He apologized to the fair-haired healer, Nate's mom. "You need a fighter's ring to square your pube hairs away; we can sort that out right quick. I'm sure Micah would be more than happy to call our people in from the fields for a little Corps entertainment this morning."

I guessed he'd rather watch us duke it out.

"Jesus." Cannon pressed his knuckles to his temples.

"Christ." I sank into the last open chair.

We grinned at each other.

"I'm not shitting you, Liz," Cannon said as his grin evaporated.

"I know. I get it. Have my back, I'll have yours. I just didn't think you'd be riding my ass the whole way, too." Mug of hot coffee in hand, I took a sip before launching for the umpteenth time into an abbreviated version of what went down during my evacuee-escort detail from Alpha to Beta at the outbreak of the Revolution.

Shepherding a ragtag group of refugees north with winter approaching, we'd gotten close to the mountainous Catskills commune outside of Beta. We'd been halted on the road when our trucks were ambushed by their Freelanders. Bullets had tin-canned the transports. Pinning us down on all sides, they made sure our return fire was useless. Within minutes, we were overtaken. Held captive by the people I believed killed my dad, I'd lost my lid—shouting, biting, punching. Begging, pleading, asking for the truth. Eventually, I got my answers, and they weren't what I'd expected. No one had heard of Robie Grant, and none had recalled a murder of that magnitude. He hadn't been sent to the front. It was all a wash job.

I peered around the table. "Not a single one of them was lying. I've been lied to enough that I can smell it a kilometer away."

Taking a long drink of coffee, I swallowed down the anger and sadness that had been my constant buddies for more than a decade. "They let us go. I thought it was damned foolhardy. But they were Freelanders. What are you gonna do, huh?"

Long ears peeping through clouds of white hair, Hills imparted a nugget of his wisdom. "We don't believe in taking innocent lives."

"Should've told them that before they opened fire in the first place. Besides, no one's innocent in a war." That included me.

Cannon's voice echoed around the room. "You could've taken a bullet."

"I'd take a rain of them to know the truth."

"Liz."

"Cannon." I grasped his hand. I knew he thought I was headed on a reckless mission. "For once, don't be a pigheaded shitheel."

Nate took his hand from me, clasping Cannon's white knuckles in a gentle hold. "What happened then, Lizbeth?"

Lizbeth was the name only my mother and father had called me before him…and Farrow. I sat back, letting a grin slide across my mouth. "Then your friend Farrow showed up, right about the time we were approaching Beta, when I was pretty damn sure I'd be put into action for your brother, Linc, and his Beta Corps. That was a close one. I thought I'd have to kill Revolutionaries and Nomads—Freelanders—whose vision I was starting to share." I nodded to Cannon. "The rest is good as Old History, sir."

Cannon was no longer officially my commander, not after blowing his cover sky-high about his sexuality, which was as good as a death sentence in the eyes of the CO. But old habits die hard.

Nate turned to Hatch, the resident inventor who monitored transmissions to the commune. "Any word from Farrow?"

"Not yet. It's too early," he replied.

Farrow was a family friend to Nate and his estranged brother, Linc, working all sides of this FUBAR situation with a feminine aplomb no one could pull off but her. She was to be my eyes and ears once I reached Beta. "My rendezvous is set up with her anyway."

Cannon snorted.

"You got a problem over there?" I asked.

"Yeah, I've got a problem. In fact, I have issues with the whole stinking thing. For starters, I don't see how a forty-five-kilo woman is gonna keep you walking the straight and narrow."

I gave a snort of my own. "I'm surprised you'd know anything about being straight, lover boy." Cannon blushed, making his hard and handsome visage appear sweet and boyish. I plowed on before he could stutter his way through his only vulnerability…Nate. "She's not tasked with being my damn babysitter."

Cannon's face cooled with his tone. "Someone needs to keep a leash on you."

My sidelong smirk slid to Darke. "The only one who'd know about the proper way to handle a leash is Darke. Let's leave that to him and Leon."

That was a direct hit, too. The brawny man's crush on Leon was as obvious as the telltale russet flush under his smooth brown skin. I couldn't even make another quip about their flirtation because his longing for the pretty-faced, twenty-year-old street hustler and his self-enforced denial was too painful to be comical. The man had lost his two life partners last autumn, casualties of this brutal war. I could only assume Darke had willfully decided not to put his heart on the line again, although it looked like he wasn't being too successful with his emotional lockdown.

A few days before Farrow had left, Leon moseyed up to us, saying he was ready to sign on and join us in Beta. The sweet, sexy boy was getting his heart beat up and broken every day from Darke's hot-and-cold emotions.

I figured that wouldn't go down well between the overprotective pair of Darke and Cannon, both of whom had a vested interest in Leon, but I listened with mild amusement as he tried to con his way into our operation. Idling on the edges of our discussion, Darke appeared not to be listening, but his big shoulders had turned rigid as rock.

Farrow had smiled gently at Leon. "You're gonna have to let me think about this now, Leon, but you might-could prove useful." I had to agree. The kid was wily as hell as well as easy on the eyes. "Ah reckon you'd be good company for mah brother."

That comment had sparked Darke into action. He'd pulled Leon away from us, parked him against one of the outbuildings, and proceeded to kiss him with such heat, his hands running along Leon's lean waist to settle on his hips, it was a wonder the building didn't go up in flames. We'd walked away when Leon arched into the embrace, his loud groan carrying across to us.

Now, as then, Darke mumbled a few excuses and strode out of the meeting hall. Tipping my chair back, I looked out the window and, sure enough, he'd snagged Leon by the hand and was leading him down the dirt road.

Hills tugged on one of his long earlobes and cleared his throat. "Let's talk strategy."

I didn't know what the old goat knew about strategy, but I'd go with it. "We're planning a three-prong, long-term attack."

Nate pulled his chair forward. "Infiltration first."

"I've got that covered. Then I need to dig out the missing intel on my father, convince Linc to give up everything he's ever worked to attain, and take Beta down." All without letting on that I knew Beta Commander Linc Cutler's identical twin and his mother closely, or that I was on friendly terms with the Freelanders and was a Revolution sympathizer. In the civil war of the

Rice/Cutler family, Linc had followed in his notorious father's footsteps while Nate had finally freed himself from that man's reins to return to his mother's roots.

I couldn't let any cracks show from the time I landed in Beta to the time I left, hopefully in a blaze of glory instead of with my carcass carried out in a body bag.

I decided to play it down even more when Cannon's glower re-formed on his face. He didn't need to know that I was feeling a few nerves, or that I hadn't been sleeping, or that I was scared the truth would turn out to be uglier than the lies I'd been eating all these years.

I was a soldier, after all.

"Just a day in the life, Big Papa." I played his familiar line about our messed-up situation back at him.

Fist pounding the table in front of him, Cannon got ready to let loose when Eden cut in. "I want Lincoln out of there."

I joined Cannon in grumbling under my breath while I thought, *No added pressure or anything.*

Rubbing his mom's hand for a moment, Nate swiveled to his man. He calmed the beast with a few quiet words and a quick brush of his lips, and Cannon's shoulders relaxed from their punched-up place near his ears.

Brushing his finger along Nate's jaw, Cannon whispered, "I know, baby."

Their apparent affection for each other would've given me an-other round of the sweats, except, if any two people deserved to be together, in love, it was them. They'd been through hell and back a few more times than anyone warranted. Hounded on their trek from Alpha to the Outpost bunker, working through attraction, suspicion, sabotage, betrayal—you name it—just to end up with Cannon being arrested for wanton corruption of a Company officer. Not to mention finding out Nate was Alpha CEO Cutler's son must've been a big kick to Cannon's nuts.

But they'd come through it.

Aside from his blatant snit about my self-imposed assignment, I'd never seen Cannon so happy. A day in the life was never gonna be the same for him; nor should it be. He'd found contentment, joy. Hell, seeing Cannon like this made me wonder just how much pain he'd been in, hiding his sexuality all those years and fighting to maintain rigid laws that went against his very nature. It also made me wonder what I was missing out on. After my mom committed suicide, the Corps and Cannon had become my family by choice. I'd since given up on one and watched another move on while my past was littered with those hitting-it-hard hookups. I envied Cannon and Nate's intimacy, craving companionship born of enduring emotion.

But thinking was for pussies, and I wasn't one of those, even if I had one.

Cannon jerked his seat back from the table to loom over me. "It's too risky."

I stood up, too, forcing him back a step. "You've made your objections clear, sir." I tacked on the *sir* just to placate his stubborn ass. No way in hell would I let Cannon risk his life fielding this operation. He had too much at stake. Unlike him, I didn't have anyone waiting up for me at the end of the day, so it made perfect sense to go in alone.

"Fuck's sake, Liz. You're going in there with your balls hanging out."

I looked down my body and back up his. "Good to know you think Linc will be more distracted by my hard-core gonads than by my feminine charms." Charms I'd only just discovered.

Commander Linc Cutler was my starting point in Beta, my only link to the Corps. I hoped to get close enough to either him or his father, CEO Cunt Cutler, to hack into their high-clearance D-Ps, where I could search out info on my dad and the InterNations plans for the Revolution. *Linc, well, his name is fitting, anyway. He just doesn't know it yet.*

Letting me pass before him out of the building with a wry twist of his lips, half fond smile and half simmering sneer, Cannon caught up to me in two strides. We walked down the single road cutting through Chitamauga Commune side by side, falling into an easy march. Just like old times.

It was cold as a bitch out here, and Cannon's ears, nose, and cheeks quickly turned pink. The Freelanders were preparing for their midday meal in the mess hall, and we stepped to. It was a large, brightly lit wooden structure with long tables sided by benches, where all the families and newcomers, refugees and Revolutionary stragglers, ate together. Most mealtimes were so noisy with chatter and laughter it was hard to hear myself think, which was always a good thing.

Ambling on, Cannon asked, "Getting an early start in the morning?"

"Sure as the cock crows." I winked at him.

He barked out a laugh before getting his serious face on again. "Blondie and I are flanking you, at least part of the way."

I started to interrupt when he pulled me into his arms. Through his strong embrace I felt him shaking. A giant tower of power and strength, he'd always been my steadfast comrade. Now I was getting ready to go it solo.

"Caspar."

"Keep that damn mouth shut and let me hug you for once." His gruff voice ruffled the short tufts of my black hair.

Surprised by the suddenness of his emotion, I felt tears burning the back of my throat.

He leaned back and attempted a grin. "There. Now when Blondie and I have to turn you loose, no good-byes."

"No good-byes, Caspar." I kissed his cheek and spun away.

* * *

Still in the grip of winter, March's icy wind ripped through my flak jacket, eating through any warmth the torn material had afforded me. I'd made it through Beta's four-meter-high walls fortified by bayonet-sharp razor wire, sneaking in through the east gate. Farrow had promised it would be open. I owed her flowers or something when this was all over.

The northeastern gale howling in my ears, I'd hustled to Sector One without any mishap. This was one time I was thankful for the Company's strict adherence to homogeneity. Each of the sixteen InterNations Territories was gridded the same, so I didn't need my decommissioned D-P's navigation system to lead the way. I'd lived here before, too, and not much had changed except from the destructive forces of war. The poorer sectors hugged the outskirts so the select didn't have to hobnob with the poverty-stricken citizens. Closer into City Center and the Quadrangle—the heart of operations—tenements transformed into shiny high-rises and affluent businesses.

I'd gone rogue, been reported MIA, and was presumably wanted. Now I was getting ready to walk back into a Corps stronghold. Maybe I am a little reckless.

Clusters of soldiers roved the streets like packs of hungry dogs. It seemed like the curfew was well in effect and the fighting held at bay, at least on this night, but the ragged war-torn evidence was everywhere. Rubble lining formerly pristine streets, buildings with blast holes, and armies of tanks screamed the Revolution was alive and well. On the other hand, the barred gates, the impenetrable fortress of the Quad, the watchtowers, and giant building-wide Data-Paks spewing the latest CO promos all looked like an unstoppable iron fist.

After the commune with its colorful glory even in the dead of winter, with its celebration of life even when they'd suffered harsh losses of their own, Beta was freezing cold, not just because of the minus-zero temperature. I might've been raised a city girl, but I'd been shaken and taken by the Freelanders ideas. I'd never be the same.

Keeping my head down, I fell in step with a patrol. I laughed along when they traded jokes about the shit-smelling wildling Nomads and too-dumb-to-fuck Revolutionary rejects. I didn't let my hands shake or my shoulders stoop, thankful they must've

thought my less-than-stellar uniform was due to a hard day slog-
ging it out on the warfront. I'd spent most of my career learning
how to blend in and stay off the radar, shining only in my role as
first lieutenant.

Anonymity was second nature, but damn, I was feeling
twitchy.

It'd taken two weeks to cross the Wilderness—land left to
Mother Nature's hands and husbanded to fresh fertility by the
Freelanders—from Chitamauga, located in the lower Appalachi-
ans, to this northeastern colony. We'd deviated from Alpha-Beta
Route Two, and it would've taken a lot longer had it not been for
the bitchin' snowmobiles Farrow had delivered for me, Cannon,
and Nate, thanks to her family's scrip, which she siphoned off to
help fund the insurgency. That ride was as sweet as my motorcy-
cle left behind months ago in Alpha.

Seemed I'd left just about everything by the wayside since this
war started, perhaps long before that. Family, friends, thoughts of
a fulfilling life…

Caspar Cannon. True to his word, he and Nate had kept pace
with me, our snowmobiles running on fancy fuel cells only the
elite could afford. Turning back three days ago, Cannon had
maintained his *no good-byes* policy while Nate gripped me in a
long hug.

"I want you to know, Lizbeth, you're not obligated to bring my
brother back."

"Nate, I'll—"

His gentle drawl quieted me. "Hush up, now. You have a mission of your own and a duty to the Revolution. If anythin' hap-

pens, you make sure to get yourself out. You are priority number one, darlin.'"

"Fuck."

"Now, now, none of that language. You know what my momma would say." He'd swiped a tear clinging to my cheek before Cannon could see it.

"Take care of that big bastard for me, will you?" I'd asked.

He'd nodded and stepped back, linking hands with his husband, whose somber features were too familiar for me to look at. I'd raised my hand, a salute Cannon and I shared, before speeding away through the snowy nation.

The commune—Nate, Cannon, and Darke—had become Central Ops for the entire Revolution, but only Darke could answer my call for help henceforth. Cannon and Nate had been branded enemy number one. They'd be killed on sight. In addition to the cool warrior who would be my point man when shit got ugly in Beta, I had Farrow as my liaison to the commune and the other side of the war, because I was about to go deep cover. My rendezvous with the woman was scheduled for tomorrow night. I was cutting it close, especially if Commander Cutler decided to stick me in the brig for being AWOL. I had to make sure he bought my story.

By now I was downright itchy.

The double-reinforced steel gate in the sky-high barricade of the Quad opened before me and the other soldiers. My pulse pounded as I squared off with the four cornerstone buildings where InterNations business was beaten out: Company HQ, the hospital, the Tribunal—home to RACE, Repopulation and Civilization Enforcement, the court, jail, and killing grounds for those who committed homosexual crimes—and my former home away from home, Corps Command.

Walking into another one of CEO Lysander Cutler's lion's dens, the flat titanium heels of my lace-ups rang on the polished marble floor. My cap was in place if a little filthy. I kept an unemotional mask on my bruised face. The latest swellings were caused by my own fist a day ago. I had a survivor's role to play, and I aimed to make good. I canvassed Beta Corps Command, waiting for my retinal scan from the outer doors to send up the expected alarms. Wearing a shredded uniform more dirty than dark blue, my first lieutenant insignia smudged and hanging off the breast of my shirt, I looked like I'd had an orgy with about a dozen dynamite sticks.

I'd figured the surest way to get Commander Cutler's attention was to serve myself up. It might not have been the smartest move in my arsenal, but I waited for my latest date with disaster without a nervous tic on my body.

Not until the rapid-blast guns—pathetic pieces of shit compared to my pair of Desert Eagles—of the five troopers I'd clocked lounging against the black pillars inside Command locked on my location. I strived not to flinch when their sights found me.

Gun muzzles met my temples, their cold barrels promising chambers of pain if I so much as twitched as I was marched wordlessly through the halls into a soundproof gymnasium. I knew immediately what the strategy was. Lock her up; then make her sing for her momma.

Steeling myself for the blows, I sucked in a breath as I was disarmed. The breath exhaled with a whoosh when the first fist hit my stomach. I doubled over, biting my lip. I was just stupid enough to stand tall, meeting the second and third knocks with my face.

With the unending lashings from five pairs of hands and boots, I didn't get a good look at my assailants. Their questions came on repeat, ringing in my ears with no rhyme or reason. What's your name, slut? You got a rank, soldier girl? Who are you *working for? Where have you been for four months?* My answer to every accusation was a gob of blood splatted at the closest beater-upper.

They obviously hadn't been trained in the fine art of interrogation by Commander Cutler, or if they had, it'd been a slapdash operation. But that didn't matter. A punch was still a punch. And that shit was starting to hurt.

Blinded by pain, I coughed into my hand. My guns were too far away to do any good. I braced myself against a wall, arms covering my head. Even I couldn't survive five-on-one.

Nearing the point of blacking out, I heard the door crash open. One tall wall of barely leashed man strode into the room. They all dropped their punching-bag fists before he said a single word while I gasped for one deep breath.

"Who gave you the order to interrogate this prisoner?"

"The c-command came from CEO Cutler, s-sir," the little rat bait with the truncheon fists stuttered.

"The CEO is not in charge of this or any other Corps operation. They fall under my jurisdiction." Crackling blue eyes leveled every rookie in the room until the smell of fresh sweat coming off his nervous soldiers joined the iron tang of my spilled blood. "Does it look like she was anywhere near snitching to you?"

The dumb nuts stupid enough to answer in the first place replied, "No, sir." His red hair was a total match for his red face.

"Where did you learn such sloppy tactics, soldier?" Sir asked. His back to me, shoulders stretching his uniform, he grilled his insubordinate.

When no answer came from any of the troops, Sir pivoted toward me. His jaw snapped as he scanned me top to bottom. I made sure the beat-ass didn't show in my precise military bearing, even though every tired, torn muscle cramped.

With his finger pointed in my face, he gazed around the room. He settled on the jar-faced dickhead who'd commandeered my beating.

"I didn't hear your answer, soldier." His words were drawn out like silk over the edge of a sword. He waited long enough for the trooper to start flapping his gums. Then, before he had a chance to get any more irate, he simply whipped out his fist, flattening the redheaded blunder boy.

He galvanized the rest of them with, "Have I been sent any other ninety-day wonders?"

"NO, COMMANDER, SIR!" went up the deep chorus.

Fucking Linc Cutler. I should've known it. I'd never seen anyone control a room of fuckwits like that except Cannon. I sized him up while he seemed to mull over whose ass to kick next.

He didn't look like Nate apart from their eyes, but Linc's were storm-ridden blue, not fresh as fucking flowers. And like a thunderstorm, his earlier look had hit me with lightning force. He was built slightly larger, a fresh shave clearing every single whisker that dared to appear on the straight line of his clenching jaw. His dark blond hair was shorter, his shoulders wider.

Linc's powerful presence caused a delicious spiral of heat between my legs, and beneath my ripped shirt, my nipples tightened. Thoughts of his big body against mine pressed the air from my lungs. My immediate attraction to him was unexpected, and worse, unsettling, as the sensual line of his mouth became a single neat slash while he watched my perusal. One eyebrow cocked—in interest or disdain, I couldn't tell. I inhaled silently and slowly, training my sights on my Eagles spun out across the floor.

"Good. Clean up this mess. And bring Lieutenant Grant to my office." Neither did Linc speak like Nate, whose southern patois was a soft and passionate song. He hadn't once raised his voice or broken a sweat.

And he sure as hell didn't worry about getting his hands dirty.

"Sir, yes, sir!"

Unimpressed by their late show of rank and file, he swept a steely appraisal over me a second time, springing a new leak in my formidable armor. This time it was derision paired with a hint of admiration, or maybe I was just headed for a concussion. Dizzies from getting my face punched in would be easier to brush off than feeling breathless and kneeless because Linc had found me interesting enough for a twice-over.

He kicked my twin Eagles to me, saying, "Make sure those stay on safety, and get her a goddamn clean uniform. She looks like someone pissed all over her welcome-home parade."

Stalking from the room, he jammed the elevator button, his gaze swinging to mine and holding for several pounding heart-beats before the doors closed between us.

Everything about him denoted coiled power, and I made no mistake about it: Commander Linc Cutler was a man made of deadly detachment. I got the distinct impression he was gonna blister my ass from one end of Beta to the other. If I thought Cannon was bad, Linc was about to introduce me to a brand-new level of suck.

I'd wanted to get his attention. Mission accomplished.

Chapter Two

Half an hour later, I wasn't quite knocking in my boots when I made my way to the elevators lining Corps Command's gleaming hall, my five armed guards down to four, care of Linc's quick strike. My face battered, nerves frazzled by the hyper awareness of my new commander's unconcealed strength, I was *slightly* shaken. My head was still screwed on tight enough to run a visual scan of my captors, cataloging their weaknesses, formulating a plan of escape I knew I wouldn't use.

The four grim-faced goons ushered me off the elevator at the top floor of Command, along a plush carpeted passageway, and into an office lacking any trimmings apart from a large desk. Live cams bolted into opposite corners of the room while a D-P screen on the wall spit its proregime, antirebel hate, and a tall man faced the slit of a window into the Quad below.

The troopers backed away from me, out of the office, closing the door behind them. I watched Linc, releasing a smile. His guards had left me fully armed and operational with my two babes, chrome Desert Eagle .44 mag dates from hell, holstered on my hips. Seeing him unarmed—hands pressed behind his back—made me think he might be as foolhardy as the Freelanders, but I doubted it.

I didn't have to doubt for long.

Sharp jaw, full lips, and his arrogant nose showed in profile when he calmly mentioned, "If you even think about going for your sidearms, you'll be dead before you make a move, Lieutenant Grant."

My gurgled laugh hurt my bruised ribs. "I might be willing to test that theory."

Movements fast and liquid, he came at me and cornered me under one of the cameras. Hands braced on either side of me, Linc's breath brushed across my temple. "You're in no position to test me, Liz."

Hot restraint rolled off him. Not a single muscle moved, from the breadth of his chest, held a scant space from my breasts, to his rugged shoulders, straining the seams of his shirt.

My gaze flashed to his, the burning blue brightness unraveling my protective shell. No man had ever affected me like this. My short fingernails tapped the holstered Eagles in warning. A warning that had no effect on Linc as his breath dragged deeper, filling out his chest until it came flush to mine.

I wanted to grab the soft-looking strands of blond hair falling behind his ears, drag him to my lips. I wanted to heft my gun and shoot a hole in the middle of his forehead.

I couldn't do either of those things. My hands were tied. Not because of his threat, but because this man controlled the entire

Beta Territory Corps. He was my lifeline to the information I needed. And I couldn't very well make him sing like a canary if I cut out his tongue to wear like a pretty little memento around my neck. Not to mention that would put an end to Miss Eden's hopes for her son's redemption.

He rolled away from me. "I see we understand each other." Straightening my shoulders, I kept my mouth shut. I remained as far away from him as possible. If he could disarm me with his presence so easily, I'd need to build a thick wall between us. "You cleaned up." At his desk, he glanced at me with the half-dismissive, half-appraising look.

Yeah, I splashed my face with some cold water, getting a good gander at my split lip and black eye. As usual, pretty as a picture. I'd hung my head under the stream of water in the sink, slowing my respiration, bringing my game back online. I'd joined the Corps because of my dad's death. I'd believed in every one of my missions. I'd given up everything I'd ever known to join the Revolution. *I am alone here.*

Sucking it up, I smart-assed Linc in reply. "As directed. I didn't think you'd want me bleeding out all over your carpet."

He grunted, giving nothing away. "You've been AWOL for almost four months, Grant."

I stood tall and silent as he assessed me, the new uniform tucked in as tight as my thoughts. There was nothing of Nate in Linc's appearance, identical twins or not. His hair was darker blond, shorter, and swept off his face in wayward waves. The sharp lines of his cheeks ran down to a sumptuous mouth he pinched tight as a sphincter he didn't want breached. A thin lick of a scar bisected his left eyebrow, and most likely he wore more wounds of war beneath his clothes.

"Did you really think you could take up assignment where you left off, with no punishment, no questions asked?" Long, strong fingers spanned his desktop. "I could cook you up for treason."

"I thought I'd kill some Nomads, just like I've always done, sir."

His jaw pulsed violently. "Your sterling reputation isn't enough to keep you out of the brig. Are you in collusion with Cannon? With my brother?"

"Your brother, sir?"

"Nathaniel Rice. The homosexual groomed to be Alpha's CEO before he took up with Cannon and they blew the Outpost and hundreds of superiors to smithereens."

His cavalier attitude toward his own brother and my friend grated on my nerves.

"The official word is they both died in the explosion, but I think you and I both know differently." He stepped closer. "Where have you been, *Lizbeth*?"

Lizbeth. He knew. He knew my past, my father. But he wouldn't find out my secrets or Nate and Cannon's whereabouts. "I lost track of Cannon in October. I was held hostage by the Nomads at Catskills."

"That so?" He removed my cap, calloused fingers pulling it gently free of my hair.

I pressed him back. "You think I liked my imprisonment? Have you tried on starvation, beating, interrogation for size lately?" Snapping the locks off my holsters, I laid both guns on his desk. "You can take my weapons. You can question my loyalty, but you can never understand torture like I have."

Linc lifted my chin, and I stared back at him as coolly as I could, willing myself not to recoil from the searing heat of his touch. "If you're asking where my allegiance lies, the Corps is my calling. *Regeneration, Veneration, Salvation.*" I recited the CO slogo like the robot I'd once been.

Linc's whisper glided to my ear, his proximity electrifying me. "What about *Live in Freedom, Love at Will*?"

"You think I'd believe that after what the Nomads did to me?"

"You're going to make me work to bring you down, aren't you, Lieutenant?" His lips hovered beside mine.

I didn't move, didn't shiver from his closeness. He held the answers to my father's death or at least knew where to find them, and that was all that mattered.

"Yeah, I am." I stepped back from him.

Linc sat on the edge of his desk, hitting me with an intense gaze. His drawl came out low and deep. "You got a status report?"

His intimate tone sent a flush to my system. "Beaten to shit, sir, but still breathing. Thanks for asking."

"Make sure you keep that up." He handed me my cap. Frowning when our fingers brushed, he pulled back quickly.

Maybe he was feeling the same conflicting emotions as me. Equal parts flaring attraction and natural distrust overwhelmed me. He watched me head to the door, gaze locked on my retreat. I wanted to shove a barrel down his throat and let it go. I wanted to rip his uniform off and take him in my hand, my mouth.

At the door, I halted. Dignified of manner, albeit dripping blood, I asked, "Am I dismissed?"

"Not quite." He came closer, his brief show of weakness once more concealed. Or maybe I'd imagined it because, Christ, looking into his now deadly eyes was the same as deep-throating the stock of a rifle. "Stoic woman, aren't you?"

"Comes with the territory."

"You might earn your stripes back yet, Prisoner Grant, depending on how you save face. You're going to have to prove your dedication."

When he slipped by me to open the door, I saluted the latest badass on the block. "Commander Cutler, sir!"

"Second Lieutenant." He saluted, a searing touch of his fingers on my breast relieving me of my badge.

"You mean First Lieutenant."

"You've been demoted."

Goddamn. And this was the man I needed to cozy up to? If I was attracted to assholes, how come Cannon had never done it for me?

I walked out the door, head high, not looking back.

* * *

Blowing into cupped hands, I stomped my boots, coaxing feeling back into my numb feet. Stinging spikes prickling my toes reminded me they weren't frostbitten yet. I paced back and forth in the gloomy alley behind the med center, pulling my visor low to hide my black-and-blue eye. The sliver of night sky above sparkled with stars, cold as gemstones.

A soldier slipped around the corner. I backed into the shadows, hunkering with distaste behind a wheelie bin of bone-cold bodies waiting for the morning's detail before they were incinerated. With the death toll from the war rising, there was no time for last rites or burial. No room either. Graveyards had already overflowed from the Purge and the Plague before. Though it was inconvenient for a career soldier, I was always uneasy around dead bodies.

Heels snapped on concrete, heading my way. I balled my fists, ready to lunge when the soldier stopped a half meter away. She let out a low, lusty laugh.

I punched to my feet and strolled into the open. "Nice togs, Farrow."

Maintaining connections with every faction, Farrow was a runner between Beta, the Revolution, the commune…and now me. She was my scout during this lonely vigil, no longer my lover. We both knew a hands-off policy was in effect as of now.

Perfectly pared fingernails brushed her Corps jacket. "Ah might just keep the uniform, Lizbeth."

Silky blond hair framing her sweetheart face, Farrow took one look at my battered mug and winced. Her fingers moved toward the cut on my bottom lip but stopped short. "Ah see you've made contact with Linc. He made a meal of that gorgeous face, girl."

One night after my gym-room punch-up, I was still contused. My dismissal from active duty had meant an inactive day of full debriefs while I recited lies. In Command Central, the glowing green D-Ps on the table spitting up-to-the-minute war stats, I'd sat surrounded by higher-ups. The sixteen near-identical Territory flags flapped on their poles against the bland walls. They were a silent reminder of my past dedication, my recent defection.

Commander Linc had sat back from the table. He waved away all the lie detector scanners, saying I'd likely beat the machines and he'd monitor the truth of my answers. Keeping up the sham was already exhausting. At the end of the day, I was glad to be escorted to the in-house barracks. The austere room with bunks against the wall bore no personal effects. I didn't need any more distractions. Linc Cutler was already under my skin, and he'd done nothing more than watch me, blank-faced, all day long.

Throughout the evening, explosions had rocked the floors, clattered the steel arms of the cots against the wall, making the halos flicker. The Revolution was here.

"Actually, he put a stop to my *interrogation*," I said to Farrow.

Why I blushed over that admission I had no idea, unless I was turning into pussy-pants Cannon all of a sudden. My fingertips hovered over my lips as if swollen from kisses, not bruised from fists…as if Linc had touched me.

Farrow swayed closer. "Oh, Ah see."

"See what?" Shoving my hands into my pockets, I frowned.

"Don't you worry none, sweet girl. This is gonna work out to our advantage."

"This?"

"You and Linc."

I scoffed. The only way Linc and I were happening was in a pistol-drawn standoff, not flaming-hot fraternization, as her impish grin implied.

"*Mm-hmm*. Those Rice men sure do have an effect." Green eyes glittered beneath the sweep of her hair.

"He's a Cutler, cut from the same cloth as is his father, not a Rice."

"Well, now, don't let that fool you. Ah've known both these boys since they were knee-high. Sometimes there are reasons for what we do, reasons no one else can understand until they break through the defenses. That's your job."

The stench of day-old corpses was as unnerving as her line of thinking. I stalked to the end of the alley, taking in clean air. I was pretty damn sure I didn't want to get in that deep with Linc even if he allowed it, which was unlikely.

I shot back, "I know Miss Eden wants her son back, but she shouldn't have abandoned him in the first place."

Farrow's cheeks lost their healthy blush. "Lysander Cutler abused her. He threatened her. He used her. He killed her daddy when he expropriated their land as surely as if he'd pulled the trigger, land that was finally put back to rights as Chitamauga Commune." Farrow's fair eyebrows scrolled together. "Lysander and Linc may be father and son, flesh and blood, but they are not one and the same."

With my silence hanging between us, she joined me at the far end of the deserted alley. "Speakin' of Daddy Cutler, he's taken control of Beta, Gamma, and Epsilon—all the remaining Continental Territories. He's campaignin' for the InterNations governments of the other twelve Territories, too. It's beginnin' to look like the Revolution is workin' in his favor for centralized leadership."

I wasn't surprised Cutler had staged his own internal coup, declaring martial law. If the Revolutionaries didn't win the war, any resemblance of governance provided by the InterNations agreement would be a thing of the past. The InterNations was laughable, but at least it was majority rules, committee driven. Sure, the majority was despotic, allowing for no new blood to enter the gene pool, but it looked like a picnic compared to One Rule by CEO Cutler.

"This just gets better and better."

Farrow brushed snow off her padded shoulders. "He'll want to tap into you."

"Who doesn't? He's had a big boner for me since Alpha days."

My D-P pinged in my pocket before she could answer. Digging it out, I turned my back on Farrow. The commander had handed it to me after my hours-long inquisition as a sick consolation prize or something, letting me know it was low-level clearance and, of course, had been fitted with a homing beacon set to locate me whenever he wanted. *Purely as an added insurance policy*, he'd said.

You're not in your quarters.

Guess who? Linc's message melted some of the cold encasing me, a fact I found fascinating and twisted, all because he'd checked in on me. Never mind the reason the levelheaded asshole was pinging me was because he still thought my story smelled rank.

No, sir. Checking up on your prisoner? I zinged back, ignoring Farrow, who watched over my shoulder.

Prisoners don't get walking privileges. Don't make me regret my leniency. Next time the tracking device will be implanted up your sweet backside.

Probably his boot tip, too. I read his thinly veiled animosity loud and clear across the wireless, but at least the commander thought I had a cute ass. *Jesus.*

I needed some air, sir.

Linc messaged: *You've been out long enough.*

Roger that. I'll be bedded down and halos out in five minutes

Three minutes and make sure of it, or I will.

I took note of Farrow chuckling at me while I expelled a curse over Linc's final message.

"Linc will have an assignment for you in two nights' time, somethin' that has little to do with your Corps trainin.'"

A pang of unease tanked the pit of my belly. I started to interrupt, but she hushed me. "Ah can't prepare you for it. Linc needs the element of surprise on his side, and your performance has to be genuine."

"My performance? This doesn't sound promising, Farrow."

"Go with it. And make him trust you as much as possible between now and then."

Fuck. Trust was the name of the game, and I probably wouldn't have too many chances to gain Linc's. "How'd you come by this info?" I asked.

"I'm not just a pretty face." She winked, slapping a compress she'd taken from inside her flak jacket into my palm.

"And I'm not a pretty face at all."

Her gaze roamed from my lips to my eyes, the color so dark they usually appeared black, lifting to the jagged ends of hair falling into my eyes. Farrow smiled wistfully. "You have no idea, sweet thing."

She retreated, and I held up the compress. "What's this?"

"A poultice, darlin'. It should do the trick fixin' up that precious face." She winked again, green eyes bright and playful. "Momma Eden showed me a thing or two."

Momma Eden. Nate and Linc's mom. Everyone had some sort of family, except me.

* * *

Early the next morning, I sat on a long galvanized bench in the locker room. Surrounded by cool metal and tall mirrors facing the shower cubicles, I was down to my bra and panties. I stared at the floor, head in my hands. Water from my recent shower dripped from my hair, puddling at my feet.

The room was featureless and uniform, like everything else about the CO. No homey charm, no color, no warmth, the locker room made me miss Chitamauga even more, and I wondered what Cannon and Nate were up to. Probably just rolling out of the Love Hovel, holding damn hands and heading to the mess for another morning of chatter, food, and company. Shit, I even missed the damn mutt and its whiskered maw, slobber and all.

I was waiting for my orders, ready to get into the field even if it meant a day of drills with the commander barking in my ear. With his constant barrage of criticism and verbal beat down, I'd focus on following instruction rather than the thoughts filling my head after another night of too few hours' sleep.

Last night Linc had appeared in my dreams. In the first he'd pointed a gun at me, grinning behind the loaded weapon while I listened to the rounds chamber one by one. A bullet exploded from the barrel toward me as his lips curved wider.

A second before impact, the scene had disintegrated into a dream just as troublesome. It wasn't a bullet flying toward my face, but Linc's full, firm lips descending over mine. I'd moaned when his mouth made contact, deep and fiery excitement replacing fear of imminent death. Soft and wet, his tongue rode the seam of my lips, his mouth sucking on mine until I'd guided him inside. Large hands held the back of my head, thumbs running slow circles beneath my ears, and when he'd withdrawn, his pupils swallowed the blue of his irises in a show of deep desire.

Remembering his masculine lips taking exactly the kind of kiss he wanted from me, my groan reverberated around the coed locker room. A near-silent whoosh of air alerted me to the door opening. I watched in the mirror as Linc strode around the corner. He halted when he saw me half naked on the bench.

Jumping to attention, I gave a precise salute, which he slowly returned. Linc's stare roamed over my body with male interest as I relaxed my stance. From the swell of my breasts in serviceable black cotton, the long line of my legs leading to a triangle of black fabric barely concealing my sex from sight, his survey was thorough, candid, and it made my nipples pinch tight, my pussy swell and moisten. Enjoying the rush of endorphins, I took my time unfolding a long-sleeved shirt, pulling the formfitting top down until I was covered.

He cleared his throat and finally shifted his gaze to the mirrors behind me. "Status?"

My status at the moment was a little bit confused but a lot more aroused. That Linc hadn't left the room to let me dress in private excited me in a dangerous way. I looked over his body to find he was affected by our close quarters as much as me, his cheeks ruddy, his eyes bright, and a distinct thickening where his pants hugged his groin.

Dropping down on the bench, I chuckled, the still-enflamed curve of my cheek smarting. "Living the dream, sir. Living the dream."

Linc folded his arms across his chest, where handsome double-stacked HK45s were holstered. "Are you always this smart-mouthed?"

Only when I was trying to outmaneuver his type. I wasn't living the dream at all. In fact, memories of the latest batch of chimera drifted back to me, Linc killing me…Linc kissing me.

"I try not to be, sir."

"I don't believe you."

"That's a running drill between us, too," I said.

His eyebrows lifting, he silently conceded that point.

"Sir, permission to ask you something?" The heat drumming through me during his intimate appraisal fled. I had to believe there was more to Linc if I had any hope of persuading him to give up his Corps-groomed path and return to the commune with me.

"Ask away."

I rubbed a towel through my damp hair. "Where were you during the Gay Plague?"

"Is this question mission oriented?" He scowled, a clear reminder in his cool expression and crisp question he was my superior and I was the only one required to answer to him.

"Call it curiosity."

Linc leaned in my direction. "I wouldn't have taken you for the curious kind; it's a pointless emotion."

"I find most emotions to be pointless, but you could humor me."

"Humor you, huh?" He gave a deep laugh and shook his head. Thick waves of hair dipped across his scarred brow in appealing disarray that made him look his young twenty-five years for the first time since I'd met him. Four years my junior, he'd always been the rising star of the combined military and regime efforts.

"I was fourteen, getting broken in by my father. He had me traveling between all the Territories, making sure my name was known. He set me to work early." The bitterness in his tone left no room for misinterpretation. Work meant killing Nomads, settling unrest among civilians with an unshakeable soldierly will, arresting and executing homosexuals.

"You've always been the prodigy."

"Not always. That was my brother." As he walked closer, until his boot caps nearly brushed my bare toes, his voice softened, the brusqueness gone. "Do you know Nathaniel?"

My neck craned as I looked up at him so far above me. "No, sir."

The quick flash of distrust extinguished from his eyes. He

moved to stand opposite me, shoulder slanted against the shower block. "Was that all you wanted to know?"

"What about the Purge?"

The Purge predated the Plague by a good forty-plus years, coming to a finish in 2020. It was the first ELE, environmental eradication caused by overpopulation of the earth and a by-product of overconsumption of natural resources until the world, governments, and billions of people were wiped out.

"The Purge?" He shrugged. "Humankind took advantage of the earth. They kept plugging into the grid, taking more than it could handle, devouring everything in their path. No one could've stopped it, not that any but the most hardheaded tried, their scientific finds ignored. When the dust cleared and the deaths were mopped up, my grandfather came into power in Alpha, my father after him." Linc sat beside me, calloused palms rubbing together.

"And you're next in line."

He exhaled long and loud, sending me a sideways glance. "Yes."

"Does that bother you?"

He flicked his eyes back to the wall. "It's not supposed to."

His shoulders were so stiff, I fought the powerful urge to caress away the tension, but he surprised me first.

Squatting before me, Linc smoothed that wayward hair off his brow. "And you? What's your story, Liz?"

The whisper of my name from his lips brushed against me like the feather tips of a tender kiss. Beneath his steady look, I felt my pulse speed up. "Getting my heart broken…That's what I was doing during the Gay Plague." I took a halting breath, tasting the mint of his mouthwash, smelling the cleanness of his soap and shampoo. "My family was destroyed, my mom and dad, dead. Their deaths pushed me into the Corps so I wouldn't be an orphan anymore. I still never..."

"Still never what?" Gone was the gruff commander. In his place was a man who stared so deeply into my eyes I was tempted to tell him everything.

"I still feel alone." I had never experienced the kind of love my parents had. Looking at him, I couldn't believe I was offering this information so easily. I felt my cheeks burn. I averted my gaze.

The gentle touch of his hand sliding up my arm to clasp my neck was more comforting than I dared to admit.

"I feel alone, too," he said. My eyes flicked to his, where truth shined. "Perhaps not as alone as you." He withdrew his hand slowly, then rose to his feet.

Linc turned away, and I could see the transformation into Beta Commander take over. He rolled his neck and clenched his fists, his posture as rigid as a board. When he swung around to face me again, his lips were firm and flat.

"We should get to work."

The tangle of emotions he'd woken in me slipped right down to my belly, where they knotted and twisted. But I didn't let it show, instead returning his cool nod. In that instant, the wall went back up between us. Linc made for the door, and I returned to getting dressed. An emotional regroup was in order. I was beginning to feel Linc was more of a danger to me as a man than as my Corps commander.

But I didn't have much time to consider it, because soon he

returned, shoving a duffel at me. "New uniform. Outside in ten. I'm making you active."

I unzipped the tote. Looked like my assignment had arrived earlier than Farrow thought.

"And, Grant?"

"Sir."

"You're going to want to keep a lid on that curiosity of yours." His sharp tone was a clear warning.

Outside, he handed me a CheyTac 408 system long-range rifle. A classic and the best of the best, it packed its own portable PDA for accurate weather, wind velocity, and distance readings. I checked the scope, then slung it gently over my back, treating it as if it was as precious as a newborn baby. Linc had to have up-to-the-minute info on me to have picked this exact rifle.

Head to toe in winter white and gray camo with padded parkas, we blended in with the snowy scenery. Gloves, masks, hoods, every inch of skin was covered. I recognized Linc's oceanic eyes, snagging mine from behind his goggles, no suggestion of the man who'd just conversed with me in the locker room revealed. A squad of ten others joined us. We marched to the tank, a streamlined black behemoth throttling just inside the Quad's gates.

As the tank roared through the city streets, I slid the viewpoint window open, taking in Beta by daylight. Fat snow flurries called up the flaky fire ash in Alpha when Sectors Four and Five went up in flame. Low-flying clouds hummed across the sky like drone planes. False reads on billboard-style D-Ps tallied the CO's triumphs over the Revolutionaries, reporting FarAsian Nu was holding steady, combat coming to an end on the continent of Europa and that insurgents in Kappa had been defeated. Every single headline I read was a spoon-fed lie. Civilians scuttled along like a slick black river, arriving for work that probably meant overtime at the munitions and food depositories. The roads were crowded because of the influx of evacuees from Alpha. Everywhere, soldiers kept guard, shepherding civilians, guns ranging around, ready to fire at any tango.

We arrived at the outskirts of S-4 and jumped out. Following the commander's signals, we stayed in tight formation, hauling ass through one ransacked street to the next. The poor area had been bombed to bits, windows shattered out, buildings busted up, but it appeared the rebels hadn't been contained yet.

After scrambling to the top of a warehouse, crawling through snowdrifts on our elbows and knees, we were lined up on the edge of the roof, overlooking a busy command center of dissenters. They were made up of a hodgepodge of Revolutionaries, distinct in their still-sleek city garb, and shaggy Freelanders with their mismatched clothes and weapons. They bustled around the open space surrounded by the blown-out walls of three other warehouses and the one we recon'd from.

Three men stood guard over crates of ammunition stacked in the middle. A computer deck stationed under a makeshift lean-to of corrugated steel, an open fire worked as a warming and refueling station in the opposite corner, and thirty or so nonconformists loitered around.

The group of hostiles had no idea they were sitting ducks.

Linc's low whisper carried across the whistling wind. "That

speech your ex-commander gave lit a fire under Revolutionary ass. They've become more organized, more daring."

What he said was in direct contrast to the D-P spin I'd just witnessed. A jolt of camaraderie for Cannon and the rebellious hordes swept through me at the mention of his speech when court-martialed in November. Nate had broadcast it live over all of the InterNation's D-Ps. The moment Cannon thought he was going down at the Outpost, he'd openly accused the CO of crimes against humanity. He'd cautioned those in cahoots with the government that their allegiance would bring them nothing but death because the Freelanders had the stronger cause, the legitimate right to fight for love and freedom.

"It might've backfired. They've become fearless to the point of stupidity," Linc heckled.

I bristled beside him, adjusting the dope on my rifle.

He shot me a look. "What was that you said in my office about killing Nomads?"

Pushing the goggles up to my forehead, I sent him a mutinous glare. "I said I had no problem doing it again."

"Maybe it's time to prove it," he challenged.

What I'd like to do was strangle his nuts in my hand, prove him to be a real pretty soprano instead of a bass tenor. Nerves jumped around in my stomach so much I felt like puking. I didn't want to kill these people.

Make him trust you, Farrow had said.

I had to kill or it was all over.

"It seems my father has a vested interest in you from your time in Alpha, and he so helpfully supplied me with your files."

The sudden stroke of Linc's thumb across my cheek stung me through and through. I didn't like this side of him. "Strange that beyond your history with the Corps, there's little in your work-up. I'd suspect you're hiding something in your personal life."

"No such thing as a personal life, sir."

"Were you close to Cannon?"

"Define close." I trained my eyes forward.

Huddling against me, his mouth warmed the side of my face, unwanted tingles triggering a flush. "This is close, Lieutenant."

"He never molested me on or off the battlefield." My voice was even, my meaning clear.

Linc retreated from my verbal slap, muttering, "Fuck."

From the corner of my eye, I saw him watching me, his expression not the usual meticulous mask. With another mumbled swear, he signaled two snipers to stay put and keep cover while he motioned the rest of us away from the ledge. "We're going to round them up for questioning. Detain only. Do not engage unless necessary. Repeat: Do not engage!"

Relief swept over me so fast I had trouble finding my footing on the ice-slicked fire escape on the way down.

We raided their holdout from all sides. The rebels scattered in different directions, ducking into offshoots of alleys. I didn't wait for more orders. I had no intentions of rounding up or detaining anyone. I hauled ass after a long-haired sprinter to tell him to get the fuck out of Beta until the Revolutionaries came up with a solid plan to bring it down.

Cursing the snow that blinded me, I swung the rifle over my

back. Lost in the maze of alleys, I took a turn and stopped short. My breath froze in my chest. In front of me stood the Freelander, gun raised. I tried to backtrack, but my way was blocked by another one. Training their guns on me, they cornered me against a wall.

I could have taken them out. I knew exactly how to do it. Instead I swallowed the tears back up my throat, blinking away the ones burning my eyelids. Even if I had my gun in hand, I wouldn't pull the trigger against these people, who were only protecting their way of life. They could be anyone I knew. They could be Darke, or Micah, or Nate.

"I'm sorry," I whispered, prepared to die alone, a failure to the Revolution, my friends, my father.

I heard my name shouted before Linc blasted into the alley. I ducked out of the way. Guns went off above my head, but when I looked up, the Freelanders were still standing and so was Linc. I had only a second to note the frantic fury on his face before he pushed me behind him. I scrabbled for his arm, sure he was going to fire.

"Drop the weapons unless you want to meet your Maker right now." Harsh and cold, his voice sliced across the narrow alley.

Two soft plops sounded when they threw their guns into the snow at our feet.

"Now, get the fuck out of here unless you want to be taken to the Quad with your friends."

As soon as they scurried away, Linc locked on to me. He grabbed my arms, scanning me for injuries. He was making sure I was all right when I was anything but. I spoke through tears clogging my throat. "I'm sorry. I choked. I couldn't…"

He exploded in my face. "You choked? You nearly got yourself killed, Liz!"

Yanking away my helmet, Linc tossed it aside. As soon as he saw the tears—weak and worrisome—he curled me against him. "Jesus Christ." His voice was muffled against my hair. "This couldn't have been easy after everything you've been through. Maybe it was too soon to return you to duty."

I spanned his back with my hands, holding on to him. I'd never been one for coddling, but it felt good to be protected, even if it couldn't last.

When he withdrew, I asked, "Why didn't you shoot them?"

"It's not a good day for killing."

"It never is."

I saw the tug of his dimple before he picked up my helmet. Then he smiled, and it was so warm my heart fluttered. "Maybe we chose the wrong calling."

The lighthearted feeling fled when we trudged to the tanks. There were no deaths but plenty of casualties on both sides. The wounded and prisoners were loaded up while Linc and I took point. He kept looking at me so much I wondered if I had my uniform on backward. Or maybe a hair out of place. Perhaps my lipstick had smudged, as if I even knew how to apply it…

"I'm fine," I said.

"You are not fine." Hoarse from shouting, his voice rasped from his throat. He held my face between hands that were warm and firm. Our mouths were close enough to kiss, but only harsh words hissed from his lips. "Do you understand we are up against more than the rebels, Liz?"

I wasn't sure if he was trying to warn me and, if so, what that warning was. Only one thing was certain. I was getting under his skin as much as he was mine.

Chapter Three

I'd become a precision-honed sniper, dedicated to my deadly craft, because I never wanted to look into the eyes of the mark I took out. Close-combat killing bothered me no matter how many times I pulled the trigger, no matter how necessary it was. The aftermath troubled me more, a cruel blow I'd been on the receiving end of from the trooper who'd heartlessly delivered the news of my father's death to my doorstep. It was one of the reasons I made a point of accompanying Cannon on the bad-news detail back in southeastern Alpha Territory when he was in charge of the Elite Tactical Unit and I was his right-hand woman.

Today I froze—unable to pull the trigger, unwilling to even raise my gun—not out of fear but because I no longer wanted to be that killer.

Making the right decision left me no less shaken. Though I'd shed no blood, it was still on my hands in the name of the Company. More than that, that Linc had rescued me sent me into a tailspin. I'd always taken care of myself. I'd never been on the receiving end before. I couldn't forget the worry on his face when he'd barreled into the alley, yelling my name.

In the locker room, I shivered from more than just cold. Stripping off my gear tinged with blood, I pushed it into the laundroshoot. After slamming a shower onto hot and stepping inside, I stood beneath the water cascading over me until the chills stopped.

Then I returned to my bare-bones barracks, sat on a bed, and shoveled in a few mouthfuls that tasted like crap from the tray I'd collected in the mess hall. All the while I glared at my pack. I pushed the food tray away and wrenched the pack closer. Digging below my spare clothes, I retrieved a few blank pieces of paper.

Stilo in hand, I made sure the door was shut and started writing.

March 7, 2071

I'll never be like Dad, the healer, creator. His proudest achievement was the Clone Project. Pets for Territorian children: dogs, cats, fish. He was a surgeon and a scientist.

My talent has always been about destruction.

I remember when I was nine or so, Mom sat beside me, braiding my hair. "Daddy's taking you to the shore today."

The shore was many kilometers away; it had been a rare treat for us to travel there for a day out. Our bare feet padded into the sand, hot from the sun. I'd run ahead, trying to catch up to the Pan-Atlantic pulled so far out by the low tide; my lungs ached by the time my toes curled into the salty, frothy water.

Dad laughed, watching me. He wouldn't laugh now. Maybe he's with Mom in the afterlife or wherever. A couple days after his death, Mom closed herself inside his office. The hollow echo of the one gun Dad kept even though he'd never handled it correctly rang out. I opened the door. She slumped onto his desk.

Mom had pulled the plug on herself, but I wouldn't. I couldn't. I'd sheared off my hair, the lengths Mom had braided every morning when I was little. I cut off the last piece of my past and grabbed the Corps train with both hands, fighting my way to first lieutenant status and no further.

I sucked it up every damn day until I met Caspar. En route from Epsilon to Alpha, he sat ramrod straight, uninterested in anything or anyone until we stopped on the side of the road and hopped out. When he leaned back, looking at the great blue sky above, a smile opened up his face. "The Corps is some kinda family, right?" I asked him.

I quickly tucked the pages under the edge of the mattress when the door of my room skated open unannounced.

"Whatchu got there, soldier girl?"

I guess I didn't hide them fast enough.

The coffee-skinned woman slung her tote onto an empty cot, then tried to grab my papers. I knocked her hand away. Mashing the pages into my back pocket, I rose in front of her. "None of your business."

She jabbed me in the stomach, pulling a sucker move that

made me grunt while she said, "Everything that goes on in here is my business, girly."

"I beg to differ." I sent her a slow smile just before I buried my fist in her button-cute face.

"Wrong move, my sister." Grabbing my hair, she rammed my head down toward her knee. I twisted around, gripped her hips, and threw her onto my cot.

She groaned as her face sanded against the slab walls. She quickly recovered. Leaping at me, she had her fingernails at the ready to rake down my face.

I grabbed her wrists before she made contact, sneering into her face as she tried to twist away from me. "Don't know if this is the usual initiation for Beta bunkies, or just how you say how-do, but you need a lesson in manners."

"I've heard all about you, Lieutenant Liz Grant. And I don't think you're legit even if the commander does. Traitor." She spat the words at me.

Well, that wouldn't do. I added another punch to her face, reeling back when she went for the hair-grabbing, nail-raking move again. She shoved my shoulder until I came up against the wall. I watched her wind her fist back, but slammed my boot into her stomach first.

Both of us were breathing hard when *soldier girl* shot me a glare. "I'm his first lieutenant, and I don't trust you for a minute."

"Oh yeah? And I've been stripped of that status. So knock yourself out." I opened the door. "Or better yet, get out."

"Sabine's my name; better 'member that." She didn't look ready to back down, fingers traipsing to the blade strapped to her thigh.

"Mine's bitch, or your fucking nightmare. Take your pick, and take your shit with you while you're at it."

Defiantly leaving her duffel on the cot, she sidled past me. "This ain't over."

"Hope not. I love foreplay." The door slid closed in her face, and I punched the wall after a ten-second count.

Great. My roomie was already suspicious of me. I had to get rid of the evidence of my writing fast. Hoping it was late enough most of the others were out on the midnight watch or safely snuggled into their uncomfortable beds, I moved between the shadows of the corridor on the first floor of Corps Command toward the stairwell that only went down.

Doors whooshed behind me as I descended two levels, softening my boot steps. Generators hummed, on second-string status. Red lights strobed, hurting my eyes. Arrows on the floor painted yellow led to various control rooms. I budged a solid door open with my shoulder, blinking until my sight adjusted to the gloomy underground tomb housing the incinerators.

I hoped my blood-painted fatigues from earlier had made it into the furnaces, too.

Pulling the mouth of an oven open, I threw the sheaf of papers inside. Orange flames licked the paper, tendrils of heat turning my weakness and words to flame.

At my back, another heat shivered up my spine. Linc hadn't made a sound, but I felt him. Hunched in front of the furnace, not looking back, I asked, "Let me guess. Little Miss Piss tipped you off?"

His footsteps rang while he ranged closer. "Are you having issues with LT Burr already? She just returned from a mission."

Sabine Burr, snitch bitch, a burr in my backside.

"Nah. We're destined to be best friends." I closed the iron gate of the furnace and swiveled around to perform a desultory salute. "Commander."

"Grant." He ambled closer.

"If Burr didn't come crying to you, then why are you here?"

"I was looking for you. Plus, I could ask the same of you." Perspiration tracked down my neck, and he watched it with avid attention before asking, "What are you burning?"

"My bras."

A grin lit up his whole face, putting Nate's pair of dimples to shame. "Maybe I should fish them out."

"Help yourself." I stepped aside, hoping to break the strange intensity growing between us.

"I think those were personal records you'd rather not have anyone see." Tilting his head to the side, he gave some serious attention to my chest before adding, "Not your brassieres."

"I think the heat's getting to you, sir."

His advance brought him against me. "What are you hiding?"

My face tight from the fire, from his nearness, I turned my head aside. "A dick that could probably rival yours."

Fingertips coasting under my chin, he tipped my face to his. "I don't buy that. I think you could be very soft if you wanted to be, Liz."

"Call me Grant." My heart battered in my chest.

Linc's whisper licked my ear. "Grant, is that how you like it? Cold, impersonal?"

Yes.

"Or long, hot, *personal* for hours on end?"

Clamping my tongue between my teeth, I let the wash of lust roll over me.

"What were you burning?"

"I like to write sometimes, okay? It helps me clear my head." This was the second admission he'd coaxed from me in just a few hours. I pushed Linc away and tried to move past him.

He blocked me. "I haven't dismissed you yet."

Linc's fierce visage was as smoldering as the dark chamber. I stood my ground, watching his broad shoulders disappear from sight as he moved behind me. Thick forearms hitched around my waist, pressing me flush against his chest. His arousal was rigid and heavy against the small of my back.

"I like it when you tell me the truth, Liz." His tongue darted and withdrew from the nape of my neck, making way for a husky whisper. "Now, do you remember what General Order Number One is?"

"Division-wide prohibition of sex during wartime, sir." My voice sounded breathy while I recited the military policy stating there was a "no sex for soldiers" law in effect.

Warm lips grazed my hammering pulse point before moving up to my ear. "Very good. Think you can keep it up?"

I spun around. "I can maintain protocol, Commander."

"We'll just see about that." A smile flirted around the edges of his lips. "If you're done burning those bras, come with me."

Led to the prisoner cells by Linc, I worked hard to keep my breathing steady and my eyes straight ahead. Immediate panic replaced the languid arousal he'd caused in me. I wasn't sure I could withstand any more interrogation or a lockup.

I almost laughed with relief when he stopped me in front of several cells holding the rebels we'd taken prisoner that morning. If he wanted me to question them, putting on a show for him was something I was more than capable of.

He surprised me when he handed me his key card. "We've learned all we can from them. Release the prisoners."

"What?"

Taking me by the shoulders, he marched me up to the door of a cell. "Let them go."

"But Cutler's orders are to execute all rebels."

Pulling my hand up, he passed the key card over the scanner and the door slid open. Beneath his impatience, he watched me with interest, almost as if he was amused by my hesitation. "Are you gonna do the rest, or will we be here all night? By which time I'm sure my father will have found out and we'll both be in trouble."

He started lining up the released prisoners in the corridor.

"They'll just be sitting ducks out there." I voiced my last concern, then did as he bade.

Ushering the thirty-odd men and women through the halls, we hurried them to an unguarded rear entry. Outside, I was absolutely stunned by what I saw. Linc had arranged transport to get them outside city walls under the cover of night.

"Why are you showing me this? Is it a trap?" I asked after we'd loaded the last of the rebels.

His hands suddenly cupped my face, fingers warm and strong.

His steady gaze held mine, showing unmasked emotion. "I'm not out to get you. I will never try to trick you." His touch slid to my neck before he moved away. "We can't work together if we don't trust each other."

My skin tingled from his slight caress. The trucks rumbled through the opened gates, and I stared at Linc's back, his shoulders straight and broad, his hands at his sides.

"Do you trust me, Commander?"

He turned his head, and his carved profile softened for a moment. "More than I think I should."

"Me too," I whispered.

Pivoting around, he jerked his cap so it lowered over his eyes. "You're dismissed, soldier."

Being around Linc was beginning to be a much more precarious predicament than I'd originally thought. He'd saved me and protected me. He'd shown me he wasn't just his father's grunt. His mere presence in the short time I'd known him disrupted my usual self-discipline, flooding me with sexual heat. More than that, being near him filled me with a longing for something I didn't think I could have. Him.

* * *

As predicted, daylight meant drills with Linc howling beside me about how shitty a sniper I was and maybe I should just go back to being a lone wolf, for all the good I'd do the Corps. For every target I aced, he sent the bull's-eye back two meters until I was wiping sweat from my eyes and snow from my scope. There was no mention of the inferno building between us even when he stood behind me, pulling my hips to his to perfect my aim. As if I needed lessons.

Lieutenant Burr worked beside me, hissy-fitting and missing her marks, earning a lot of scowls and no personal tutelage from Linc apart from harder trials that wrecked her thin thread of concentration.

I could've felt bad for her. I didn't.

Five grueling, dirty, hungry hours later, I trudged into the barracks hoping for a message from Farrow, some connection to Cannon, a goddamn care package. Instead of any of those things, what I found on my bed confused the hell out of me. Next to a nest of shoes that bore no resemblance to my lace-ups, there was a dress and something pale gray, lacy, and about the size of my hand.

I tapped on my D-P, messaging Linc: *What is this garment?*

When there was no immediate reply, I slipped a finger under the hem of the dress, fingering the expensive, stretchy material.

"I believe it's called a frock." Linc's deep voice registered behind me.

I turned to find him standing inside the doorway, one arm bracing it open. His sensuous grin triggered a surge of warmth just where I didn't need it. Sweeping my hand down the frock, I muttered, "Fuck."

"Well, no." He slid closer, lifting the dress and holding it against me. "Although, if you replaced your hard edge and your Class A's with this dress, maybe."

"You've got a problem with a woman in uniform now, Commander?"

"Not at all, Lieutenant. I'm just wondering what you look like underneath it."

My body clenched in reaction to his liquid tone. "I think you got a pretty clear view of that yesterday morning."

His deep chuckle rattled me even more. "I don't think it was an adequate viewing at all."

I drew a gun, prodding the lacy piece of nothing onto the barrel, waving it in his face. "And this?"

His fingers rubbed over the sheer gusset. Eyes hazy blue and hooded, Linc laid the undergarment down on the bed with care. "These are panties, unless you'd rather go without, in which case I won't put up an argument."

Arrogant bastard. "I am not getting dolled up so you can trot me out like some fancy tart."

"Would you mind reholstering your weapon?"

After I slid the gun home, he took my hand between his. "Let me start again. Will you be my date tonight?"

He seemed half teasing and half tentative, flustering me in a different way. "I didn't think dating was allowed."

Releasing my hand only to lace his fingers through mine, he pulled me a step closer. "If you're referring to that General Order, we were talking about sex last night, not dating."

"I was not talking about having sex with you." Indignant, I pulled my hand free.

His deep laughter made me smile until he said, "Maybe that was someone else, then."

I went for my guns again, but he stilled my hands before I could wrestle them out of the holsters. "Relax, Liz. I'm joking.

There's no one I'd rather be with tonight, and I certainly wasn't with anyone else last night." He ran a nervous hand through his hair and peered at me. "In fact, I don't normally flirt with my soldiers at all."

"No kidding. You usually shout at us until we cry."

"Does that mean you're impressed with my flirting skills?"

Oh, I wasn't about to admit that. "I think you'll have to try harder."

"I'll see what I can do later, then." He winked as he walked to the door. "I'd really like you to wear the dress for me, Liz. Meet me at my apartment in an hour."

* * *

After a fast, scalding shower, I reconsidered the outfit Linc had given me. I even laughed when I found he hadn't included a bra, no doubt because of what I'd said last night about burning all of mine. The dress fit like it was made for me. Rich, stretchy, charcoal-gray fabric snugged my form in a way that made me feel feminine yet not frilly. The cutouts around my shoulders showed a glimpse of skin. The black leather lacing from thigh to hip on the sides and the long silver zipper between my breasts to my belly made me feel sexy and strong.

I'd never dressed for a man—hell, I'd hardly ever gotten fully undressed for one—yet Linc had nailed the essence of me after spending approximately thirty-six hours in my presence. An unusual impulse made me hope he liked what he saw. 'Cause if he didn't, I carried a small pistol strapped to my thigh, not to mention the razor-sharp heels I could use to disarm him if my appearance didn't. I made it to his door upstairs in Command just as he swept out. He scanned me with a growing smile. "Beautiful."

I had absolutely no experience accepting praise unless it had to do with my work as a soldier, so I simply took the arm Linc offered.

* * *

Seeing us reflected in the mirrored surrounds of the elevator, my heart beat faster. We made a sharp-looking couple. Linc's civilian suit accentuated his broad shoulders and chest, smoothing down to his trim hips and long legs. A tie was notched to his rugged throat. His hair, not sun-lightened like Nate's but a darker gold, swept off his brow and temples. He was handsome, a hint of the commander always exhibited in the scar on his eyebrow. My short black hair slicked back, my lips plush with a splash of wine color—the only cosmetic I'd used from the compact provided—if I leaned toward him, I could leave the imprint of a kiss on his chin.

Linc captured my eyes first, in the glassy wall, then my hand within his. He hummed under his breath, daring me to withdraw from his purchase. His mouth relaxed fully, and a sensual curve topped his upper lip, beckoning me to lick it. His fingers threading through mine sent sensation speeding through me. As alarming as it was to be fascinated by Cannon's Fuck Bunny's identical twin, the attraction between us gathered velocity.

Charming, handsome, even funny, Linc was not just an order-barking badass. He made me feel wanted as a woman. It was hard to remember I was here to find information and send it back to the commune, because for the first time in my life, I felt a little frivolous—all because of his attentions.

And frivolous was not something I needed to be at this moment. Tamping down the excited energy flowing through me, I was determined to act like the trained soldier I was, not some silly woman who could be bought by pretty dresses. Accepting a winter wrap from the trooper stationed at the door—because now we were doing valet service around here—Linc pulled the fur around my shoulders. I barely withheld a poisonous laugh at the bullshit charade Beta Corps had become since the onset of the Revolution. We should be out on raids, busting chops, dodging bullets if Linc truly believed in this war.

Blazing halos outside blinded me, but Linc escorted me carefully down the sixteen stone steps to the waiting new-spec, low-riding Cruiser. Encased in a buffer of silver, it slunk to the ground like a growling animal and was done up in bulletproof glass and armor. A monstrous black tank gunned ahead of us, and one prowled behind, providing fire and cover. Passing HQ, I was reminded CEO Cutler was most likely holed up in there, hatching plans for my friends' downfall. That thought hardened my resolve even more.

Exiting the Quad's high walls, revving all the way to the south gate, we were waved through, into the Wilderness. It was only then I glimpsed our driver in the darkness. If it wasn't the red-haired jar-faced jag-off from my welcome-to-Beta-beat-up. Obviously, he'd been downgraded more than me.

"Hey, Ginger." I slid my fingers off my brow in a lazy salute, enjoying the sight of his cheeks flaming in response.

During the rest of the drive, I took in the quiet moonscape speeding past. We rolled deeper into the forest on a secondary road, getting closer and closer to Catskills. Linc watched me dispassionately. He probably measured every one of my uneven heartbeats, trying to dig out my motivations. I wasn't the only one who had experienced a major shift in mood from the start of our *date*.

Forty minutes later, we stopped outside a castle constructed of rough stone blocks. Double doors opened at the top of the sixteen steps—sixteen for the InterNations Territories, the same as the buildings in the Quad. At the foot of the hills, forest all around, this would be a good place to off someone. Linc insisted on helping me out of the Cruiser, hands on my hips, thighs brushing mine. Our breaths, misty clouds of frost, clung, heated, and evaporated. Music, laughter, and light clamored from the mansion. Inside, Linc pulled off his gloves, handed them to a liveried minion, and took the stole from my shoulders with a suggestive stroll of his fingers.

The mansion was opulently detailed, and guards armed to the eyeballs stood to attention at one-meter intervals. CO scrip oozed from the furnishings, paintings, and dressed-up perverts in attendance. The dark wood-paneled room we entered was crowded, but I cataloged it, quickly mapping windows, exit points, jackasses.

The jackasses were in abundance. Leather-bound boys, bitches in tit harnesses, hair in vibrant, twisted formations. Makeup ranged from nonexistent to black kohl to off-the-wall body paint.

So this was what the corrupt CO got up to while they sold their citizens into the daily drip of *less is more, make do or do without*. Territorians worked their way through endless monotonous days with little recreation or entertainment, held hostage to the D-P indoctrination. Abortion: illegal. Homosexuals and *deviants*: disenfranchised and hanged. Sex toys: outlawed. *Is it any wonder a mutiny has been incited?* Regardless of Gen Order Number One, passions ran hotter during wartime, as evidenced by the men and women, hetero-sex only, drinking, undressing, sucking, kissing, and all-out fucking around us.

"What's this?" I asked as deep suspicion curdled any sweet thought I'd had about Linc.

A muscle ticked in his jawline. "The Club."

"And I'm here because?"

"You haven't quite proven yourself to all standards yet."

Oh Jesus. This is what Farrow meant. Talk about an instant mood killer. If I hadn't already caught his intense scrutiny in the Land Cruiser, I would've been floored. "I thought that's what last night was about." Smug bastard, making me get all dressed up so he could parade me around like a cute CO party girl.

"Then this should clinch it." Handing his coat to a passing servant, he leaned in to murmur, "Your assignment tonight is to smile and pretend to enjoy my company."

The pistol strapped to my thigh was beginning to look like a great way to give Commander Linc Cutler a long kiss good night. I didn't bite back my sharp retort. "I'm afraid that might be beyond even my stellar capabilities."

We were interrupted by Sabine hustling up to us. Her voluptuous form almost fell out of the molded green sheath meant to suck her in. I hated her on sight, again.

"I ain't had a chance to debrief, sir."

Linc looked blankly over her head. "And now is not the place."

"Commander, all due respec', but—"

"Lieutenant Burr, find my father and tell him Liz and I have arrived." He dismissed her with a flick of his hand.

His father? I almost teetered in my preposterous heels.

"Permission to speak freely, sir." Burr's continued desperation was enough to put me off the nibbles being passed around by immaculate servants.

"Denied. Now run along."

"The CEO's here?" It was do-or-dig-a-grave time. I couldn't let any cracks show.

The hard formation of Linc's face revealed even fewer cracks than mine. "He's very keen to speak to you."

His hand at my lower back propelling me into a second smaller room did nothing to stanch my nerves, and neither did the scene revealed inside. Pale rose leather chairs filled with occupants were arranged under hanging cylindrical halos. Low tables were laden with crystal decanters of liquor, as well as men and women writhing on the shiny surfaces in various states of undress. They were all well groomed, attractive, and giving free rein to their debauched desires.

A decadent exploration of heterosexuality, this would be the CO's answer to the nonstandard-issue Amphitheater frequented by *aberrant* civilians. The last I'd heard of an Amphitheater was the one held outside Alpha walls the night this war started. It'd been Cannon's birthday, and he'd been present when it was raided. He got away only because Leon—the kid who was as much a hero as a hustler—pulled the tornado alarm to warn the revelers. That move had landed him in the RACE brig from which Nate had broken him out, bringing him to the commune…and into Darke's life.

I noted a trio of black-haired vipers sizing up Linc, nudged forward by a demurely dressed older woman. Wearing nothing but the most transparent lingerie, they rolled their hips together, mewing at him in open invitation. They were true CO whores, but I supposed you had to make your scrip somehow.

Other than the trio of tarts, there were no blatant threats, but those were never the most lethal kind. My fingers itched, and the pistol was burning a hole against my thigh. Everyone seemed to be out to get their rocks off, but I wouldn't hesitate to unload a bullet into the Jacks, Jills, or Johns if anyone stepped out of line.

Everyone included Farrow. It was a great big fucked-up reunion. She waved her fingers at Linc and glided our way. The innocence of her ethereal white gown was undercut by studded leather gear that cupped her breasts and ran around her neck. She looked part angel, part bandit, and that pretty much summed her up.

She allowed Linc to kiss her hand, then swept an arched glance over me. "Utterly delicious, Linc. Wherevah did you find her?"

His rough palm was a hot brand on my hip. "Farrow Monroe, please meet Lieutenant Liz Grant."

"Oh yes. Ah've heard of her from Alpha days. Quite the asset to your squad, isn't she?" Then the mischievous little minx mentioned, "Perhaps even more of an asset to you?"

I thought my eyes were gonna bug out of my head, and I definitely wanted to spit out a rejection to that sideline to my mission in Beta. Linc beat me to it, drawing me to his side. "I think the lieutenant could prove herself valuable indeed, Farrow."

I wanted to tighten the strap around her throat to cut off her tinkling laughter. *The wench is gonna get hers.*

"Oh, there's Bas. Bassy! C'mere darlin'. Someone Ah want you to meet," Farrow called to someone behind me.

A tall, rangy youth beamed a pleasant smile at Linc and me. He gripped Linc's hand and turned to me. "And this is?"

"Lieutenant Liz Grant, a rather famous soldier from Alpha."

Wide pink lips brushed my knuckles, his long, soft hair, bleached white at the tips and dyed black at the roots, fell across my wrist. "Lovely."

"Liz, this is Sebastian Monroe, Farrow's younger brother."

The young man Farrow mentioned pairing up with Leon. Seeing him in his leather pants and a snug shirt through which nipple piercings glinted like the black diamond stud in his nose, I thought she might be onto something. His eyes were guileless and a beautiful shade of violet. *Yeah, he might be just the new bad boy for Leon.*

"If you'll excuse me, ladies, Bas." Linc worked his way through the crowd, touching an elbow here, exchanging a salute or a word there, veering away from the touchy-feely hands of *I got what you need tonight, big boy* ladies.

Bas bowed out, too. Smart boy, because I was seething inside, on the verge of beating his big sister's pert backside. Seeing all these possible perps out of uniform—hell, half of them out of clothes—I didn't know who was upper-echelon Corps or a government official. In fact, I hadn't been prepared at all.

I hissed at Farrow, "You could've warned me."

Breezy laugh bursting out, she said, "Ah told you, that couldn't be, and now you see why. Linc is comin' 'round to you."

"Anything else you can't tell me but I should really fucking know?"

"Ah'm not exactly sure where Sabine's allegiance lies. You wanna watch your back around her." Reaching for a glass of fizzy alcohol, Farrow marked a couple standing alone in a corner.

Linc and his LT Sabine.

My eyes narrowed as a charge of jealousy pumped through me. "It looks like the commander needs to watch his cock around her."

"Maybe you should watch it for him."

I grabbed a drink of my own, forgetting about ladylike sipping to swallow it in one gulp. "If you're asking me to get emotionally involved here, I need to know why."

"Linc is vital to winnin' the war and startin' the new Republic." She patted her already impeccable hair. "'Sides, y'all could do each other some good."

"Jesus Christ, Farrow. It's a revolution and you're playing matchmaker? You ought to stick to Leon and Sebastian."

Beneath her lighthearted charade, her shrewd green eyes found mine before she made a smooth getaway. *Goddamn her.* When Linc's gaze locked on me with the force of a taser, I started my own retreat. Weaving around masses of bodies rolling against one another in lazy gyrations to the jazz-toned music—another item banned by the CO—I explored one room after another. I tried to shut out the memory of Linc's fingers on my neck, a soft caress from a hard man. In a rowdier section of the mansion, I was knocked into a gambling table by some stupid young buck who was asking for a payload of bullets in his drunken face. I reached for my thigh, where my gun was hidden.

A deep voice swept like velvet across my temple. "Easy, Lieutenant."

My defenses deflated as I peered at Linc. "Why did you bring me here? To flaunt your famous prisoner?"

He pulled both hands through his gold waves and exhaled. "My father has owned this house for decades. It was built long before the Purge. He ordered me to make it a viable stronghold when he came here instead of the Greenbrier Outpost, where he was supposed to meet Nathaniel."

"He never intended to see your brother?"

"Let's just say they never got along and leave it at that." He stared off at some distant point, a place where his memories were stored out of reach. "Sometimes my father likes to take part in the destruction firsthand, and sometimes he prefers to watch from a distance as the dirty work is done for him. The basement here is a network of tunnels, artillery-proof bunkers, and escape routes."

"That's great, but I really have no interest in architecture."

"Just store that info away, please." Linc pulled me around to face him. "I brought you tonight because you're still on the watch list, Liz. I can't promote you to full status anymore, not with—"

"Martial law in effect." Meaning CEO Cutler had the final say. He nodded.

"You want me to get my stripes back?" I asked.

His suit jacket stretched across his shoulders when he took a long breath and blew it out. "I'm finding I want you in many ways."

Heart stuttering, I relished every ounce of heat in his look, every rough syllable of his words, knowing I should work through what he'd divulged instead of watching him moisten his lips. "Are you trying to use our chemistry to back me into a corner?"

"I told you last night I wouldn't trick you, and a corner is the last place I want to back you into," he said with a sinful smile before the full import of tonight settled between us. "You need to solidify your reputation as a Company supporter, not just a career soldier. You still have a target on your back. Follow my lead, Liz."

Follow his lead *is starting to sound like falling into bed with the man when I can't be certain he isn't setting me up for a fall.* At least I had my exit strategy, care of his intel on the mansion's lower level, should things get shady tonight, which looked about to happen with Cutler's unswerving approach.

His bodyguard grinned insolently at us from his left flank. A long sheath of straight black hair swung forward as he performed a reluctant half bow in our direction.

"Welcome to my home." CEO Lysander Cutler embraced his son, then pointed his hawkish nose and predatory eyes toward me.

Contempt rippled from him. He'd had a stiffie for me since

day one in Alpha. It was a miracle he'd never taken me into HQ for strafing just because he didn't like me. Last time I'd seen the asshole CEO, he'd been wearing a white towel, dripping blood from his neck, the victim of a botched assassination attempt on his life a couple months before the Revolution.

"Prisoner." His blue eyes were nuggets of distrust and hatred.

"Lieutenant." Linc stood shoulders above his father, lips so tight they were tinged white.

One knobbed knuckle ran down my arm to my wrist, circled in bruises from the grip of my welcoming committee a few days ago. "You trust this traitor, son?"

"Lieutenant Grant has been in action. She performed well. She won't be a problem to the regime."

I swallowed hard at Linc's blatant lie on my behalf.

"*Not a problem* is not the answer I'm looking for." *Cuntler* roamed close enough I swore I could smell oily death diffusing from his skin. "Perhaps she needs to make a show of honor tonight."

Bile rose up my throat. I swallowed it down along with the desire to shove my shoe so far up his ass he'd be eating his scrambled prostate for breakfast.

"That won't be necessary, Father. I've got our brat well in hand."

The CEO nodded to Linc. "Well, good. That's good. I always could rely on you."

I let out one small breath of relief only to have it hitch in my chest when he continued. "Care to prove it?"

I didn't look at either of them as the bottom dropped out of my belly. I couldn't be made to shoot someone, not tonight. I wasn't a merc. I'd rather die not knowing what happened to my dad.

Linc led me into the center of the room, cautioning, "Easy, killer."

The small bubble of a laugh choked inside my throat.

"Just a kiss. Let's show 'em how it's done."

A kiss, not a kill shot. "What?"

"All in a day's work, Liz."

Of course it was, for him. He'd been through public sex ceremonies, establishing himself as a dedicated future Breeder.

"You are such a swine." I smiled up at him through gritted teeth.

"There's that smile. I don't think they're convinced it's genuine though." His taut lips relaxed into a teasing grin.

I jerked my head aside on a puff of silent laughter. The laughter died when Linc's hands encased my hips. "Remember, you're being evaluated."

Holy shit. I guessed General Order Number One didn't extend to the uppity whoremongers. It didn't make a dent in the rest of us during deadly times either. I could attest to that firsthand with my short-lived fling with Farrow. I also blamed the *we-could-die-at-any-moment* mentality for the way my body reacted to Kinky Linc's touch. A hush swelled over the crowd of people waiting for their hit of voyeurism. I closed my eyes.

"I should've said it before, but you look incredible in uniform. Fuck, you look great out of it." I opened my eyes to his boyish grin sliding into something more rakish, obviously remembering me in nothing but a bra and panties. "But I like this side of you too, all woman."

"Linc." The spicy scent of his cologne and the closeness of his large, muscled body catapulted deep craving through me.

Eyes deep and blue lowered to my lips. "Are my advances unwelcome?" His words ran hot strips across my vulnerable flesh.

"No." I yielded to him in surprise, delight, desire when his tongue stroked his bottom lip before he tucked his teeth into the pink flesh I wanted.

"Let me kiss you?"

"Yes."

A short curse and hungry groan later, Linc curled his hands around my shoulders, moved into my hair, and slanted my mouth to his. Firm and moist, his lips tasted mine. Slow and tender, he plucked at me until I reached around his back, spanning my hands across the width of muscle.

He asked for no quarter, easing his tongue into my mouth. What started out hesitant became a wild, slippery tangle, our hands grasping, mouths gasping.

Savoring the last licks of his lips, pressing for more, I listened to his growl. "You are tying me into knots, Liz."

I cupped his face, sucking his full mouth, tonguing inside one last time.

Hands running up my thighs, he shook his head when he found my party favor strapped there. "Always packing."

I dragged my palm down his chest to his trousers, lighting on the thick roll of his erection that jerked beneath my fingers. "So are you."

Another passionate kiss passed between us, barely there touches promising so much more. It was public; it was a turn-on…yet it felt totally private. I took everything Linc gave, desperate for more, my body surrendering to his. When his thigh parted mine, I rode against his leg, so swollen, so ready for him.

"We have to stop."

I blinked up at him.

Lips red from our kisses and his cheeks flushed, he grunted. "Goddamn, Liz. We have to stop. I won't do this here, in front of them."

The reminder of where we were and why we were kissing was like a bucket of cold water dumped over my head. My pride stung as I withdrew from his embrace. "Maybe you won't do me at all."

Our terse whispered exchange didn't go unnoticed by Cutler. I hoped our intimate kiss and Linc's testament about my active duty convinced him I wasn't working for anyone but the Corps and that I was one hundred percent for the CO.

Linc's expletive was low he as took my elbow. Threading us through the throng, he swiftly made our good nights. "I just saved you from another grilling from my father. You owe me."

Anger spiked in me. "What did you get out of it?"

He stopped and stared at me before dropping his gaze. "A kiss from you."

His quiet admission affected me nearly as much as his lips on mine had earlier, but that wasn't the answer I was looking for. "Why would you help me get into Cutler's good graces?"

"Ah, now that, that is because I am my father's son and I want to stay one step ahead of him. You're a high commodity, whether you're a true soldier or a traitor, and for the moment, you're mine. I plan to keep it that way."

Slinging the fur over my shoulders, he helped me into the Cruiser. Seated beside me, he sent Ginger in motion. "The next time we kiss, Liz, it won't be in front of an audience, and it won't be an act." His whispered words were warm against my ear.

It hadn't been an act at all, at least not to me. A ball of fire inflamed my sex. A ball of fear rolled around my head. Linc's magnetism was the focal point of it all.

Deep cover? This is shaping up to be more like deep shit.

Chapter Four

Several days later, a loud rap on the door woke me. Since our kiss at the sex party, Linc and I had been outmaneuvering each other in the avoidance department. Suited me just fine. Luckily, Sabine was experienced in the same area. Her duffel remained on the cot across from mine, unpacked, and the bed retained its drum-tight blankets. We'd been careful about keeping opposite hours so we wouldn't have to look at each other's face or attempt murder while the other slept. I was beginning to wonder just how much of a coincidence it was that I was forced to room with the one soldier who clearly had misgivings about me.

Whoever knocked on the door wasn't giving up. Sabine would've simply barged in; so would Linc for that matter. I pulled on a pair of pants to go with the tank I usually slept in and slid the door open.

Ginger stood outside. "Commander requests your attendance in his apartment."

"Fine. Give me five while I pull myself together."

He waited outside until I was ready. Stopping off on the way to Linc's rooms, I brushed my teeth, washed the sleepy grit from my eyes, and completed my ablutions with a grim face.

Upstairs, Ginger's knuckle rap was met with a booming, "Enter."

I elbowed the boy out of my way and strode inside on my own. A short hallway led into a cushy lounge area. Clean and impersonal, the space was just like Linc, everything contained and closed away. The barely risen sun worked hard to get into the room through the thin slits of the tinted windows. Linc stood against one of them, arms crossed over a regulation black tank top, biceps bulging, his blue eyes tracking my entrance. A slight tilt of his chin when he saw me unarmed.

The anxious jingle in my belly was due to his silence, not the thorough see-through stare accompanying it.

Swaggering farther inside, I sank into one of the thickly cushioned seats, my stomach grumbling at the vast spread of food on the low table in front of me. Steam tooted into the air from a silver carafe of rich-smelling coffee. Eggs, spicy, crispy meat, warm, fresh bread, and whipped butter—all expensive and virtually unattainable foodstuffs—sang to my appetite.

Linc took the chair opposite me, pouring a cup of coffee he dosed with heavy cream. "Dig in."

Although sudden hunger drove sharp hooks into me, I crossed a leg and linked my fingers in my lap. "You shouldn't have gone to the trouble. I don't need a breakfast-time brush-off with the boss to get it, sir. You did your job at Cutler's, and I did mine. We're clear."

After taking a sip from his mug, he set it down. He poured another cup, leaving it black, sliding it toward me. "Actually, I don't think we're clear at all."

His quizzical look gnawed at me. It went much deeper than anything a simple meal could relieve. Preferring not to dwell on the tense feeling stretching between us, I loaded a plate and tucked in. Companionable silence enveloped us as we ate, but sexual interest, palpable and intense, sizzled in the air.

When I cleared my plate, Linc served me seconds, those damnable dimples deep in his cheeks. "You've got a hearty appetite."

I finished chewing. "My mom used to say I must've had a third leg to pack it all away."

Linc folded his hands on the table. The scent of his aftershave wafted to me, spicy and manly. As always, his hair was neatly swept back, his strong jaw smooth. His muscles tempted my touch, from the grooves of his shoulders to the thick pad of his pecs dusted with gold hair at the edge of his tank top.

"Do you have any siblings?" he asked.

"You know I don't."

A tight nod of acknowledgment meant *touché*. We both knew he'd been into my files. What Linc didn't know was I had firsthand gen on him too. I was familiar with him in ways he couldn't even begin to fathom.

After a dragged-out curse and a brush through his hair, his hands returned to the table. They were splayed open, as open as his expression, which was torqued in pain he probably never let show. "You know about my twin, Nathaniel."

"Your family's history is public knowledge."

"I'll bet you believe, like everyone else, the story that my mother died when we were eight."

Something from the night at Cutler's must've burned Linc so badly he was digging out long-buried memories. Quietly sliding to the chair next to him, I took his hands in mine. His skin was clammy to the touch.

"It was on the D-Ps, even in the broadsheets my dad used to save. Big headlines at the time. I'm sorry."

Even though I knew it wasn't true, for a moment this bond of lost mothers connected me to him.

He closed his eyes. "It was all a lie. A cover-up so Lysander, my father, could save face. She left him because he beat her. She abandoned me, us." Resentment threaded through his words, and I couldn't blame him. A helpless boy left in the hands of a monster. "Nathaniel left too. He came back, or at least pretended to, working for *Sandy*. Long enough to bring on the Revolution. But for most of these years, I've been alone with our father. I don't know if either of them are alive anymore, my mom or my brother."

I gulped back unbidden words, blinked back hot, fast tears. Linc was so vulnerable in that moment—young and hurt. I ached for him, thinking about the desolation of his one-gun upbringing by Cuntler.

He scrutinized me, searching for answers I couldn't provide. "You don't look shocked."

"I'm not sure what you want me to say. I don't know why you're telling me this."

"Me either. Forget it." He stood up, pacing to the other side of the room. "Maybe we should forget about the other night, too."

I wasn't fooled by his bluff. I'd been there, too. A lost mother, dead father, nothing to hold on to but career-minded motives. It pained me not to tell him about Nate and Cannon, about his mom and the commune, but he could be playing me, the consummate tactician. Emotions had no part in these war games, and neither did my heart.

Nonetheless, I walked to him. "I don't want to forget it, Linc."

Such large hands found mine, bringing my fingertips to his mouth, brushing them across his lips. "It's Lincoln. My mom named us." His short smile sent a pang of sympathy through me. "At least she was strong enough to leave him. She'd be dead for certain if she'd stayed."

I couldn't process the magnitude of realizing his father was capable of such a crime while he continued to work for him, doing the *yessir* gig every single damn day.

"What about you, Liz? Do you miss your mother?"

His question hit me like a gun butt to my stomach. "Yes," I whispered.

"None of that should've happened to your family."

"It is what it is."

"Is it?" Linc quirked his head. He lifted my palm to his chest, just a thin shirt separating his skin from me. His loose black pants lay low on his hips, leaving a stretch of taut skin, a trail of gilded hair, and the deep grooves of his pelvis on display. A thick bulge beat against the fabric.

"Is it what?" I asked.

He tilted my face up. "You must get lonely."

"Loneliness is a state of mind I don't visit often." I lied to him. Our initial attraction was building toward something that seemed impossible to control. I kept losing my footing around him. Looking for a way to cut through the magnetism between us, I marched away from Linc. I schooled my face into a blank mask.

He was fast, barring the doorway with his body, bringing his mouth close to mine. A press of my toes and I could kiss him, get rid of the games between us.

"I want you to know, Liz—" He broke off, stepped away. He turned his back, his guarded profile sharpening. "I want you to know, Lieutenant, I'm keeping my eyes on you."

"I have no doubt, Commander." We were back in play, the promise of intimacy stowed neatly away.

"I want you to make a clean sweep of S-4."

"Roger that."

"You've been fully reinstated per my father's orders. It seems you managed to impress him. Congrats." He opened a chest of polished wood, laying out his weapons for the day and his Command-access key card.

"Yessir, thanks."

He smirked, roaming closer. "EO 23987 is in place."

I recited it. "Executive Order. Martial law under CEO Cutler. His InterNations council is in charge and all advisers report to him."

"Excellent, Grant. And the people at the party? Many of them are on my father's committee?"

Once again, Linc stressed the gravity of my situation. The EO

and the CO sex club meant Cutler kept his council sweet with
a side dish of corruption he documented for future bribery. The
only reason I was allowed to go along last night had to be because Cutler was trying to decide how he could best use me for
the regime. His plan was total InterNations domination, and by
God, he'd do anything to attain it.

And that included using his son, too.

Linc had his father to contend with and I had mine to lay to
rest. We were at two opposite ends of a war that would do more
than just end lives. It would destroy families, ruin relationships.
I had no right letting any burgeoning feelings for this man come
between me and my endgame, but they were there nonetheless.

"Take Burr and Johnson with you to S-4."

"Johnson?" I echoed.

"I believe you call him Ginger."

"I work better as a single operative, sir." And no way in hell was
Ginger Johnson tagging along, or Sabine.

The door pressed open. Linc's arms bracketed the frame. "I can
trust you on this?"

"Affirmative." As the door slid closed, I leaned against the wall,
catching my breath.

* * *

I ran through the gridded streets until checkpoint Charlie inspecting my credentials aggravated me beyond patience. Then I
networked the fire escapes and rooftops, bouncing from one to
the other. Fat snowflakes dusted Beta in a pristine vision, hope-

fully the last snowfall of March before spring took hold.

The first snowstorm I remembered from my childhood, Mom had taken me out into the wintry white world. I'd bounded along behind her like one of the pet-puppy clones Dad had created. I'd giggled when she turned around, popped her eyes wide and, grinning, fell back into a tall bank of snowy fluff. Skimming her arms and legs wide.

When she'd jumped up, black hair arranged with a halo of fresh white, she'd laughed. "Snow angels, Lizbeth. Make one!"

There were no angels here, just snow devils and desires sifting down on me. Predator drone planes scoped the sky above, fully armed unmanned vessels that were half helicopter and half blast-off rocket, able to take off from standstill in a powerful vertical thrust. Buzzing above me and flying away, the spy planes were the latest devices against the Revolution.

Deep in Sector Four, I halted on the same rooftop Linc had given orders from a week before. What I saw below was confusing—and utterly brilliant.

Taking the place of the group we'd wiped out was an ultra-urban guerilla army that had to be backed by big money. They looked fully trained, orderly…and incredibly young. The fact they'd moved into an area we'd already swept through—believing the place to be off the Corps radar—was a highly clever operational decision.

Scanning a one-kilometer radius through my CheyTac, I got a clean shot on three fully weaponized tanks sporting a symbol and slogo I'd never seen before. A six-pointed star and the words *Posse Omnis Juvenis* were decaled on the sides in stark blocky white detailing. The dead language instilled in me from my dad's teachings, I quickly unscrambled the Latin: *Power to All Youth*.

While I watched, the tank closest to my position snarled to life. Keeping low to the roofs, I followed as it gained ground closer and closer to the north gate and the bridge that bordered S-5. The tank stopped and ten youths spilled from it. They slouched into a factory that was alive with activity, releasing gray smoke into the air. I kept flat to the wall, lowering myself to the ground from the building opposite, landing in an alley. More militants came and went from the warehouse next to the factory. Young men and women who wore black garb like it was armor. There was a lot of armor decorating their faces, too. Piercings and elaborate tattoos abounded. Their hair took CO slick several steps further, colorful stripes embellishing Mohawks, braids, and close-cropped skull cuts.

I went out the back of the alley and ran down two blocks. Crossing over to the guerillas' side of the street, I ranged closer. Squatting against a huge metal container, I peered inside the grimy warehouse window. Nearly fifty youths roamed the open area, and on one end of the large room, bunk upon bunk lined up against one another. Their barracks.

I continued to survey the goings-on, slipping behind the barracks for a better vantage point of the factory. Blacked-out windows on all the floors frustrated my efforts. No doubt about it, there was a lot of manpower here. They had tanks and artillery in the abandoned sector between shaken-down tenements and half-demolished depots. And who knew what the fuck they were making in that factory?

Someone's raising a private army of highly skilled youths. The question was, who? I didn't think Linc expected me to stumble upon a scene of this magnitude when he'd sent me out on what should've been an afternoon's easy jag-off mission. Reaching into my pocket, I pulled out my D-P, ready to take some snapshots for Linc.

And then, *Oh shit.* Oh, holy shit. Squishing between the soot-covered wall and a graffiti-painted Dumpster bearing the *Posse Omnis Juvenis* mark, I made myself a shadow as Sebastian Monroe marched past me less than a meter away. *Bas, Farrow's little bro.* Rifle in his hands, black-rooted bleached hair shoved off his face, he clapped the shoulder of the boy who'd been pushing his crew for the past thirty minutes of my recon. They spun away from my hiding place.

"Hey, Sarge." The boy in charge greeted Sebastian. He was stocky and muscular, probably twenty or twenty-one. His eyes penciled in with kohl, his buzzed hair a startling shade of electric blue, he had a tattoo circling his wide throat, bearing the same words emblazoned on the tanks.

"Sarge." Sebastian laughed, shaking the hair out of his eyes. "Let's leave that to the Corp, yeah, Taft?"

Taft smiled and slid his arm around the blond boy's waist, landing a pinch on his ass. Sebastian punched him away, rubbing his behind. "Fuck, Taft. Y'all need more gadgets to keep them hands of yours busy? Ah already told you, I'm downright virginal. Savin' myself for my Validation of Union."

"Aw, c'mon, Bassy." Taft wrapped his hands around the back of his friend's neck and brought him forward for a quick nip of his mouth. "You know the Company isn't ever gonna be homo friendly."

They strutted away while I scrambled backward. *So Bas was beta dog to the alpha leader of this group.* I definitely couldn't engage them. I probably couldn't report them to Linc either. With Sebastian in cahoots with this so-called Posse, it didn't seem too far-fetched to think they might be on the Revolutionary team.

I decided to keep this fresh info hush-hush for the time being.

* * *

My head swimming with conspiracies and factions and who-the-fuck-knew what else, I skipped my room once I returned to Corps Command. In no mood to clash bitch swords with Sabine, I headed straight for the showers, hoping a hot one would thaw my frozen toes and help me think.

With my head bent under the blasting spray, water sluiced over my tense shoulders and down my back. Right then Commander Linc barged in. I shouldn't say *barged*—not this time. He was silent as a stealth weapon. Deadly as the drone Predator too.

He drew up quick with a rough curse. "Fuck, Liz."

My head whipped beyond him to the bank of mirrors, where I saw myself as he did: a long, sleek body taut with lean muscle. Finding his eyes, I drowned in his devouring gaze and turned around under the shower's spray. He locked sights on my sex. My thighs pressed together, slick lips swelling under his hungry regard.

"Do you always conduct Beta business in the locker room, or is it just me you're stalking, sir?"

Jaw ticking, he strafed closer. "I came for a report."

"Here's a report." I flicked water down my navel. "The water's hot."

Breath ragged, he caged both arms on the shower's open sides. "Woman, I am so close to coming right now."

"Care to join me?" Under my touch, my nipples drew even more erect. I liked breaking Linc down, testing him, tempting him. I needed the man in a state of mindless desire. Since seeing his key card laid out in his room earlier, I'd been forming a plan. Now was as good a time as any to implement it.

"Maybe you should get out."

"Maybe you should sit down before you fall over, sir."

He shrugged off his holsters and reached into the shower. Calloused palms slipped over the suds pouring down my body until he scraped across my nipples. The aroused buds in his hands felt so good.

"Yes," I whispered, writhing beneath his firm touch. *Too good.*

"I want to suck on you until you scream, sweetheart."

There was none of the softness in his words that had started our sensual kiss at the sex club, and there certainly wasn't any of the empathetic connection from our breakfast of truths. This was filthy-hot, on-fire, totally unstoppable wanting.

"I thought we were forgetting about what happened at the Club."

His possessive kiss stormed my defenses, his tongue cruising past my lips, thrusting in time to his groin against me. "This has nothing to do with the Club or those people. You keep tempting me beyond my control, Liz, and I won't be able to stop myself."

Compelling attraction snared us together in a moist embrace until I withdrew from his mouth, flipping off the shower. Brushing past him, I slung a towel around myself.

Linc fingered the edge where it knotted between my breasts. "What did you find out today?"

Besides the fact we can't keep our hands off each other? "Sector Four was all clear." Technically a small lie because the Posse factory and barracks were situated in S-5.

"Anything else?" Fingers tugged open the towel's drapes, finding my waist. His thumb rubbed my hip.

I gasped, "No, sir."

"I like the way you say *sir.*" His meandering thumb rolled up to my nipple, stroking back and forth.

I leaned in to his caress. "I like the way you touch me."

My eyes skated down his chest to his pelvis, and I moaned. He filled out the uniform pants, a solid cock straining against the blue fabric. A small part of me was weirded out—it was almost like eye-fucking Cannon's man, with Linc and Nate being twins. But whereas Nate was a soft touch, Linc was hard. So, so hard.

The halos, constantly fizzing with the unsteady electrical grid, blinkered off. I stumbled forward in the sudden darkness, catching myself on…*Oh my God.*

Linc grunted, shifted. That wasn't his weapon in my hand, but it was hot as freshly fired metal, rigid as a gun barrel. The weight and heat of him in my palm made me want to push my hand into his pants and feel that naked cock. Fingers snapped around my wrist. Linc pulled my hand slowly down his length, my fingers fully engaged with his flesh. And he was big. If Nate was packing the same, no wonder Cannon walked so…stiffly.

The halos came back to life. I snatched my arm away, my eyes wide. Linc's cheeks were flushed, his lip narrowly curled off his teeth. My palm was on fire from the feel of him. I waved it around in front of me, an added distraction to the dark-out move I'd pulled while I'd cupped him.

"Was touching me that bad?" He sneered.

"Next time I want a gun in my hand, I'll go for my Eagle."

"Good idea." Spinning around, Linc banged out of the locker room. I had no idea how the man managed to march with that *cannon* between his thighs.

As soon as the doors shut, I sank onto the bench. I pulled his key card from beneath my towel. I'd stolen it in the few moments the room had been pitch-black.

There was no time to savor the thrill of victory, and I wasn't all that happy with the way Linc had pounded out of here, angered. Pushing those thoughts aside, I dressed and headed to the basement. Thankfully, the halls below were empty. I bypassed the furnace room and slipped inside the one housing the mainframes—the backup singers to the D-Ps on the upper floors. I'd managed to sneak down here a second time to conceal a slim key card replicator. The device had been hatched by Hatch, naturally, for just this purpose. The bespectacled whiz kid had more contraptions than Cutler had schemes.

The room was as still as a catacomb. Dungeon-like halos on the walls cast eerie shadows as I recovered the little machine. I slid

Linc's card in one end and waited ten seconds for my copy to spit out the backside. I pocketed both, slinked along the corridor to the boiler room, and destroyed the replicator in a furnace. *Leave no trail.*

What seemed like a hundred floors upstairs, I dried my sweaty hands on my thighs before knocking on the steel panel door to Linc's quarters. I pressed it open when he said, "Come in."

He came around a corner wearing a wary smile.

"Sorry to interrupt you, sir." My breath left in a rush, remembering the sensual pitch of my voice and his response when I'd said *sir* to him last, not a half hour ago.

"I'm not."

"I thought I left something here this morning."

"I wish you had." His suggestive grin smoked.

This was such a dangerous game, and I was on slippery ground.

"Mind if I have a look in the lounge?" I asked.

He stepped back. "Help yourself." Dimples peeked from his cheeks as he repeated my words from the furnace room.

Leaning against the wall, he watched me. His hair was disheveled, and a graze of golden stubble sprinkled his chin and jawline, topping his upper lip where the bow of his mouth had tasted so good against mine.

Another knock on the door made him wheel away. I took the opportunity to shove the key card among his holster and badge on the chest in his living room. From the short hall, his low voice rumbled before he returned.

"Find anything worth your while?"

"No. I must've been mistaken." I started past him.

From behind, Linc blanketed me with his body. He curled his arms around me as I reached the door. "I don't think there's anything to mistake about us, Liz, so don't start lying to me now." After a brief all-too-intimate moment, he let me go and opened the door.

My heart lurched when I saw the raw emotion in his eyes. It echoed the way he'd looked at me the night we'd let the Freelanders go. As if he was searching for something in me, not to betray me, but to figure out if there was more between us.

He brushed my cheek with a gentle caress. "Have a good night."

I snapped to attention. "You, too, sir."

I had the key to Linc's office, the first step in discovering the truth about my father's murder. This was a triumph, but I didn't feel victorious. I'd used Linc. I'd trespassed the unspoken Corps code, and there was little valor in what I'd done.

Chapter Five

Stealing into Linc's office, I had zero-minus five minutes to ransack the place and get out. I hopped onto a chair and short-circuited the wires of the two spy cameras, looping them on a five-minute delay. Hopefully, Hatch had got it right, because I sure as hell wasn't a gearhead. I moved the chair back into position and headed to Linc's desk. After pulling open the drawers and rifling through the contents, I eased each drawer shut in turn. In the bottom of the final drawer, my fingers slipped across a slightly raised area. I depressed the slider and it levered up, revealing a hidden compartment. Inside was a slender machine I lifted out in shaking hands. My dad's digi-diary, recognizable because of the half-worn-off Pet Clone puppy-dog decal I'd decided to decorate it with when I was ten. The last time I'd seen the diary was several days before his death, while he dictated notes onto it.

The small pad hummed to life when I passed my fingers over it. Suddenly, I was staring at a grainy image of my dad.

"Oh my God, Daddy."

Pressing the heel of my hand to my eyes, I scrubbed away tears. I hadn't seen his face for eleven years, and he looked so close, real enough to touch. I crouched behind Linc's desk, listening intently as the date stamp scrolled across the bottom of the screen: *17-May-2060*. Just a month and a half before his murder.

The Pneumonic Plague is not reacting according to the trial tests. A cure seems impossible at this moment. Quarantines have proved ineffectual at containing its spread.

He looked haggard, sleepless, his face gray and drawn.

I've been unable to pinpoint an origination carrier. Since the outbreak last spring, the Plague metastasized almost immediately. The common terminology—Gay Plague—has incited fearmongering. The misnomer isn't an accurate portrayal of its spread.

Two minutes left on the camera loop, I scrolled ahead.

Date Stamp: 14-June-2060

Lysander Cutler shadows me in the labs. Although he's not a scientist, he's good company, a reassuring figure. Peg joined us for dinner last night. She was utterly charmed by the man.

My mom met CEO Cutler? In this memocast, Dad looked more relaxed, dark brown eyes even twinkling a little.

The Alpha CEO is a dedicated family man like me, raising his twin sons on his own since his wife died seven years ago. I have to admit—he broke off, grinning like a boy for a moment—*I'm a little awestruck by his charisma. I hope he can find a way to stay in Beta, perhaps take up the helm here. I'd like for Lizbeth to meet Nathaniel and Lincoln.*

Oh fuck. My dad had been taken in by the CEO's schmoozing. I felt sick to my stomach, my mind racing at the implications.

Date Stamp: 20-June-2060

Lysander convinced me to stop the Pneumonic Plague research. He says I should focus on the cure instead. He's right; of course he is. The samples and data I've collected are contained and sealed in my secondary lab on level ten of the medical offices in the Beta Quad—

I had no warning as the door to Linc's office tracked open. The motion-sensor halos bloomed back on. *This is worst-case scenario.* Flicking off the diary, I crabbed under the desk, thankful for the full-to-the-floor sides and front shielding me from view.

Linc grumbled to himself. "Now, where the hell did I…?" His boots were in my line of vision while he sifted through the documents on his desk. Reaching for the drawers, he got real close to my hidey-hole. Less than two minutes—way less—before Hatch's neat trick with the cameras reverted and I'd be well and truly fucked.

His D-P blared, and he answered it with a bark. "Yeah?" He continued to rummage through the desk.

Jesus. Hurry it up, Linc.

The return on the D-P was loud and clear, overriding the furious pound of my heart. *"Commotion in the Quad courtyard, sir."*

"What do you mean, commotion?"

"Uh, I think you better check it out for yourself, Commander."

"Goddamn it." His palm slammed onto the desk, rattling the metal above my head. "Get lieutenant on the horn."

Forty-five seconds… I started praying, mouth moving silently.

"Which one?"

"Jesus Christ. Burr. Get Burr. I'll track down Grant."

Fuck, fuck, fuck. I fumbled to power down my D-P just as

he pinged me. At my nonreply, he growled a vicious curse and stormed out, presumably on the warpath for me.

After I replaced the digi-diary, I quickly checked out the diversion that had saved me by the skin of my teeth, peering into the Quad below. *Oh Christ.* A black tank painted with a white star, loaded down with machine-gun turrets, trolled the perimeter of the Quad. Under the ultrabright halos below, I caught a glint of electric-blue hair. *Fuck. I hope Bas isn't stupid enough to shit in his own mess kit.*

Seconds to spare on the cameras' feedback loop, I hit the door running.

I legged it to Farrow's fancy condo while the *commotion* in the Quad warranted all attention, hoping the nut-fuck would buy me some time. Locating the address she'd given me, I buzz-buzz-buzzed the penthouse at the top of the needle-like glass and steel structure. I was jittery as hell. If I'd had any sense at all, I'd have hidden some fucking civvies somewhere along the way a few days ago so as not to draw attention to myself.

Livin' the dream, that was me.

I buzzed again, and finally Farrow opened the door. Her green eyes grew round an instant before she tugged me into the apartment.

"This is a big risk, sweet girl." She swept past me into a sunken crimson and cream lounge area.

"No shit. And I wouldn't be here if it wasn't for your little brother."

"Bassy?"

I scowled, flipping my cap against my thigh, then sailing it onto a velvet banquette. "Yeah, Bassy. Listen, I came across him with a big group of very well organized—and armed—youths. I'm telling you, Farrow, I don't like the looks of them. I can't tell what allegiance they have, if any. I'm hoping you can clear this up before everything goes to shit."

"Oh mah lord, Liz." Trembling hands smoothed down the front of her dress. "You're sure it was him?"

"Dammit, yes. You don't know what I'm talking about? You've never heard of a group called *Posse Omnis Juvenis*?"

"Power to All Youth?" She shook her head.

"What about terrorist factions?"

Farrow pressed her fingertips together below her chin. "Ah haven't had any news from my runners about that kind of unorganized activity."

"They weren't unorganized, that's for sure. They aren't working for the Freelanders, the Revolution?" I asked, knowing the answer already. "What would a gang of twentysomethings be doing with three tanks and enough gun power to make them a contender in the war? Not to mention they've overrun a factory in S-5 and are working it good?"

"What are they building?"

"Couldn't see in—blacked-out glass."

"Sebastian passed his exams two years early." Farrow paced the room.

Sheer dread climbed up the back of my neck. "In what?"

"Accelerated Applied Engineerin."

"In other words, Bas is a genius at building shit." I let out a long sigh, wondering what he could do with his talent and for whom.

Farrow nodded and rubbed her hands up and down her arms.

Walking to her, I cupped her shoulders. "Don't worry, okay? I haven't reported any of this to Linc and I won't."

Her lips bent into a brittle line. "It's too late not to worry. Ah shoulda kept a better eye on him."

"He'd have found a way to circumvent you anyway, if he's as smart as you say." I gave her a hug until she relaxed. "We'll figure it out. At least you've got an in with this group through Bas, assuming he doesn't know about your Revolutionary sympathies."

"No, he doesn't know. The brat thinks I'm just a flighty socialite."

That made me laugh, but I sobered fast. "We've got bigger problems anyway."

"What else?"

"The Posse are in the Quad right now. I saw the leader, Taft. Sebastian seemed pretty close to him," I explained.

Resolve tightened Farrow's delicate features. "Ah'm gonna beat Bassy's ass until he cain't sit on it for a week."

"I didn't see him in the Quad."

"Ah don't care where that scraggly little possum is, Ah'll find him" She hurried down the hall, reappearing several minutes later in head-to-toe leather, tucking a gun into her waistband.

Good-bye, socialite; hello, badass operative.

I gathered my cap and got ready to follow her out.

She pivoted in front of the door. "Ah forgot to mention, we've got anothah situation."

Goddamn it. Can this night get any worse?

"Leon's here."

"Here in Beta?" *Yeah, this night could get a whole lot fucking worse.*

"Here, down the hallway, in the shower."

"What? Jesus Christ. This is not good, Farrow. Where's Darke?"

She opened the door with a final glance at me. "You'll have to ask Leon about that. Ah'm gonna go wring my baby brotha's neck. I'll get a message to you, sweet girl."

That's assuming Linc lets me live through the night.

Great. I had a pissed-off commander to attend to, but instead I was stuck minding the runaway. The runaway made his appearance a few minutes later, strutting down the hall, a towel draped around his neck. His finely shaped torso was bare. A pair of loose pants hung low on his hips, and his light brown hair clung to his neck. Leon's gold-brown eyes glittered to life when he saw me.

"Liz!" Loping over, he enfolded me in a hug.

I smiled against his shoulder. *Shit. The kid is more of a puppy dog than I ever was.* "Big Papa is not gonna be happy." I took a seat on the red settee.

"Big Papa?"

"Cannon."

A nod followed his knowing grin. "Big Papa, *mais oui.*" Elbows braced behind him on the glinting metal bar, Leon stretched his legs out, all his pretty muscles on show. "Cannon knew I wanted to join the freedom fighters. He don't own me."

I had to admire his balls. "Uh-huh. And this fuck and flee has nothing to do with Darke?"

His chin lowered, and so did his voice. "We're not fucking. He can hardly stand to touch me."

"Hell, the way he kisses you, that's not the mark of a man who doesn't want you." I leaned forward and brushed his hand. "He can hardly tear his eyes off you, Leon."

"Not after the last moko session."

"The what?"

"Tattoos, the way they used to be done, with a bone awl. Darke asked me to give him a moko as a tribute to Tammerick and Wilde." Tears stood out on Leon's lashes.

"Aw, shit. That's just plain cruel. Why would he make you do that? Better yet, why did you agree?" A sharp spear of sympathy twisted through me.

I'd never seen Leon angry, but now he was infuriated. "I can't let no one else do it. Don't wan' any of them touchin' him. And if it hurts my heart to mark his body with…" He gasped as twin tears rolled down his cheeks. "With Tammerick and Wilde's names so he can remember how much he loved them, that's what I gotta bear."

My voice rasped with pain for him. "No, you don't have to bear it, baby."

"*Mais*, I wanted to." The willful jut of his chin was struck from stone. "Last time, he be all stretched out on the pallet in Smitty's forge. All that big brown body, bare down to his ass. I like to bite one day, *se derrière*."

"Leon."

"No, I need to say this, Liz. Okay?" His gold-flecked gaze found mine.

When I nodded, he continued. "Right across those big shoulders, he's made me do it. You know how much pain it takes to have that shard of bone piercing into the skin like that? No one been able to touch Darke but me since they died."

"That's because he feels something for you even if he won't admit it."

He shrugged. "Maybe that be. I don't know. At first I jess like to make him laugh, but he wasn't smilin' that day. I hated to hurt him anymore; told him so, too. He rolled over and got ahold of me. *Do it, my angel, my devil. Make it so I'll never forget them.*"

"Shit, Leon." The tears gathered in his eyes were mirrored in my own.

Leon wiped his face and sniffed. "When it was done, I told him, *I want my name on you, too,* cher. *Tous quelque chose,* all of me, it's his for the takin'."

"You should never give anyone that much power."

"Don' matter. Darke couldn't get out of Smitty's barn fast enough."

One man devoted to his lost lovers, the other determined to give whatever he could. Their plight reinforced what this Revolution was about. Lives were not the only thing at stake but the freedom to choose whom you loved, how you loved, no matter what gender. *Freelanders*—their very name was a call to arms.

"He was scared."

"Then he be a coward I don't need." Leon wrenched away from me.

"You don't believe that."

"Don' matter what I believe either." Turning around, his smile fell far short of his saddened eyes. Arms wide, he tried on a loose grin. "'Sides, look at this spread! Never seen the likes of it."

Darke's grief for his lovers had pushed Leon straight into the war zone. He'd grabbed some rations, his Colt, stolen one of the snowmobiles, and set off for Beta. He'd hardly slept during the trek but shrugged off the fatigue with a weary half smile. "I ain't no good at keepin' my emotions to myself. I had to get away. I can't help I got a hankerin' for the man."

I hated to break it to Leon, but he had more than a hankering going on.

"*Mais*, easy come, easy go, no? Like you and Miss Farrow."

What he potentially had with Darke was nothing like the free and easy downtime Farrow and I had enjoyed.

I ruffled his damp hair. "You really are insane."

"'S why you like me." He winked at me. "I saw you lookin' at my body."

"Boy, you got enough to deal with without making eyes at a fucked-up Corps foot soldier and Freelander supporter with abandonment issues who wants to jump her new commander's bones."

He gaped at me. I slammed my mouth shut. That was probably more truth than I'd ever admitted out loud or even to myself. I blamed his sob story. I blew straight threw that admission with, "You decided to put some distance between yourself and Darke."

"I guess so."

"I suppose he's hot on your heels."

"Don't know that he'd bother." Leon jumped onto a high stool and leaned his head on his hand.

And just when I was about to tell him why Darke was gonna bother, a not-so-subtle knock reverberated through Farrow's apartment. I sent Leon an I-told-you-so look and drew out both Eagles just in case, shooing him away. He paid no attention to me, tagging along into the foyer.

I peered through the peephole to see Darke outside. I yanked the door open and beckoned him inside. Wearing a knit cap, woolly winter gear, looking bigger than ever and not a little bit unhinged, Darke shut the door. Then he went immediately for Leon.

I stepped into his path, his ruddy cheeks reddening even more under the deep brown tone of his skin. "It sure took you long enough. What was that? You gave Leon a whole three hours' head start?"

"He was gone twelve hours before I knew it. Get out of my way, Liz."

"Not so fast, lover." He wasn't getting past me until he settled the fuck down. The stark lines of his handsome face spoke of fatigue, but the deep frown smoothed slowly away with every glance at Leon.

"I need to make sure he's okay."

I lashed out. "You got two eyes. Use them. And by the way, you big ass, this is a fine time to get concerned about Leon's welfare."

Black eyes swiveled to mine, and his jaw leaped with tension. "I am always thinkin' about him." His shoulders dropped, and he tugged off his hat. "Let me pass, please, ma'am."

I stepped aside. "Only because Miss Eden would be proud of your manners."

Leon withdrew from Darke's hand, but he let himself be guided to the lounge. I leaned against the wall, ready to step in if Leon's heart took one more hit.

Darke's body vibrated; his hands trembled with the effort of not touching his boy. His voice growled, "Tell me you're fine."

"I be fine." Tilting his head back, Leon bared his claws. "An' I was fine before you got here." He prodded the big chest in front of him. "I been fine all my damn life. You think I'm too innocent for you, Darke? What do you think I used to get up to in Alpha? How do you think I made money?" Leon's eyes narrowed. "I don' need you right now."

"Leon, angel—"

The smaller man swung away from him. "Not now. You don' get to call me that now."

Darke watched him leave the room. "Shit."

"Do you realize what you're doing to the kid?" I'd taken my life into my own hands a few times tonight already; no need to stop now. I shouldn't call Leon *kid* anymore either, not after that standoff. The supercharged atmosphere between him and Darke was the primal attraction of two highly sexual men.

"You do not wanna get into this with me, Liz." Darke was barely leashed, one step away from going after Leon.

"Bullshit, I don't."

Muscle by muscle, he made himself relax. Scrubbing large hands over his face, he admitted, "Fuck. I know...I just..." He sank into a chair that was much too fragile to bear his weight. "I can't have him, and I can't let him go."

"You better sort this mess out. I'm assuming Cannon's await-ing word from you?"

"Yeah." He looked utterly miserable.

"*Y'all* better haul ass to the Catskills commune then, and I'll touch base. You're here now and it ain't a good thing, because the situation just went squirrely." I kissed his cheek, cold from the outside still frosting over him. "Just leave Leon alone, if nothing else, Darke."

I left him to put the FUBAR circumstances to rights and to soothe Leon's battered ego. I had my own deep well of crap to dig myself out of, and the night wasn't even half over yet.

I didn't think Linc was gonna let me hit the sack without some extensive excuse-making, boot-licking, and ass-kissing. The last time I'd seen him, I'd been hiding under his desk and he'd been about to hunt me down so we could take care of the *Posse* playing chicken in the Quad courtyard.

* * *

"Where's my gear?" I called out as I stomped into the bunkroom.

Sabine was there, *surprise*, but my stuff wasn't where I'd left it, always tidily packed in the event I had to reassign myself to another part of the InterNations once Linc discovered I was a Revolutionary decoy. In the days we'd been roomies, I'd learned about Sabine's mission before she returned to Beta. She'd traveled cross-continent like the good little toy soldier she was, delivering CEO Cutler's new edicts to high-ranking Corps staff in other Territories.

She was her usual grumpy, dumpy self when she rolled off her bed and stomped her feet to the floor. She looked at me with distaste. "Commander moved you out a couple hours ago. He said you need to report to him. In his quarters."

"But I was thinking we could trade beauty secrets," I goaded.

"Yeah, I saw how you got all dressed up when the commander took you to the CEO's party. It's disgusting the way you've got your sights on him, trying to use him to solidify your allegiance."

Whoa. If the undeniable draw I felt toward Linc was about keeping my position safe, I could think of a thousand other less-messy ways to go about it. In fact, being intimate with the man bordered on stupidity because every time I got close to him, I wanted to know who he really was. I wanted to find out about the soldier who rose to such a high rank at so young an age. I wanted to comfort the boy who'd been left to a despicable man who had no right raising children.

Taken aback by Sabine's accusation, I said the first thing that came to mind. "And I saw how pathetic you were when he didn't give you the time of day."

"You got it all wrong, girly. I'm not about Linc Cutler. I'm fighting for the CO. I'm fighting to keep CEO Cutler in power."

I swallowed my retort, leaving before I said something I'd regret.

I made my way upstairs. The superspeed of the elevator made my head reel but not as much as the day's events coupled with Sabine's finger-pointing. The visuals and sound of my dad rang clearly through my mind. My stomach clenched to think he'd been so thoroughly taken in by Linc's father, but I didn't know to what aim and I wouldn't be able to find out until I broke into the labs across the Quad compound. Not to mention I was starting to think I was in a shitload of a mess—my dad, the *Posse*, the Freelanders, the Revolution. Then there was Linc.

I was a ball of nerves by the time I reached his floor.

His door glided open as I approached, my progress clearly tracked by the cameras lining the corridor. *Lovely*.

Linc scooped me inside and locked us in.

I wanted more than anything to tell him the truth, but I couldn't. I wanted to be held and assured everything was going to be okay even if it wouldn't be. For fuck's sake, what I really needed was a hug.

Trying not to appear as lost and vulnerable as I suddenly felt, I said, "Burr said you were expecting me, sir."

His forearm came to rest on the wall beside my head. His hand rose to my face. Watching me closely, he trailed his fingertips to my lips. "So I was, several hours ago."

One touch from Linc and too many sensations swirled inside my body.

One look at him and I was twisted up with the desire to come clean. Shaken by what Sabine had said about the two of us, I wanted to know if he thought the same. Or if he felt the way I did—as if our burning attraction was on the verge of becoming something far deeper and so much scarier.

"Were you intentionally disregarding my messages, Liz?" Rich, husky, his voice sent webs of silken desire to my rapidly moistening sex.

I tried to clear the thickness from my throat. "No, sir."

"Sir?" The half smile that slid up his cheek was full-throttle sex. Sex with dimples, sex in another tight black tank top, sex in those low-slung, soft cloth pants.

I was suddenly having trouble breathing. "Linc."

"That's better." He unleashed a full smile, and I about fell over from the force of his good looks before that smile became something more sinister. "Now that we've cleared that up, tell me where the fuck you've been all night and why my coms went unanswered."

Raising my chin, I said, "I thought I was getting my monthlies. Sir."

"And were you?"

"False alarm. The cramps must've been from the gray matter stew we were served in the mess hall for dinner."

His laugh broke free. "Gray matter stew?"

"Yes, sir. Some of us don't have the luxury of fresh vittles delivered to our quarters."

A wicked gleam shone in Linc's eyes. "Now you do."

"Now I do what?" Was he really letting my excuse slide? It was hardly airtight.

Curling a hand around my neck, he pulled me close enough for a kiss, close enough to feel the steady pound of his heartbeat against my breasts. Close enough to whisper in my ear, "Now you have that luxury too. You'll be staying here. My father's still keeping tabs on you, and I want you safe."

Worry skittered through me. "Why?"

"I have a vested interest in you."

"I'm a pawn. That's what you mean." I broke free of his embrace.

"To him you are." Linc leaned back against the wall.

"And you?"

When his eyes slid shut, weariness slipped over his body. He shook his head. Instead of answering me, he shoved off the wall and took my elbow in his hand. He led me down a side hallway into a well-appointed bedroom. My pack sat on one of the low chairs. Silver-gray bedding was pulled back on a bed whose platform was almost at floor level. Muted halos glowed over a variety of belongings on the dresser—a watch, a pistol case, a faded, framed photograph. Masculine items, Linc's belongings. This was his bedroom.

I started to back out, but he barred the way. "I'm not taking the sofa."

I gulped. "Then I will."

He shut the door, spinning me around. "No, you won't."

Oh no. This isn't gonna fly. I don't need another reason to fantasize about the man. Kinky Linc Cutler was so damn hot I nearly combusted on sight. I wanted him too much for anything about this to be safe.

Brooking no disobedience, he pointed to another doorway. "Washroom's through there. Get ready for bed."

I all but fled, collecting my duffel on the way. I raised my face to the mirror, swearing at my tell-all reflection. My cheeks wore a pink blush. My tits rose and fell while my heart rate went rapid-fire at the idea of spending the night, many nights, alone with him. I was in heat for the man and it showed. Hopping into the shower, I cleaned up from my run to Farrow's and back again. I dressed in clean panties and a tank top. It didn't really matter what I wore. He'd already seen the goods. Besides, it was gonna take full-body armor—maybe even an anaphrodisiac—to ward off his lure over me.

Linc sat propped up against the pillows. Sheets pooled around his hips, showcasing deep pelvic cuts. His chest was dusted by a scattering of golden hair that arrowed into a line bisecting his six-and-then-some abdominals.

His invitation was so low I barely heard him. "Get in."

The sheets smelled of him—spicy, musky male—and his warm bulk pressed against my side, the heavy muscles of his thigh against my slimmer one. Shutting my eyes, I lay as rigid as a plank. He strained over me to click off the halos, his biceps brushing my breasts, a caress that wasn't accidental. I fought not to arch against him as he pulled away from me.

Suddenly, I wished I hadn't bothered with clothes at all. I wanted to wrap myself around Linc, ride up and down his thigh. I wanted to watch him come all over my belly.

Cramming my eyes more emphatically closed, I ran through all that had happened that night, ending with the one article of information Linc had failed to tell me. He'd made no mention of the *Posse Omnis Juvenis*, a fact I found both suspicious and curious. At least I wasn't the only one keeping secrets.

"Are you cold?" He broke into my reverie.

I shook my head, which brought me up against the thick bulk of his shoulder. No. I was on fire from my head to my toes, toes that curled with every husky sound of his voice.

"Hot?"

"You could say that." I smiled in the dark.

"Yeah, you are one hot woman, Liz." I heard the sheets rustling and then his rough voice. "C'mere. Let me hold you."

"Linc—"

"*Shh.*" He shifted to his side and kissed me softly, once and twice, mesmerizing me with his lips sweeping against mine. "I haven't stopped thinking about you since that night at my father's. Hell, I've wanted you in my bed since you returned to Beta. You're the bravest woman I've ever met."

Oh God.

He bent to my neck, sucking and tasting. "You're so beautiful, sweetheart. Been making me crazy."

Arms stealing around his shoulders, I curved in to him, and the kisses went wild. Our tongues writhed; my thighs widened to cradle him. I ran my palms down his back until I landed on his ass, gripping both hard crescents.

Leon's story, his pain and desire, urged me into an undeniable, hungry state. Starving for Linc, I decided to grab what I wanted. I wouldn't be like Darke, always wondering, never taking. *It could all end tomorrow.* I needed to be with this man, to feel him inside of me.

Linc punched up on his arms, huffing with frustration. "Too many goddamn blankets."

I squeezed his rear. Slipping my fingers down, I tried to reach where his balls nested. I felt powerful when he threw his head back and groaned. "Well, it is your bed, sir."

"Yes, it is, and I want you out of it, out of your clothes, and in that chair, now." He moved onto his back, tossing the covers off me.

Beside the bed, I dropped my tank top and panties to the floor. Linc's gaze traveled all over me, as tangible as his touch, his breath coming faster. He licked his lips and pointed to the chair.

Rolling my hips, I walked away from him. I tilted my head back and ran my fingers through my short hair, giving him the ultimate view of my body. Being completely naked for a lover was nearly a first for me. This time, the most important time, I wanted to be utterly bare. I glanced over my shoulder. Linc's hot gaze roamed over me. I'd never felt this desired as a woman—for one night, a soldier no longer.

"Jesus, Liz. You're about to kill me over here. I could look at that ass for hours."

"You just wanna look?" Reaching the chair, I put both hands on the seat and bent over, spreading my thighs as I went. I was wet, ready for him.

He stood slowly, but I could tell his control was slipping by the catch in his voice. "Touch yourself for me."

Linc's command hummed through my veins. I glided one finger through my slit, swirling it around my clitoris.

He groaned. "Suck it. Suck your finger."

I moaned around my own taste, then straightened to face him. "This definitely violates Gen Order One."

"A bunch of other shit, too." His face tight with desire, he stalked forward. "Tell me to stop and I will."

Close, *God,* closer, heat poured off him, and his briefs hardly contained his enormous erection. "I don't want you to stop. Don't stop."

He didn't, not until his body made contact with mine and I cried out. My nipples grazed his pecs, the soft hair arousing my flesh. His hands cupped my bottom. I skimmed my fingers from his neck down his rugged chest, watching the flat brown nipples turn into satiny buds I eagerly sucked.

"I want you in the chair, Liz."

Saluting him with a smoky laugh, I complied. I slid to the edge, my toes pointed into the carpet, my back arched. I offered myself to him, aching for him. "Is this good for you, baby?"

He lowered to his knees in front of me. "Yeah. Let me see those pretty li'l darlin's." The drawl he usually tamped down broke free. "Give 'em to me."

Turned on like never before, I closed my fingers around my breasts. My nipples were drawn up between my fingertips, dark and tight. The first rake of his tongue guided me into his mouth, tugging a moan from my lips.

My breasts filled his palms, his lips, and while he lapped from one side to the other, his words scattered across my skin. "Damn, I've wanted to taste these tits since I saw you in the shower. Do you have any idea how hard you make me, Liz?" He bit down and sucked until I shouted, grabbing his hair. "I want you wet, hot, and all over me until I feel nothing but your sweet, juicy cunt."

Shivering with need, I spread my legs wide around his torso, slipping my pussy against the ripples of his stomach. The long draws of his mouth, his fingers trailing lower, caused escalating sensations inside me. He explored my mound. Skimming through the soft curls, he spread my slippery arousal around until every bit of me was soaked. Then he thrust two fingers inside, his thumb circling my clit.

"Your pussy's so plump and wet."

I could only moan.

His satisfied rumble of laughter shook against my peaked nipples. I came apart with a sharp cry, holding his wrist, keeping his fingers inside me.

Pulling out with moist suction, he swiped the wetness around my breasts, sucking it off with hungry laps. He stood up and bent over for a kiss, working me with his tongue until my head rested against the back of the chair.

When Linc dropped his briefs, I didn't beat an eyelash. His long, solid cock came into view as he straightened. Mouthwatering, thick, the head more than a mouthful, it reared up from a thatch of light brown hair under which two heavy sacs cuddled the root of his cock.

I took him in my hand. "Oh, yes."

He grunted and moved closer. I weighed his balls in one hand, languidly pistoning the length of his shaft with the other. He was thick and hard against my palm, and a drop of precome pearled on the hooded tip. Rubbing it over his head until it glistened, I listened to Linc groan, watched him become even stiffer.

I circled my fingers around and around until his thighs quaked, and I knew he wanted to drive his cock up and down my fist. Catching the glazed blue of his eyes, I tilted my head sideways and slurped along his shaft. I bestowed the lightest kiss to the tip before heading down the other side until his entire cock was darkly colored with desire and slick with saliva.

"It's too good, sweetheart." He slipped from my hand, pressing me into the seat.

On his knees before me, he tilted my head to the angle he wanted until we were plunging—wild and greedy—into each other's mouths.

Lips skating to my neck, my collarbone, my earlobe, he asked, "Are you untried?"

I hauled him back by a handful of hair. "You really are a barbarian, aren't you?"

His expression was arrogant as hell and only half ashamed. "I meant have you been with many men?"

"Enough."

He tugged my breasts and jerked me forward. His aggressive torment turned me on.

Voice seductive, he said, "Yeah? I'm gonna make you come, sweetheart, until your hot little pussy flutters all around my cock and you beg me to fuck you some more."

I licked a line up his throat to his ear. "You won't find me arguing about that."

He laid my legs over the arms of the chair until I was wide open to his stare, his fingers, his cock. Guiding his length up and down my pussy, we both watched my lips part over his thick root. I grabbed the seat, working in counterpoint thrusts as he pumped up and down the outside of me.

"You gonna take my cock, Liz, or is it just a gun you know how to handle?"

"Why don't you shut the hell up and give it a shot?" I spread myself open for him.

On a long groan, he buried himself inside me. So deep, heavy, and hot. Pinning my thighs aside, Linc withdrew and thrust again. Each slow departure punctuated by a perfect, smooth lunge that pitched me into another orgasm, flooding my body with lush sensation.

He snapped his hips faster. Beads of sweat slipped between our bellies, and his hair hung in his eyes. He licked his lips and grunted, brow furrowed. I pushed forward, sliding my hands down to grasp his ass, adding to the force of his thrusts. Our lips met, slanting sideways, tongues coiling together. And then Linc was so out of control, he couldn't kiss me anymore. He groaned at my mouth until his head fell back and his hips jolted harder.

As another climax sped toward me, he pulled me off the chair, onto his lap. I was draped around his tensed body as he urged me up and down his cock, holding my weight on his thighs. Thrusting harder, tighter, deeper, and yelling, he filled me. He filled the aching void of my body, my being, howling as he let loose and came while I shattered apart again.

Our kisses were breathless and slow, no longer urgent. Linc's hands slid to my hips as he lifted me back onto the chair. Slick and wet, his cock withdrew from me. His chest shined, his muscles still flexing from exertion. He stood, turning to fix the pillows and blankets we'd tossed aside on the bed.

My gaze wandered up his strong legs to an ass to die for. His broad back was banded by taut muscles...and a goddamn moko. A black, primitive design of an American eagle of Old History days marked the wide stretch of his shoulders. Thick whorls of ink filled in its wingspan from shoulder to shoulder. Beneath the hooked talons that dropped to his spine, the word *Libertas* underlined the majestic, extinct bird of prey. Latin, like *Posse Omnis Juvenis*, this brand meant Freedom. Unlike the synthetic, brightly colored tats of the guerillas, Linc's was clearly made in the manner of the Freelander moko Leon had described.

While I lingered on the sight and possible implications, Linc's back flexed from his shoulders to his gorgeous glutes, and then he slowly swiveled toward me. He latched his arms around my waist and carried me to the bed, where he laid me out gently. He covered me first with his body, then with a sheet. Kissing my cheeks, my neck, he roved lower to my breasts.

I tugged his hair to draw him to my face. "What does this mean?"

Linc gave me a lazy smile of pure male satisfaction. "It means I'm still keeping my eye on you." The heart of his palm began a slow, sensual grind over my aching clit. "And my hands."

My belly hollowed with need, and my hips circled against his hand. I muffled my moan against the underside of his biceps. I couldn't deny my body's reaction to him, but what pulled at my heart was more than pure sex.

He thrust into me, hard, fast, and to the hilt. He captured my gaze and never looked away. "It means I want more of you."

I rolled him over, molding my flesh to his. This wasn't how I'd imagined the night ending. With no family, virtually alone, Linc gave me the connection I needed. Stretching out on top of him, I kissed his chest, his neck. I found his hands and tangled our fingers together. We moved together, slow and sensual. And everything about being with him felt right when we were like this.

Chapter Six

In the Corps Command war room a week later, we ran through strategies. Ginger and his groupies, the assholes who'd roughed me up my first night in Beta, were paying close attention to the D-Ps. Today the airwaves sang about the trouncing of Omega Territory in the former Middle East by the CO and Corps. It was another devastating defeat, if it could be believed. I imagined it was more false reporting to keep morale up.

Linc was all business to my right. He squinted at the latest hot spots popping up on the glowing geo-map of Beta Territory. The contrast between this man who controlled Beta Corps and the one who commanded my body was striking.

The morning after we'd fucked, I'd woken cautiously. He'd had me in every erotic way, sometimes with his hands gripping my hips and hair, holding me in place while he pounded into me from behind, sometimes slowly rolling his hips, lowered on top of me so every inch of his muscled body rubbed against mine. While he'd slept, I'd memorized his face. Relaxed, he looked so much younger, no longer torn by the weight of the war. I'd kissed the slim scar on his eyebrow, the strong jaw raspy with new stubble. I'd curled my arms around him, amazed when he murmured my name in his sleep. He held me even closer. It was the first night I'd slept without nightmares of my father's death plaguing me.

Finding Linc absent from the bed when I opened my eyes, I'd rolled face-first into his pillow. I wallowed in the last of his warmth. I'd enjoyed the pleasure still humming through the tips of my breasts and between my thighs. I'd heard the outer door open and close. Hushed footsteps accompanied by a low musical hum that made me smile into the pillow.

He'd halted in the doorway, one foot crossed over the other. My heart slammed with his slow, thorough perusal. A domed tray in his hands, he'd strolled over, gaze on me the entire time.

He'd uncovered the tray to reveal a massive serving of breakfast in a can, notorious on all Corps chow lines. "Thought you might be missing your mess hall special, what with all my *luxurious vittles* you partook of last night."

I'd narrowed my eyes at him. Leaping off the bed, I'd sauntered to him. The tray rattled when his hand shook and he took in my naked form. "You evil, evil man." I'd winked and set the tray aside. I moved in for a kiss that Linc returned with immediate passion.

I left him wanting more, climbing back in bed. "No more of that until you feed me properly."

His chuckle echoed as he left the room. Returning a minute later with another platter, Linc sat beside me. Our real breakfast consisted of fresh eggs, baked bread, and juice, which we shared from the same plate.

"I suppose you think you're funny with your little joke about the mess hall grub."

"Yep." He grinned.

I shoved a corner of toast into his smug mouth and laughed.

Living together, fucking like mad—we could give Nate and Cannon a run for their fuck-bunny money—working side by side, we made a crack team. Linc respected me as a lieutenant and wanted me as a woman. Before him, my only allowance to femininity had been my personal quarters in Alpha, and I'd have sooner cut the nuts off anyone than share my longing for color, frills, pretty things. With Linc, I was more a woman than I'd ever been, as well as the fiercest military operative. Our time together was marred only by the secrets wearing me down.

In the days after I moved in with Linc, we'd thrashed the units' ass. We put them through maneuvers, making them testify their allegiance to the Corps with blood, sweat, and sobs. They were almost worthy of their uniforms now. Lieutenant Sabine Burr continued to act like I was climbing the Corps ladder with Linc's cock as one of the rungs. I still needed to sort out her sourpuss face, preferably with my two fists: *Worst* and *Nightmare*.

There were other things to worry about that ranked higher than her. Watching Freelanders mowed through and Revolutionaries plowed down by Predator planes while I maintained my good-soldier farce. Beta was up in arms, up in flames, and the dust never settled. Then there was the Posse faction and Farrow fretting over Bas's involvement.

"Water's being rationed, food shipped in, but the supply lines are drying up." Linc tilted a massive D-P screen in my direction.

On it I could see the civilians in Omega lined up for the gravy train comprised of a column of Corps food and water trucks. The terrain was desert harsh, and the people were sunburned, their lips cracked.

The water and food shortage was nothing new, a phenomenon begun with the Purge and its earth-wide devastation. It was why the CO had created its own food banks filled with genetically harvested provisions and why each Territory had a water-processing plant. No matter what the news was—whether or not it was true regarding both sides of the war—CO resources were stretched thin. Or maybe Cutler and his dignitaries across the globe were using starvation tactics to add a new level of *Oh Holy CO* promo to its remaining on-the-fence populace. Delivering aid and appearing to be the heroes in this scenario while the Freelanders and Revolutionaries perpetuated the war was a canny tactic.

"It's the same all over the InterNations, sir." I scanned through three more government channels broadcasting from various Territories, the news getting more dire.

Ginger's troops took one of the portables off the table and huddled beneath the rows of Territory flags all bearing the same gold bars and blue slogo: *Regeneration, Veneration, Salvation.* They loudly bragged about taking down the *butt-ugly Nomads* and *undergunned Revos.*

Ginger was beginning to piss me off, again.

Linc pushed the hair off his forehead. Today the untamed golden waves brushed low on his brow. My fingers itched to curl into the locks and smooth his worried frown. "Beta should've been better prepared. Refugees are still streaming in. We can barely contain the war at this point, let alone feed a thousand more hungry mouths."

Starvation and dehydration, fighting, and hope for survival clouded the horizon with fear. I had too many worries of my own—bring Beta to its knees and Cutler with it, deliver Linc to his mom and brother, discover who had assassinated my dad—to stop and comfort Linc, yet I traced his knuckles where they pressed onto the long titanium table.

"We'll figure it out." I whispered, making sure Sabine and the rest were happily yapping about who was gonna bag the biggest body count during our next mission.

Spreading his fingers beneath mine, Linc swung his storm-blue gaze to me. "Will we?"

My throat went dry. I wondered if he was referring to him and me. Moving my hand up his forearm, I squeezed the taut muscles. "Yeah." Sliding away from his intense stare, I asked, "This setup, with the workers concentrating on the war effort, the sewage backed up, and water running short…are you concerned about a resurgence of the Plague?" I kept mentally playing back my dad's memocasts, trying to figure out what the Plague—the Pneumonic Plague, not the Gay Plague, as it had popularly been called—had to do with his death.

"It was stamped out a decade ago." Linc hitched one hip onto the table. He sent a look to his crew, where they hunkered over the D-P. "But if we can't get control of the sewage treatment and overpopulation by the warmer months, then I'd say conditions are ripe for a new outbreak."

"It's already April."

"That means we've got a lot of work to do, Lieutenant."

"Double that." My hand hovered over the haunting D-P display, turning it off. "Beta can't last much longer on its own."

Linc gathered the others close, barking orders for the night's details. After dismissing the troopers, all but me, he called into the guardroom, "Take the cameras offline in the Central Command. I'm conducting a private interview and am not to be interrupted."

As the door snicked with an airtight lock, a sinking sensation fell all the way to the pit of my stomach. *Busted.* The D-Ps disappeared down into the table while I remained stock still. I swallowed my fear and looked over to find Linc watching me. He'd shed his cold calculation, lips forming a sensual curve. Softer than sleep, his blue eyes were slumberous on me. Linc was so gorgeous my breath caught.

"What, sir? Couldn't wait to get me alone?"

"Exactly that." His fingers ghosted over my lips. "You are so damn beautiful, Liz."

I melted into his touch, closing my eyes. The thrill of his words wandered up and down my spine.

The velvety depths of his voice shot another quiver through me when he pulled back. "How are you holding up?"

"Fresh as a fucking daisy, sir." I saluted.

"You like flowers?"

"Not so much. They make me sneeze." I grinned.

Linc chuckled. "Your tough-girl routine turns me on." He yanked me to him with a hand traveling into the waist of my camos. "I also like how hot and wild you are when you let yourself go on me. We'll have to be fast. Can you take it?"

"I think I've proven myself capable of handling you, Linc." Backing out of his embrace, I threw off my cap and gun belt. "The question is, can you take me?"

Our race around the room was littered with teasing grabs, squeals, and laughs. Chairs tossed aside, flags waving in our wake, we ended in a mock tussle. Linc took me to the floor. Ripped the shirt from my breasts, tore through my bra, and palmed my breasts. I threw my weight against him and shoved him off of me.

I crouched low, beckoning him to me. "Got enough balls to follow through with your brag, baby?"

Linc pulled his shirt off, unbuckled his belt, and popped a couple buttons on his trousers. He peeled down the smallest jock strap imaginable, the wealth of his wiry hair and the base of his rigid cock coming into view. Framing his groin with both hands, he answered, "You know I've got the balls, sweetheart; you had them in your mouth last night."

Passion flashed through me, remembering the taste of his silken, heavy orbs on my tongue. Our fists up, we circled each other, breath coming quickly. He swiped across the space separating us, slapping my tit, pinching my nipple. Arousal screamed down to my sex.

"Look at that." Linc's voice was hoarse, his touch rough as he cupped my breasts. My nipples swelled, and he started raining light slaps over the pin-tight points until our mouths met and our tongues coiled.

I came with a shout when his next series of spankings landed on my breasts.

I trembled in orgasm while Linc grunted, "Still gonna fight me?"

"Every step of the way." I unsnapped his pants the rest of the way and crammed my hand inside, filling my palm with his thick, hard shaft. Lifting him free, I gave two loose strokes of the solid length. Linc's hips jerked, and he shouted my name.

Vectors, sectors, the grid offline, Linc and I were lit up. Shit was unraveling at a rapid rate, but I shoved it all away. The only thing that mattered was getting him inside me as fast as possible. I was on the table in two seconds, the rest of our necessaries ripped away. Linc prowled on top of me, his cock ready. Magnificently male, he peered at me with a mischievous glint.

"So help me, Linc, if you so much as—"

Thumping me hard with his cock right on top of my clit, he pushed one arm behind my thigh, opening me further as he slapped his shaft onto my wet flesh. I screamed with each strike, and he groaned, face a mask of erotic concentration.

"Oh fuck!" I was frenzied by shattering shots of pleasure. His cock looked ready to explode when he finally plunged inside. I came the moment he entered, deep and long. He was so hard I felt every ridge as he lunged in and out. Hands gripping his back, I could barely withstand his thrusts. I sped through several orgasms; then he started shooting. A volley of semen landed on my sex before he buried himself inside me again. Hips pumping, cheeks caving in, he came with shuddering, full-body pulses I felt all the way inside my belly.

"*Ah*, fuck." His face came to rest at my neck, hands caressing my sides. "Fuck, Liz."

I moaned when he thrust a few more times, teasing me with the full, wet tip of his cock. Wrapping my arms around him, I kissed his shoulder where a deep old scar raised the skin.

"I want to stay right here." His rugged voice lifted chills on my neck.

I moved my hips against him. "Right here?" I wiggled my back on the cold, hard table. "Or right here, in Central Ops, on top of me?"

He rose, irises ringed in black from spent desire. "Did I hurt you?"

I pushed my hands into his hair to bring him down for an un-hurried kiss. "No, baby. You felt good. It was perfect."

A lazy smile crept over his lips. "*Hmm*. I think we better move out."

When Linc withdrew, I noted the pink flush to his cheeks and ears and chest. I watched him sort out our clothes. He dressed me, trying to make the buttons line up with shaky hands. He kept his head ducked the whole time. It wasn't until he had some sem-blance of his uniform on that he took a deep breath. He smudged his thumb across my lower lip and started stepping away.

I grabbed his wrist. "Wait." After the tearing-it-up sex, I was drowsy all over. I had to get back on mission, an increasingly dif-ficult task where Linc was concerned.

"What is it, sweetheart?" Even while he said the endearment, he scoped the cameras lining the room, making sure they blinked red instead of green.

"Permission to go off duty for a couple hours, sir."

"Why?" His measured look fissured another crack in my armor.

"Being in Beta brings back a lot of memories. I just need some downtime." I didn't have to fake the pain and vulnerability I showed him.

"Your mother and father."

My eyes welled at the tender touch guiding my chin up. I never expected this level of comfort or understanding from Linc. Our kiss long and soft, I looped my arms around his waist.

He pulled away and knocked my cap. "Keep your D-P on and be careful."

"Affirmative." I saluted.

Linc turned back at the door. "One more thing, Grant. You understand my father's endgame, right?"

"Total Cutler control."

"We're going to make sure that happens."

My stomach took a nosedive, but I held my salute. "Copy that, Commander."

* * *

Lying to Linc was becoming second nature, and it was eating away at me. Maybe he felt the same way. He'd never mentioned the nighttime visit by the *Posse Omnis Juvenis*, which made me wonder why he didn't want me to know, what he was hiding.

Dressed head to toe in black, I left Corps Command by a less-guarded door. I snuck around the edges of the Quad's cornerstone buildings, slipping down alleys and keeping tight to the walls. In the square where Taft and his tank had blazed trails, the massive D-Ps droned on, illuminating the area in harsh light. I had to skirt around CO Headquarters to reach the hospital and med offices, both of which were constantly patrolled. With watching eyes everywhere, there wasn't a whole lot of wiggle room.

At the rear of the thirty-story-high med building, I jumped up, catching the lowest rung of a fire escape. Silencing my steps over the metal grating, I sprinted up to floor nine, using a compact pry bar to jimmy a window. I darted into the stairwell once inside. Approaching the next door, Level 10, I eased it open to scope out the bright white corridor. Two guards were holding a raucous conversation about a meter and a half away from me. I squeezed the door shut, waited a forty count, and checked again. Bingo. One of the guards was gone, the other strolling away with his back to me.

Coming up behind him, I dealt a hammer blow to the back of his head, followed by a soft drop to the floor, incapacitating but not killing him. I tied the lanky man up with a length of wire and stowed him in a storage room, bringing the butt of my gun down on the lock from the outside.

It took another thirty seconds to locate my father's secondary lab. His name was still on the metal plaque outside, all these years later. There wasn't a retinal scan or thumbprint ticker, but a digital code box bleeping in red, awaiting the correct password. Hearing a pair of footsteps approaching, I gave myself one chance to get it right before I had to fall back. Dad had been sentimental to a fault, a trait I'd stricken from my life over the past few years. Rubbing the butt of one Eagle for luck, I gave the password a shot. *MarvMillionfish#39* was his first successful clone pet project, the common name for a millionfish being guppy.

The box blipped green. I stepped through in the nick of time, quickly sliding down to the floor against the door. I stayed low and worked my way around the dark room from center to center. Lab stands stood empty, storage units frosted over and void of contents. Nothing was out of place until I hit a long steel table running down the side of the lab where glass beakers—scores of them—had fallen out of a stand and lay broken all over the floor and worktop.

Underneath the scattered glass shards on the table, a stack of large papers were fanned out. I shuffled through them, more and more confused. There were no notes, just dates, most of them within the past six months but the oldest going back twelve years, and the initials DCIC—PPII Infestation. The images were blueprints, schematics that looked like mechanized insect species.

"Shit."

Apparently, someone had been here recently, and this information could prove useful to Hatch or Farrow. I had to get it to them, but it was too chancy to steal and even more stupid to upload the images onto my D-P not knowing who was monitoring it. I made a split-second decision. Leaving everything as is, I backtracked all the way out of the building and then the Quad, running whenever I was sure nobody was watching.

At Farrow's, I knocked repeatedly until door opened. I swung inside before she had a chance to blink. And before she had a chance to speak—and probably lay into me about hazardous visiting hours—I held up a hand, caught my breath, and slouched into one of her luxe armchairs.

"Just give me news about Cannon and Nate, good news, preferably," I said.

Both her delicate blond eyebrows rose, but she humored me. "Cannon's bitin' at the bit to get to Beta, and Nathaniel's continually talkin' him off the cliff."

I released a long breath and braced my elbows on my knees. "They have no right coming here and messing up my operations. Hell, I'm doing a bang-up job of that on my own."

Her soft skirt brushed my legs as she knelt next to me, pretty green eyes wide and disarming. "Is it Linc?"

How to answer that? Yeah, it was Linc. The man was all over me and I didn't want it any other way. "I don't want to talk about that bullshit."

"Oh!"

"Oh?"

"Ah warned you about them Cutler men." Farrow preened beside me.

I glowered at her. "You didn't warn me about him. You practically spread my legs for him, Farrow."

"*Mm-hmm.* He's gotten to you."

"Gotten to me, in me, inside me." Her eyes widened. "Farrow, I can't use him."

"You don't have to use him, sweet girl. You have to like him, make him interested in you. Ah can tell by that look on your face he already is."

I shook my head.

Taking my hand between hers, she tried another tactic. "If we don't have Linc on our side, we will nevah win this war. We need Linc at the helm, to step up and regroup the government of the Territories."

"You're asking too much." Every time Linc and I talked about the war, I knew I was gonna pass all the information on to Farrow. It was for the good of the movement, but the ongoing betrayal was not good for my heart.

"Ah'm givin' my damned heart up, too, Liz. Bassy, he's shuttin' down on me. He's nevah been this way. I can't get anything from him—not even a smile or a joke."

Much as I wanted to commiserate with her, I'd already wasted too much time on my own goddamn sad story. *This is getting ridiculous.* "Put Leon on him."

"Darke ain't gonna like that one bit."

"Darke can suck my left nip for all I care." I shut that argument right down. Darke needed to suck something anyhow. "I came here because I need a burn D-P, pronto. I broke into one of my dad's old labs and found some very weird shit that has nothing to do with his official projects. I figure if I can get it to Hatch he might be able to break the schematics down."

The disposable in hand, I completed my round-trip back to the med building. I added another guard to the appropriately named *storage* closet, cuffing the first on the head with an extra blow to buy some additional time. I sealed the broken lock with a filament patch. It would have to do.

Inside Dad's lab, I raced to the table and hauled up short. It was all gone. The stacks of blueprints, every last one of them, even the shattered glass had been swept up. *Fuck!* My plans for a docu-drop to Hatch ruined, I tapped out to Farrow: *Plans are gone.* Before she had a chance to reply, I hooked up to Hatch. I gave him as much of a description as I'd committed to memory and sent the shit I'd seen with the Posse too. Then I put the D-P in a basin and set it to self-destruct. Ten seconds later all that was left was a pile of black ash that evaporated while I watched.

I knew I should get out before the situation went totally tits-up, but I was not goddamn leaving without something to show for busting my tail for two hours. I made my way to the interior office where my father would've done his record keeping. I smashed open the door, done with being subtle, especially if someone was already hot on my trail. The foul mood I was in, I could do with a little hand-to-hand to loosen shit up.

Dad's big D-P emerged from the desk, glowing to life when I pressed a button. I tapped in the same frickin' fish name as before and nearly laughed when a page of links opened up as if by de-sign. *At least tonight isn't a total bust.* Everything was ordered by dates, reaching as far back as 2042, when he'd taken his esteemed position in Beta, but I didn't need to time travel that far.

Clicking on the January 2059 documents, I scanned through scientific formulas that read like gobbledygook.

I opened a new file: *Pre-Plague Results: 14-February-2059.* Columns and columns of acronyms—presumably pa-tients—tallied up to the same end result: *Test success; subject de-ceased.* The initials *R.G.* in my father's handwriting signed off on each page of dead subjects.

A later document coded *Pneumonic Plague Formula Notes: 30-March-2059* blinked open under my command. The telecast type read:

The mutation is live, viable. Genetically altered plague, my brainchild at the CO's behest, will be ready to spread in three weeks, targeting the growing rebel subculture. It's taken months of research and trials, but in the end it was a simple matter of gene-splicing I've used for years on the pet clones with the deadly virus. The result is genius with its ability to adapt and outlast curative measures, living on air molecules until able to invade a new host parasitically. Its toll will be devastating. The CEOs are pleased. I received a personal note of commendation from Alpha CEO Cutler himself.

What? Horror and shame slammed through me, followed swiftly by bile rising in my throat. The year 2059 was when Cannon's younger sister, Erica, and his parents had been wiped out by the Plague.

No, no, no.

Document: *Live: 31-May-2059*

InterNations Plague Event has gone airborne. Subjects planted in all sixteen Territories have been reported infected, the surrounding area swiftly making black marks on the geo-maps.

Gruesome realization at my father's hand in the Plague sickened me. The idea it had been manifested and controlled by the CO repulsed me. It really had been designed to target the *deviant* masses, my dad the mastermind behind it all. Something didn't add up between this new data and what I'd watched on his digidiary in Linc's office recorded a year later.

I was too numb to cry, too shocked to shout all the rage

burning inside me, but when I heard boot steps outside the office door, I rallied. I was not too fucked up to fight. Even better? When I yanked open the door, I found Sabine fucking Burr-in-my-butt snuffling around outside like an overblown hog. And she still had a chronic case of bitch-face, which was perfect timing, considering if I didn't bust some chops, I'd probably break apart.

"You following me, you ugly gash?" I snatched her off her feet by her collar, letting her toes dangle.

She hawked right in my face, a wad of spit hitting my cheek. "Somebody ought to. I see you got Linc tied around your finger, but you ain't foolin' me, soldier girl."

"I'm not fooling him either. I'm fucking him. And you can call him *Commander*, grunt."

With that, I polished her plump brown cheeks against the wall, one side and then the other, adding a burst of force when I slammed her forehead into the ugly block wall. Dropping her to the floor, I kicked her in the stomach.

"I got one sure shot up the ranks, and you keep fuckin' it up for me, Grant." She gasped.

I shut her up by adding pressure to her windpipe via my boot. Underneath her cocoa-colored skin, Sabine turned an unsightly shade of purple that really didn't go well with her hair. Slithery as a snake, she pulled her ice-pick blade and sank it into my calf. That's when this *sistah* hit boiling point.

I yanked out the knife. Straddling her torso with my knees on top of her shoulders, I pressed the sharp tip to her carotid. Flesh compressed, and the first drops of blood beaded on the blade.

"You're not the only one handy with a shank. Got any last words before I grease you all over this floor?"

She struggled, getting nowhere but a deeper wound. Sabine spat, "You don' know who you're working aginst. If you keep asking questions, the answers you find ain't gonna be to your likin'."

There was truth tainted by fear of death in her gaze. "I already found that out tonight, which makes this your lucky day."

I threw the knife to a steel-topped table, where it screeched and found purchase. Leaping off Sabine, I rearranged my cap and then checked my leg. I'd had worse nicks cutting myself shaving. LT Burr had a weak wrist. I walked out the door without looking back. She knew she was lucky to be left breathing. *Leave it to her to mop up the mess.*

I made it to Corps Command, head swimming with disease and a heart full of hurt. My trust in Dad destroyed, I was absolutely alone, bereft, newly disillusioned. Barely aware of my surrounds, I sent the elevator up to Linc's floor. I couldn't tell him what I'd discovered. I didn't have the first idea how much he knew about my dad's involvement. I only hoped his father's filth hadn't reached him by that point. He'd been only a teenager at the time.

When I walked into Linc's quarters, he put down the D-P and papers he'd been working on, meeting me at the end of the hall. No words, no questions, he folded me in his strong embrace. All of a sudden, this man felt more like home to me than the memories of a false childhood I'd cherished all these years.

Twining my arms around his neck, I kissed him from the corner of his lips to the bow. Fiery anger melted to slow-burning desire. "Make love to me, Linc. I need you."

Chapter Seven

Jesus, Grant." Linc moved away, pacing back and forth.

Not exactly the reaction I expected. Of course, through all our nights together, the sex had been hot, but we'd never mentioned love. It wasn't an option. I should've asked him for a fuck or shut the hell up except I craved a connection with him that went beyond the physical. I thought we already had it.

Stupid, stupid.

I wouldn't stick around to be spurned. I'd had enough heartbreak for one day. Make that a lifetime. "Sorry I asked, sir. Must be something in the water. I just felt dizzy for a second."

His eyes frosted over, glacier-cap cold.

I'd bunk down in the lobby. Hell, I'd even spend another night with sad-sack Sabine.

Linc spun me around before I reached the door. "What do you want from me?"

More than I deserved when I was double-crossing him every chance I got. Such great yearning leaped inside me, a longing for someone to watch out for me, to wait up for me. I swallowed thickly, not answering.

The answer must've been in my eyes. His lips melted to mine, a slow, sensual spark of mouths speaking the language of desire, maybe, finally, love. Pulling back, he cursed. His fingers sifted through the short strands of my hair. "You can have it, Liz. Anything, everything."

My heart beat faster. "Be close to me, Linc. That's what I need."

His slow blink revealed a hot blue gaze burning out of control, and his fingers tightened and then loosened in my hair. Gruff and dark, his groan crept inside me. "I wasn't supposed to get attached to you."

"That makes two of us."

I searched his face. He looked like he wanted to say more. I did, too, but words could wait. I needed his touch, the comfort of his body. The rest would come. It bubbled up inside me, a purity of emotion for this man, my lover.

Linc carried me to our bedroom. Throwing back the covers, he laid me down. "We're going to take it slow tonight, sweetheart."

We undressed each other, the badges, the holsters, the guns set aside. Clothing peeled off beneath hands that touched every bared expanse of skin. Our bodies warmed, then heated even more when Linc lay beside me, our legs entangled. Rubbing against each other, our mouths forayed south but always returned for delving, hungry kisses.

I pulled the hair at the nape of his neck where too-long waves curled, damp with sexual sweat. "You feel so good, Linc."

He looked up from the sensual tonguing he gave my tits. A

smile graced his lips before he scooped my nipple into the fiery depths of his mouth. He sipped his way down my stomach. My palms on his shoulders guided him lower.

"Is this what you wanted?" He asked, growly voice washing across my sex while he penetrated me with two fingers.

Shaking my head, I guided him over me. I pulled his thighs until his engorged length levered over my mouth, and his knees were split beside my head. I grasped his firm buttocks and he my ass, and we embarked on a slow, wet ride of warm, sleek tongues. He thrust into my mouth; I gyrated up to his. I buried my nose just beneath his sacs. The covers, the pillows fell off the bed, and all I heard was sucking, sweet and low.

I lapped his shaft at the same leisurely pace he suckled my clit. Moving his head from side to side, I heard his murmurs as he ran his tongue up one side of my pussy and down the other before plunging inside to ring me. I rubbed his cock across my closed lips, waiting for him to beg me to take him inside. I nibbled the broad crown. I washed his length over my face and down my neck and painted my nipples with his preejaculate.

Fingers digging into my thighs as he spread me further, Linc grabbed his cock and pushed it into my mouth. I took him with a starving moan. My head lifted off the bed and slammed down with each hard thrust he gave me. Three fingers inside me, he swirled his tongue over the nub of my clit. It swelled, aching from his attentions before he stopped.

Linc swiveled over me and settled between my thighs. We were slippery from cock to cunt and in between from our own juices and sweet, clean perspiration. Licking and biting the taut tendons of his throat, I rode against his turgid shaft. Linc shuddered and slowly, so slowly, seated himself inside me. My breath hitched; my back arched. Our hands together beside my head, he lifted his chest and I watched him enter me, stretch me.

"Takin' it slow, sweetheart."

I nodded, unable to speak. He was so hard inside me, I squeezed down and he groaned.

His large hands cradling my face, he whispered, "Look at me, Liz."

His cock withdrew all the way with a wet sound, and I panted, needing him back inside me. He thrust again only when I met his gaze. First the thick head and then his whole length inching inside.

"Oh, more, Linc. Please give me more." This was more than sex. It was a communion of hearts and bodies.

As soon as he hit the farthest reaches of my body, he ground against me, pubic hair rasping my clit. Then he dragged out again, all that long, strong length little by little until his head tapped the entrance of my sex. Over and over again, Linc rode me with the same measured drives, the same slow egresses until his arms wound around my waist and my hands grabbed his hair. Our mouths came together with combustible kisses, murmurs, clashes of tongues, but he never hurried his pace, not even when I clenched around him in the tight flash of orgasm.

We'd almost run out of bed. My leg hung off it, toes pointed onto the floor, my body stretched out beneath him. Bracing himself on his fists, Linc dragged my thigh over his hip and went at it.

I dug my fingernails into his ass and screamed every time he lunged. "Yes, yes!"

His head fell back, but he tried to keep his eyes open, on me, even when his cock swelled inside me, exploded inside me. Even when I curled up and cried out and bit the thick muscle of his shoulder.

"*Ah, ah!*" His booming shout of release echoed around us.

Lowering us both to the bed, he continued to release inside me, hips kicking in tight circles as if he'd come all night. I couldn't speak through my constricted throat when he bundled me against his body, one mighty thigh thrown across me. I kissed him instead. His fingers, his palms, the silken skin of his arms.

I laved his jaw, then whispered in his ear, "Thank you."

Smoothing hands down my back to my bottom, Linc brought me closer. His short chug of laughter died abruptly. "Don't ever thank me for being with you, sweetheart. Just—"

I propped my elbows on his chest. "Just what?"

His gaze delved mine. "Just promise me you'll be smart and stay safe, because I don't know what I'll do if you get hurt."

"Linc." I rubbed my forehead against his.

We stayed that way for a while before he lifted me in his arms.

"Where are you taking me now?"

"I'm gonna take care of you."

I grinned at the hint of his drawl and the intimate caress of his words.

Inside the glass brick walls of the shower, Linc did take care of me. Fingers glancing off the thin puncture wound from

Sabine, his head tilted in curiosity, but he didn't ask for answers. Instead he lathered my body and hair with gentleness, his big hands used for killing as gentle as a lover's. I did the same for him. My brow furrowed as I counted his many scars, the one on his shoulder the deepest. Lingering over the eagle moko across his upper back and outlining the word beneath, I scooped hot, sudsy water over him.

He returned me to bed. When he entered me—both fresh and clean and warm—he didn't have to ask me to look at him. I was all in.

I was in over my head.

Later, as we nestled together, we were peaceful, yet the war raged on just outside.

* * *

I woke with a start a couple mornings later. The communion between Linc and me had begun the night I'd discovered the hateful truth about my father. It'd lasted through two days of tactical training, rebel raids, and nights of lovemaking. But there was no hope for our future. We were trapped in lies, fighting for opposing sides of a war, for Christ's sake. My head was still screwed up about my dad, and coming clean with Linc was impossible.

Linc was long gone, probably starting in on the reports and duties and details of another day of Beta combat before the sun even rose. I found a piece of paper and my stilo and barricaded myself in the bathroom.

April 15, 2071

Linc ordered me out yesterday morning. "There was a secu-rity breach at the med center last night, in one of your father's sealed labs." I held it together under his steely stare, the one that reminded me of the cold bastard Beta Commander I first met, as he asked me to question the guards who'd been dis-abled.

I hustled over there like my ass was on fire, hoping to save face before I got shafted by Linc. The guards stared at me like lumps on a log. I must've knocked a handful of their brain cells loose. They couldn't give a worthwhile description of me. I sent them off with a warning they were looking at their new bitch-mommy if this type of shit went down on their watch again. I think they soiled their britches.

My report to Linc was curt and concerned, playing the bereaved daughter/solid soldier angle. I breathed again only when he approved. "Good work, Lieutenant."

Yeah, I'm good at my job; always have been. Maybe that's the problem with this inside-out asshole of a situation. Because I'm thinking I can cut Linc loose when I have to. It's in my makeup. Especially since finding out my sentimental dad got in bed with the bad guys, the ones who decided eradicating an entire subpopulation was an excellent strategy for total Com-pany dedication.

My D-P cut my bleeding-heart moment short. I looked at the sender—Linc. *Surprise.* If he was pinging me, he was prob-ably already on the lookout for me. I hurried to hide the latest journaling bout at the bottom of my pack, inside a roll of socks. Half a minute later, Linc's unanswered blowback had piled up. I started with the first, figuring the rest were him letting me know the tracking device launched up my ass still wasn't off the table.

New alert. There's an Amphitheater event outside the perimeter tonight. We're going undercover.

My fingers tapped quickly before he could make another backdoor threat. *I'm not sure it's wise to mingle with the natives.* Because no way did I need to find myself in Freelander and Revo crosshairs at a fucking orgy with Linc breathing down my neck.

His bounce back was just as fast. *I won't stand for your insubordination, Grant.*

I chuckled. The man hadn't seen insubordination yet. Wait until he got a load of my endgame, forget about his dad's. I bit my lip, typing: *No insubordination intended, sir. Your wish is my command.* Oh, he was gonna love that one. I hit send and waited for his high-handed reply.

Instead I heard the tone of another D-P behind me. *Shit.* My body vibrated, fine-tuned to Linc's, and my skin tingled. I hadn't heard his footsteps, but I felt his arms coming around me. I gasped when his open-mouth kiss landed on the side of my neck, a seductive press of tongue and lips traveling up to my ear.

"Are you on board?"

"Depends." I gasped when his tongue darted around my earlobe. "What time is this detail?"

Turning me to face him, Linc's lips found mine. "Twenty-two hundred hours."

"That's fourteen hours away. I don't need that much time to prep."

"Maybe I do." A suggestive smirk highlighted his dimples.

"Don't you have work to do, Commander Hot Gun?"

"I do, on you." He started undressing. "Remember, my wish is your command."

He rolled his shoulders out of his shirt, and my laughter was breathless. "I think you should delete that message."

"No chance." Linc pressed me against the wall. He shed our clothes and fucked me hard. His hands clasped my bottom and my heels on his ass spurred him on, our teasing jibes and deep-throated groans shaking our bodies. His powerful thrusts shaking the wall.

At nightfall, we got ready. The difference between my getup for the Theater and the formfitting, femme with a fuck-wish dress from the CO sex club was startling. I pulled up the black leather pants, tucking them into my jackboots and easing a knife inside a secret sheath. There was no bra, *again,* and nothing to wear beneath the jacket except a low-cut, silky white tank. The black leather jacket hugged me like a glove when I zipped it to my neck. Linc tugged the zipper until the leather parted below my breasts.

I resituated the zipper between my tits. "Jesus, Linc. If you want to truss me up, why not just tie me to the bed?"

In laced-up leathers that made his big gun show, he whipped me close. "I might just yet, later." His jacket was as formfitting as mine, and I tried not to stare. His harsh blond good looks suited this sleek black gear as much as his daily uniform.

When we left Command Central, the mood got a whole lot

more serious. Shoulder holsters housed my Desert Eagles on my back, and Linc was likewise armed, reminding me shit could go from grand to grievous at any given moment.

Linc drove the same bulletproof Cruiser as before. This time there was no Ginger chauffeur and no armed escort paying lip service to the vehicle prowling the burned-out streets of Beta. Every block we went, Linc's mouth tightened and his knuckles turned white, seeing his city gutted and falling to ashes.

Entering the Wilderness, he relaxed, easing the vehicle through dips and curves. All I felt was unrest and unease. I kept a close watch for hidden threats, Freelanders, or the Posse.

"You know what you're in for?"

I turned to Linc. "Illegals getting out of control and asking for the death squad."

"How do you feel about that?"

I didn't like his line of questioning. "We've all taken the heterosexual pledge, sir. I stand by my allegiance to the Corps, the Company, and the Breeder program."

"What about Cannon and my brother?"

I was acutely aware of his close study. "What about them?"

"They're homos." His blank profile gave nothing away.

Struggling to remain unaffected, I said, "I wouldn't know. I've told you the last I heard from Commander Cannon was last autumn as Alpha fell, when he was en route to the Outpost under your father's orders."

Linc let it ride. I couldn't believe the man who was so tender with me would write his brother off like that. The inside of the car became stifling with unasked questions I might never know the answers to. Once this mission ended, Linc and I would be over. Reaching across the seat, I took his hand in mine. There were tears in my eyes, but he'd never see them. He pulled me closer, wrapping his arm around me as he drove.

We entered the grounds of the Amphitheater through gates twisted off their hinges and rode down a long track. We stopped in front of a palace that had been bombed nearly to earth level. The mansion was a thing of Old History, a lesson we'd learned about capitalistic greed. Once owned by a baron family brought to its knees like all the other first-tier families of the former United States, hit first by the Purge and then razed out of existence by the CO.

All that remained of this classical beauty with its *For the People* gilded-era idealism were the western portico and a high-walled set of rooms. The Catskills mountain range—home to the closest Freelander commune—provided the backdrop. And Cuntler's manse was too close for comfort. *Stupid oversexed fucks.*

Melting patches of snow crunched beneath our boots as we navigated around the ruins. Buds on the last remaining trees hungered for spring's full sun, ready to burst forth. Linc guided me up the steps of the entryway, where revelers spilled from twin sets of doors, the glass panels long gone. The portico provided sanctuary to Jacks and Jills in every *perverted* permutation, but this time it wasn't to gain government favor and they weren't trading in flesh. Their genuine hunger for one another rose up in heat waves. Hands seeking, mouths searching; it didn't matter if it was man on man, two women together, or an indistinguishable web of both sexes.

At the entry, our credentials weren't checked and neither were our weapons. The guards let us inside as if we were any other harmless hedonists. Old Man Hills would've declared trust. I thought it was just plain stupid.

The sheer volume of the music shivered through me. The immense crowd inside pushed against us as one solid mass. A shell of a structure, the soaring walls reached to the sky, no ceiling to shut out the night above. Linc hooked his arm around my waist, weaving us into the seething sea of people. Glaring strobe lights circled the grand-scale room, illuminating neon graffiti slashed on the walls. *Libertas; Live in Freedom, Love at Will; Fight for the Right; No More Corps!*

Even with the apparent political message, the people were all about party time. Freelanders were in abundance, their unshorn hair and homespun threads marking them. Scores of freedom fighters in black and red, leather and lacings, latched on to one another. Younger crowds hung together, pierced and tattooed, with sculptural hair shaving; they took their hard edge to the extreme. I wondered if I was looking at a few of the Posse's radicals.

A man with a yellow Mohawk stomped around onstage, his throaty voice calling out through a miniature apparatus fitted against his mouth. Barbell piercings laddered down his abs, disappearing into his tight pants. I'd never seen live musicians—rarely heard music at all, in keeping with the CO prohibition—except at Chitamauga. This growling sexual call to arms had nothing in common with Nate's guitar or Smitty's banjo playing.

A gathering of this size was asking for trouble, especially so close to Beta, the Catskills, Cutler's. Linc kept his arm around me but loosened his hold when we sensed no immediate threat. In fact, the only danger came in the form of me losing control and joining in on one of the erotic ensembles with Linc. He started grinding against me, his breath teasing my nape, his hand moving around to my hips.

"What are you doing?"

"Staying in role."

His hard cock strained against my ass. I slowly shook my head and bit back a smile. Sometimes I forgot Lincoln Cutler, Commander of Beta Corps, was just a man. And right now, he felt purely male, wrapped around me, moving us with the rhythmic, pounding music.

"If I'd known we were staying in character tonight, I'd have brought my handcuffs and a whip."

He swung me around, lips curling into a wicked smile. "I might even let you take it out on me."

We'd run out of room, Linc backing me into a corner. We kissed as the ravening rumble of bass music pulled us closer. It was so hot, so many packed bodies, a veritable meat market of forbidden activities going on around us. Linc looked like arrests and interrogations were the last thing on his mind. We had a tug-of-war with the zipper of my jacket until his grin flashed in triumph and he slid inside. His whole hand massaged my breasts. The music swallowed my cries.

A spark of bright blue sprinted across my vision. *Taft*. I followed the electric dart of his close-cropped hair and saw the boy on his knees, sucking a cock with great gusto. If it was Sebastian he gave head to, I was gonna need to do some serious damage control. The muscles of his back shifted with each head bob, but the boy he blew wasn't Bas Monroe. *Thank fuck for that.*

The guttural vibe of the song gave way to something softer, a lush sensory exploration. Linc pulled me around, giving me a view that jarred my senses.

I was immediately riveted by a tall redheaded woman seized between two men, her bottom filled by the cock behind, her cunt opening for the shaft of another man in front of her. The front man sucked her pale pink nipples, breasts lifted to his mouth by the man soldering her ass. Between the two, she shook, taking each piercing lunge with an arch of her hips back and forth.

There was no question she was getting off on the double-fuck, and so was I. "Oh God," I moaned.

Linc held me against him. "Want that, sweetheart?"

"I'm not averse voyeuristic pleasures. I don't see the difference between this and what I observed at the CO Club."

"The difference is *that.*" Linc pointed to a big black man kissing his male lover.

Darke and Leon. This was a full serving of *Oh shit. Forget about Taft being present.*

Linc was stern. "It goes against the laws of nature."

"And the laws of the InterNations governance," I replied automatically, my stomach roiling.

Leon's silver ring sparked off Darke's short hair. Reclining against the wall, Leon moaned and Darke's hand delved into his pants. I turned Linc's face to mine, kissing him like my life depended on it. My cheek against Linc's chest, I glanced at the two men. Darke's face flushed russet red and words tumbled from his lips.

In return to whatever Darke said, Leon yanked back, tugging his pants closed. His mouth moved fast before he disappeared into the throng. Darke ground his teeth down to the gums, by the look of it.

Way to lay down the law, kid.

No sooner than Leon vanished, Linc stepped forward to greet someone. "Here's my little mole."

Farrow stood before him, of fucking course. Why not add her to the mixed bag of trouble? Dressed in an oxblood catsuit, her blond hair was loose to the middle of her back and her green eyes were both crafty and playful.

His mole. "Farrow." I nodded in her direction.

"Pleasure to see you again, Lieutenant Grant." She turned to Linc, tucking her hand around his elbow as if they were about to go for a stroll around the gardens annihilated decades before. "Ah see y'all got my information."

I knew she had to play both sides of the game, but did she have to put me in the middle? This all-points-converging shit made me twitchy.

They conversed for a moment while I played deaf and dumb; then Farrow said, "Ah'm purely parched, Linc. Go an' fetch us some drinks, darlin'?"

Placing his hand on my waist, he hesitated.

Farrow's lips spread in a cunning smile. "G'on, now. I'll look after your girl for you."

I shook off Linc's hand. "I can handle myself, thanks."

"Yes, you can, and me too." Backing away, Linc merged with the masses.

"Mind telling me what we're doing here?"

"Ah thought Linc could use a little eye opener, see that sometimes there's more to life than what he's been used to." Farrow grabbed my hand. "His entire existence has been nothin' but a steady diet of indoctrination and dogma. It's a wonder he nevah cracked, Liz. It's a wonder you've been able to reach him."

The weight of her words suffocated all but the most sympathetic feelings toward Linc, but I wasn't ready to admit that. I tugged my hand from Farrow's. "Oh, he definitely wants more, with me. He's been trying to get into my pants all night."

Her eyes sparkled like gemstones. "You gonna let 'im?"

I shivered at the possibility but shoved that tempting thought aside. "You aren't getting off that easy, Farrow. Leon and Darke? You couldn't keep a leash on them?"

"Leon's getting in with Bassy and the Posse, as you asked, and Darke's the watchdog."

Watchdog? At last observation, Darke had looked like he was being hounded to hell and back. And wait, what? "Bas? Sebastian's here too?"

Linc was making his way back through the crowd toward us. Farrow whispered, "Yes, and Ah'm none too pleased about it."

"That makes two of us, because Taft is here as well, so I'm pretty sure that means there are more of the Posse's diehards in attendance."

I zipped my lips and my jacket just as Linc approached. He handed over a drink, and a smirk, directed at my chest. "If you'll excuse me for a few more minutes, ladies, I have an informant to meet."

Farrow took a dainty sip. "If it's that Denver, you be sure to keep both eyes open. Nevah did trust that one."

As soon as Linc was out of hearing range, Farrow navigated us through the half-naked maze to the other end of the room and through a squat doorway she shut firmly behind us. Leon and Darke were inside, propped against opposite walls. The small square room contained remnants of pipes and fixtures from the lavatory it once housed. Farrow tossed her drink into a drain hole, but I downed mine. The liquid courage could come in handy.

"Saw your man out there. Ain' he somethin' to think about on a long, hard day. *Cet homme est beaucoup amoureux.*" Leon's meaning was crystal clear. "Now, if he be the one back in Chitamauga, I mighta set my hat on him."

Massive muscles across Darke's bare chest stood in stark relief. He growled like an animal, listening to Leon talk about another man.

"I think you've prodded the beast enough for one night, Leon. Tell us what you've got."

He shoved a hand through his mane of hair and dragged it to the back of his neck. "Sebastian ain't givin' me a whole helluva lot yet, but I be workin' on him." He winked. "I do know dis. *Posse Omnis Juvenis*? They're workin' for CEO Cutler."

Farrows lips popped open; my brain backfired; Darke cursed up one side of Beta Territory and down the other.

Even though Farrow hated the idea of working Bas over for intel, and Darke looked ready to throttle someone, anyone, whenever Leon said Sebastian's name, I slapped Leon on the shoulder. "Good work, kid."

We needed Leon to get into the inner circle to find out what the Posse was making in that factory of theirs. I was willing to bet whatever it was would be used against the rebels, especially since Cutler was backing them. Darke paced back and forth. "I wanna bring up my militia."

"It's not time yet. We don't know what they're planning," I cautioned.

"I'm getting the word to Hatch, Liz. They'll go to Catskills, and I'll prep everybody. We can't wait for the whole Breeder bombshell to go live while my people are yanking their cocks back in Chitamauga."

Farrow added her concerns. "Ah'm worried about Bassy bein' involved in all this."

"He'll do us more good inside."

She spun on me. "I don't want mah brother in danger."

"Think about it, Farrow. You know this is the smart move. Leon will watch his back." I stood my ground until she reluctantly nodded. I peered behind me at the two men and rolled my eyes. "And Darke will be all over Leon's."

Leaving the antechamber one after the other at delayed intervals, we blended in with the partiers, no one—that is, Linc—the wiser. My mind was on overdrive. Between all these factions, the CO, the Corps, the Posse, it felt like everyone was fucking everyone else over big time. If I could lay all this shit out for Linc, we'd figure out a solution, but no way was that gonna happen. Especially since his pops was head of Posse ops. Maybe Linc already knew everything about them. Maybe he was in on it, too. But why would they have broken into the Quad last month?

No sooner had Farrow emerged from the side room than a squadron of five Pred UCASs—Unmanned Combat Air Systems—flew in formation overhead. Thinking it was the usual nighttime buzz-by, which wasn't exactly best-case scenario, considering where we were, I watched with the rest of the crowd as the black aerodynamic drones whined above our heads and out of sight.

Meeting Linc's eyes from several meters away, I wondered briefly if the planes were all part of some sort of setup. But then the music strangled out. The sudden silence was filled by the screaming rush of speeding jets. Linc's eyes widened on me as everyone else turned their faces to the sky again.

Dread crawled all over my body. I was shouting before I knew it. "TAKE COVER! TAKE COVER!" Frantically searching for Farrow, for Leon and Darke, I screamed until I was hoarse and pulled my Eagles from the shoulder holsters. "EVERYONE, TAKE COVER NOW!"

Firing into the air got their attention faster than my yells. People hit dirt all around me. I stood in the middle, guns aimed at the incoming threat. I glanced around. Linc was running at me, roaring, but I couldn't hear him because the drone planes arrived on site.

They opened fire on the interior of the Amphitheater. Linc slammed into me, driving me to the floor. He covered me with his body, tucking me under him as whizzing bullets chewed into the marble floor of the vast room. Those were the most grating sounds. The softer ones, by far more horrifying, followed by fast, low grunts as bullets hit bodies. With five armed airships to share the workload of plowing through a couple hundred people, the raid would be over in no time, with no one left standing to tell about it.

Linc rolled off me. Grabbing my hand, he hauled me through the room. We zigzagged to the portico. Outside, the scene was just as dire. People frantic in the face of outright, unprovoked carnage.

Adrenaline pumped through me. Linc shouted into his D-P, clenching my hand until it felt like my fingers would break. "CEASE FIRE! Abort, abort!"

His commands were to no avail. The terror didn't stop. The planes banked the opposite side of the mansion. In that brief respite, we made it to the Cruiser, followed by fifty or so people. My heart leaped out of my chest when I saw Leon, Darke, and Farrow among them. No sign of Sebastian, not a single electric-blue hair in evidence from Taft. The UCASs were unmarked. For all I knew, this could the work of the überbrilliant Posse.

One of the bombers dropped twelve mini-gliders from its hatch. They advanced ahead of the squadron at alarming speeds. Flying low to the ground, the unmanned gliders, kitted out with machine guns, came into firing range. The *patter-patter-patter* of their bullets took down one, two, three people on the outskirts of our group before Linc and I took aim, pumping the flying monkeys full of lead.

Rage lit Linc's eyes. "They've gone rogue." At the back of the

Cruiser, he opened the gate. "This is an unsanctioned attack, Grant."

What I saw in his eyes—the need to protect innocent civilians—matched what I saw in the back of the Cruiser, a cache of high-powered assault rifles. Leon and Darke were right there beside me, though we couldn't exchange a single word. Linc didn't stop to question their allegiance as he tossed a rifle to each of them and me. We clambered to higher ground—the roof and hood of the Cruiser—yelling at the civvies to hit the ground.

The squadron made its return visit. Linc raised his rifle. "Open fire!"

I aimed and shot, aimed and fired, the repeat from the four rifles sending up a deadly ear-splitting salute. Of one single mind, we focused on the lead plane and its fuselage. When it seemed the motherfucking drone was indestructible, it finally burst into flames. By the time it nose-dived into the main part of the manse, the sonic boom of its bad landing deafening me, we'd hit and lit the second and third planes.

The others scattered.

The roar of the crashing planes, the loud shower of gunfire ceasing, I heard moaning, crying, wailing. I heard screaming.

"Bassy! SEBASTIAN!"

Jumping off the Cruiser, I reached Farrow, who was running from person to person, from the wounded to the dead, searching for her brother. Tears streaked down her face. I jerked her away from a twisted, broken corpse.

My voice was harsh, my throat sore. "He must've ditched, Farrow."

She looked at me wildly, shaking me off to return to her search.

"Listen to me right now before Linc catches on." I grabbed her again, squeezing her arms. "I didn't see him or Taft during the attack. I think the Posse might've had something to do with this. And that means Sebastian's safe. You need to go home and wait for him."

When she finally nodded, I returned to Linc. He was clapping Darke on the back. In that moment, he reminded me so much of Cannon and Nate, my heart flipped over.

I heard him speak to Darke and Leon. "You men should join my unit."

Despite the butchery of the night, I nearly smiled. *That'll be the day.*

When the smoke lifted, the mansion's main building had been cleaved by two of the UCASs. I pressed the heels of my hands to my eyes and sucked in a few fast breaths in order to control the tears threatening to blind me.

Linc wrapped his arms around me, turning my face into his shoulder and away from the slaughter.

"What do we do now?" I asked. "What about the casualties?"

His voice was gruff beside my ear. "They'll want to take care of their dead. The best we can do is return to Beta, buy them some time, and find out what the fuck happened here tonight."

Chapter Eight

Linc hauled ass back to Beta and through the Quad's gate. He met me at the front of the vehicle, cupping my face briefly before he pulled his hands back. His face stony, he gutted all emotion from his stark blue eyes.

"I want you to go inside and wait for me." He jerked his chin at Corps Command and spun away, heading to HQ.

His brisk march delivered him to double-reinforced doors, and he didn't have to wait for a retinal scan before they yawned outward, swallowing him up.

The adrenaline rush from the ambush ran dry, but my emotions were firing on all cylinders. Upstairs in the apartment, I tried to forget the screams and cries, the sounds of bullets eating through flesh and tissue. I scrubbed my face and hands in frigid water until my skin chapped. I settled into the main room, placing my guns on the table alongside the four rifles that had been discharged earlier.

Painstakingly cleaning each of the weapons, I unloaded and

disassembled them. I kept my hands occupied and my mind on the mundane. I didn't want to remember the deaths, the drones, the destruction any longer than I had to.

The only thing that got a halfhearted smile out of me was the moment Leon and Darke had sided with Linc and me to take down the five planes in a show of unrehearsed teamwork and a shower of gunfire. After Linc's performance at the Theater, his dedication to defending the people no matter what faction they belonged to, I believed for the first time he was within my reach. We might have a future, one where the multiplying lies gave way to honesty…and the world wasn't on fire twenty-four seven.

I'd made it through oiling only the third rifle when the door slammed on its track. Linc strode down the hall and into the room, eyes seeking me out. A giant mass of a man in black leather and blond hair, his fiery expression scorched me. I had time only to stand before he was on me, lips on mine, tongue curling inside and hitting every recess of my mouth.

I pulled back. "What happened?"

He growled and shook his head. "Need you now." His hands shook, too, as he clasped my face. "Jesus, I need you. Tell me to stop if I'm too rough, Liz."

His tone sent sparks up and down my spine, immediate warmth between my legs. I tore at the zipper of his jacket, sliding my hands inside and digging my fingers into the ropy muscles of his shoulders. He groaned, then shredded the tank top from my breasts.

The circles of my nipples stood taut and swollen for him, and he fell on them with long, hard sucks. "Yes," he grunted.

Clawing the top off my back, Linc bit one peak and the other. I grabbed handfuls of hair when he finally placed a deep kiss on each nipple before the flat of his tongue soldered a line straight down my belly to my pants. We both grappled with the zipper, scrambling to tear the trousers off. He ripped them from my legs and sheared my panties between bared teeth and aggressive fingers.

When he'd exposed me, he rocked back on his heels, staring at my pussy. "Holy shit."

Dampness tracked down my inner thighs from his look alone.

Fingertips grazed my belly, my hips, the tops of my thighs. Linc blew out a gust of air. "Holy *shit*, Liz."

I stepped up to him, my legs straddling around him where he kneeled. "I thought I'd surprise you. Before all that…" He raised his eyes, crackling blue irises that slid back down my stomach to my smooth, bare lips. "You didn't have to. I liked you just the way you were."

But his chest was filling and emptying fast, his cheeks tinted pink, and his hungry gaze didn't move beyond my freshly shaved sex.

I sat down on the sofa and spread my thighs. "I think you'll be eating those words."

The man who so rarely showed a reaction became unhinged. A feminine thrill shot through me, intensifying when Linc parted my outer lips, tugged my ass forward, and launched a hot, wet assault with his mouth. I held the back of his head, the back of the sofa, and swiveled my pelvis against his face. He moaned with every taste, and a climax bore down on me within seconds.

Linc didn't stop, even when I was screaming, thrashing. He only moved me off the cushions and straight over his face. Pressing my legs wide, he balanced me with his hands on my ass. After I'd come a second time, body crossbow tight, he pushed me back. He loosened the suede lacings at his groin, parted the leather, and his cock leaped out. Framed in black leather and the thatch of dark, golden curls, his cock was pulsing and slick. The head reached up to his abdomen, dark in color and ready to fuck.

With a wild look in his eyes, Linc lifted me into his arms. My legs curled around his hips. I sucked viciously on his neck and chest and dug my fingernails into his back. I arched away from him, and he steadied me with a hand shoved into my hair and one spread over my ass as he lowered me onto his shaft. He slammed my back against a window.

"Holy fuck!" I yelled.

He leaned away, just a breath of space, shaking as he held back from ramming into me. His kisses on my mouth were just this side of completely losing control. "Too rough, sweetheart?" His voice sawed out of him.

"No." I gripped his shoulders, lifted up, and dropped back down his length. "Faster."

"Yeah."

He blasted inside of me, fucking me with the same raw urgency I returned. The life-threatening situation we'd survived, the deception on all sides boiled down to a savage connection of bodies. My breasts ached from his teeth and tongue, and I drove my heels into his ass. Banging me against the wall, the windows, Linc grabbed hold of my neck in his teeth, groaning with each hard slam.

I yanked his head back and licked his mouth. I reveled in the unyielding thrusts opening me, stretching me, until I couldn't breathe anymore. I found his fingers beside my head and grabbed his hands as he braced his arms on the wall. Three more lunges, coming at me from the balls of his feet, beautifully brutal inside me, and Linc roared. I flew apart as an orgasm ripped me away from Beta, away from war, away from betrayal. Until our screaming release tore us apart and threw us back together in a heap of heaving chests, trembling legs, hot, well-worked skin.

The guns I'd been cleaning lay on the table; our clothes were tossed all over the room. I was draped over Linc as we left everything behind and he carried me to the bedroom. Entwined together in bed, I smiled when he rolled me over on top of him. I frowned when I remembered his bleak expression after meeting with his father. I wanted to know how Cutler had spun the attack on the Amphitheater.

I splayed my hand over the washboard of Linc's abs, listening to his slowing breaths. "What did the CEO say?"

He tossed a forearm over his face. His lips hardly moved. "Standard protocol against the enemy. He claimed to have no intelligence of our whereabouts before giving the order." He squinted out at me. "Although I'm not sure that would've stopped him."

My heart ached. "Jesus, Linc. How can you stand it?"

"It's my job, my calling. It's been ingrained in me since birth, and I believe in it." Lowering his arm, he showed a closed-off version of himself.

I didn't believe that bullshit for one second, but I recognized his look. I was losing him to Cutler. But not tonight, and not without a fight.

I shifted into a sleep where howling bombs rent the earth, razing Beta. A nightmare of people on fire screaming for my help, their mouths as wide as their horrified eyes, their hands reaching for me. And I was helpless. In the morning, when I woke, it was with ghosts surrounding me, not Linc's solid arms. I remembered the shadow lurking in his eyes, the one I hadn't managed to erase during the night.

* * *

I couldn't destroy my own demons either, not if I kept ignoring them. Thinking about Linc and his vile father gave me a final reason to lay all my ghosts to rest.

April looked pretty, at least, and there were no wailing air-raid sirens. If I squinted to take in the blue sky and bright sun, I could almost forget the hellish surrounds I strode through. Birds didn't chirp in Beta, not like they had in Chitamauga. The commune felt like a lifetime ago. There were no children on the streets as I walked along the grid system through Sector One, no dogs either. Everyone was head down and grim faced. Feeling all-around awful for slipping out on Linc again, I hunched my shoulders further.

* * *

In line with the civilians, I wore their sleek garb all in black, attracting no attention. The black I wore was in mourning for the murdered civilians at the Amphitheater. I was still in shock that my father had created a weapon meant to kill instead of cure, that he'd helped Cutler. But then again, I'd worked for the CEO, too, just as blindly. This was one slippery mess, mission be damned. Cannon had been right. I wasn't prepared to take this on. By *this*, I meant Lincoln Cutler. I thought—hell, I knew—I was in love with the man. He'd protected me when I was in danger. He'd provided comfort when I needed it. He'd proven himself to be a solid leader who watched over his troops like they were his family, trying to keep them safe even in the midst of a war. He took care of me when I felt most vulnerable and never made me feel weak. How could I not love him—the strong commander, the intense lover? And now my mission was one bad move away from being scrapped because of a man I wasn't supposed to fuck, let alone make love to, *or* goddamn fall in love with.

I'd dug my hole so deep I couldn't even see my way out of this grave of deceptions. I'd stolen his key card, broken into his office, lied about being off duty, lied about being on duty. I'd used him to get intel on my dad and used him to stay safe from *his* dad. I'd agreed to be his second in charge, have his back...not stab him in the back. I knew his momma, his brother...I knew all about Cannon and Nate's loving relationship. I'd never told him a single word about how I felt for him. Just him. Linc, minus all this shit.

Christ.

Two blocks away from Farrow's building in Sector One, I took the elevator to the top of a similar soaring skyscraper and trudged to the only door on that level. I had a hard time punching in the numbers and letters, but the code still worked. The doors swished aside, opening to my family's condo. In my grief, I hadn't sold it. I'd just walked out and straight into the arms of the Corps. All those years I'd pretended I wasn't looking for something more until Linc stole straight through my defenses.

Taking a deep breath, I stepped inside. The doors whooshed shut, leaving me in an airtight tomb. The air smelled stale, and everything from the entryway to the sitting rooms, bathrooms, kitchen, and dining room was covered in a hermetically sealed vacuum. Clear plastic sucked over the furniture, artwork, and possessions collected by my parents during their life together. Everything had remained untouched since the day I'd left when I was eighteen, my entire family dead. Everything, that is, until I pushed open the door of my dad's study.

A digi-diary sat on top of the undisturbed seal on his massive desk. My throat immediately raw, a frown puckered my forehead. "What?"

I rounded the desk cautiously. My hand hovered over the small digital tablet, identical to the one in Linc's office, down to the same worn puppy-dog decal.

I looked up when a flicker crossed the shadows in the doorway. Leaving the diary on the desk, I held out my hand. "Linc?"

He entered the room. Keeping his back to the wall, he stared at me with an unreadable expression beneath the low visor of his cap.

"You followed me?"

He removed his cap and held it against his thigh. He didn't come forward, and the only movement in his face was the tic in his jaw. "I know why you came back here. I know why you came to Beta, Liz. I've known all along." His face was all harsh angles. "You won't leave without the truth about your father, and I can't bury it any longer. I don't want to."

Oh God. He knows. My lips were dry, my palms sweating. "Linc, I—"

"You don't need to explain anything to me." His nostrils flaring, his eyes flicked to the diary and back to me, suddenly showing the stormy depths of sadness. "I wish to hell you'd never come to Beta."

I straightened my back as if he'd slapped me. My throat worked and worked to swallow, but I couldn't because I was choking on pain. "I don't understand what you're saying."

Pacing forward, he caught me in his arms, whispering in his deep voice, a straining voice. "And I don't regret a single moment with you. You should know that."

"I don't regret it either. I'm sorry, Linc. I was going to tell you. I just needed to find out—"

He stared at the floor as he pushed me away. "I need you gone. Out of my life. Just disappear. You're screwing everything up."

My lips trembled, yet wild venom raced through my veins. "You look me in the eye when you say that, Lincoln Cutler." I punched him on the shoulder, and he turned his head aside. "You goddamn look at me, Linc."

A tear rolled down my cheek, and when he lifted his face, he tracked it before turning those cold, clear blue eyes to mine. "I need you out of my life, Grant. You're a liability to the Corps, to the Territory, to me."

More tears followed, and I let them run down my face unchecked, staring him down. He cursed suddenly, dragging me against him. Fingers caressing the tears away, he raised my face and kissed me, arms cinching around my back. He kissed me for minutes, and it was unlike any we'd ever shared. Our mouths and my tears and his harsh groan a despairing and desperate farewell before he tore away from me.

He pointed at my father's diary, the same one he'd had in his office at Corps Command. "Everything you want to know is in there. I know which memocasts you watched."

Shock rattled through me.

"You need to go a week or so forward." His voice cracked. "I don't expect to see you again."

I stood there shaking my head as he backed away. I could tell his face was a hard-won mask because he had to take a couple breaths and clear his throat before he spoke again. "I'm sorry. Good-bye, Liz."

Good-bye? I threw the first thing I could find at the door as soon as he was out of sight, my knife. I yanked it from the doorframe and wielded it anew. Screaming and wild, I slashed into the plastic on the desk, the chairs. I ripped it through the vacuum seal until air puffed inside, and all the artifacts of Old America my dad had collected were out in the open. Sweating and sobbing, I dropped the knife to the floor, bracing my hands on my knees.

The familiar scent of his leather-bound books wafted over me, bringing memories from my childhood. I would curl up on the little sofa while he worked away behind the desk, shooting a joke at me every so often until Mom poked her head in with an indulgent smile for us both.

I ached for all I'd lost. I ached for Linc's touch. I was pretty sure I didn't want to know what it was in my dad's memocasts that would make him drive me away. I didn't think I'd seen the last of loss as I cradled the digi-diary in my palm, wiping my eyes.

With a deep sinking in my gut, I passed my hand over the tablet and scanned past the summer 2060 entries I'd already watched.

Date stamp: 26-June-2060

Dad looked like hell. Face gray and waxy, he had new white streaks in his black hair and purple pouches beneath his eyes.

I found out why Cutler wanted me to stop the source search earlier today. Why he's been shadowing me in the labs. He wanted to make sure I'd stop meddling, that I wasn't remembering.

Dad looked behind him, and his voice became almost inaudible.

The lab tests, the data, the details of all the deaths I'd logged…It's all come back to me. They've been nightmares for a while now. I haven't been able to sleep in the same bed as Peg for weeks because I keep waking up, haunted. They weren't nightmares. It was the truth.

He slouched in his chair. His normally neat shirt was half unbuttoned, tie askew, face ashen.

I helped engineer the Pneumonic Plague, what the Company renamed the Gay Plague to use as an internal and deadly deterrent against all deviants. Only a year and a half ago. I was honored by the request from the CEOs who cited my dedication to the job and my willingness to join the Company mission to curb the rebel faction. I thought I was creating a better world.

His laugh cut through me and died out quickly.

A God complex is what they used to call it, that kind of hubris, the arrogance that consumed me enough to take pride in applying the scientific method to a biochemical weapon of death. I believed the slogo: Regeneration, Veneration, Salvation. I believed in them. I believed I was better than all the civilians I gave a pledge to serve as a man of medicine.

We were supposed to be saving humanity. I gave the CEOs the perfect weapon for murder from the inside. Liz can never know. She's my sun, so bright. I can't—

He ended the transmission. Rocking back and forth over his diary, I called up the next entry.

Date stamp: 28-June-2060

The memories come fast now. It's gotten out of control. The Plague is on the rampage. The human death toll fractured all my fidelity with the Company's policies. I am a scientist, a healer. I am not a killer. I don't want Lizbeth to remember me as a killer.

I hissed through my tears. We'd been shafted by the CO so many times, so many years ago. I was sickened just sitting inside one of their Territories. And I'd done their dirty work again.

I remember it all. Last summer, I cracked apart under my conscience, and they gave me a choice. I'm a coward, an absolute coward. Lysander told me I could be executed or have my memories of my part in the Plague erased. I chose the latter. I'd been thankful for the second chance. They sent in my counterpart from Delta Territory, the doctor I'd worked with in creating this abomination. Dr. Val.

Fuck! I'd met her. She'd been a rising star, on the same path as Linc except her specialty was genetics like my dad. She'd been invited for dinner a few times, her cool smile never meeting her eyes, her eyes taking everything in. I hadn't gotten the warm fuzzies from her then—dubbing her Doc Evil—and now I fucking wished her dead.

She wiped my frontal lobe clean, using a highly evolved form of MKUltra. Not clean enough. The shame, guilt, remorse, it's a virus inside of me. The death count keeps climbing. I have a responsibility to the citizens of the InterNations. I can't let this go without blame, without taking the blame myself.

I couldn't stop watching even while I gagged on the truth.

Date stamp: 29-June-2060

Lysander knows. He saw through me the second I didn't look him in the eye. He gave me one final out. I'm not sure why. Anyone else would be a body bag in the morgue by now. It's a gag order. They'll tarnish my reputation, the humanitarian scientist as the creator of the scourge of our generation. I don't care about that. They can take their insurance policy and shove it up Corps ass.

My snuffled laugh at Dad's bravado didn't last.

I'm going to whistle blow. I won't have much time after the announcement.

I sucked in a breath at the end of the transmission. Hurriedly pressing the next, I watched my father. His skin was slack around his jaws, hands shaking as he raked them through his hair. It was the day before he left home that last time, having been ordered unexpectedly, inexplicably to the Wilderness.

30-June-2060

I've been locked out of my labs. I won't toe the line, though. I'm tired of hearing about the bad fags, the good breeders, the hated rebels. I'm...tired.

I never meant to go out this way. I've loved my family, my calling, my life. I love Lizbeth and Peg. This is my only dishonor, and I will make it right.

They have a plan. Total eradication of the insurgent subnation, but that doesn't matter. The plague has mutated. It's beyond control. I cannot stand by that. I don't believe their feed anymore. I spoke to Peg the other night. I told her. I had to. I told one last lie, too. I couldn't stand her heartbreak. I swore to Peg it would be all right. The important thing now is she knows the truth. Lizbeth might never forgive me. She doesn't have to. She only needs to stay safe, be strong, make sure this never happens again.

I forgave him in an instant. I would never understand what hell he'd been through, but I'd given my allegiance to the CO and the Corps, too. I'd voluntarily conscripted, believed.

I was wrong about CEO Lysander Cutler. I wish he'd go back to Alpha and take his aspiring young soldier with him. There's nothing more I can say now. It won't be long. I think I know who's going to kill me.

Chapter Nine

Oh God. Oh God.

I paused the diary. My body shook all over. My hand clamped over my mouth as horror ripped through me. Horror not from staring down the barrel of a loaded gun—real ones I'd faced down and the imaginary one I'd dreamed of my first night in Beta—this was dread I couldn't evade or outrun. Remembering that terrifying nightmare when Linc grinned at me from behind a loaded pistol he pointed at my face, I almost dropped my dad's diary. I'd never felt so alone, not when I'd answered the door to the trooper baring news of my father's death, not even when I'd found my mom bleeding all over the desk behind me. None of it came close to the all-consuming dread punching me in the gut until I doubled over.

This was worse. Far, far worse.

I clicked play with a shaky finger, closing my eyes, listening intently.

It's too late for me, so I'm going to tell the truth. I know I won't

be coming back. Cutler has me followed every time I leave the house.
The boy is as sly as his father—the soldier, the future commander.
Yet I feel his presence even when he remains out of sight. I don't
imagine the CEO will want to get his hands dirty with my death.

Lincoln Cutler will be my executioner.

"NO!" The scream tore from my throat.

I slammed the diary to the floor. Hauling myself to my feet,
I reached for the desk, hanging on to it as my legs fell out from
under me. My heart hollowed out, a pain so intense I could only
stand there and keen until all sound dissolved. Breath rushed in
and out, hoarse and loud, a reminder I was still alive. That I'd
have to live with this pain every single day and it would slice me
open until I died.

The evidence tucked inside my jacket, I took a final look at my
dad's office, knowing I'd never return, just like him. There was no
return from this. I stumbled into the wall on my way out, nearly
tripping to the floor, but I righted myself and started a blind
march to the door.

Dad hadn't gotten a chance to tell anyone about the
Plague…the *Pneumonic Plague*. The Gay Plague. Linc Cutler
had cut him down before he'd had a chance. I wasn't gonna let
that happen again. Anger ramped through me, ignited me. He'd
used me, kept tabs on me, *fucked me* for a reason. And I'd been
worried about his father's filth reaching him. By the age of fourteen, he'd already been fully contaminated.

The enormity of Linc's duplicity on the heels of every other
deception I'd had shoved down my throat was too much to bear,
but at least he was alive. I didn't have to suck this one up. His pa-

thetic *I'm-sorry* move was nowhere near enough to put out the inferno of hate blazing inside me. Contempt, vicious and violent, propelled me. And one other thing.

Hope. One small nugget of it, stupid and in vain. *Maybe Dad was wrong.*

Linc hadn't revoked my privileges. I marched into the Quadrangle, up to Corps Command, straight through the doors. *Stupid, arrogant sumbitch is gonna regret that.* The elevator flew up while I checked my weapons and replaced them in my holsters.

I banged inside the same way he had after he'd debriefed with the CEO, nearly running the doors off its tracks in my haste. Only I wasn't looking for a fuck. I was gunning for a fight. Linc showed no shock at all when I stormed inside the apartment. Much like my first entrance into his office, he stood with his back turned, looking out the narrow window. Suited up, ready for another night of doling out the death he seemed so adept at, his impassive mask was fully in place when his face swiveled aside.

"You're sorry?" I stood in the middle of the room.

"I thought I told you to go." His voice was cold.

"You told me you didn't expect to see me again." Crumbling for an instant, I ranged closer. "Tell me it's all lies, Linc." *Please.* I didn't want to hate him. I didn't want to believe it.

He spun stiffly around. "I can't." Truth shone from the bright torch of his blue eyes.

Rage took hold of me, and I flew at him. My fists pounded against his chest, into his stomach. He weathered every blow without flinching, grunting with the impact but keeping his hands at his sides. His nonreaction made me even more crazed. Throwing him against the wall, I punched him in the mouth, splitting his lip.

"I saw the pictures of his remains! You did that? You fucking did that, you animal?" My fists bloody and swelling, I hunched over, on the verge of vomiting. "Why? Why?"

"I had my orders."

"That's it? Because you were ordered, *when you were fourteen years old,* to kill a man—my father—you just went along with it?" My head kicked up. "Have you no feelings?"

Linc pressed his tongue to the drops of blood on his bottom lip. "That man was going to squeal. *That man* made the fucking Plague, Liz. He wasn't innocent, and neither am I. I told you, there is no excuse. He was going to blow apart my father's future."

"You make me sick." My rage mutated into disgust. "Maybe you don't regret a single moment with me, but if I could erase every single memory of you from my head, pretend your soiled hands never touched my body, I'd do it in an instant with no re-grets."

Stonier than ever, he nodded.

"You have nothing to say, do you?"

He leaned against the wall, warily watching me. "I didn't stick around, Liz. I took the shot and left the scene immediately. I don't know what happened afterward." His voice fell. "I was just doing my job."

Just doing his job, ordered by his father to kill a man when he was still just a kid. How many times had I killed without ques-tion? And I wasn't an impressionable teenager looking for a pat on the head or a hand up to the next rung of the CO's deadly ladder I was expected to scale. I wasn't influenced by the demands of a despotic dad who owned almost all political control of the entire InterNations. He'd done his job just like I was doing mine. Except his had included murdering my father.

I slumped into a chair.

"Are you all right?" Concern crackled in his voice.

I shook my head, cringing from his outstretched hand. "No, I'm not okay, and I might never be again."

Withdrawing from me, Linc pressed his back to the wall and lowered down to the balls of his feet. "I didn't know you then."

"Maybe not, but you knew who I was the second you heard I'd turned myself into Beta. You said so yourself. You had a special interest in me." Another pulse of revulsion hit me. My life, my emotions had been played at every turn in this master game. "Why would you let me break into your office?" I thought about the moment in the locker room, my victory at snatching his key card, the power I'd thought I wielded over him.

"You're the consummate soldier; you tell me. You used me too, Liz." He pulled the replicated key card from his pocket, waving it in front of me. "I wanted to see how far you'd go, *sweetheart.*"

Of course. He wasn't stupid or sloppy enough to let himself get heisted even if he was getting a hand job at the time. I should've burned that bitch of a card the same day, but it wouldn't have mattered. He'd already known everything.

"It was all a setup."

Linc gained his feet in one graceful move, a tall shadow looming in front of me when I matched his stance. "That's right."

I pushed against his chest, and he manacled my hands in his fists. "You sent me on this wild-goose chase and watched every minute of it! You watched me fall apart, you...*Oh fuck*...You knew what I'd found in the labs, when I came back." My heart cleaved apart anew. "You knew I'd found out about my father's part in the Plague because you wanted me to see it. Linc? How could you? How could you?"

He held my hands behind my back, a grim scowl on his face. "Because you wouldn't fucking stop. You kept asking for trouble. Trust me, Liz. You have no idea how deep this goes, how far up it reaches, or the vast repercussions you keep bringing down on your head, a head I've been watching over." Tightening his fingers around my wrists, he leaned in to my face. "For a smart girl, you sure don't know when the hell to call it quits."

I should've called it quits right then and there, but like he said, I wasn't smart enough. I was reckless, hotheaded, and hurt beyond scope. "I asked you to make love to me that night because I had nothing left. And all along you were messing with my head?"

"I made love to you because I wanted to."

Tearing my hands free, I slapped him so hard across the cheek his head recoiled. "You filthy pig! I can't believe I ever let you put your hands on me."

He blinked at me. "The diary today, your home, your father... what I did. That wasn't part of the plan, Liz. That wasn't a trap."

"Oh yeah? What was it? Another cheap shot to my heart?"

"I had to come clean."

I slid away from him. "I hope you feel good about that, because I sure as hell don't."

"I don't feel good about anything, and I haven't for a long time!" he roared.

I felt no pity. There were two wars I was fighting now. The personal and the pan-InterNational, and between Linc and me, the battle lines were drawn. I still had my mission, to get the best intelligence possible back to Chitamauga, where those worth fighting for, fighting *with*, were waiting for me. "I'm leaving."

"Good. I don't have time to play house with you anymore." A cruel smirk curled his lips.

"You don't know how to play house, Commander. You wouldn't know the first thing about family. What you did to me? You made me a hostage."

I started down the hall to the bedroom, but he swooped in front of me. "A hostage? I kept you here against your will? Did I, Liz?"

"You lied to me." I glared at him.

His dark laugh washed over me. "*Touché.* We're even because you lied to me, too. But I never coerced you, because you made sure of that, didn't you?" His hands on my hips dragged me to him. "Every time we were together, there was nothing between us but passion." His erection tilted against my hip, beckoning me because he spoke the truth. I'd used him just as much. I'd wanted him with the same undeniable attraction.

God help me, I still did, my body responding to his. "I need to go."

"You're a Corps officer, Lieutenant Grant. Your strategic retreat is what I've been waiting for."

He goaded me beyond control. Hooking my leg behind his, I

took him down to the floor in a tangle of limbs. "Goddamn you, Linc! I want the fucking truth, all of it. I'm not leaving until you spill." I jerked my gun out and pressed it to his temple. "I'm not leaving so you can carry out your daddy's master plan and make like nothing happened, just one of his killing machines."

Linc leaned in to the barrel, daring me to fire, no fear showing in his irises.

I fingered the trigger, then released it, rubbing the butt across my forehead. "Where did you do it?"

"At the mansion." Head knocking back against the floor, he shut his eyes.

"At the sex club, at Cutler's house? You dressed me up, showed me off, and kissed me there, in that place where you murdered my father?"

"If that's what you want to believe, then yes. I did all those things." Lightning fast, he grasped my arms and drew me down to him, his lips pressed to my ear. Desperation tinged his voice. "I was doing my damnedest to protect you."

"I should've been protected from *you*." It galled me that though I struggled, I couldn't break free of his hold.

His lips moved down my temple to the corner of my mouth. "I would never hurt you like that, Liz. I took you to the house because of the tunnels I told you about." He dropped his head back, peering at me. "Someday you might need to run from more than just me."

"Shut up. SHUT UP!" I clawed to get away from him, from the sudden truth shining in his eyes. Scrambling from his embrace, I watched with satisfaction as he winced with the words I flung at him. "Just shut the fuck up. I don't care about the house or the tunnels. I don't care how you've convinced yourself to go on living regardless of what you've done."

I backed away from Linc, foregoing getting my shit from the bedroom in favor of getting the hell out as fast as possible. Not a single thing he'd said made a damned bit of difference. He was guilty, guiltier than he knew. "You have two lives on your hands. My mom committed suicide days after we got the news. I found her bathed in blood after I heard the pistol go off."

The color leeched from his skin.

Tears streamed down my face. "You took my entire family away from me in one week, Linc. One fucking week."

He shook his head at the floor, pinching his thumb and forefinger over his eyes. When he slid his cap off and raised his head to the ceiling, I saw the silvery tracks of wetness glinting on his face. And I saw something else, something that froze my insides.

I saw an unemotional young trooper standing at my door. I remembered Linc in my father's office hours ago, cool and unreachable, eyes hidden beneath the low visor of his cap. I slid to the floor, broken. "Oh my God."

"Liz?"

I could barely raise my head. "It was you. You're the trooper. You're the one who told me he was dead." I didn't even raise my voice. "You assassinated him, then told us about it?"

This cruelest blow spun me inside out.

"It wasn't my choice." Linc knelt before me, but I lurched away. I couldn't allow a single pang of sympathy for him. Blame had to be placed: on him, the CO, and CEO Cutler. "I was following my father's orders."

He whispered, low and intense. "I had to prove myself."

A part of my heart cracked open with Linc's avowal. I crabbed my way up the wall, locking my legs in place so I wouldn't fall over. "And me? What were you doing with me?"

In answer, Linc sent a final look into my eyes before he stalked into the lounge. He gathered his guns, his D-P, suiting himself up, shutting me out.

I caught his arm. "Keep your enemies close. Is that all I was? Is that why you had me in your bed, why you gave me back my stripes and stripped me bare?"

"I saved your ass, Grant." Grabbing my chin, he snarled at me. "Do you imagine for one single second we are not being watched? Think about it." He shook me. "I'm the CEO's son—the one who stuck it out—you're the known consort of the CO's number-one enemy. *You are not fucking safe.*"

I jerked back, a bark of laughter breaking free. "And I feel so very safe with you now. You murderer."

I watched his hands tremble as he replaced the visor on his head. "If you'd known me then, would you do the same thing?"

Bewilderment shuttered his eyes. "How can you even ask that?"

I slammed my fists against his chest. "Because I fell in love with you," I howled. "I fell in love with a monster!"

I went for my weapons. Linc didn't even try to stop me. Perfect calm replaced my hysteria as he tried to digest what I'd said, that I loved him. Both Eagles in my hands, the butts a solid, comforting weight in my palms, I pushed one point-blank at his heart—where there should've been one, anyway—and the other in the middle of his forehead, beneath the dangling lock of hair.

Maybe he could've unarmed me. Maybe he could've tried to charm his way out of this, but he didn't. He said, "I wish you'd do it. I've waited to make my retribution to you." His fingers on mine notched the trigger. "I'm already dead from the guilt I carry every fucking day."

I shut my eyes. My hands were shaking, my fingers useless. *I can't kill him.* But that didn't mean I wasn't above wounding him if he came after me. I trained both guns on him as I retreated to the door and angled half outside, checking up and down the empty corridor.

I sent a last look to Linc. "I won't end you. You'll have to live with your burden." As I did, *every fucking day.*

Chapter Ten

Outside, the spring rain poured over me, coming down as heavy as a sheet of bullets I couldn't escape from, didn't even try to. If I was looking for cleansing, this was as close as I'd get. I'd prided myself on being able to read people, but Linc had thrown me for a loop since day one, right up to the last minute upstairs. Part of him assuring me he was out to protect me, the other half complicit in the CO's most corrupt plans. I didn't know where to find the truth in him; maybe I never had. Linc was no guiltier in this dance of war than me, but his duplicity ran far deeper; it was more devastating. And I'd run out on him because ending it this way—fresh with rage over what he'd done to my family—was an easier solution than listening to the doubts seeded inside my soul.

No moon, no stars, the night was black, black, black. The rain had no intentions of letting up. At least the wet pinpricks hid the tears on my face even if it didn't do a goddamn thing to quench the unstoppable ache in my heart. Breaking down in the middle of Beta S-1 was not an option. Throwing my head back, I opened my eyes wide, blinded by the fury of drops, blinking it all away.

I don't regret a single moment with you.

A debilitating twist of agony ripped through me. I fell against an abandoned storefront, then stumbled into a side alley. Holding myself up with one arm against the wall, I shook my head. I had to hurry, to get to Farrow's before I lost my shit with all my defenses down. *At least Linc isn't dogging my ass for a change.* I charged through the despair brought on by that thought, running out the opposite end of the alley. The unyielding rain crackling as loud as gunfire popped onto my shoulders and blasted into the ground at my feet.

Except it wasn't just the rain making rifle-loud shots. It was guns, a lot of them. I'd dashed right into the middle of full-fledged street combat taking up the entire block west of Farrow's place. *Oh shit.* Dodging back undercover, I swiped at my face and drew my weapons. As I leaned out the side of the alley enough to get a good look, I gathered I'd stumbled straight into a melee, because I hadn't dealt with enough shit for one day. The whole block teemed with fighters, the rain making their movements look slow and shimmery until a body dropped, a pool of crimson diluting in the wet street.

Everyone was dressed for Dark Ops. The two camps were indistinguishable except for the faint glint of metal insignias on the Corpsmen and -women versus the six-pointed star and *Posse Omnis Juvenis* decaled on the back of the paramilitary jackets. Looked like Power to All Youth had decided to come out to play. They couldn't have picked a better moment if they'd sent me a personally engraved invitation to their pissed-off party. The Posse bastards wore ventilated full-face masks, the Corps in night visors; all combatants were unrecognizable, but I knew one thing. The Posse worked personally for Cutler, so that made them my number one target.

I leaped into the street with a screaming war cry. Shoulder to shoulder with a trooper, I dodged a spray of bullets. We advanced, the Corps as one body with one mind: Kill the enemy. The rain took visibility to nil; good thing those big white stars made such excellent bull's-eyes.

Taking on the young guerilla band should've tweaked my conscience, but I was beyond that now. I couldn't understand why they'd engaged the Corps, but they worked underground for Cutler, so they were out for Freelanders and Revolutionaries. If I had to throw my cap in the ring once and for all with the Corps, I was all in tonight. Especially when the trooper beside me spun on her heels and dropped dead to the ground.

"No!" Crouching low, I all but crawled down the street. When the next bullet whistled too close to me, I attacked, making clean kill shots in front and to both sides of me.

There was nothing impersonal about this, no shield or sniper rifle to hide behind. I would have a million nightmares about this night, but maybe they'd take the place of the ones I already felt brewing at Linc's betrayal. Coldhearted as a mercenary, I did the job I'd learned to hate, so enraged that adrenaline pushed me harder.

Our frontline collided with theirs. Then it was just a bloody mash of bodies and that sickening soft close-contact force of bullet to flesh. I felt a piercing in my biceps. Hot wetness tracked down my arm. I swung around and pulled the trigger on the tango.

My breath rasped in and out and still we went at it. I just needed some goddamned peace and quiet. I just needed...I hadn't realized I was still crying until a salty wash slid between my lips. Looking wildly around, coming to, to the brutality of the scene, I heard the first pump-gun before the sound of dozens more registered.

"GAS!" I shouted as the first canister jetted through the air. I pulled my jacket up over my nose and mouth.

The Corps soldiers pressed a button on their visors and the bottom levered over the lower halves of their faces, giving them an airtight oxygenated mask. I wasn't so lucky. Thick bright green fumes created a smoky screen rising from the ground, its eerie vapor fingers reaching higher. I kneeled over a fallen soldier and gently pulled her night visor free; then I buckled it around my face.

I'd always hated these contraptions. They had the makings for a claustrophobia attack. It took an effort to steady my racing pulse, slow my breaths and take stock of the situation. The Beta Corps had gotten smart since I'd arrived. Instead of falling back as the Posse would expect, they kept a steady approach.

I stuck with the squad, eyes straining to see through the murky green sea in front of me. Walking gingerly among fallen bodies, I halted only when I heard a muffled shout. "Look lively, Sarge!"

I knew that growly voice. I raised my Eagle for a final shot. *Taft.* I held the gun primed, but maybe I should let the blue-haired extremist survive the night. I needed some answers, and if I could make him shit his tight britches in the process of getting

them, that would be a bonus. Besides, I had bigger concerns—because Taft's *Sarge* was Sebastian goddamned Monroe.

I pivoted around, and my stomach bottomed out. At my rear, a
lanky youth with hanks of platinum hair beneath his black mask
had a straight-armed gun shoved in his face. It was Sebastian.

I slunk silently closer.

"Well, well, well, lookee what I caught."

I recognized that ugly voice and the thin, hard lips emitting
it. MP Jenoah had fast-tracked in the ranks since arriving from
Alpha if she'd gotten in with the Corps. The ballsy broad was
one step above an animal only because she knew how to wipe her
own ass instead of licking it clean. Cannon had told me how she'd
worked Leon over until he was nothing but a pulpy mess, and
now she had her standard-issue weapon stuck in Sebastian's face.

"You another one of them Posse punks, you little prick?"
Jenoah angled the barrel beneath his strong jaw. "You adolescent
fuckwits got enough brass to bang the Corps?"

I watched Sebastian's throat rise and fall with a hard swallow. I
stepped closer, running through the best strategies to disarm her.

Jenoah pressed her gun into his skin until it hollowed around
the barrel. "Any last words before I pull this here trigger and
decorate the inside of your fancy helmet with your brains, little
boy?" Her hand went to his groin and she twisted his nuts in a
cruel grip.

Sebastian bit into his lip as she lowered the gun to his pelvis,
hammer still live.

"Ain't gettin' a woody on me now, are ya?"

I figured Sebastian could do without a nut more than his

pretty face, so if my move went south, no harm done. Sneaking as close as I could without alerting Jenoah, I slammed between them, forcing Sebastian behind me.

Taking off my helmet, my hair instantly matted to my skull by rain, I bit out, "You spatter my brains out, Jenoah, you better make sure it's clean through. You hear me?"

The gun wavered. She frowned, trying to pigeonhole me with all three neurons she possessed.

I inclined forward, letting the gun eat into my throat as it had Sebastian's. "Lieutenant Liz Grant. Now, get that gun out of my face."

She holstered the weapon, not without hesitation. I raised mine, with no compunction. There was a time and a place, means and motivations. If the Corps was ever to be recovered, made stronger and better for the people, *for all people*, not all of them would survive.

"On your knees now."

She bent her legs, stooped into a puddle, knees on the ground.

"Visor off," I ordered.

Sebastian was stiff behind me, a wall of palpable energy.

Jenoah unsnapped her helmet and laid it aside. Black rage hit me from her eyes.

My hand shook this time. I was doing this close range, fully conscious, completely in my mind. "This is for your hatred. This is for Leon Cheramie. You are not going to a better place." When I pulled the trigger, I kept my gaze on hers. She dropped instantly.

I grabbed Sebastian's arm and ripped off his mask. "You stupid son of a bitch!"

Frozen in place, he stared at Jenoah's body.

I grabbed his chin, snarling words similar to the ones Linc had said to me earlier, finally understanding what he'd meant. "This is a fucking war, Sebastian. We are going to kill; people are going to die." I yanked him away, hoping Taft was busy dicking someone else. "Let's make sure it isn't you." With that, I tore off his star-emblazoned jacket and crushed it underfoot lest he become the next Corps target.

Bodies clotted the thoroughfare. Flashes of the green gaseous smoke waved in the air. The fight hadn't died down, not one bit. I hurtled past a soldier, spun around, and clenched his shoulder. Not even the visor could hide the freckles on his face.

"Ginger!"

He swerved to me but kept a steady aim down the street, earning my immediate respect. "Lieutenant, ma'am!"

"Either get the hell outta here or get the commander ASAP."

"He's half a block away. I'm staying till it's done."

Keeping a close cover over Sebastian, I sent him forward at a fast run. *At least he made it out of the Amphitheater in one piece.*

When we turned the corner and the combat became an echo of gun chatter, I pulled him by his scruff until we were face-to-face. Sebastian was handsome as hell and too fucking delicate to be getting nuts deep in this, evident by the vulnerable quiver of his lips. He lowered his eyelids over those almond-curved violet irises, but I snatched his chin up.

"You don't belong here, baby boy."

"Lieutenant Grant?" Even his voice was sweet, hungry.

"Keep that pretty mouth shut. I want to let your sister get first crack at you, you little shit."

I was shell-shocked by the time we reached Farrow's. His fingers trembling just as badly as mine, Sebastian coded us into the apartment. He pulled up quick at the gun barrel that greeted us from his sister's ironclad grip.

She dropped the weapon to her side and ushered us in, eyes flecked with alarm. "Ah don't even wanna ask, do Ah? Jesus, Lizbeth. Are you bleedin'?"

She took hold of my arm, and I flinched from her gentle touch. Her voice softened. "What happened, sweet girl?"

Extreme shock was setting in. My teeth chattered so hard, I stuttered. "I c-c-can't…I don't want to…t-t-talk about it."

"Oh good. So y'all just busted down my door, lookin' like the hind end of a yard dog, and you aren't gonna tell me a thing? *Mm-hmm*. We'll see about that. Bathroom's that way, so git. As for you, Bassy…"

I'd let them chew over each other for a while. The bathroom became a steam-drenched enclave once I'd turned on the shower. I stripped and fell against the wall as sobs broke out of me under the hot spray of water. All the pain and fear I'd held inside ran out of me in tears. Even while I cried over Linc, I couldn't forget the way it felt undeniably right to be with him in this very same position while we washed each other and then made love. The way only he had ever satisfied me enough, in my body, in my heart.

Farrow slipped in silently and shut off the water. She helped me up off the slick floor. Wrapping me in a towel, she eyed the fresh wound on my arm trailing blood down to my fingertips.

"Let's bandage that up. Is Linc expectin' you back tonight?" She pulled out a first aid kit and sat me on the commode.

I swallowed through the dryness in my throat. "He's not expecting me ever again." I watched her patting the wound. She kept her gaze on my arm, leaving me a shred of dignity—while I sat naked, wrapped in a towel, sitting on her toilet as she took care of me like a baby. "I can't save him. I can't do it. He doesn't want me, and I'm not strong enough." Then I started blubbering…like a baby.

Farrow's lips thinned. "He's got you slung over a barrel, has he? Ah can't help you unless you tell me what happened, darlin'."

"I fell for him. You thought I could free him from his father's vise, but I can't. He's a machine, a monster." Pain gripped me from inside.

"What did he do to you?" She threw the detritus of gauze into the waste shoot and faced me.

"He set me up for the biggest fall of my life. He made sure I'd find my dad's digi-diary, his lab work…" I crossed my arms over my chest, attempting to hold the stinging bitterness inside. "He made sure I'd find out my father created the Plague."

"It makes sense." I could see her sifting through what she knew of my father, the Plague, fitting pieces of the ugly puzzle together.

I charged to my feet. "It does not make sense! He was my father! He was supposed to be a savior, not a man who engineers a disease to slaughter thousands. There's *no* sense in that." I turned a bleak gaze to Farrow. "It was on my dad's diary. Linc murdered him."

A wave of sadness reached Farrow's eyes. Her fingers clenched mine, a hold so tight I started crying again.

"I went back to Command even though he told me he didn't

want to see me again. I don't know what to believe. He did it. He admitted as much, and then he..." A deep breath burned my lungs. "He didn't deny anything, but he said I was to get away from him and Beta because his father was watching us, me, waiting for a slipup."

That's why the CEO always had it in for me. He wanted to make sure I remained in the dark about my dad and the truth about the Plague. Why he made sure his favored son was on top of the situation, on top of me. But Linc had tried to set me free, given me an out after he'd handed over his heart, knowing I would crush it as he had mine.

"Oh fuck." My head hung low. "Linc wants me out of here because he wants me safe."

"He took up arms against the drones to prevent a whole lot of collateral damage at the Amphitheater, Lizbeth."

"I know. I know."

"There's still hope for him, more than ever. He's not lost, not to this war, not to you." She looped an arm under mine and walked me to her bedroom.

I slipped into a silky dressing gown she handed me, speaking softly. "We made love."

"You love him."

"I don't..." Of course I did. There was no use trying to deny it. Love was stupid, blind, misguided, and almost always a mistake. Therefore, being in love with goddamn Commander Linc Cutler was a given. "God, how pathetic."

"Pathetic was when Ah found you on the roadside outside this here Territory way back in November. You've been nothing but an excellent soldier, a strong friend, a passionate lover since then." She slipped a pair of short KA-BARs into the knee-high boots she zipped over her calves. "Remember what Ah told you then?"

"How could I forget?"

"A pussy in the bush is worth more than a bushel full of pricks, and Ah see you got rid of the bush."

I chuckled for a moment, my face flaming.

"About Linc, bless his heart. Ah will make that Breeder bull a sterile steer mahself if he so much as looks at you wrong ag'in." Cool and cutthroat, Farrow unsheathed one of the blades and twirled it in the air, catching it in a solid grip. "Ah might even let Cannon lance his sac for hurting you."

Farrow started for the door. "But you know Linc didn't understand the repercussions back then, don't you, Lizbeth?"

I wasn't sure of anything yet, except… "I need to talk to Cannon."

She handed me the usual untraceable D-P. I didn't accept it, keeping my palm held out.

Farrow asked, "Problem?"

"I need to see his face. Get me on a video feed."

She hedged. "Ah don't think Hatch has that capability."

"Bullshit. Hatch has all kinds of tricks up his sleeves. Do it."

She returned with a flashier D-P. I heard her murmuring to Hatch and then Cannon's deep rumble, loud and clear. "Get her for me."

Farrow left me to it, heading back to Sebastian to finish hashing it out.

Staring at the D-P screen, I almost started crying again. I

hadn't seen Cannon in more than two months, but his scowl pressed as deeply between his brows as it had during our last meeting with Hills and the co-op crew.

He growled, "You look like you've been dropped face-first from a Predator."

"Don't pull any punches or anything." I held the D-P tight in my hands, taking in the stormy crags of his face. "How do you get Nate to fuck you with that ugly mug you got going on there, sir?"

Cannon swept both hands over his close-cropped trim and smirked. "Where's my salute, Lieutenant?"

"'Bout the same place it always is. Wanna see it?" I motioned down to my crotch.

His laugh let me breathe again. "Goddammit, woman. I miss you."

Raising a hand to my eyes, I wiped them clear. "Miss you, too, you big bugger."

"What's happening up there? We've had coms from Darke. He wants to enlist the militia *tout-fucking-suite*."

"Give it another week." I looked aside. "I'm not sure I can hold it all steady right now. I might need an out."

He leaned into the screen, filling it with his face. "Don't you give me that crap, Grant. There is one out, and that is victory, however you make it happen. Don't make me regret allowing you to go in alone when you know it's the last thing I wanted to do."

"Fucking hell, Cannon, do you *ever* take the stick out?"

"If you feed me one more line of horseshit, I'll—"

"Don't make me say it," I begged.

The harsh planes of his face melted with sympathy that cut me closer than his glare. "Whatever the fuck's going on up there, you better tell me, Liz. You called me; you needed me."

"My dad helped engineer the Plague. A couple years later, Linc killed him at Cutler's command. Not much more to say than that." I left out the whole *my heart is tied in knots* problem.

I must've worn it on my face because Cannon swore himself purple, then cursed some more. "You stupid fool; you fell in love."

I was saved from answering by a slow southern drawl in the background. "Is that Lizbeth you got there?"

Of course the sound of Nate's voice and the visual of his face so like Linc's triggered more tears.

"Jesus fucking Christ, Liz. You're a mess." Cannon visually cataloged my tear-streaked face and red-rimmed eyes.

"You're a fine one to talk about falling in love with the men in that family. Don't even think about telling me off. I've done enough of it myself. He's a Class-A asshole. Sorry, Nate."

The background crackled when Nate whispered to Cannon, Cannon assuring him, "I'll fill you in later."

Great. Now my lousy love life was gonna be Freelander fodder.

"I can't go back to Command. I can't go back to Linc. It's not an option." I sounded pitiful even to myself.

"You listen to me, Lieutenant. I promise you when I meet Linc Cutler, I intend to *infiltrate* his face with my fucking fist until he's breathing out of his ears and seeing through his nostrils."

"Oh, Big Papa, I missed you." For the first time, I welcomed his protective edge. I felt so far away from him and my starting point in all this.

"I missed you too, girl. That's why I won't let you opt out. You're in too deep and you respect yourself too much. No matter how much I want to kill Linc for what he's done to you, you have a mission."

Aw shit. Taking a deep breath, I straightened my spine, got back on point.

"You steady there now?" His brown eyes became flinty, as relentless as my objectives needed to be.

"Damn straight." I wasn't gonna let Linc run me off my assignment, and I sure as hell wasn't going to let him walk away with my heart in his hands. "How are things holding in Alpha?"

"There was a coalition appointed from Shoals Commune and Alpha native rebels. They're doing the cleanup, rebuilding." He smiled in wonderment. "We're still not sure how this new government is gonna work if we win this war."

"*When* we win the war."

"That's the fighting spirit." He crossed his arms behind his head. "Kappa and Nu Territories across the pond are on board. Omega in the Aafrican continent continues to be a hotbed."

I mulled that information over. Omega had been reported several weeks ago as being well in hand by the CO. "And you think this campaign in Beta is important."

"Important? Fuck, Liz. It's pivotal. Cutler is *there*. If we oust him, if we gain control of Beta, we can clinch the rest of the Continental Territories."

I popped my knuckles one at a time, grinning when he winced at the sound. "I like those odds, but there are a lot of tangos up here."

"What's new?" He shrugged. "This is a different war, Liz, but you know it inside and out. Bring the factions you can together, and thrash the rest."

"Working on it."

Lifting his hand as if to caress my face, Cannon let it drop along with his voice. "I'm right here, you know?"

My throat bobbed, I goddamn blinked at a bright halo-light to burn my tears away. "I know."

"You let Farrow take care of you tonight. Back on spec tomorrow."

"Double that, Caspar."

"Good night, Liz."

I found Farrow in the lounge, pacing a tight circle. "Where's Sebastian?"

Dazed eyes met mine. "I told him some home truths, that I'm not just a displaced Old History debutante kickin' up my heels. He skedaddled."

"Jesus. Now is not the fucking time for him to go all rebellious teenager, Farrow."

"He's in over his head. I want Leon to tail him tighter."

"I'll do you one better. Starting tomorrow, I'll be his constant shadow. The boy won't be able to take a leak without me knowing about it."

Farrow had been pulling on a padded leather jacket. She peered over. "You gonna clear this with Linc?"

"Linc can kiss my ass; then go straight to town on my—"

The apartment door slamming open silenced my diatribe. Linc strode into the room, filling it with black-dressed, rain-drenched fury, while I stood in the middle dressed in some silky confection of a robe instead of the full-body protection I needed.

I spun on Farrow, hearing Linc's loud breaths as he tried to bring his hammering respiration to heel. "You ratted me out?"

"Oh, sweet girl, you'll thank me for it tomorrow." She patted my arm and swept out the door, shooting back, "I'm gonna go kick some sense into Bassy. Y'all break anything, I expect compensation in full."

I wasn't gonna thank her for shit. As for reparation, that would come in the form of my boot print on her ass. Bristling with refreshed rage, I tried to swivel past Linc where he barred the entryway. He caught my arm and I flinched.

He dropped his hand to my wrist, his voice hoarse. "You got hurt out there."

"You hurt me more than any bullet could."

His features wrenched in torment. "Please let me look at it. I need to make sure you're okay."

"You didn't show the same concern for my well-being earlier." I stood rigid while he parted the loose sleeve up to my shoulder.

A thick fringe of eyelashes hid his eyes from mine as he stroked the bandage with his thumbs. Faint red blood seeped through the gauze beneath his gentle touch. "Did Farrow clean you up?"

Yanking my arm away, I bolted past him, but he was faster than me, framing the doorway with his bulk. The muscle in his jaw ticked like my racing heart. "How deep is it?"

My eyes narrowed. "Not as deep as the wound you caused me."

He turned into a predator. Slinky movements belied the wild

emotions he held in check as he cornered me against the wall. "I asked you a question."

"It's a graze," I spat at him.

Bound by his presence—a warm, masculine mass pressing against me—I stopped fighting. His hands were firm and rough on my hips. "I know what you went through out there tonight. I know that kind of combat fucks you up."

"If you knew anything about me, you'd know *you're* the thing fucking me up."

"I know you chose to remain a lieutenant instead of climbing higher. I know that sniper rifle you're so good at wielding isn't the only shield you hide behind." He lowered his face to mine. "I came here because I had to make sure you were unharmed."

Sliding from under his arms, I marched into the lounge. "Now that you've seen I'm just fine and dandy, you can go."

"Not so fast."

I turned to him, hands out in front of me. "What more do you want from me, Linc?"

He cocked his head. "Why'd you come to Farrow? You hardly know her."

"You introduced us. And I'll ask you again, what do you want from me? If you're just here to feed me more lies, I've had my fill."

"I want the truth."

"I thought I did too." I turned away from him, fumbling onto the sofa.

Suddenly he was before me, on his knees. "I can't change any of that. I don't know how to make it right, Liz. But I gave you my truth. It's your turn."

"I owe you nothing." I pressed my head against the back of the sofa, trying to get as far as possible from the spell of his words, the heat of his body, the honesty blazing from his eyes.

His head hung low, forelock of hair falling over a dirty mark on his brow. "If you feel anything for me, anything at all, please, Liz."

Uniform tattered and wet, fresh from battle, he'd come to fight for me. I wasn't willing to give in. "You gave me one version of the truth. Was that all of it?"

He rested his head in my lap. My fingers clenched just above his hair, aching to stroke him when he admitted, "It's not that easy."

I slipped my fingers down his neck, trailing through his damp hair. "No, it's not." A hard shudder coursed through his body. "Did Ginger make it?"

"Yeah, but there were a lot of losses, on both sides." He reared up, clasping my hands against his face, a long tremor working through him. "I thought I'd lost you when you ran out of Command, but that was nothing compared to what I felt when I got the Mayday code from Johnson, that you were on the scene. Fuck, Liz. I've never been so scared in my life."

The painful intensity of his words burrowed into my heart. I couldn't pull away from him.

From the shell of my ears to the curve of my neck, his fingertips traced the lightest touches as if he was reassuring himself I was there before him, solid, breathing, alive. "I know I don't deserve your forgiveness for what I did, the way I told you, the lies I tried to make you believe. I wanted you to go, get away from my father, before he got to you too."

He held me as if I'd break apart within his hold. His voice vibrated with emotion. "I would do *anything* to keep you out of danger, Liz. I will give everything I have to keep you out of his hands. Do you understand that? Even if it means making you hate me."

Hating Linc would've been the easy route, the weak road, but I was no coward. Loving him meant strength, balls, and more trust than I'd ever given anyone. He wasn't asking for absolution; he was asking for understanding.

Tears clotted my words and my breath hitched, but I joined my hand with his. "I don't hate you, Linc."

A deep exhale—more groan than breath—slid over the side of my face. He watched me for a moment before relief swept through him and he carried me down onto his lap.

The comfort of his touch loosened the last knot inside me. The shakes hit me hard and fast. I told him what had been haunting me all night, what I couldn't admit to Farrow. "I could've killed Sebastian tonight."

"What was he doing out there?" Linc's murmur drifted over me, settling some of my tremors.

Grasping his shirt to keep him close, I shook my head.

"We have a lot to discuss." His whisper slid along my cheek, his parted lips following to my waiting mouth.

I gasped at the soft stroke of his tongue, the hungry mesh of our lips.

Bruised by battle, starving for each other's touch, we held on.

Chapter Eleven

I didn't want to think about the grim facts of war. Anything could tear us apart again, as it surely would. Linc's mouth against mine, he moved us onto the sofa, one knee pressed between my legs, parting the robe to my hips.

Hauling my thigh over his hip, he ran his fingertips behind my leg to my ass, cupping it, squeezing. I pulled off his jacket, the wet shirt, too. I pressed my lips to his chest with every sculpted plane revealed, reveling in the chills rising up his abdomen. Linc smelled of smoke and ash, rain and gunpowder. And man.

His chest holster clunked to the floor. Combat jacket, D-P, and visor followed suit, each with a loud slap, the only noise to be heard. We didn't speak. Words had no place here, not yet. The truth would come, and the pain of it might not allow the surrender we needed.

I ran his belt through the loops, lashing it aside. His eyes flickered to the coiled leather.

When I arched my back, the silky robe fell away to frame

my breasts and aroused, pinked nipples. "You wanna tie me up, baby?"

He lowered his lips to one breast while both hands roved up my spine, tilting me to him. He tongued a wide circle. "If it means keeping you close to me, I don't see the harm in that."

Latching on to the bud, he sucked vigorously. His width was a muscular mass between my legs. I pressed my heel to his erection, and he growled against me.

"Foot fetish, too?"

He plucked the button and zipper of his trousers open. Shaft in hand, he slid the velvety length of flesh along my instep. "Woman, when it comes to you, I have every kind of fetish."

Linc's hand coasted down my belly to my center, his fingers slipping lower and twisting inside me. Aching need had me rotating my hips. Wetness spilled from me, saturating his palm. "Ah, yes!"

Grabbing my ankle, he kissed the scar on my calf. Linc released the robe from my shoulders and ran one palm along the middle of my body to my clit, meeting the deft fingers plunging into me. "You put yourself in way too much danger, Liz."

I pushed him off me until he stood, fists opening and closing at his sides, awaiting my pleasure. I held his gaze while I touched each scar on his front. His cock rose up from his open pants to his stomach, leaking pearls of liquid I salivated to taste. "You're the most dangerous man I've ever met."

He tried to step back, but I curled my foot around his calf, keeping him in place. "Lose the trousers."

His stare was half-mast, wholly hot. I stroked my nipples,

peaking them between my fingers for his perusal. Everything sizzled with heat between us. Linc shucked his trousers and briefs, slinging them aside to show off his lean, cut pelvis, long, hard cock, and broad thighs.

"You're also the most careful and tender, the most considerate." I leaned forward, licking the shiny tip of his shaft, easing it into my mouth with teasing, moist kisses. "And by far, the sexiest."

His fingers dug into my shoulders. "Jesus, Liz."

"*Mmm*." He was salty, hot, a firebrand on my tongue and in my throat. He thrust deep, and I loved it. His hand at the front of my neck felt the arch of his cock going deep down my throat. Savoring the taste, I closed my eyes, swallowing.

His hips were up to my face, the crisp curls surrounding his cock against my lips, his scent—male, musky, unmistakably mine—was in my nose. My fingernails drove into his sectioned abdomen, pulled the arrow of dark blond hairs, yanked him deeper as my mouth was deliciously bruised from his use.

He pulled out. "Not yet." Voice rich and sexual, Linc wrapped his fist around his base, shuddering from head to toe.

When he tossed me onto the sofa, my hands scrambled up his back. Bringing me close inside his embrace, he penetrated me with languid ease.

My back rose along with a scream on the verge of my lips. The sofa dented by his knees bending mine farther apart, he groaned. "Just like this. We're gonna come just like this, sweetheart."

I grappled for purchase on his shoulders, that silent howl finding voice on his next slow lunge. "Yes, *yes!*"

Each long ride inside and out of me drew my pussy around his shaft. I quivered around him, gripping him with my arms and legs, with my heat. He stroked inside, stretching me to the point of fullness. Crashing together, his hips pivoting against mine, I licked his ear with a hoarse whisper for more. My palm wet with us, I teased his sacs as his thighs tensed. I moaned when his measured thrusts turned hard and fast.

Linc abandoned himself inside me, driving my breath from my throat, all thoughts from my head. He withdrew at the moment my body was tight for release.

His words—harsh and potent—fanned over my lips. "Tell me again. Say it when I'm inside you."

Arms stretched beside me, he slowly sank into me, watching my need for him play out on my face.

"Tell me." He held still, muscles quaking, an animal desperate to slake his hunger. His hips rising, his thick shaft emerged—wet, shiny, beautiful. It danced above my body.

My hands on his flexing ass, I thrust him inside, amazed I could take him. I rejoiced in my heart's acceptance. "I love you, Linc!"

My body a vise, I compressed around him. I keened against his throat as he pushed higher inside me, jetting his seed into me.

Afterward, I couldn't move. Linc stayed inside me, the male animal hardening again. I cupped his ass and laughed when he grumbled into my neck. *It would be so easy to stay like this.* He shifted under me in a slick move, retaining his tight hold around me. High on endorphins, drugged by sudden exhaustion, I fell into a light snooze.

His chuckle was my first alert I'd dozed off. A big hand cupped my hair. "Tired, darlin'?"

I smiled. "You can't blame a girl for nodding off after that."

He hooked me a little bit closer. Linc was the first man to make me feel treasured, honored with every touch and look. Splayed out beside me on Farrow's dainty sofa, one arm stretched behind his head, he was gorgeous, strong. More than that, he was mine if we could make it through this night. I nuzzled the dark blond tuft of hair at his armpit, nipped the ropy deltoids, and listened to him hum in satisfaction. His hand lazily stroked my back to my ass, one finger slipping into the crease.

His hair was rumpled, eyes crinkly. He was perfect…just waiting to be shattered.

I could forgive him. I already had. He'd done nothing I wasn't capable of, culpable of wanting to do myself. I'd wanted to kill his father all along and I *knew* who he was. Linc hadn't known, not for eleven years, how it would hit me or even who I was. I'd withheld just as much, maybe more from him, and the knowledge knocked against my heart. It was time to come clean.

I stood before him, gathering his hand in mine. With Farrow gone for the night, I wanted to make the most of being outside Quad walls. We walked down the hall, and he trailed a solitary knuckle down my spine.

"You know your way around Farrow's place pretty well, Liz."

Trying a door, I found a linen closet. My eyes slanted to Linc's as he backed away from me, a small grin on his lips. "Maybe not that well."

The next room was a guestroom, as luxuriously appointed as

the rest of the apartment. I led Linc inside to the bed. He pulled back the covers and slipped inside, his hand held out to me.

Curling in next to him, I met his eyes. "You were right earlier. We do have a lot to talk about." I captured his hand, determined to hold on to him during these very hard truths. "I knew Farrow before I came to Beta. We all have someone in common."

"Nathaniel." His thumb—rubbing up and down my palm—stilled. "I asked you about him your first night here and you lied to me."

"Of course I did. You just about told me you'd string me up on charges of treason simply for being AWOL, to say nothing about having data on Nate."

"Nate, huh?" Taking his hand from mine, he blew out a breath. When he peered at me, suspicion angled his brows together. "Are you saying you trust me with this now?"

"I have to. If I didn't, I'd be digging my own grave beside a lot of my friends."

He turned his back on me, feet hitting the floor. "You're telling me because you have to trust me, not because you have any faith in me."

"That's not what I meant, Linc, not at all. I have to ask you something, though."

"Shoot."

"How do you really feel about him and Cannon?"

He rounded on me then. "Do you honestly think I didn't know what my brother was, Liz? I grew up with him. We're twins, for God's sake. There's some kind of…connection between us. I knew. I always knew about him." His hands falling to the bed, he lowered his voice. "And I always knew it would get his foolish ass killed."

"Do you disapprove?"

"Does it matter one way or the other?"

Fear that this might not work, that Linc was made from the same gay-hating mold as his father, made my heart plummet. "I have to know I'm not endangering them by disclosing anything more," I whispered.

"What matters is that he's safe. I don't give a shit who he dicks or who he loves. I care a fucking lot when he puts his frigging neck on the line for another man, especially since I gave up so much of my own life trying to protect him." Linc rose and started to walk away from me, but I gripped his hand.

"Please don't leave me."

He stood, unsure, looking down at me.

"You put up such a tough front. You've fallen in step so completely with your father." I shook my head at his scowl. "And I know there's more than that, baby."

I laid my head on his hip, hand running up his side. I felt the slow, infinitesimal shift of his defensive stance until he exhaled. His fingers drifting into my hair, he clasped the back of my head to hold me closer. "I've never told anyone what it was like."

"You can tell me."

He sat back down, shoulder to shoulder with me. "We were only eight when Momma left. I'm assuming you know the real reason why." His gaze swerved to me and I nodded. "I resented her for that, for abandoning me. I held on to that anger for a long time. I was just a fuckin' kid, but we were never allowed to be kids after she deserted us. When I was twelve, I guess I had a turn-ing point. I figured out Daddy's hard ways and rigid upbringing suited me, which made sense. What mother would want to stick around to watch her child become a coldhearted bastard, just like the one who hit her until she had to run away?"

I fumbled for his hand, but he flinched away from me. "I was an excellent little trooper for Father; Nathaniel wasn't. I played right into Dad's hands until the night of our Proving Ceremony before we turned eighteen. In honor of his twin sons, he pre-sented us together. I went first, strutted up to that fancy bed in front of everyone and climbed in like I owned the world—and I did, back then. I can't remember the name of the girl I was with. I've been with so many women since—that's the sick thing about this whole government. It's one rule for the masses, another for us officers and executives. No such thing as monogamy…Excess and greed everywhere you look, until the disgusting overindul-gence sneaks up on you and you see it for what it is. Sex so you don't have to feel. Fucking so you don't have to think about what you're doing every single day."

"I have a lot of hate, Liz." Linc planted his elbows on his knees, his face buried in his hands. "I don't remember those women, didn't give a shit most of the time, not until you."

I dug my fingers into my thighs, wishing I could take some of his pain away.

"I remember Farrow though, that night, when Nathaniel couldn't complete his ceremony with her. Wouldn't go through with it, because he was too honorable. Such a sweet girl; still is, if you can put up with her back-assed words."

He looked over when a small laugh slipped from me. His voice was rough. "I still wanna know about you and her."

"We'll get to that."

Facing forward, he nodded. "So after Nathaniel failed and got sent on a survivalist mission, the one that would've seen him killed if he hadn't been found by the Freelanders"—my eyes filled with tears when he called them Freelanders instead of Nomads—"I started rethinking some things. I couldn't change my position with Father, but I could make sure that shit never happened to my brother again. I swallowed my doubts—doubts that multiplied a few years ago when I learned all about the Gay Plague and its genesis."

"Linc, none of this is your fault."

He swung around, face tensed. "You tell that to the families of all the people I've killed!"

We both realized what he'd said at the same time, hurt collapsing silently between us as the distance widened.

"Always primed to be Father's successor, I'd already been on tours—killing sprees and publicity hand in hand—the most excellent spit-polished commander. So I redoubled my efforts, playing my role to keep Nathaniel safe from our power-hungry dad. And killing your father was only my first proving ceremony."

Horror crashed through me over what he'd been made to do at just fourteen. "Oh God, Linc."

"No, don't. Don't sympathize. Don't even look at me." He fended me off with both hands.

I could only watch him stand and pace around the room.

"I didn't want to lose another one, not like our mom. I took the heat. I knew what I was doing. I've been copacetic, Liz, through all the blood on my hands. I pushed Nathaniel away as best I could because if Dad found out he was gay…" A sneer distorted his mouth. "He'd kill him. I stayed on point because he beat our mother, and I couldn't fucking live with myself if he beat my brother, too."

Grabbing his hands as he passed me, I brought his palms to my mouth. My tears trailed between his fingers, fingers that remained as unresponsive as his voice.

"I can take anything for the people I love to make sure they're not hurt. All those times I asked you about him and Cannon, I just wanted to know if he was okay, Liz." A shaky hand disentangled from mine, warming my cheek. "That's all I wanted. I'm not going after him. I love him."

"You sacrificed everything for him."

"I don't regret it." He stood strong before me.

"He's good, Linc. He's safe. I'm sorry. I should've told you before." I closed in on his unbearably stiff frame, holding him tight. "He's in love, happy. He's with your mother."

He nodded, his features rigid, not allowing himself relief from the pain of his past.

"I came here to find out about my dad, but I'm also here to bring you back to them. I'm part of the Revolution, Linc. I'm with the Freelanders." His stoic silence shook me. "Eden and Nate, they haven't given up on you."

"Maybe they should."

"*I'm* not giving up on you."

Passing his fingertips over my cheeks, a long, unreadable look passed over his eyes. "That's a lot to take on."

My heart tripped in my chest. "Yes, you are."

His laugh rasped out. "You really were holding out on me."

"There's more. Farrow's not who you think she is." It was my turn to dig in and hope he understood.

"Seems no one is."

"She delivered me to the Outpost when Nate freed Cannon. I was there. She's underground; she has to have immunity, Linc."

"Fuck, y'all have been playing me together?"

"No! No." I rose from the bed only to meet the wall of his body, solid with tense muscle, but I wouldn't back down. "Farrow was only ever thinking about you when she brought us together. She figured I could get to you in a way no one else had."

"She got that right." He spun away, heading for the door.

"If I had to listen to how you killed my father, you will goddamn stand here and hear me out, Lincoln Cutler."

He pivoted. "What else have you been withholding from me?"

I love you. The words I wanted to say to him over and over again remained lodged in my heart. What emerged was entirely different. "Farrow and I were together."

"Jesus Christ." He hunched over like he'd taken a strike to the gut, hitting me with an accusing look. "Are you a dyke now on top of everything else?"

I stomped up to him. "Don't make me hit you for that."

His head turned aside as if I'd already smacked him, blood rushing to his cheeks. "I may not care who Nathaniel screws, but

I definitely have a major problem with you being with anyone else—male or female—but me. We clear?"

"Crystal, and it's over. We ended it months ago, before I met you, before I came here. I needed her! I needed a person to be with without any fucking subterfuge. I never knew how much I could feel for someone until I met you. I don't know what I am, except in love with you, you pigheaded mule."

The back of his head beat against the wall. "You turn me inside out every goddamn time I think about you, Liz."

"Ditto."

"Fuck." He squared his jaw. "It's over with her?"

"Yes. I love you, Linc. I have never said those words to anyone." I pressed a kiss to his stubborn chin.

"Maybe you shouldn't. Maybe it would be best if you went back to the commune, as far away from me as you can get."

"I know why you're doing this, and you can shove that idea up your ass sideways."

Self-hate torqued his features. "I don't know how you can even look at me. What you said this afternoon, about my soiled hands." He lifted them up, weapons of death. "I don't know why you let me touch you, make love to you. I can't stand myself. I may have lost my mom, but I killed your father, your mother too. You were right. I'm an animal. You shouldn't...I shouldn't be here with you..."

He'd borne so much on his shoulders, all alone, for all this time. I wouldn't let him push me away. "You said it."

"Said what?" Anger twisted his face. Anger at me, himself, my deception or his, it didn't matter, none of it mattered.

"Make love, you made love to me, Linc." I cupped his face. "You love me. You love Nate." He tried to rear back, but I went right with him. "You have proved your worth by your selfless deeds and you're stronger because what you did, you did selflessly, right down to telling me about my dad when you knew it was the sure way to get me to leave without looking back." Restless hands stilled on my hips. An anguished groan vibrated in his throat. "I'm not going anywhere, not without you."

He ducked his head to my shoulder, his own shaking.

When he lifted his face, his cheeks were damp, blue eyes resolved under the moist sheen. He stepped me back a couple paces from him. "I'm not that good, sweetheart. Don't be fooled. You weren't the only one with a mission, and I had motives up the wazoo for stickin' to them."

"But you didn't." I smiled as his accent slipped into a low drawl. He probably didn't even notice it.

"I thought about it. Secrets to safeguard. And then you, traipsin' right into my life, tearin' it all apart." Taking my hand, he guided me to the bed. He laid me on it, climbing in next to me. "What is it about you that changes everything?"

I kissed his fingertips and murmured, "I don't know, but it's the same for me."

He rolled onto his back with a laugh. "You're this hard-core, hard-ass, sexy-as-fuck lieutenant who strolled into my office, about to pull your weapons on me. I should've known there and then I wasn't getting away with anything. I was only supposed to keep an eye on you."

"You did that to top specs."

"My eyes, Lieutenant, not my hands."

I smoothed my lips along the soft skin of his shoulder. "I prefer both."

A world full of possibility resided in his azure irises. "I found something in you I never went looking for, Liz. I can't help thinking I'm putting you at more risk by letting you stay."

"Oh, no man's ever *let me* do anything."

Rising above me, Linc pinned me down, but it wasn't a playful move. Seriousness lined his tight lips when he bent to kiss me briskly.

"What is it?"

"I'm not fucking around when I say you shouldn't be here, and I'd be a smarter, less-selfish man if I made you leave."

"Something happened that night after the Amphitheater, didn't it? It all changed when you came back from HQ." I listened to his pulse thud against my ear. "That's when you decided to tell me about my dad, isn't it?"

Sweat pricked on his brow.

"You came at me with a vengeance."

"I'm sorry for that. I was too rough. I know—"

My fingertips on his mouth silenced him. "It's not that. Don't you ever apologize for needing me. There's something else, isn't there?"

"Yeah."

"What did Cutler say that night?"

He stared at me, speaking in a low voice. "He said I better get rid of you or he'd blow up Beta with you in it, that the little show at the Amphitheater was just a test run. It was a warning shot from him to me, about you."

"Fucking hell, Linc. He could've killed you!"

He shrugged, faint sadness in the downturn of his lips. "He figured I'd survive like I always have. He's convinced I'll keep up the Cutler name, that I have to since Nathaniel already forsook it." Passionate with conviction, Linc kissed me. "That's never gonna happen, not while he still lives to threaten you and my Territory."

Safe in his embrace, I settled into his side. The rain had stopped slashing outside, no more machine-gun rattle to raid my sleep.

Linc's deep voice rumbled through his chest with a question I should've expected. "What do you know about the *Posse Omnis Juvenis*, Liz?"

The question reminded me this wasn't just idle lovers' chitchat. Even though we'd made love and could make plans to get out of this shitty Revolution alive, together, maybe…the poignant thing was we still straddled two sides of the cause.

I could cut and run, or go with my gut. "I've gathered some intel on them."

"You didn't give it to me."

"Issues of loyalty stood in the way. That won't happen again." His silence unraveled the slim thread of peace we'd brokered tonight. "I happened on them when you sent me for a clean sweep of S-4. They've got a factory and bunkers. They're manufacturing technological warfare, as far as I can tell. Sebastian's dick is practically being sucked by the egghead in charge of the group."

"And they're bought and paid for by my father," Linc finished. "I knew about Bas. I've had Johnson on him."

I almost snorted. That boy had more tails than a mutated Gen-1 Clone Project. "Since you know I was hiding under your desk when the Quad alarm came in when they busted into the compound, how's about telling me what they were after?"

"Just to cause trouble, it seemed."

That was before I broke into my dad's lab, where someone had already busted shit up and then disappeared a whole lot of info in the form of the schematics. It was before the attack on the Amphitheater by the UCAS drones, drones hatching unmanned exterminating machines much smaller than any we'd seen before. And the attack was commanded by Cutler, who controlled the Posse.

"You left my father's classified labs up so I could find them."

"I'm not proud of that, Liz—"

I sat up abruptly. *DCIC* those papers had been stamped. *D* for *Drone*... *C* for *Clone*. I didn't know what the rest stood for, but a cold chill raked down my back. "They played the distraction game."

"What?"

"I think it's possible they got into my dad's lab that night because the place had been turned over before I got there." The information gnawed a hole in my head, but I couldn't piece it all together. "Why wouldn't Cutler gather the files he wanted himself? He has access."

Linc blew out an expletive. "Because he doesn't want to get his hands dirty. What else did you find there?"

"Schematics, plans that—" My pulse skyrocketed. "Holy shit. Plans for small-scale drones that made the mini-gliders that came after us at the Amphitheater look like first-generation child's play. Someone's putting a whole lotta shit together, Linc. I tried to get pics of the plans, but they'd been removed before I could."

The laboratory had been torn apart, all but my dad's private records. The truth crawled over me with sickening realization. The Revolution had escalated beyond our imagining.

"What happened to the samples?" I asked.

"The Pneumonic Plague samples? The last few were cooling on ice when I was in there, kept for curative research purposes only." Linc locked steady eyes on mine. "When your father died, most of the intel was supposed to go with him, Liz."

"But we both know it didn't."

"The Plague project was killed. Dr. Val made sure of it."

Coldness flooded through me, and I started to shake. Linc rubbed his hands down my back, taking the chill away with his touch and the fear away with his words. Low and powerful, his voice dipped against my ear. "We're gonna figure it all out, sweetheart. I promise."

I burrowed deeper against him for a long moment, trying to relax into his warmth. Then I sat up, trying to shove him over onto his stomach.

He raised an eyebrow at me. "Got a problem looking at my face?"

"Maybe I just like your backside better." I pinched his ass so he yelped. "Roll over. I want to look at your tat."

He lay on his front, the hills of his biceps forming a pillow beneath his head. He sighed when I slid my fingers along his back.

I gave him another pinch and he jumped, covering his rear with a hand. He growled, "I may not be on board with strafing, but I reckon I could come up with some way of punishing you, vixen."

"Baby, I tired you out so much you look about ready to melt into the bed. Don't make idle threats."

"C'mere." His eyes glittered.

I leaned over, loving the taste of him on my lips, the slow generosity of his lazy kiss.

Sitting back, I outlined the eagle on his back from one stylized wing to the other, caressing his shoulders while he shut his eyes and moaned. "Tell me about this. Tell me about *Libertas*."

"Freedom. It's my way of throwing my hat in the ring with the Freelanders. Even though no one's ever known it."

Tears gathered in my eyes. "It's beautiful, my love."

The smile on his lips was wide. "Say that again."

"My love." His eyes crinkled and a deep breath lifted his shoulders, spreading the eagle's wings. "So you don't think of them as savage Nomads in need of euthanasia?"

"My mom's one of them. How could I?" He pressed up onto an elbow. "I had to keep up the charade, swear her off, then Nathaniel, too, because the little prick couldn't keep his dick in his pants—"

"That's exactly what I said to Cannon. Not that you're one to talk, *sir*."

"I didn't hear you complaining between screams." He laughed when I punched his arm. "I found a way in with the people at Catskills about four years back. They gave me news of her and I tried to keep them out of the line of fire." He frowned. "I haven't been very successful at that lately regarding anyone."

"You've been pulled in too many directions, Linc. No one can blame you for what's happened."

"I blame myself."

"Hey." He peered at me warily. "I don't blame you," I said.

"When my dad moved his operations to Beta, my liberties were cut short. That's why I kept hounding you about Nathaniel. I haven't had any word on him."

"I am so sorry, baby." I caressed his back and massaged his shoulders. I stopped when my fingers came to the deep, ugly scar I'd noticed before. "What happened here?"

"Father saw the eagle and threatened to cut it out of my skin. He demonstrated with a knife." Linc spoke so nonchalantly, as if that sort of abuse was just part of daily life.

"That bastard. I'd like to garrote his cock with a slip wire." I hissed.

Rolling over, he brought me down on top of him. "I don't want you getting anywhere near him, Liz. You're to stay away from him at all times."

"Linc—"

"No excuses, no buts." He gripped my shoulders until I looked at him.

"Is that a command, sir?"

"As if you'd listen if I said it was."

His grumble made me smile, but I nodded my assent. "Since we're talking about the Freelanders, I should tell you something else."

"Not sure I can take much more, Lieutenant."

"Sure you can. You're a big, strong man."

He groaned in response.

"You remember those two guys at the Amphitheater? The pair who helped us shoot the UCASs from the sky?"

"You better not tell me you were doing them, too."

"Hell no. Darke's hung like a bull. I'd have to limber up before that." Linc cooled beside me, his frosty stare imbued with unwarranted jealousy. *Men and their cocks.* "Oh, please. Don't throw a big dick contest about that comment. You've got more than enough to spare."

"*Hmm.* What about them?"

"They followed me up from Chitamauga. I'm working with Darke and Leon, and all of us with Farrow, for the Revolution."

I thought he'd fallen asleep while silently digesting my final bit of important disclosure, but he opened one eyelid and asked, "If Darke's the big dude, Leon's the punk with all the hair and the pouty mouth?"

I snickered. Linc had nailed Leon's blow job lips to a T. No wonder Darke couldn't let him go. "They're camping out at Catskills."

"They're good people."

"The Chitamauga militia is on the way."

Linc wound his arms around me. "Good. We could use 'em."

My eyebrows rose. "You're taking this remarkably well."

"Only because you let me take you all night, sweetheart." Blue eyes dancing, he winked. "Besides, when this is over, I'm handcuffing you to my bed until you swear allegiance only to me."

My heart pounded with the implications of *after*, but I threatened, "We'll see who gets tied up first, baby."

He chuckled, enfolding me in his arms. A keen sense of happiness and peace settled over me as we drifted to sleep, replacing the anguish that had fractured me apart for too many years to count.

Gray predawn light woke me. Already alert, Linc was watching me, a lively glint in his eyes. "Your team needs you. You're a born leader. We have a lot of work ahead of us if we're gonna take Beta back from my father."

I stretched against him, enjoying the luxury of his naked body before pecking him on the chin. "I know. I'm coming in with you, baby."

"I need you." He proved it with a possessive, demanding kiss. Easing up, Linc brushed his lips over my closed eyelids to the edge of my ear. "I love you."

Those words were so hard fought for, caught up in so much pain and death, punishment and deceit. Love and hope would win out; they had to.

I reveled in his kisses and gruff whispers, clasping him to me. "You shouldn't say things like that, sir. I'm liable to get lightheaded," I teased, but my voice was breathy.

He smiled, rugged features relaxing into youthful handsomeness. "Then what? You'll have to let me hold you? Take care of you? Look out for you?"

"All those things, I hope. I love you, Lincoln."

His eyes flared with deep emotion. "You honor me." The fingers that caressed my face in wonder were gentle, making me feel cherished, precious.

We borrowed a few more moments, murmuring to each other, but the war waited for both of us and we wouldn't shirk our duties.

Linc had gathered our weapons and clothing, folding two neat bundles at the end of the bed. "We're gonna need the support of our troopers if we intend to save Beta from the inside. We'll have to tread carefully."

I tucked my shirt into my trousers and bent to lace up my boots. "Turn them against your father…Is that what you want?"

"It's what I've wanted for a long time, what must be done. I just didn't know how to do it alone."

"You're not alone anymore."

"I know." He cupped my face, his gaze never wavering from mine. "I want you to know, you're more than my lover, Liz. I plan on making this a permanent thing. I will make it right between us."

"It already is." I guided him softly to my lips.

"Not enough. Not yet."

I could wait. We had so much to accomplish. All of it hinged on us walking back into Command, where we'd have to weed through our crew to find those who sympathized with the Revolutionary cause.

Determined and sure, Linc led me outside to the streets. The rain had cleared, the combat on the next block cleaned up. The only trace of battle lingered in diluted puddles of blood. Soldiers roused from their watchpoints with precise salutes to the commander and the lieutenant, which we returned smartly. The sun broke through from a breathtaking dawn, paving the streets and high-rises in a rosy glow that reminded me of the Beta Territory I grew up in, before the Plague, when my family was whole.

It reminded me what Beta could become again, under the right leadership, under Linc. His hand brushed mine once, intentionally, as we came to the Quad's tall wall.

The gates opened, granting us entrance, and we walked through, together, united in our mission.

Chapter Twelve

April 26, 2071

It's been only a week since Linc and I put it all out there. May and mayhem are coming fast, but we're hanging tight. The Plague, my dad's murder, the Company…it all crashed down, but Linc was there.

His hard-core head is on straight, but the glimpses he's given me into his boyhood break my heart. I asked him about the photo on his dresser, the only personal effect he's allowed himself. In the picture is a sunburned, full-bearded man, big as an Old History house, and a young blond woman standing on a rambling porch. The photo is Eden and her father—Hamme Rice—at their family home the summer before Cutler came into their lives and tore it all apart block by block until all that remains now is a dictatorial father, two estranged brothers, and the matriarch trying to bring her boys back together.

Via yours friggin' truly.

The photograph itself is a rarity, something Linc hid away when Cutler pitched out mementos by the hundreds after Eden left. The fact Linc kept it and gives it pride of place…that just nails it for me.

This is a man worth fighting for, fighting alongside.

I asked him about the Beta team he sent after Cannon and Nate, the crew that slaughtered Darke's militia during an ambush. "Bunch of fuckups went rogue. I've only ever wanted to keep Nathaniel safe. I'm the older brother. That's my job."

When I laughed and asked him older by how much, he unleashed his grin and confessed, "A full five minutes."

Fuck. Even though he wisecracks through these moments, the strain is there. The worry over Nate…and now me. I haven't made his load any lighter. But we're sharing the burden.

I regarded the pages spread out before me in the lounge of Linc's quarters before grabbing a steel bowl and layering them inside. I sparked a match and watched the small flame waver in a sudden draft. A hand reached out, grabbing my wrist, stopping me from igniting the paper. I hadn't heard Linc come out of the shower. Now I was wishing I could get Hatch to invent combustible paper to do the same self-destruct dance he'd pulled on the burn D-P.

Towel hanging low on his hips, Linc hunkered down beside me. He blew out the blaze. Flinty smoke whispered between our faces. "I can't stand the thought of your words turning to ash."

He turned his hand from my wrist, capturing my palm and pressing a kiss into the middle.

I tried to pull back, but he strengthened his grip. "I don't like you knowing about my weakness."

"Maybe you should've kept to your bra-burning story that night, then."

"You wouldn't let me off the hook."

"I'm not asking to read them; nor would I ever trespass. And it's not a weakness, Liz." His lips dipped to my fingertips.

"I just don't want my tits and things getting in the way of my job."

He reared back and laughed. "Tits and things? I'm assuming *things* are emotions?"

I rolled my eyes. He removed the pages and folded them neatly, placing them in my lap.

"Have I told you how gorgeous you are?" My heart started tripping. "How hot you make me?" He pushed his hand into my short hair. "How you're one of the best soldiers I've ever met, regardless of your tits and things?"

Swallowing a sigh of pleasure, I purred. "You may have mentioned a couple of those details on a few occasions."

"A few?" He stood, yanking his towel free with one hand and tossing me up over his shoulder with the other. "It appears a demonstration is in order."

I squealed—I goddamned *squealed*—squirmed, and thumped him on the back as he bore me down the hall. He slid me down his fully aroused body, his hands going to my face and mine to his very fine ass.

"We have a meeting in thirty." I gasped.

"We'll just have to make it a quickie, sweetheart."

* * *

There was no such thing as cut and run or a clean getaway, not in the bedroom and not in the war room. This time the war room had relocated outside of Quad walls to an armory in the middle of S-2. It had been swept for bugs, the cameras given the lens-scrub treatment.

Linc stood in front of his amassed soldiers, fully in charge. Feet planted wide apart, gold hair brushed his brow and the tips of his ears. He was dressed in his dark blues, filling them out to perfection. Bearing military precise, he scanned the fifty leaders riveted by him. These were the troops he'd culled from the thousands he commanded in Beta. Men and women who had the highest marks as operatives and analysts. Linc had kept a keen eye on each of them through years of training as they made their way through the ranks. They were the least likely to be informants because of one special element they shared in common.

"Soldiers, I've brought you here because from the time I enlisted you to my squads, you've had a difficult time curbing your rebellious natures."

A handful of faces turned bright red, Ginger included. That was a given, one I enjoyed as a small highlight to this masterful show. I almost laughed. Apparently, Linc wanted them to drop a load in their drawers before he brought them on board.

"Dissenters, at one time or another, all of you. I don't have enough fingers or toes to count how many times I figured each of you for future deserters of Beta Corps team." He started working his way through the troopers, their rigid-plank posture becoming shifty with each turn he made among them. He let his words hang for several beats, peering into every face branded with a *holy-fuck-he's-gonna-kill-me* expression. "You've never been totally driven to uphold the Company program. That's why I know I can count on you now.

"In the event I'm wrong, I've ordered Lieutenant Grant to take you out if you breathe a goddamn word of what I'm about to tell you." I sent a salute and a toothy grin, pulling out both Eagles and crossing the chrome barrels over my chest. "Hell, I think I'll alter that order." Linc rounded on a tall dude with a scar snaking down the side of his face and into the collar of his shirt. The only person present who wasn't sweating bullets or doing the *gonna-piss-my-pants* dance. "If you so much as *dream* about this new mission, I'll cut your fucking tongue out and feed it down your throat while I pack your own fist into your asshole. We clear?"

"Affirmative, Commander!" Scar-face saluted. There wasn't even a damp spot at his armpits—color me impressed.

"Music to my fucking ears." That music resounded when the others called in with their salutes and their heels tapping the floor. "I have one final question before we go any further. Do you love your Territory?"

"Sir, yes, sir!"

Linc marched to the front of the armory, taking his place beside me. "Excellent. This is what's happening with the Revolution. The D-P feeds you're seeing? False. The Nomads needing a beat down? False. The Revolutionaries we've been ripping through? That's gonna stop right now."

No one dared let a whisper escape as they maintained their stance in the full beam of Linc's hardened glare. "There's a guerilla group working the streets. We're gonna put the heat on them. My lieutenant is heading it up. What I need from you is your very best soldiers brought on line, in line. I need numbers, people. I need devotion the likes of which you've never committed to before, because we are not messing around. No more *Regeneration, Veneration, Salvation*...We're stamping a brand-new slogo on our chests and it goes like this: *Live in Freedom, Love at Will.*"

A shocked silence reverberated through the building and lingered so long I popped my safeties off, Ginger doing the same. If this was a mistake, we were gonna kill it right here and now.

"Do I have a problem?" Linc's voice boomed. "Since you've all black-marked your records for opposition in the line of duty, I'm waiting to hear your pledges, soldiers."

There wasn't a foot shuffle in the place. Not a single dropped head. Scar-face stepped forward first, hand to his chest. Five more came next to him. The others pressed into line, all orderly, gear-tight.

"I want leadership I can rely on, and I need it fast." Linc moved on to the next stage, pointing out Scar-face while I let out a long exhale. "Vance, you head up ballistics—weapons from tanks to munitions. Stockpile that shit. Moxie!" A woman with a skinhead and large blue eyes jerked her chin at Linc. Earrings lined both her earlobes and up around the cartilage, dainty chains linking those piercings to the two in her delicate nostrils. "You're in charge of re-cruits. Bring me manpower. If any fucker starts falling apart, put a bullet in their head. And take that shit off your face before I rip it out. We don't want them to have any kind of advantage."

"Got it, Commander."

The rest were divvied up with duties—bullets, brains, and brawn. They single-filed out the side door an hour later, leaving the hollowed shell to me, Linc…and unshakeable Ginger. I was beginning to think the boy had a boner for his commander.

Leaving out the back and locking it down, Linc and I matched our steps down the road. Our fingers brushed, curled together, and came apart.

"Sabine wasn't there."

"That's right." His head angled toward mine. "She lost that privilege when she stuck a shank in your leg."

Good enough.

At the sound of jogging footsteps coming from behind, we swiveled as one, dropping down, raising firearms.

Ginger all but rolled into a ball. Hearing the snick of our com-bined guns being taken off the mark, he shuddered to his full height. "Fuck, you two!"

Linc cocked his head.

"Sir and Lieutenant, I mean."

He toed up beside us as we took the roads toward the Quad. Talk about a romantic stroll in a war-torn city or a threesome I wasn't ready to give airtime to.

Ginger took off his cap, red hair all aflame around his face. "I was on the Posse."

"Yep." Linc stepped into an alley.

"Well, what's my appointment, sir?"

"You're almost at the head of the helm, son." We pressed on down the dew-damp narrowness, Ginger's footsteps faltering.

"I think that's a bit unwarranted," I remarked, glad Ginger lingered behind so he couldn't see my grin.

"Wait. What?" He caught up again.

Linc clasped his shoulder. "You done good. Apart from beating Grant's face to shit and cheering on her strafing her first night in Beta. Your momma never taught you manners?"

His freckles melded together beneath the sunrise of a blush. "I didn't know. She was on the watch list…She kept mouthing off…"

I snickered.

Linc held on to Ginger's shoulder a little tighter. "Yeah. We're gonna have to work on your parlay technique. You're with me from this point forward. You sell me out, I'll poach your nuts."

I could literally see his nuts shrinking. Ginger shoved both hands in front of his groin. "You sure Lieutenant Grant doesn't need my backup?"

I was touched, truly, but I didn't need Ginger riding my fumes when I pulled the plug on the Posse…Plus, red had never been my color.

"Are you questioning Grant's skills?"

"No, I…No, sir…Shit. I just think I might be useful to her."

"She's got it under control, and never speak about Grant as if she isn't standing right beside us."

I saluted the two of them while Ginger continued to gawp.

"Run along, Red. You have a full fucking night of reports to get together. Good luck with that. I like my dossier by oh five hundred. You're my brand-new liaise with all those soldiers who nearly soiled their cammies tonight."

Ever the eager trooper, Ginger ran off to Corps Command; no la-la land for him tonight. Linc's unreserved conviction in my abilities—plus his effortless command of his people—sweltered through me.

"You were ruthless back there."

He slanted me a look. "You liked it."

I'd almost melted into the floor during his speech, and I was ready to take him on in a deserted alley. Hell yes, I liked it.

* * *

The only secure place for Linc and me was his chambers in Command. Even before our night of reckoning, he'd taken every precaution to fail-safe the apartment using false vid-feeds and making sure only his key cards—one for each of us, new every twenty-four hours—popped the door lock. Linc's presence beside me on the sofa went even further toward increasing my sense of refuge.

The night was late. We'd been awake since dawn, and work wasn't over. I busied myself with the thorough cleaning of our cache of weapons. He scanned updates on two D-Ps, the one linked into the Corps and CO and a second handed over from Farrow, through which his new leaders contacted him with field reports. Oiled rag in hand, I rubbed the barrel of Linc's Heck, running through a variety of unchaste thoughts regarding oil,

Linc, the rock-hard column of his cock. Beside me, his arm brushed mine as he shifted in his seat. I hid my smile by concentrating on the firearm, glad I didn't have to walk around with a tattletale cock showing the entire world when I was in an extreme state of horniness.

The clever bastard was either at the top of his game at mind reading as well as tactical maneuvering, or he just figured handling guns made me think about handling *his gun,* because he casually lifted his far arm, slowly undoing the buttons down the front of my shirt. He was still checking his dual D-Ps, one dimple sliding into his cheek. Heat slammed through me, but I managed to keep my hands on a steady rub-rub-rub motion he glanced at several times.

"Need I remind you I have a fully loaded weapon in my hand, Commander?"

Setting the D-Ps on the table, he eased back into a relaxed pose, thighs open, arms on the back of the sofa. "And I already told you, I've got one of my own, ready to be fired, sweetheart."

"Perhaps I should test the wares?" At the first barely there pass of my fingertips up Linc's hard length, he pulled in a tight hiss and rolled his hips up.

His voice came out rough and low. "I think that's an excellent idea."

I squeezed the solid shaft in my hand, slowly releasing the snap and scraping the zipper down. Fingers circling him, I stroked, steady and sure. "My favorite toy to play with, hot as metal, all man." I leaned over, licking the droplet leaking from the tip, spreading his moisture over my lips. "All you."

He wrangled my pants off my legs and finished the job on my shirt before lifting me over his hips. "Toy?"

My mouth homing in on the late-night golden stubble shading his jaw, I said, "Popgun."

"You'll pay for that, wench." He grabbed my hip and his cock, guiding me down until wet flesh met thick, rigid arousal.

"I hope so."

My breath caught as he lowered me onto him. Working in at just the right angle, Linc spun me close to immediate climax.

His groan coasted along every nerve of my body, centering me with him in this moment. "Good?"

I kissed him, tightening around him. "Living the dream…"

* * *

Another few days, and this was not living the dream. Waking up beside Linc, prepping for each day and coming down every night from all the double-agent agenda with him…yeah. Trading notes, making plans, making love, that was just the beginning of the dream. I hoped we'd have time to build a future together, but it seemed to get farther and farther from our reach.

I was fully entrenched in *Posse Omnis Juvenis* muck. My cover had to be authentic down to a T. That meant taking extra care with my appearance because the geek faction got hard over who had the best hair gel, tats, piercings. Dressed in stomp-some-ass boots, my own well-worn leathers, hair twisted into razor-sharp spikes, I accessorized with my girls: Desert and Eagle.

My first morning out tagging along with Leon and Sebastian,

Linc had done a double take. Then he'd stepped up to me, shutting the door I'd been about to exit.

"Darke and Leon will be out there, right?"

"Yes."

His "oh-shit" quota hadn't hit the roof when I'd told him about my friends the Freelanders nor my relationship with Farrow, but I had a feeling he was gnawing through several unsavory possibilities while he blocked the door like an unmovable monolith.

He finally exhaled. "I'm glad I've seen them in action. I have every confidence in them."

Okay.

He grabbed me to him, laying on me a possessive kiss, a mark on my soul, a stamp to my heart. I had to lean against him when he finished.

"I'd rather be out there with you." He'd released me but remained stationed in front of the door. "So we're clear, I don't like you in danger. I don't like putting you in danger. I love you, Liz."

"I'll be fine. Just playing in the toy shop with the young'uns."

He'd pulled my head up, eyes and mouth stern. "Don't you dare play this down."

I'd put some strength into my voice and backbone into my stance. "I won't. You can be sure of that, Linc."

"Good. If Taft makes you, you kill him. No second thoughts."

"No second thoughts. Got it."

His words still sent a shiver through me. Linc's powerful affirmations of love tingled inside me. I wanted more of that, more of him. I wanted this Revolution over with so I could enjoy some of the goddamned peace always just beyond my reach.

Peace wasn't on my docket for today. Instead I was prepared for day three of trying to get in good with the Posse while Leon and I stood guard for them, outside of the S-5 factory. The plan that made the most sense was to take the Posse down first, amputate Cutler's underground, homegrown artillery. And that shit was not happening. Taft's crew was tight-lipped. I needed to get closer. Nothing short of the firsthand intel about what they were building would do.

Darke was on a different watch guard drill that meant he stayed on point from several rooftops away, scoping the place, us...Leon from the sights of his rifle. I could practically feel his impatience rolling like heat waves from that distance. He was probably getting baked up there on his black-topped roof under the searing spring sun, but I bet he reveled in his skin getting as blistered as his heart, watching Leon play up to Sebastian, Sebastian play up to Taft. I had a ringside seat to it all, one I didn't want.

I peeked at Leon. The grin on his lips didn't make it to his eyes. It was clear in the glare he sent to the rooftop Darke recon'd from that he was still on the outs with Darke.

"So, it's all working out for you two, then?" I went to pull down my cap, hands quickly punching to my hips when I remembered I wasn't in uniform.

"Yeah, dat be about right."

I started to grab his hand, thought better of it since no doubt Darke could easily pop a bullet between my eyeballs if I so much as touched his *angel*. Then I was thankful I'd curbed my big sister moment because the doors of the warehouse grinded open. Sebastian's platinum-blond head slipped out, and he beckoned me inside.

I blew Leon a kiss and mouthed, "Time to play."

In return, he made a slow jerking motion with his hand in front of his groin.

Little prick.

Sebastian led me to Taft. Up close, his buzz-cut electric-blue hair resonated with the crackling blue of his stare. He may have been a good seven years my junior, but the boy had presence and, judging by the lockstep operations inside the factory, he had a mind to match it.

"Who's this, Sarge?" he asked Sebastian.

I lounged on one leg as if I couldn't give half a shit about being invited inside the inner den.

"Lizzie," Bas improvised.

Taft strolled around me, the metal piercing threaded through his tongue clacking against his teeth. "Why do we need her?"

"Since Red did a runner, we're down one. We need some new meat, and she's tough on the outside, tender on the inside."

Red aka Ginger was back at Command, hopefully not rubbing his crotch and going all *Yes, sir* on Linc.

I endured another half-minute head-to-toe inspection before Taft gave his nod of approval. I was sent straight to the chain gang to take my place with the other grunts, putting minute pieces of machinery together.

Everything anyone explained to me sounded like sheer gibberish, but there were bits and shit that bolted into other gears, so it was pretty much like putting a gun together. It was piecework, every finished component swiftly removed from the conveyor belt, boxed up, and stacked. The gadgetry looked like the DCIC schematics and the miniature clone garbage that had attacked us at the Amphitheater…That was all I needed. No doubt about it; this constituted a legit threat I had to neutralize.

Keeping my head down the rest of the day, I took surreptitious sweeps of the factory. The stacks of boxes grew into high walls, so the separate widgets were being assembled off premises. And we couldn't let them get off premises.

I made a lot of sly scans of Sebastian with Taft, too, and what I saw didn't settle my nerves one bit. They conversed throughout the day, sometimes seriously, sometimes jokingly, Bas never letting on that his loyalties were wavering. Taft constantly flirted with the younger man. He shrugged off Bas's rebuffs as if it were no biggie, but when Bas turned back to work, the glances Taft stole time and again were the looks of a man in love with someone unattainable. I'd been around Darke and Leon enough to know the anguish on Taft's rugged features was all about unrequited love.

No matter which way you looked at it, there was a bond between the two that went beyond the brutality of war. And this was gonna end badly, even if Sebastian didn't realize it yet.

My fears over that specific scenario were proven correct when Leon, Darke, and I met up with Sebastian that evening in the decommissioned armory Linc used as a secondary war room. Already pacing a wide circle when I slid in the back door, Sebastian took no note of my entry. I nodded across the room at Darke and

Leon propped against opposite walls, just like at our oh-so-fun tête-à-tête at the Amphitheater, while Sebastian muttered up a storm to himself.

I sidled closer, wondering if I'd have to slap him to pull him out of his downward spiral. "He been like this long?"

Darke spoke. "'Bout five minutes. He was already cruising his little lap circuit when we got here."

Shock over the day—hell, maybe over the whole year—was setting in, and it probably had a hell of a lot to do with the daily deception of his friend. *Fuck.*

"Nano Biomimicry, that's all he'd told me, the Nanos, because he knows I like to design the really tiny robotics."

"Come again?" I asked.

Sebastian ignored me. "He never mentioned armin' them." As if he'd hit a brick wall in his thoughts, Sebastian did a one eighty and started off in the reverse direction. "I can't believe Taft sold out! Used be all about makin' things smarter, better, for the people. For All Youth. That was why I signed on." Blond hair swinging over his shoulders, his round-and-round march reflected in the blacked-out panes of the building. "He's gay, for God's sake! How could he get in bed with that homo-hater? I know why. The coin, of course, and I bet that bastard Cutler promised him a place in the New World Order."

Okay, I needed to shut this kid down now. Getting right in Sebastian's path, I stood my ground and he halted before me. It seemed that minor interruption to his circular route was enough to pull him back to reality. One that made him squat before me, head in his hands.

"So, I take it you didn't know what you were designing, or at least why you were making it?"

His eyes shot up, filled with guilt and sadness. "'Course not! I just knew I was gettin' paid to hang with a bunch of my buddies, makin' the type of nanobots I'd be messin' around with on my own anyway."

"Nano-whats?" I asked.

He rose to his feet, mouth opening for what would probably be a long-winded explanation I didn't have time for.

"You know what? Never mind. Just speak fucking English to me."

"We have to blow it all up," he said.

I was way cool with that plan since it aligned so beautifully with my own. For the first time since I'd been in Beta, this was something I could get totally on board with, with a lot of flash-bang.

Seemed Darke and Leon had similar thoughts of *hell yes, we can* because their wide grins were mirror images, until they glanced at each other, dropped their eyes, and did the maudlin shuffle.

One genius plan in place, my pack filled with an assortment of fireworks of the right kind, we reconvened at 0300 hours, which was the perfect time to torch something in my estimation. I'd alerted Linc to all that had transpired, and though it was evident he wanted to come along, he restrained the protective urge. The four of us—Darke, Leon, Sebastian, and I—eyeballed the blocks leading up to the barracks and factory in silence. A silence that came back to us tenfold. The closer we got, the more deafening the quiet became. There was no movement inside the barracks. There were no lights on in warehouse, and not a single vehicle on the street. Even the Dumpster with the Posse tag had been removed sometime between nightfall and now.

We broke into the factory through all four ground-level entrances. The area lit by tiny halos on top of our weapons, I rotated in place. The room was cleaned out. There probably wasn't even a dust bunny rolling around on the floor. No machines, no boxes, not even a *kiss-you good-bye* love note taped to the wall.

"God fucking damn it!" I hissed.

The others added their own creative curses to the mix. Motioning for them to stay put, I retreated the way I'd come and infiltrated the barracks. Same deal. The place was absolutely wiped clean. Taft was onto us.

Back in the empty factory that had been buzzing with activity during the daylight hours, Darke, Leon, and Sebastian each staked out an entrance and performed sweeps at intervals. It was just a shame there was nothing in there to guard, destroy, or deliver back to basecamp for further examination.

"The barracks came up nada, too." I walked over to Sebastian.

Darke's deep voice rumbled. "The little shit relocated in a hurry, probably with the CEO's assistance."

Sebastian wore a glare ill suited to his pretty-boy face. "Taft played me."

"We can still make sure there's not so much as a piece of rubble to come back to," I said.

I opened my pack, preparing to wire the place to blow. I stopped all unnecessary movement when a high-pitch beep sounded. Followed by another louder alarm. Then a few more in closer succession until the noise was a steady *beep-beep-beep* countdown.

This was not a hit-the-deck moment. This was get-the-fuck-out-now-before-we-die. "RETREAT!"

"*Merd*—" Leon didn't finish his sentence. He was too busy gunning for the front door with the rest of us.

Shooting into the night, the four of us ran at a hard, fast pace into the alley across the way, hoping to some distance because who knew? Maybe the whole block was triggered to go up. And wasn't Taft really, truly, a bloody goddamn genius?

My heart knocked hard, but my legs pumped faster. Breath scraped out of me. I heard the boom seconds before I felt a blazing heat that seemed to peel the clothes off my back before it seared into my skin. When I looked back, I saw the factory and barracks detonate like dry tinder covered in kerosene. The entire sky burst into orange flame, a blaze that curled its incinerating fingers in our direction.

My thighs churned, and I checked beside me to make sure all three were there. Cement, glass, brick, and pavement flew like massive boulders in every direction, and every direction pointed at us.

A huge body folded over me, over Bas and Leon. The wind knocked out of me when we hit the ground as one unit. Rubble and the offshoots of fire barreling toward us, all I could do was shut my eyes, scream inside my head for Linc, thankful he wasn't here.

Chapter Thirteen

I swallowed through the burn of my throat and limped home to Linc. Sebastian stepped up, providing a shoulder to lean on while I hobbled along. His brain must've gotten knocked around, not just because of the blast. His best buddy had basically taken out a death warrant on him, yet he put one foot in front of the other as I leaned heavily on him.

We hadn't died. It was a frigging miracle. A miracle named Darke. He'd saved our lives, getting hit by the worst of the detonation. We'd all shouldered together to get him to the stripped-down Cruiser he and Leon used for their back-and-forth from Catskills. His clothing had been flayed off, to say nothing of his flesh. Not a single groan of discomfort had passed his paled lips as we'd traversed the alleys. We'd loaded him gently onto his stomach in the backseat of the vehicle.

I'd stayed long enough to watch Leon punch his fists into the door, then drop to a squat in front of Darke's. He grabbed those big hands in his, wrapping their fingers together. The tracks of several tears made clear streams through the soot on his cheeks. "No more, Darke. *Pas plus va-t-et-vient.* You coulda been killed."

Their reassuring murmurs were exactly what I'd needed in that moment, from Linc.

Beat-up as I was, it wasn't lost on me what I'd thought about when I volunteered for this solo mission, so cocky up in Cannon's face, that I didn't have a warm body to go home to, just more nightmares. In Linc, I had everything I'd wanted, and the close scrape of the explosion worked another round of discharges inside my heart. Linc and I might never get the chance to live a simple life. There was no time to spare.

In the long corridor at the top of Corps Command, Linc opened the door. He took one look at Sebastian and sent him inside. He grabbed my waist, holding me vertical when the world spun out beneath me.

"You do not do this shit again." His voice grated so deep it was nearly a growl.

"Sounds like an ace plan."

A shudder ran through him. He hauled me up into his arms, and I must've blinked out for a few minutes because I jerked to in the shower, hands flailing.

"*Shh. Shh.* You passed out there for a few minutes." He'd climbed into the cold spray with me, both of us fully clothed.

He turned the water temperature up, the wet warmth overriding the shivers of shock cascading through me.

"You scared me there, Liz." The words were barely audible, his blue eyes incredibly bleak.

I wrapped my hands around his neck, crying quietly while he rocked me in his arms.

"You're too strong. You don't have to be this strong." His voice shook. His hands did, too, as he undressed me, breath tearing in and out of his chest in great gusts. Those tender hands took measure of my wounds, and his arms were ever enfolding me.

After he'd done a once-over for injuries, he drew me against his front. Linc discarded his clothes with one hand, keeping me upright against him, his solid flesh shoring me up.

Linc settled me as nothing else could.

"Fuck, Liz." Straining wet forearms ran above and below my breasts.

"It's okay." I rested against him, letting him keep me steady. Support that anchored me to the earth when everything else washed away like the ash at my feet.

"Not okay, not at all." His voice was gruff, but the hands cleansing me remained soft.

"I've survived worse."

Those hands stopped, fingers curling into his palms, palms he braced before me on the glass. "Yeah, so have I. That's not the fucking point." He pounded a fist with each word spoken. "You think I can live with you stretching your neck out and not being there to back you up?"

I was too tired to put up a brave front. Sliding around to face him, I laid my head against his shoulder. "Tell me there's more. Tell me this will end, or I don't think I can finish it."

He turned off the water, swaddled me in a towel. Fingers running along my back, Linc held me firm. "We will finish this, Liz. We will. Don't go AWOL on me again."

Sobs overtook me, but Linc held me through each jerky motion. He whispered those sweet murmurs I'd heard between other couples, never believing this sort of belonging would ever be part of my life.

"You're too formidable for your own good." He carried me to the bed. Unrolling the towel from around me, he pulled the blankets up.

"Ditto that," I mumbled, sleep just beyond my heavy eyelids, but I needed him beside me first, to ward off the war, the nightmares.

"Be right back, sweetheart. Just gonna check on Bas."

Minutes later, broad muscles rippled against me. Linc shifted me into the lee of his shoulder.

"How's Sebastian?" I slurred into the shadowed stubble on his throat.

"Sleeping it off; no worse for wear. I commed Farrow. All good now, all good."

His hands swished slowly up and down my back, halting for a moment when I said, "I love you, Linc. You're a good man."

The slow motion of his caresses and quiet declarations eased me into sleep. Whispers of love and hope. A place where war didn't exist. A time when worry wouldn't eclipse life and the daily grind would be something we could laugh about.

A world in which we didn't live in fear.

And we could love.

And our love would grow, unburdened.

* * *

Getting your ass fried, having a front-row seat to buildings going up in flame, dodging bullets were all part and parcel of being a soldier in the middle of a war. We had damage control to take care of, new plans to make, and priorities we still hadn't tackled. I hadn't been carted away from Command by Cutler's goons for potentially traitorous activities. Either he didn't know about my penetration into the Posse or he had bigger dicks to suck.

Still on the scent of the juvie geniuses, we had all feelers out. Going from what I'd learned and seen, Hatch was trying to figure out exactly what uses Cutler had planned for the miniature drones. Meanwhile, Sebastian worked his cute little butt off trying to reconnect with his pal, which placed him in a potentially dicey situation.

Linc's frustration showed in the firm set of his mouth and his wildly disheveled hair as he watched me fill up on breakfast before doing the rounds with our new *For the Better of Beta Troopers.*

I shoved the plate away and wiped my mouth. "What?"

Linc's mood hadn't lightened since I'd returned with my ass dragging two nights before. He'd made love to me with force and total possession bordering on aggression last night. I'd welcomed his demanding body, Linc's need for me strengthening my resolve we'd beat this war. Afterward he'd held me in his arms until a couple hours ago, returning to the cherished tenderness I imagined no one had seen in him before.

His thick biceps straining the sleeves of his shirt, he leaned his elbows to his knees. "Tell me you kept your father's digi-diary."

"Of course. It's in the bedroom with my—"

He held up a hand. "Just promise me you'll let nothing happen to it."

"I'll guard it with my life; you know that. It has the truth about the Plague on it."

"So it does." He nodded, a half smile curving his lips.

"What?"

He raised his voice to a higher pitch. "What?"

Skirting the table, I landed in his lap. "Are you mocking me?"

"Nope." He grinned and bent to kiss me, but I swiveled out of reach.

"Do you have plans for it I should know about?"

"Not yet, not quite, and I don't want you privy to information that could get you in trouble."

"Bit late for that." I rolled my eyes.

"It's classified."

"Classified?"

He merely grinned at me, and it was good to see his blue eyes with that beautiful sparkle lighting them up.

"Classified, you say?" I pulled his shirt up his chest, biting and sucking one flat, silken nipple. "I'll show you classified." Good luck to him withholding information from me. I'd have him begging me to *declassify* his cock in less than two minutes. Then we could talk strategies while I teased him into a priapic state—

Our D-Ps beeped at the same time. I grabbed mine and handed Linc his off-spec handheld. I read my message.

"Did yours tell you to get out to the Catskills commune ASAP?" Linc asked.

"Yeah. You?"

He nodded while searching my face. The color must've drained from it. "You think it's Darke?"

"He was in pretty bad shape." My hands rubbed up and down my arms to take off the sudden chill. I didn't want to face the possibility Darke might not have made it. "But why would they alert you too?" I asked.

Linc glanced away, expression wiped of all emotion. "Good question. I don't have ties with the group."

I grabbed his face, holding firm when I saw the disappointment he tried to shutter. "I didn't mean that the way it sounded."

"You're right, though. I'm connected to no one." Vulnerability shadowed his voice; misery shaded his eyes.

My hands went around his neck, fingers coiling into his hair. "You have your mother and Nate. Fuck. You belong to me, Linc." I yanked his hair until his eyes flipped up.

"Maybe I shouldn't."

"Don't give me that bogus noise. You can't get rid of me that easily. Sorry. Not gonna happen." I slipped off his lap. "Now get your shit so we can head."

"Damn, woman. I thought I was the commander here." He pocketed the D-Ps, his gaze lingering on the high points of my figure, T & A.

I fastened on my holster and swatted his ass in return. "You can command me all night long, babe, so long as you can keep up the full salute you've got going on in your pants."

* * *

It wasn't every day a Corps commander and first lieutenant strolled into a Freelander commune without being frisked, frigged by the barrel of a gun, or shot at immediately on approach. Dressed in our dark blues, weapons to our teeth, we couldn't have made a bigger spectacle if we'd stripped down and run around naked. Or maybe then we'd have fit right in; things could get pretty wild during a celebration.

As it was, our appearance had little impact on the goings-on, meaning we were expected. I took stock of the place. Long hair, homespun clothes, motley crew of weapons on the militia guarding the outskirts…check. Kids running around barefoot with an assortment of farm and domestic animals tagging along, you betcha. Crop fields and fruit orchards were in full spring bloom.

After weeks of being caged inside Beta with its soaring steel, glass, and grimy concrete, its escalating conflict, I took a long, bracing breath. This was what we were fighting for. *The right to be.*

On the graveled main road, I spotted the usual rustic outbuildings. The meeting hall–our endpoint—sat in pride of place in the center of the commune. What was inside made me stop in my tracks for several heartbeats.

Yeah, Darke was present, looking like shit-on-a-stick, but sitting, smiling…*alive.* It was the other presence that made me start at a full run from dead stop, barreling straight into Cannon's outstretched arms. There was no way to be cool about it. Tears and babbling and nonsense came out all at once as soon as he plucked me into his familiar hug.

"Fuck, Lieutenant. Are you on your monthlies?"

I thumped him hard on the arm and continued to snivel.

He rocked me side to side, whispering, "You're gonna scare me shitless if you don't start mouthing off soon. But I like this, too, Liz."

I nodded and gulped, swallowed and swiped my eyes. "You stupid dickface. What the hell are you doing in Cuntler Territory?"

His loud laugh lit me up inside. "There you go."

A deep cough made me look over my shoulder. Linc's glare was icy.

Lounging next to Darke on a bench, Leon's gold gaze skipped between the clearly alpha pair of males. "*Tiens, les bon temps…*"

Because I needed to break up a fistfight between my former boss and my…boss, or beau, or lover. *Shit.* I disentangled myself from Cannon, taking a last caress of the new laugh lines on his face. "Wait. If you're here, then—"

"Lizbeth, girl."

I swung toward that rich drawl, happiness ringing through me anew. Nate stepped up from behind Cannon, sweeping me into a tight embrace. It looked like the militia had arrived on schedule, with a couple unexpected sidekicks. "You done good. We're so proud of you."

"*Proud* wasn't the word I used on the journey up here," Cannon mumbled.

"Oh, let me guess, sir. I'm a hothead, foolhardy, shit-for-brains…"

Cannon's head appeared beside his lover's long, dark blond

locks. "All of those, and brave, courageous, a soldier among—"

"Asswipes," Nate said, and the three of us laughed together until another clearing of the throat broke us apart.

Leon piped up. "Yeah, da show be about to start."

I backed away toward Linc and Cannon stepped off to the side. We left the two estranged brothers facing each other. Linc's face was a fortress of withheld emotion.

Laying an arm around his waist, I squeezed him to me. He trembled all over. "It's going to be okay, baby."

Once he struck eyes on his twin, he didn't let go. The years of distrust, anger, and despair stretched between them, thick as rope. Rope that could either bind them together or tear them apart.

A woman with black hair streaked with white stepped between the two. "I'm here to mediate this meeting."

Linc stalked past the woman. "Don't need to mediate shit between me and my brother."

Threatening of visage, scary in his undeviating march to his twin, I worried about what he might do. Apparently, I wasn't the only one, but I trusted Linc, whereas Cannon looked like he just wanted to kick ass to protect his man.

Linc veered around the mass of muscle in his way, not sparing a glance at Cannon. "Don't need his lover keeping me from him either."

I thought about rushing between Linc and Nate before they clashed, but as Linc toed up to him, strain dropped off his body like ice melting in the sun. He pulled Nate into a hard hug, a gasping growl of a sob breaking free of his throat.

Nate hesitated for less than a second before he clutched Linc's back, clinging tight. Blinking away tears for the second time, I sidled over to Cannon, entwining our hands together as we witnessed a moment no one believed would come to pass.

Linc's voice came out muffled. "I just wanted you safe, needed you out of Father's reach."

"I get it. I get it, brother."

Shit. The waterworks were not letting up.

Cannon bumped my shoulder. "Need a hanky there?"

"Fuck you and the tractor you rode in on."

He clapped me on the back so hard I almost spilled face-first onto the floor. *Fucker.* My stumble broke Nate and Linc apart, and when Linc came around to stand next to his brother, his cheeks were a little ruddy, his eyes wet, his smile totally shaky but truthful.

And that was beautiful to behold. I walked right up to him, clasped his face, and brought him down for a hell of a kiss, such that Leon gave one of his patented whistles and Nate shuffled to the side to give us some space.

The space he abandoned was immediately taken up by a huge, not so amenable, presence. *Big Papa.* Oh, Christ.

Cannon muscled in. "It appears you and I have a problem."

"Can't imagine." Linc rolled his eyes. Whereas Nate was not quite as hard-packed with muscle, Linc was a total match for Cannon in sheer strapping size, on and off the field of battle.

Cue the dominant males throwing around their egos like heavy artillery about to go *boom!* I vacated the vicinity, content to let them hash this out. Besides, Darke deserved some entertainment during his convalescence.

Cannon pulled a hand along his clean-shaven jaw. "See, I promised Liz here I'd make mealtime of your face when I met you...you know, because of the fact you broke her heart." Lips pulled off his teeth like a dog about to attack, he added, "I probably don't need to go on."

Linc stepped into his space until they stood chest to pumping chest. "Far be it for me to deny you the *chance*."

Okay, now those were fighting words, and bones would probably get broken if this *I'm the biggest beast* BS continued. Nate clearly had the same idea, as we both got into position behind our guys.

We exchanged winks before I said, "Yeah, I think that's enough of the Big Dick Contest."

On a silent count of three, Nate and I yanked their respective pants down to their thighs, and my, oh my, who would've guessed they'd both fly commando?

Cannon and Linc assumed *identical* nut-cupping stances, not doing a whole lotta good with the size of their packages. Leon's eyes went wide and unblinking, I chuckled, and Darke started getting all het-up.

Pivoting to me, Linc gave me a serious glower.

I held my hands up. "What? I just wanted to check on that full-salute sitch we talked about earlier."

He took his hands from in front of his cock just as he backed me against a wall. "Fully prepared to demo right here, right now, Lieutenant."

"I appreciate that," I gasped when he rolled his hips, hard shaft grinding against me, "but I don't think our hosts would."

Victorious in this standoff, Linc put his clothes back to rights and pulled me to the others. He and Cannon ended up shaking hands, not their dicks, and I breathed a sigh of relief.

Small talk ensued, awkward, full of fidgeting, but Leon broke the tension with his funny, full-color comments about the two cocks totally off the table to him. Darke muttered blackly beside him. The only thing that took Darke's jealousy down a notch was the way Leon kept a hand on his thigh.

Maybe there was hope for them after all.

Just as I was getting my fill of all that was joyous and wonderful, a full set of D-Ps blared like alarm bells.

"Hatch!"

"Sebastian."

"Hey, Bassy."

"Y'all got a report, Hatch?"

I was linked up to Sebastian with Leon and Linc while the other three started jabbering to Hatch in Chitamauga.

Less than a minute later, shit was shut down, and we started moving.

"We've got a new location on the Posse from Bas," I reported.

"Hatch said he cracked the DCICs, but the connection cut out before he could divulge." Nate tweaked the double helix at the high cartilage of his ear. "Doesn't matter. We've got to haul ass before Taft moves house again." Linc checked his weapons, striding out of the meeting hall with me behind him.

Darke's baritone registered next. "I'm comin.'"

Yeah, he's coming apart at the limbs.

And suddenly I was surrounded by four dipshits and a limper who was half prostrate. I let out an ear-splitting whistle. Miss Not-Hills winced, and the boys stepped back a pace.

Pointing at Darke, I ordered, "You sit your ass back down before you keel over." I swung on Nate. "You're stupider than you look, and don't even think about giving me that southern-boy charm. You're staying put." Nodding at Cannon and Leon, I said, "You two, with me. Keep it tight."

Cannon's brows rose to heights untested, but he zipped his lips over the grin threatening to split them apart.

"You cannot be compromised," I said to Linc. "Remember? There's this little insurrection of Beta troops you're trying to keep under wraps."

"I don't want you out there without me." He pulled me against him.

"I know that, but I'm a soldier. This is my job."

"*Ah*, Christ, Liz. I'm just supposed to let you go it alone?" His joined hands on my lower back brought me impossibly closer.

I tipped my head up. "I'm coming back to you, home to *you*. This is simple surveillance. Besides, you need to stay with your brother. You've got a lot to talk about."

After murmuring his demands for my safety, he set me loose.

Nate looked on, impressed.

"Pussy-whipped," Cannon muttered with a nod in Linc's direction.

Linc countered, "Didn't think you'd know about that."

Leon joined the bullshit fest. "Got that right, Commander. He be dick-whipped by Big Blond over there."

During the drive into Beta, Cannon looked so relaxed, at peace. I couldn't get over the change in him. In fact, I couldn't shut Mr. Chatterbox up as he filled me in on the gossip from Chitamauga. Jonquil had tied the knot and she was pregnant—the girl worked fast as ever. Eden and Evangeline, Leon's *maman*, had become tight. Just how tight, he didn't deign to allude.

We arrived at the new locale to find Sebastian running rings around himself, which I'd learned to take as a bad sign. Hopping from the Cruiser Cannon left idling outside S-5's looming gate, I grabbed Sebastian's hands, stopping the windmill action.

He jerked his head toward the old, decommissioned Beta water refactory, white-blond hair swirling around his face, the black diamond stud in his nose glinting. His mouth ran a kilometer a minute the same time Cannon got an incoming message from his Blondie. I could tell he had one ear on Sebastian's mouthful and another on Nate, his face screwed tight.

"Miniature weapons of biochem warfare. That's what we made. That's what I designed!" Sebastian's gums kept flapping. "What you saw on the schematics. I only worked on the insect-sized drones, Liz, nothin' else."

Yeah, yeah, the nano-bio-bullshit.

"The Drone Clone Insect Colony, DCIC." Sebastian's pale purple eyes bored into mine. "It's an army ready to infect, and no one will even know it's happenin'"

Cannon flipped his D-P into his back pocket and ran both

hands over his head. Not a good sign. "The Drone Clone Insect Colony? It's equipped to infect."

"That's what he said." I gestured to Bas.

We moved toward the nearest leg of the water tower, keeping to the shadows.

Cannon lowered his voice. "Those notes you saw about PPII, Grant? Pneumonic Plague, Infestation Stage II."

This was my *eureka* moment, but I was ready to black out. The Plague my father helped create hadn't been killed. Cutler had coerced a bunch of brainy boys and girls to devise its newest, most-lethal delivery system.

A bunch of minibots holed up in this shithole of a derelict water tower. We had one more chance to take the bio-virus warfare offline before a terrifying All-Territories-wide crisis screwed us.

With my signal, we turned the corner, Leon and Sebastian calling softly, "At your back."

Keeping to the tower's legs, I swallowed hard. I hunkered at Cannon's side, about to latch on to a ladder.

Just then, Taft sauntered from behind the opposite steel leg. "Not one step closer or I unleash them all."

We froze, our hands held in the air instead of grasping our guns, because now we knew what the whole nano-fuckery project was about, and it could be the endgame to us, the civilians of Beta, hell, the entire pop of the InterNations.

Beckoning Sebastian front and center, Taft addressed him. "You snitched to them about the DCICs, din't you?" The guy looked rough around the edges; he sounded like a loose cannon.

And I didn't trust loose cannons. It was time to stop this.

Moving as if under a silent command, the four of us aimed over-head into the sheet-metal belly. Before anyone could unload, Taft made a fast grab for Leon.

"Thank you for bringin' a hostage." He pulled a blocky fore-arm around Leon's throat, squeezing the air out of him.

No rash moves. No rash moves, boy. I silently pleaded with Leon to keep his cool.

Towed back into the shadows with Taft's gun pressed to his temple, Leon fastened steady eyes on me.

"You got a plan?" I hissed to Cannon.

"Fuck all," he muttered.

I belted both barrels up. "You kill him, you get a gander of hell yourself."

Cannon matched my stance. Sebastian, too.

"Don't even think about playing the maverick, Bas." Taft's gun hand shook, and I feared he'd fire off from nerves alone.

"Stand down!" I shouted to the others.

"Bas might've told you what the DCICs are capable of, but you haven't seen a damn thing yet." Taft's forearm bulged with re-strained pressure as he looked right at me. "You really think I'd let you, *Lieutenant Grant*, anywhere near the genuine article? The bots you worked on in the factory were nothing but overblown replicas. You have no idea what you're up against. But don't worry. I haven't told the CEO about your defection—yet."

Taft turned his attention to Leon. He straightened his arm, holding the barrel of his weapon a trigger pull away from explod-ing Leon's head. "And what've we got us here? Leon Cheramie. Wanted for acts of a wanton and deviant nature." He rolled his eyes, clearly not fully indoctrinated but willing to go with it nevertheless, especially when Sebastian started forward.

Taft nudged his gun, the sound of a chamber loading echoing beneath the steel structure covering us. "Back off, Sarge. I might be hot for your cock, but you had your chance to play on my terms. Fuck, man, you used me against them?"

Bas took another step. "Don't do this. Let him go! I'm sorry. I didn't mean to—"

"Yeah, you did. Shut the fuck up, or I'll do him right here."

Sebastian dropped back, and Taft refocused. "Broke out of Alpha RACE in October 2070. An outstanding warrant on his arrest. Leon here is known to be a street con, a homosexual, and a scrip-charging whore because all the old men like a taste of jailbait. Lastly, he's a traitor to the Company."

Jesus Christ. Taft has the whole rap sheet on him. He must've looked into Leon's records the second Sebastian brought him into the Posse. My stomach dropped way below my knees.

"Yeah. I think Leon will do, a'right. He's gonna be the insurance policy to make sure the rest of you stop meddling in Company affairs you really shouldn't get involved in. Leave us the fuck alone, and maybe he'll be returned in one piece instead of a pile of body parts."

"I'll go. Take me instead," Sebastian volunteered. "Is it because I didn't love you, Taft? I can. You know I can. I just—"

"You think this is all about you? Baby boy, it's about forging a place in the world that's about to be turned upside down. I gave you the option of coming with me before, but you always turned me down. All that optimism you wear on your face? Just makes me feel dirty inside. Because that's what I am—corrupted." He shook his head. "I don't want you anymore, Bas. I got what I want right here. And this one puts out, from what I've heard about his reputation as a rent boy."

"Don't you fucking touch him," I snarled. "You rape him, and I will cut your cock off."

"I don't think it'll be rape." His grin made me want to scream.

"You hurt Leon, and I'll come after you. There will be no place to hide, nothing that will stop me except your death at my hands, when your last breath beats out beneath my fingers." Cannon gnashed out his deadly threat. "There is no place far enough you can run, *boy.*"

Drops of sweat lined Taft's brow. "Yeah, enough with the entreaties. Me and Leon here have a date."

The all-encompassing need to keep Leon safe was the only reason we didn't rush Taft. We watched him retreat, Leon pressed to the front of his body. Through the shadows, at the other side of the tower, there was a tank that fired up at their approach, its rumble shaking the ground.

Leon, who hadn't said a single word through the whole thing, strained forward. "Darke, tell him…*tiens-moi serré…*"

Then he was whisked from sight.

Chapter Fourteen

At the Catskills commune, I took the march to Darke's caravan alone. The daylight hours had been beautiful, those few moments between breakfast ending with Linc and Nate's reunion before the heavy had come down hard and fast.

Orange and yellow flowers crowded the foot of the faded wooden steps outside a wagon painted in a patchwork of color. The place looked far too small to contain Darke, and sure enough, he wasn't resting inside. Standing on the small stoop, he grabbed the canopy overhead, quickly going through the math when Leon didn't emerge from the evergreen forest behind me.

"Where the fuck is Leon?" Darke snarled, his ebony skin stretched tight over muscle.

It was hard to remain undaunted with him gnashing his teeth at me, but I took the steps until we were face-to-face. "Let's go inside."

"Just tell me he's not dead, goddamn you!"

"He's not. Leon's not dead, Darke." I touched his shoulder, moving him back, into the caravan.

The interior was neat as a tick and too small to contain Darke's worry. He shoved the bed aside, overthrew a pitcher of water…He crouched on the floor.

I sank in front of him. "He was taken."

A purely animalistic growl ripped out of his throat. "You were supposed to watch out for him."

"There was no choice, Darke. Taft snatched him, threatening to release the DCICs on the Territory if we got in his way."

"*Ahh*, fuck!" Scrabbling away, he curled both arms around his torso, eyes tearing up. "I can't take this shit anymore. I can't…I can't shake the fool boy off, but…" He whispered, "I should've never let him in."

"You didn't have a choice."

Darke jumped to his feet and towered over me. "I had a choice. I should've made him stay away from me." He choked on the next words. "What'll they do to him?"

"Taft promised to bring him back as long as we step off our hunt for the DCICs."

"Then you fucking stand down now, all of you. This war, this Revolution, all of your plans, none of it goes ahead until Leon comes home to me."

"You should be prepared, Darke."

Deadly eyes turned to mine. "What for?"

"Taft intimated rape."

"No. No!" A pained groan slipped out. "Why didn't I take care of him when I had the chance?

"I will kill Taft, the CEO, anyone who hurts him." A savage sneer bared his teeth.

"Darke." I waited for him to still. "Leon said something for you when he was taken away."

Tears escaped his eyelids.

"*Tiens-moi serré*," I said.

"Hold me tight." His body racked with the pain that made his voice hoarse.

Losing the man he hadn't fully accepted, one more after Wilde and Tammerick…I pushed my arms around Darke as my grief joined his.

* * *

Leon's abduction constituted another major setback. We couldn't go after gaining control of Beta; we couldn't destroy the DCICs. Taft's new *insurance policy* tied our hands. Linc, Ginger Johnson, and I kept our streamlined Beta Corps crew at the ready, but they were biting at the bit for some action. There was nothing for them to do but go about their daily business to keep their cover secure, recruiting other like-minded soldiers to beef up their ranks.

Individuals had become invaluable, life and liberty inviolable rights. Their sanctity funneled down to Leon—on this, we all agreed.

It took two damn days to get a lead through Farrow. During those excruciating forty-eight hours, I'd been in constant contact with Cannon and Darke. Darke was back solidly on his feet, most likely through sheer force of will rather than true physical recovery. Cannon assisted him with bringing the Catskills fighters up to the level of the Chitamauga militia camped out in the flourishing village. The four of us came up with a solid game plan for the takeover of Beta Territory and a coup against Cutler. Meanwhile, Nate was configuring something top secret at Linc's insistence.

All this busywork provided no new answers and very little hope, no matter how organized we were. I knew Darke wasn't sleeping. He was barely eating, and he snapped at anyone who crossed his path. He'd threatened to end more than one of his trainees' lives in the past two days, and if we didn't get a location on Leon ASAP, I was afraid how far he'd fall.

Linc and I were the only ones headed for the midnight meeting Farrow had arranged. The others were safe and sound and under wraps at the commune. We took the Cruiser into the heart of S-1, wrapped in an air of intensity and intimacy.

This late-night meet and greet looked more and more like a date, not that I'd had any experience with one of those. I'd for damn sure never gotten cleaned up, dressed up, and my heart had never knocked so loudly before. Looking at Linc sitting beside me, freshly shaved, wearing a dark blue civilian suit that sent midnight fire into his eyes, my pulse rocketed.

I reminded myself this was an assignment; no need to get giddy. "Tell me why my tits and things are hanging out again?"

Dressed in a formfitting black suit with a severe satin jacket whose lapels rested against the curves of my breasts and plunged to my navel, I was bare underneath. I felt more nude because of the lack of my Eagles than the revealing outfit, but I'd strapped a short knife to my ankle and had one sheathed at my back.

Linc snuck a finger along the line of skin between my breasts to the divot of my belly button. "You really have to ask?"

When his whole palm cupped my breast, I leaned against the headrest. "You like my body, but what's that got to do with tonight?"

"We've gotta talk to Denver." He placed his meandering hand on my thigh.

The infamous informant Denver who'd been mentioned at the Amphitheater. Distrusted by Farrow, possibly another double agent, but she'd set this up and we had no choice but to follow through. "And?"

"He's my father's bodyguard."

Shutting my eyes, I asked, "What else?"

"It's too suspicious to talk to him alone. We have to make contact at another event."

I slapped his hand off me. "I'm not prepared to see the CEO."

Event meant upscale seediness, wills tested and bent. It was the last place I wanted to be, on show with Linc before his conniving father.

Linc's hand pressed against my cheek. "I won't let anything happen to you."

I took a breath that didn't do a damn thing to settle my nerves before lacing my fingers through his. "Let's do this. For Leon."

Brittle laughter sounded as harsh as splinters of glass, hitting my ears when we entered Cutler's Beta condo. Wealth saturated this den of degeneracy, from the marble floors to the frescoed ceiling bearing the InterNations emblem, but the revelers were wound tight. An air of desperation hung over these rich surrounds, so tangible it was suffocating. It was as if this was the last party, the end of the world as we knew it.

And it might well be.

I accepted a cocktail, sipping the cool pink liquid while Linc propelled me through the grandiose marble foyer that ran the heights of two floors. I paid attention to the routes to and from the outer doors, checking others for weapons bulging beneath their sleek upper-crust outfits, noting how many guards stood watch.

Music filtered around the main room, which was equipped with semisecluded salons, each complete with a double-deep dais. The easier to fuck your night's conquest under the guise of privacy but really in full view of the partygoers. I remembered what Linc had told me about these soirées: sex in excess, fucking to forget, greed, and overindulgence. My fingers tightened on his forearm. He'd been part of this, party to all this depravity. *He'd fucked women like this.*

"Are you all right?" Linc led me into a quiet hallway.

"I'm seeing how you were." Except I couldn't look at him.

He bent his knees, getting in my line of vision. "You remember that, Liz. How I *was*. Not how I wanted to be and not who I am anymore."

Jealousy and hurt were stupid distractions at this point, ones I couldn't afford. I nodded, reminding myself he'd been an active participant to keep in good graces, to take the knife for his brother. And probably because sex damn well felt good, too, especially presented freely when all else was conscripted. In many ways, I'd done the same, and even though these scenes were prevalent at the communes, the Amphitheater, there was nothing of the give-and-take present here. Tonight it was all about take.

"I know. I'm sorry." I skimmed my fingers along Linc's jaw, then tucked my hand around his arm.

Sabine sauntered up to us. "Don't you two look cozy."

We had been, for a moment at least.

"I didn't think I'd see you here."

I wished I could say the same for her, but she had a habit of showing up at Cutler's parties.

The gash had kept her head out of range of my scopes the past few weeks, but the scar on my calf reminded me what she was capable of. I knew why Linc couldn't kick her out of Corps; his hand would've been tipped. But that didn't mean I wasn't keeping score.

I pushed past the red-dressed sow, shoving into her shoulder. "You might be Beta Corps, but your insignia is tarnished, and I can't wait to rip it off you."

As soon as we passed Sabine, we came up against a tall man with black hair braided past his backside. He was immediately recognizable as Cutler's guard from the last party. The planes of his face were crisscrossed with fine scars. A full mouth and high cheekbones led to eyes that were nearly black. A synthetic tattoo of a dragon crawled from his collar to the back of his neck. So this was Denver. A man who didn't fit the CO mold at all.

"Your father awaits." There was a rasp to his voice, as if nails were embedded in his windpipe.

I looked above to where Cutler watched the proceedings from

a mezzanine of glass and steel. We walked up the stairs in front of us while Denver followed behind, silent for all his powerful presence.

White crest of hair in place, a sneer on his lips at the sight of me, CEO Cutler was as imposing as ever. "Son." When Linc stepped forward and dropped down to one knee, my heart turned over in my chest. Only I knew what his obeisance cost him in pride.

"You continue to inconvenience yourself with Grant, I see."

A fat silver band—a Rice family ring he had no right to—circled one of the fingers Cutler used to grip Linc's shoulder. It was identical to the ring Nate had given Cannon in betrothal.

"She's proven herself useful so far, and she can get us to Nathaniel and his queer commander."

His father beamed down at him with satisfaction at Linc performing as expected, bashing his homosexual brother and his brother's lover.

Cutler loosened his grasp on Linc's shoulder. "Commander Caspar Cannon is no more than a rat I could crush beneath my boot. The waterboarding I ordered should've killed him last November, but he floated to the goddamn surface like all disease-ridden rodents tend to do. It won't go so well for his old pastime, Leon Cheramie."

I measured my intake of O2, willing myself to remain calm.

Those talons, like an eagle's, dug into Linc's neck until the fingertips turned white. "How soon can she deliver the betrayers?"

I could see Linc's jaw grinding as he continued to keep his head bowed. I would trade places with him in a heartbeat to stave off the battle Linc fought inside against one side of his family for another.

I bent beside him, clasping his father's hand. "A few more days, sir," I assured him, although I had no intentions of delivering anything to him but his own death. Forcing his attention on me instead of his son, I kissed the signet ring.

A heavy hand petted my head, the unbearable weight Linc had borne all these years filling me with revulsion. "Good girl, Grant." Cutler released us both and sat back. "Good, the pair of you." A smile like that of a contented child lined his face, bringing my hate to a boiling point.

"Denver." Cutler summoned the black-haired man. "Please show the commander"—he paused, the insult meant for me clear—"and lieutenant out."

On the street, Linc and Denver sank into blue-black shadows. "Tell me when the handoff is going down for Leon."

Denver wore a faint smile that never reached the cool gleam of his eyes. "Tomorrow. Noon at the water tower. They're shipping him out to Delta Territory."

"How many marks will be there?"

"Guess you'll have to wait and see," Denver replied.

They clasped hands. "I owe you," Linc said.

"Plenty of time for that." He disappeared into the May mist.

* * *

Never in my life had I felt like there was less time to memorize Linc's face, not enough time to tell him everything that was in my heart. The minutes had simply slipped away from us. Back inside the Cruiser, we sped away from Cutler's. I placed my hand over Linc's on the gearshift and lay my head against his shoulder.

Perhaps he felt the same as me, because instead of turning toward the Quad, he took off in an easterly direction. He drove toward an underpopulated area I hadn't explored since my early youth, when life had spread out before me.

Following the grid system streets until the vehicle rutted over ill-maintained roads, Linc drove through a high iron gate. The scrollwork was rusted, yet Vanderbilt Gate was still impressive. Headlights bounced off the trees and shrubs thriving inside Beta's only wild expanse of land.

He drove us deeper into the Central, a naturalistic stretch that used to be known as Central Park in this former booming northeastern city before the Purge. The habitat had been hacked into an eighth of its majesty when Beta barricade went up, leaving only four thousand hectares within Territory walls. The area was remarkably untouched woods and meadows.

My grip on Linc's fingers tightened, and he squeezed back, eyes on the track ahead. Stopping in the middle of a field of tall spring grasses, he cut the engine. Linc lifted my hand, placing my palm against his cheek for a moment before he left the vehicle. He gathered me from the Cruiser, kissing me as softly as the flowers swaying around us on tall stalks.

While I watched in quiet wonder, he popped the back hatch. He took out candles and a blanket. Spreading the blanket over the shaggy grass, he arranged a large circle of candles and lit them within glass globes. Soft light suffused the area, reminding me of the votives in the Chitamauga meadow after Nate and Cannon's handfasting. My pulse a little jumpy, my breath a little halting, I was touched to the very depths of my being by Linc's gestures.

"Is this a…date?" I asked.

After lighting the final candle, he stood. "I pay attention to you. I saw how you reacted to the Catskills commune. I know how hard it is for you to be here."

"As long as I'm with you, I have everything."

"Come here." His deep tone shivered through me. Then his shy smile made my heart burst. "It's not much, but…"

I went to him, slipping into his arms. "It's everything."

He took both our D-Ps and turned them off. Linc removed his holster, the hidden knives as well as mine. His dark blue gaze never left my face as he unarmed us. He disarmed me with his sure motions. He placed the weapons, the coms units into the back of the Cruiser, removed his suit jacket and added it to the heap inside. Returning to me, he loosened the buttons on his shirt all down his front and at the cuffs, rolling the sleeves up his forearms.

My body loose, warm, flushed, I waited for him, as if every item removed was another layer of subterfuge vanishing from between us. I wanted just this—Linc, his heart and body, his heat and his truth-filled eyes.

Lowering me onto the blanket to sit in front of him, he rested his hands on my sides, just below my breasts. I curled my fingers into his hair and brushed kisses over his face. I savored the roughness of shadowy stubble on his jaw.

"Should we really be out here now without keeping in contact with the others?"

His thumb swept across my bottom lip. "I don't care about the war. I don't care about any of that right now. I want to be with you, Liz—just you tonight. If Leon's capture has taught me anything…" He pulled in a shaky breath. "I don't want to go into one more battle until you understand how deeply I care for you. How much I love you."

Unsaid words screamed between us, neither of us daring to breathe them aloud in this sacred space amid a revolution.

"You are the most unexpected gift of my life. I've been alone for so long, convinced it was how I'd live and how I'd die, believing that was the way I wanted it." Linc's hand caressed underneath the plunging lapel of my jacket until he cupped my breast. My nipple rose into his palm as my lips turned to his. Driving his tongue deep, he moaned into my mouth. His free hand worked the sole button at my navel. With the black satin fabric spread wide, he pulled back. "I want to do something right, with the woman I love, for once in my life."

He took me down to the blanket, and I hissed when his mouth drifted to my breasts. His tongue captured and suckled both buds until they were engorged and wet. My pants and panties and shoes, he skimmed from my body, and I was nude to the night, naked beneath his sight. I helped divest his clothes, impatient for the feel of him, the expanse of taut muscle, his thick cock, the spicy scent of him.

The flowers were probably weeds, but they smelled sweet and fresh, crushed beneath the heat of our bodies when we rolled off the blanket. The grass was soft, the air warm. It was quiet and perfect.

As he stretched above me, his eyes glassed over with desire. Need so strong it hardened his face threw the cords of his neck into sharp relief. He dragged his finger into my moist heat. Linc drew a long whimper from me when he brought his wet fingertip to his mouth.

"Don't make me wait, Linc."

"Never. I'll never make you wait, sweetheart." He thrust into me. Our bodies forged together, hips pivoting, pelvises smacking. His chest rubbed my tender breasts, sending flames down to my belly. I sucked on his neck, his shoulder, the magnificent cut of his biceps. Stiff and long, Linc withdrew and plunged inside me until his abs, his cock, his sacs were wet from me.

I wound my arms around his shoulders, over the Eagle moko. I felt as if the bird, its wings, as if the word *Libertas* itself was lifting us up above this place, raising us above the Revolution. I soared within his strong embrace, crying as I crested the heights of love and lust. Linc buried himself inside me a final time. His climax bore him down onto me, into me, his straining muscles coming loose as he roared above me.

When he snuggled me on top of him, glistening sweat clung to his shoulders and temples. I nuzzled his chest, knowing I would stay right here forever, with him, if I could.

His chest jostled beneath me. I tilted my chin to narrow my eyes at him.

"What?" I asked.

"I'm gonna have grass stains on my ass." A thick blond eyebrow arched up.

"You are? How about me? You just about drove me down the hillside on my backside, sir."

His hands rubbing my ass, he grinned. "I'll take pleasure in cleaning you up, Lieutenant."

"I bet you will." I laid my head back down. "I love you, Linc."

His circling arms enclosed me tighter, and his lips swept across the top of my hair. "You have my heart, Liz."

He stretched an arm out, dragging the abandoned blanket over the top of us, intent to stay where he was. Content to be with me all night, alone, where no one could reach us and no one would find us.

I awoke, face pressed against his chest, and I smiled. The smell of flowers brought our night together back to me, memories I'd treasure for the rest of my days, however few there were. The sun was too low to be of warmth, early morning just beginning with the din of birds I hadn't been able to enjoy since Chitamauga.

Linc's hands flitted through my hair. I sat up and gently played my fingertips along his chest, sighing when his knuckle rubbed my nipple.

"You look good in flowers, almost as good as you look naked, well fucked by me."

I tried to glare at the man, but it was impossible when he was spread before me like a man of myth, legend, a semi-tamed satyr. "What about in my uniform and guns?"

"Hot, but I still like you naked and fucked best."

I lifted my hands to run them through my hair and came away with flowers—tiny purple cups—between my fingers. "What—"

He kissed me quickly. "It's a daisy chain. You looked so pretty, sleeping in my arms. My mom taught us how to make them, although I don't think these are daisies." He plucked a flower from beside us, inspecting it. "I'd forgotten. Thought I had, anyway." Tucking the flower into my hair, Linc joined his hand with mine. "I just wanted to see how you would look, when you were...if we were handfasted."

I couldn't have spoken if I tried. I simply nodded, hoping I reflected the same desire for such a ceremony with him as he did. I sprang to my feet and rushed to the vehicle, peering at myself in the window. Little lavender blossoms formed a braided ring through my short hair.

Linc approached behind me and I said, "It's so pretty."

"These hands are not just for death."

"No, they're not." I turned in his arms, trading several long kisses with him, smoldering heat fanning to flames between us. Linc drew back too soon. Seriousness etched his features. "I'm glad Cannon and Nathaniel are here. If anything happens to me, I've told them to get you out of here."

"I would stay with you."

"Of course, so long as I'm alive, but I need a backup plan."

The burn of fear flashed through me so fast, I gasped in pain. "There is no fucking backup plan. There's only one plan. Survival."

"I want you to go to the commune, to my mom. Tell her I never stopped loving her, that I always forgave her." Linc gathered me close as tears spilled down my face.

"Don't say that like it's the end."

A curse broke from him. "If this is the end, I could never have imagined anything better than being loved by you."

Chapter Fifteen

At 1145 hours the next day. Cannon, Nate, Farrow, Sebastian, Darke, Linc, and I were placed at strategic intervals in the shadows of Beta's looming outer walls, watching the water tower. This wasn't the time or place for remembrances of Linc's and my night spent in the Central. This was fifteen minutes away from possible mayhem, yet when I looked at the man closest to me and his fingers glided against mine, I almost cracked a smile. His love was like a fever. A hot, burning blast inside my body that made me more alive than I'd ever known.

I swept my gaze over Cannon. He stood beside Nate, their arms touching. *Fuck me.* This was also not the time or place to smile about the possibility of having my own forget-me-not, blue-eyed fuck bunny who also made me goddamn daisy chains and placed them in my hair while I slept within his embrace.

Denver had told us the handoff to who-the-fuck-ever was at noon sharp, but the area remained clear until, as the minutes to twelve hundred hours crept ever closer, so did the earth-shaking rumble of a tank. It was either Taft with Leon or more of Cutler's henchmen. The military vehicle shuddered to a halt on the far side of the water tower's legs. Sudden palpable tension rolled off of all of us.

I murmured, "If this is a handoff, where's everyone else?"

"I don't like this." Cannon echoed my thoughts.

The hatch on the tank thunked open. Leon's sweat-streaked hair showed first.

Darke strained forward, shouting, "LEON!" So much for subterfuge.

Nate and Cannon hauled back on his arms, trying to tame the wild beast he became at the first sight of Leon.

Leon's clouded golden eyes drifted across to him. Throwing off Nate and Cannon, Darke blazed forward. He stopped when a gun muzzle appeared under Leon's jaw, Taft rising after it from the interior of the tank.

"I see you're not worried about showing yourselves, then." He dug his gun into Leon's neck for good measure.

This was setup number whatever. *Jesus.* No small thanks to double-agent douche bag Denver.

His voice raw, Darke addressed Taft. "You did anything, you *touched* any part of him, I will take you apart bone by bone."

"Easy there, killer." Taft clucked his tongue, the metal ball piercing rapping loudly against his teeth.

Nudging Leon to the ground, Taft scanned our group as Darke's growl formed into a rapacious snarl.

Taft and Leon came forward, not like Leon had any choice with a gun cocked under his chin. The good thing was, he was walking on his own. The bad thing was, he looked dazed and discombobulated.

"Let him go," Cannon demanded.

Taft looked young, not the scientific mastermind, not the ringleader, but a youth in charge of some seriously bad shit that would ultimately end his life, real soon. "Can't."

The sound of multiple weapons locking on his T-zone made him swing to Sebastian. "I got a message to deliver, from the CEO."

Sweat popped out on Taft's forehead, and Leon started looking really bad. He listed to the side, eyes pinwheeling. He was not just slightly out of it. He looked completely bewildered, and I didn't like the way he kept peering at Darke in confusion.

Gun raised on a steady arm, Darke wasn't going to wait for the change in Leon's custody before he fried Taft.

I rushed him, trying to drag his hand down. "He's just a kid!" Corrupted, used, the same as all of us.

Darke just glared ahead, trigger finger pulling back.

Features blanched so white his *Posse Omnis Juvenis* tat stood out on his neck, Taft shoved Leon at us. His eyes lit on Sebastian while his prisoner stumbled toward our line and Darke was right there.

He bundled Leon into his arms, releasing a groan of relief. "Leon, you okay?"

Leon tried to draw back, but Darke wouldn't let him go. "Answer me, baby. Are you all right?"

Leon shook his head and searched out Cannon and Nate. "I know *mon vieux* Caspar and his beau"—he nodded toward the pair—"and I know them." He pointed at me and then Farrow. "But I don't know where I been, and I don' know you."

"I didn't want you to see me like this, Sarge," Taft called over. Gun slipped into his waistband, he held his hands wide.

Holy shit. My stomach dropped as I tried to keep one eye on two pairs of men who were really fucking with my heart rate.

Sebastian stomped forward. "What have you done?"

"Can't answer that. I didn't do nothing to him. I'm just the delivery guy."

They stood facing each other until Bas smashed his fist so hard into Taft's face, he wheeled around on his heels. Hand cupping what had to be a throbbing cheek and possibly a broken nose, Taft lifted his eyes to Sebastian and nodded as if he'd gotten what he deserved.

A large brown hand peeled Sebastian away; then Darke was in that swelling-up face. "What the fuck is this!" He pointed at Leon.

"You wanted your boy back; you got him."

I muttered to Linc, "It can't be this easy."

"It isn't gonna be if Darke kills Taft before we get a chance to question him."

"What the fuck did you do? He doesn't remember me?" A mighty roar came from Darke.

Unfazed, Taft said, "You might wanna rethink any move you make, killer. I told you, the CEO has a message, for all of ya."

And then total chaos ensued.

Directly above Taft's head, the shadow thrown by the water tower's undercarriage darkened. I thought about rubbing my eyes, but my hands were too goddamn busy trying to keep my guns steady. The belly of the tower retracted, and suddenly the air surrounding Taft was humming. It was *alive*, buzzing. Hundreds, thousands, millions of the DCICs—had to be that many to create a shadow so dense it was black and so long it stretched to fill the base of the water tower—circled around Taft.

I couldn't tear my eyes away. I couldn't blink. My breath was sharp sounding above the buzz of the insect drones. The colony of killers kept swarming from within the womb of the water tower. "Oh my God, Linc."

I heard him rumble beside me. The others were just as horrified, wide-eyed, openmouthed as we watched the mechanized harbingers of death swim out toward us. Hovering in the air, swooping, flying. Dragonflies, black flies, moths, mosquitoes, bees. A staggering, innumerable amount of them, and so many different species they would be innocuous, untraceable, inescapable.

That's when I holstered one of my guns and grasped Linc's hand, unwilling to let go of him. Taft hadn't been shitting me about the oversized replicas I'd worked on. These robotic insects could fly about human targets, and no one would be the wiser.

Taft threw his arms over his head and the swarm dispersed, flying straight up into the sky. "They're armed now, fully operational, ready to infect. That's the beauty of them, my little inventions. It's why the CEO wanted me, wanted you, Sarge. *We created this.*" Oh Christ, he'd been overcome, too, by lust for power. "Every one of these babies packs enough Plague II to infect fifty people."

All of God's pretty creatures made into a death squadron.

Swirling his arm in the air, the DCICs became a funnel cloud whipping off down the street and returning. They spun in place between Taft and us. "It's not a mistake you're all here, every one of you."

I dragged in a breath and shut my eyes, willing Linc to know how much I loved him, how much I'd hoped for a life with him. "If I'm infected, you kill me, you hear me? I do not want to be a carrier for this germicide."

"You're not going anywhere, and nothing's going to happen to you." His jaw was set, his eyes snapping and his nostrils flaring wide.

"Too bad you didn't think about that when Denver gave you the meet point last night. It was all so brilliantly orchestrated," Taft crowed. "Look at you, a veritable who's who of the Revolution, plus the CEO's two sons ready for a takedown. I'm pretty sure that'll be a surprise even for Cutler. The Plague strain hasn't been calibrated yet to attack specific individuals; it knows no bias. It's pretty fucking clear the CEO has decided Beta Territory is no longer salvageable."

When Taft's arms spanned wide, the massive black cloud spread out over the horizon, stretching so far it was unimaginable in its monstrosity. I was strangely awed—sickeningly awed—by this man. "How is he doing that?"

Beside me, Sebastian murmured, "He's been working on biorobotic synthesis."

"They're connected to him?"

"Looks like he cracked it," Sebastian answered.

What it looked like was Taft was about to deploy them toward inner Beta. True terror cut through me as I shouldered forward to where he coordinated the locust-like cloud. "Holy fuck. He's gonna infect the civilians!"

"No, he's goddamn not," Linc gritted out, opening fire.

We squeezed off round after round, all of us. Our bullets made not a single frigging dent in the storm cloud. Suddenly, they flew not as a flock but as singular individually minded entities. An even more alarming prospect.

"That was the CEO's message, but it's not mine." Taft's voice rang clear.

Light exploded before my eyes. Millions of flashes blazed up the sky, blinding me. Ear-splitting cracks sounded like muffled shotgun fire, and I took cover, Linc surrounding me. The flash-bang tore up the horizon, jettisoning hot metal lightning strikes toward us.

Minutes later, Linc rocked to his feet and I looked around. Gray puffs of air went off like little fireworks as the last of the DCICs self-destructed.

"Well, that was fucking anticlimactic," Cannon bit out.

My knees weakened with relief. When the smoke finally filtered away, I saw Taft holding a control pad in one hand. He'd blown up the bite-sized biochem army. He dropped the control to the ground, smashing it into the dirt with the heel of his boot.

In his other hand, he held his gun.

He aimed the pistol at his temple. "I, Taft Harding, have been an apostate to the people, to my friends, my family…the ones I love." His focus swung to Sebastian. "There's just one thing I gotta say to you, Bas. Well, maybe two." A small grin flitted across his lips. "I thought I could be good enough for you, but there's only one way I can do that now. I'm sorry."

"No!" Sebastian yelled, running forward.

"A man can't live without honor, baby boy." He looked lingeringly at his friend, his love. Then he shook his head sadly. "You're too soft for this war, Sarge." He pulled the trigger on himself.

I spun into Linc's arms. The pain and poignancy of this war slayed me. He shuffled me backward, away from the scene. His hands were on me, knocking my cap off, in my hair, on my face, over my lips.

I clung to him desperately. "He saved us."

His deep voice resounded through his chest. "Bravery, self-sacrifice. That's the way of the soldier."

"He didn't have to kill himself."

Linc rocked me in his arms. "He would've died anyway. He did what he had to do to save face."

I fought against the tears rising behind my eyelids. "What about Sebastian?"

"That I don't know, sweetheart. I don't know. But he's got all of us, and we are not going anywhere." He tipped my chin up. "You okay?"

The truth was if Linc hadn't been there to talk me through it, I'd have swallowed all this pain down with all the other crap as I'd done the last eleven years of my life. Adding to the backlog of bullshit that had festered far too long before he'd come along.

"Five-by-five," I answered, only because I had him.

He took a quick kiss, and we walked back to the group just in time to see Leon leg it to Cannon and Nate.

"This ain't Alpha. It ain't the commune, big guy. You g'on tell me what the hell is goin' down, 'cause the last thing I remember, I saw the four of you"—he motioned to me and Farrow, Cannon and Nate—"draggin' asses back into Chitamauga in December."

Darke watched from the side, eyebrows drawn down. "Leon, it's me, Darke. How the fuck can you not know me? Please, angel. I'm begging you."

Leon's eyes landed on him. "I don' remember." He spoke softly.

I didn't know how it was possible a man who had seen his two lovers gunned down, who had grieved them, could possibly look more bereaved, but Darke managed it.

"Listen, man." Cannon pulled Darke out of Leon's earshot. "The kid's all nerved up. He doesn't remember the better half of December or anything after that, so he sure as hell doesn't know what they did to him, and that's a little bit important right now. We gotta get him back to Catskills. We'll have a healer look at him, make him feel safe, yeah? Let me take him."

The battle within Darke didn't die down. "He was mine before this, and he's gonna be mine again."

"I know that. You're in his heart." Man-to-man, Cannon prodded Darke in the chest. "But now is not the fucking time."

At Darke's nod, Cannon marched away. He put an arm over Leon's shoulders and led him toward their vehicle. Sebastian was a broken heap over Taft's prone body, Farrow kneeling next to him. Darke stared after Leon, fists balled at his sides.

Linc called out, "We regroup at oh-seven-hundred."

* * *

Back at Corps Command, we sequestered ourselves in the apartment to debrief Ginger Johnson. His eyes grew wider as the story went on, and his freckles stood out like bright pinpricks splashed across his cheeks.

"But they're destroyed, right, Commander?" He sat on the sofa, twisting his cap between both hands.

"Yeah, they're dust."

"Well, that's something."

"Yeah, and that something is just the beginning of the clusterfuck about to rain down on our heads." Linc stood at the window, squinting into the evening light.

"Taft?"

"He's gone too," Linc replied.

The redhead pushed to his feet. "You should know Sabine's been riding my back recently. She thinks something's going on she's not privy to."

Linc spun around. "Just keep towing the line. We don't know where her allegiance lays yet."

"Affirmative."

He got in Ginger's face. "You've got more important things to do tonight than worry about her."

Johnson replaced his cap and pulled his shoulders back.

"Spread the word, Johnson. The timeline just moved up. We're taking control of Beta tomorrow."

He performed a snappy salute. "Yes, sir."

As soon as Ginger exited, I lashed out. "They erased Leon's memories!"

"Just be thankful they didn't eradicate him altogether." Linc's voice was cool, his gaze unemotional.

"Be thankful? He was in love with Darke! Now he doesn't even recognize him." I pulled my fists back to beat on something.

"Maybe it's for the best." He grabbed my wrists. "Think about it, Liz. My father just wrote me off in scrambling the DCICs with the intention of blasting Beta. What do you think he plans next?"

I already knew. "Total annihilation."

Clasping the sides of my face, he leaned in low, his expression finally softening. "Not many people are as strong as you."

"Leon is."

He touched our foreheads together, lips barely touching mine. "Good. He'll have to be."

I wound my fingers through his. "I would rather die and have loved you than have my memories erased of everything we've been through, even the bad, the worst, the things I didn't think I would survive, Linc."

The disciplined mask on his face shattered into fraught emotion before he whispered, "Me too." His mouth slanted fast and strong against mine, tongue thrusting deep.

Our frantic haste to be together, skin to skin, superseded everything. Beating heart and warm body to body. Clothing wasn't shed fast enough. We couldn't get to the bed quickly enough. I ended up splayed across the dresser, yanking open Linc's buckle, followed by his zipper. I hauled his combat pants down just enough; then he was in my hand—hot, solid. My knees were pressed against my tits. When he slammed into me, my spine skidded across the dresser and my neck fell back.

His grunt met my moan, and we moved against each other, grabbing everything we could—asses, necks, hair. Our mouths moved in wild syncopation, tasting, biting, licking through the groans grinding out of us with each powerful surge of Linc's cock into me.

This wasn't tender loving. This was fierce fucking, the need to be inside each other's bodies and souls, the only way we could.

I came and came again. Still he railed into me, getting up on the dresser, knees pressed against my ass, my thighs pushed so hard into my chest my breasts were flattened by the pressure of his grip on the back of my legs. I grabbed the ledge behind my head and watched him above me. Muscles corded, mouth pulled open, eyes staring into mine.

"Yes, yes. Fuck, Liz!"

Then my body released. Linc went deeper, fast and hard until he slid my legs around his waist. He gathered me in his arms and groaned rough in his throat. One large hand held me by my ass, convulsions rippling through his body.

A slow hand moved through my hair as I lay panting against him. Linc carried me to the bed, which was good, because I was completely boneless. He slid both arms around me and didn't say a word. He didn't have to. He was here. He was solid. He was alive. *We* were alive. It was enough.

"I love you," I whispered.

Only then did his body relax. Eventually, his breaths deepened, and I closed my eyes.

We'd caught a couple hours' shut-eye to be jerked awake by loud banging on the door.

I swiveled up with an Eagle. Linc leaped off the bed, his Heck in hand.

"Sir, COMMANDER! I've had word."

Ginger Johnson. I lowered my gun and covered myself with a shirt. Linc pulled on his sweats and sprinted down the hall.

I waited beside the bedroom door, listening.

"Talk to me," Linc said.

"There's movement in the city, alarms raised from S-4 to S-3, coming this way," a harried-sounding Ginger said.

"Who?"

"The CEO's Beta Corps."

"Fuck!" A fist slammed into the wall. Linc's voice came out like sheet metal grating at the edges. "Scramble our team; wait for me in Command. Lock it down. Lock our people in."

"Sir, yes, sir!"

Linc swept past me. He dressed faster than I could blink: guns holstered, key card stowed, D-Ps one and two palmed and pocketed.

"You stay here until I get back from HQ," he ordered.

We'd discussed what was gonna happen, and this wasn't how it was supposed to go down. I beat down my worry, holding all my fear inside. "Be safe, Linc."

Linc took my lips in a fast, deep kiss, a slight grin making a dimple appear in his cheek. For all those things, I was grateful.

Then he was gone. I sank against the door for a moment, swiping the tears I hadn't let him see. Then I geared up quickly. I checked my weapons, my D-P, and thought about sending up a prayer. I decided to open the chest that acted as a coffee table instead, took out our spare guns, and loaded those too.

Twenty minutes later, the doors slid open and Linc marched inside. I did an immediate check. He was unharmed. I was grateful for that, too, until he hooked my gaze and shook his head.

"He bugged out."

Linc had planned to take his father out silently, in his rooms at HQ where he usually holed up. He'd been prepared to kill his dad. My voice trembled and stuck. No man, no soldier, no son should ever have to face that.

He'd hoped to avoid a bloodbath, the kind that would come if Cutler caught wind of our plans and pressed the remaining loyal Beta Corps into action. Against us.

It was too late.

I swallowed all of that while he connected with his people—our people—and set the battle into real live color. He ordered, "Total evac of the Sector civilians pronto. Get them safe." He finished with a cold, "We are under attack! Commence Emergency Action Ops."

He slid the D-P into his pocket, eyeing the array of weapons I'd laid out.

"How soon is the militia here?" I asked.

"Twenty. Thirty tops."

He noted my gear, the cap on my head. He strode forward,

captured my hand, and placed it against his heart. His eyes weren't stormy; his vibe wasn't rocky. Clear icy blue and totally fucking solid, Linc closed his eyes for the breath of a moment. When he opened them, he said, "My father wants a full-fledged war; so be it. This will be done today."

In this moment, we were soldiers first, lovers second. We couldn't be together until this thing was finished. There would be no regroup at daybreak, and our line of attack had just been blown out of the water. Now was the time to advance, guns blazing.

Because we were gonna take Beta back.

Chapter Sixteen

Daybreak skirted the sky, but it was overshadowed by great clouds of gray smoke. People ran pell-mell through the streets of S-1 when we exited the Quad's gates. There was no birdsong this morning, just air-raid sirens and the fast crack of guns firing from far away, but not far enough.

"I said get these civvies outta here!" Linc sounded off to Ginger.

I heard the tail end of his tirade as I jacked in my earpiece, connecting with all the key players on our side of the war.

By the time we got near the action, the far outskirts of S-2, any straggling civilians had mercifully disappeared. The roads were deserted, the military action headed our way. It was the perfect place to lie in wait.

"Get in place." Linc spoke directly into my earpiece, squeezing my hand. I watched his lips move afterward beneath his helmet, a silent reminder for me alone. *Be safe. I love you.*

A compact RPG hefted over one shoulder and my rifle in

hand, I scaled the nearest fire escape while Moxie, minus her facial piercings, and cool-as-fuck Vance converged on Linc. By the time I'd slung myself to the rooftop and settled at the edge, Cannon, Darke, and Nate had joined the powwow below. What I saw behind their small gathering was awesome. Unbelievable. Five tanks flanked lines of soldiers—thousands of them—herding them toward central point. I knew Moxie and the others had been recruiting. I'd had no idea how successful they'd been. It blew my heart wide open. The sum of the numbers swelling the streets below lit the fire of hope in my chest.

Linc was on the horn to his forty-eight other handpicked Reformed Corps leaders, putting people into place. I marveled at the breathtaking scene of Revolutionaries, troopers, and Freelanders below. Each wore an article of red to signify the blood they were willing to shed for freedom, red to remember those who already had.

My yee-haw moment was cut short when a Loyalist tank fired hot artillery into our new united front. People I'd just watched, alive and well, blew apart. But not Linc. Not the others. There was no time to take a breath or say a fricking prayer of thanks. Our units scattered, keeping low and tight. Linc with his own mini army led to the north.

His voice steady through the jarring impact of his run, he demanded, "You got a mark on that tank?"

The bastard tank was too far away, with too many people in the way for a clean shot.

"On the move," I muttered into my mouthpiece.

"Affirmative," Linc returned.

Five buildings from the detonation zone, I got close enough. Locking in the target, I fired the RPG. I listened to the whistle of the rocket, the impact shuddering through my body when the tank combusted into flames.

"Tango down."

"Roger that. Maintaining northwest," Linc reported.

Breath jetting fast, I found myself in the middle of a shooting range. I was on the rooftop, my way blocked in every direction by a quad of snipers intent on me. *Fuck, fuck!* I did a running roll toward an air vent, taking a clip to my thigh. My head and body out of range of three of the gunmen, I hauled up my rifle and took out the marksman who otherwise would've had a full-body shot on me. The wound on my thigh was a graze I tied off with my red bandana. Bullets whizzed around my safe place. I unstrapped my helmet and tossed it into the air behind me as a target. A helmet full of holes was better than a head riddled with them. As soon as bullets started popping into my helmet, I sprang like a Jill-in-the-box and aimed: left, center, right. *Crack, crack, crack.* Dead, dead, dead.

Crawling to my decoy helmet, I remained low all the way to the ledge.

I'd tuned out the chatter on my earpiece during the impromptu target practice with me as the bull's-eye but couldn't ignore Linc when he rumbled over it, "Report, Grant. Stat. Stat."

In the middle of a full-scale battle and he was still riding my ass. "Staying frosty, sir."

"You take a two-minute time-out again, I'll not only strip your stripes; I'll stripe your ass."

My heart triple-timed with his threat.

"I'm counting on you, Lieutenant." *To make it out alive.* His growling voice was ripe with emotion.

I affirmed every part of his message with, "Double that."

I got fuzzy static after that, which meant my meaning was clear too. Racing along the rooftops, evading sniper fire, I cleared the high-rises of hazards. If Linc was headed northwest, so was I. Focusing on the battle below, I darted toward any hideaway I could find. I watched the red-ribboned warriors go at it, providing them cover when I could.

I'd just hurried onto a new roof-scape, gaining ground in S-3, when the roots of my hair tingled as if fuzzed by an electrical current. That current jolted straight up my spine when I recognized where the feeling came from. A Predator plane at least half the size of the rooftop hovered above me. It carved airborne sweeps to the left and then right of me, pinning me down. Red beams fastened onto critical points of my body as I crouched, rifle raised. Another Predator rose up on the opposite side of me. A pair of armed, sleek UCASs positioned to gun me through.

At least I'd had last words, of sorts, with Linc. Didn't stop me from calling out on my mouthpiece, "It's getting hot up here."

Tone thick with worry, Linc barked, "Don't care how you do it. Take the trash out or get your ass under cover."

That was a direct order.

I rolled to my back, looking right up into the fuselage of the drone plane. I waited until the second killing machine got close enough to flank the first, taking a big-brother position. Rifle hot in my hands, I let loose a short volley into the fuselage. I scrambled backward, watching the two planes collide as fire leaped from one vessel to the next.

The incinerating debris careened behind me. Metal tearing against metal screeched as I ran as if hell's mouth itself had opened behind me.

"Clear," I gasped.

This time there wasn't a cool, collected reply, only Linc's long exhale and short curse.

I kept to the high sides of the buildings after that episode, blending with shadows. Tanks trundled below, black, huge, and threatening. Some carried the *Posse Omnis Juvenis* symbol, but others were straight-up Beta Corps.

By the time I reached S-4, I'd fried three more tanks and was out of rockets. If nothing else, I could use the RPG as a bludgeon. My CheyTac rifle holding strong, I kept it raised for action. Although, surveying the scene, maybe I wouldn't be needing it here after all. Snaking up and down the thoroughfares, Beta Territory civilians weren't running for their lives. They were *fighting* for liberty.

Fighting with anything they could get their hands on: discarded weapons, debris from buildings. The streets teemed with people who were not backing down, not giving up.

The only ones giving up were Loyalist Corps troops with weapons dropped and hands raised—they wouldn't gun down innocent civilians. Maybe they didn't know what this battle was for anymore. The Revolution was turning on its axis right before my eyes.

"Give me a read, Grant," Linc burst across the coms.

"S-4, coming to you."

He sounded another long, deep exhale. "We're moving toward the bridge."

He must've hounded the Loyalist troops all the way to S-5 fringes, the final frontier of Beta before the Hudson River took over where the Territory walls left off.

Jesus. The ramparts of the old bridge were unstable, to say the least. Not to mention its lengthy span and just how much could go wrong if our team was strung out in the middle of it, over a Christly river with no escape route. In other words, it was not a good place to be.

I hurried to his location. Three minutes later, I clipped myself over the edge of a building, snicking down the tripod on my rifle, steadying the focus.

Linc didn't need me to tell him how bad this circle-jerk situation was, but apparently Moxie did. I was just in time to see her squad take to the bridge.

Sun shifted over the river, sending glassy brightness into my eyes, but I still managed to get a read on Linc.

"Behind you, left mark, high." I gave him my position.

I zoomed my sights on him. He dropped his head for a second before his voice came back. "Excellent, Lieutenant."

Linc motioned his troops forward to rearguard Moxie. He was at the head of the column. At the one-quarter point, the bridge erupted in a hail of steel, pavement, shrapnel, Moxie and her crew right in the middle of it. The explosion sent a wave of destruction outward, toward Linc, who sprinted directly into the maelstrom. Smoke thick as a cloud cover sucked him inside.

I started crawling off the roof, but I was brought up short by an arm wrapped around my windpipe. My gun knocked away, the unseen assailant hauled me off my feet. Clawing at the arm around my throat, I jerked my head down, biting my attacker. The arm only tightened, cutting off my curses. My airway constricted with no relief.

The rough scrape of my attacker's breath sounded winded. *If I can just hold out a little longer.* I wiggled, kicked, struggling. My eyesight dimmed. I was reaching blackout point.

A second earth-shattering explosion on the bridge sent a shock wave through my system. The first blast had brought Linc running onto the bridge. The second had been set off while he was on it.

"NO!" I screamed. And that was all she wrote.

* * *

I started to come around. Slowly, silently, and without moving a muscle. I was carried over someone's shoulder, my thighs, ankles, and wrists bound, my eyes blindfolded.

The noises I'd blacked out to—explosives, shouts and booms and blasts—were gone. It was dead quiet but for the *drip-drip-drip* of water leaking from a source above my head. Two pairs of footsteps rang loudly, echoing as if we were in a cavernous structure. It smelled musty and damp. The walking went on a long time while I noted the direction of each turn we made, mapping the route in my head. I clued into everything around me even though my heart screamed that Linc was…that he'd been… *The bridge was gone.*

I closed down every single response and focused on the bare minimum. Survival.

A door creaked open. The assailant carrying me slung me from shoulder to a seat. Long hair brushed along my arms as I was re-arranged. I was strapped to the legs of a chair by my ankles, and my arms wrapped around the back of the seat. I let my head hang loose on my neck.

Muffled words were exchanged; then one pair of footsteps retreated.

A knife slipped under the blindfold, quickly slicing the black cloth away. I scanned the area around me through low lids, not moving, barely breathing. The room was a dark hollow of damp brick, empty of all but me, my jailer, and the chair my ass sat on.

The tunnels I'd been hauled through, the fact Linc had wanted me to know about his father's personal underground barracks…the lack of light all figured into the fact I was back at Cutler's manse, exactly where my dad had been murdered. "I like you this way, bitch. Too out of it to run your mouth at me."

Sabine's voice hit me like a sucker punch to the stomach. We should've decommissioned her the first chance we got, not to mention the second or the third.

I lifted my head as fury pounded through me. "You brought me here to shoot the shit, or you still want to spend some girl time with yours truly? You missed me after Linc moved me in with him, didn't you?"

"Nah. I was just worried about losing my toehold with the CEO because of a slut like you. You see, I was keepin' tabs on Linc long before you came along. His daddy has trust issues.

When you showed up, you secured my position as—"

"Cutler's rat," I spat at her. That's what she'd meant... *Yeah, Grant. You don't know who you're working against.* Sabine's words in my dad's lab hadn't been a warning but a threat.

The butt of her knife crashed into my cheek. "Better than a barracks' rat."

Blood splattered my lips. I still smiled up at the round-faced whore. "This get you off, Burr? Thinking you're all powerful over me?"

"What gets me off is knowing you're gonna die here, with no one to save you."

I snorted. "It's gonna take more than a few knocks to the head for that to happen."

Her backhand hit the other side and my cheek bounced off the back of the chair, but fuck it, I could go another twelve rounds and still pop her in the gut, if my hands weren't tied.

"As I was saying, you almost messed up my sure thing with the CEO. Luckily for me, you kept fuckin' up, going to your dad's lab, cryin' to the commander. You're pathetic, Grant." She sank down before me, sliding the flat blade of her knife back and forth across her thigh.

I'd been held prisoner before. I'd been beaten. I'd learned my lover had killed my father. Sabine tapping into my weak points wasn't gonna work. I wiped the blood on my cheek against my shoulder. "Yet I'm still here."

"Not for long."

I leaned as far forward as I could, tied to the chair. "You wanna know what I think, Burr? You're pretty when you keep your cock holster shut. You're a good shot when you have your head tight. But mostly, you are a loose cannon, you got a loose mouth, and you're on the losing side of this war."

She stepped off. It seemed my words were almost as effective as my guns for weapons, so I kept at it.

"For the fucking record, and for the final time, I've been hurt far, far worse than anything you could ever dream up with your limited brain cells. So this"—I nodded around the room—"abduction? Do your worst, because you *will* die trying."

"I don't think so. No Commander Cannon to save you from this. Linc's offline," she barked in my face. "I've been ordered not to kill you, but I'm gonna love the show when the CEO gets here and gets to work on you."

"You fucked up, Sabine. You got in bed with one mean sonuvabitch snake, Cutler, and instead of having any honor, you ditched your calling to protect the people. You are an imposter, a traitor." As my words sank in, her go-to-girl grit began to waver. "Now, I don't know about you, but there's a goddamn war I gotta fight."

"You ain't going nowhere, chickie."

I rocked back in the chair when her knife pressed against my throat. "Go ahead. You could use more knife practice," I rasped.

Her blade skated under my chin to my cheek. "Maybe you won't be so pretty when I'm done. We'll see how the commander likes that."

"I'll still have Linc's love." I pressed into that blade a little harder, keeping her attention on my face and the trickle of blood trailing from my cheek.

"Not if you're dead." Sabine got closer.

Close enough.

I ripped my hands free of the plastic binding around my wrists. "I could say the same to you." Wrapping the cord once, twice around her neck, I started to strangle her. I jerked the ends tighter, watching shock and then fear scuttle across her face. The knife fell from her fingers before they flew to her throat, grabbing at the plastic strip. I gripped harder. Her eyes bulged; her mouth gaped.

Her breath gurgled, and on her dying gasp, I stated, "Like I said, *sister*, you fucked up. Your reward is a trip to hell."

I let her body drop.

I might have been able to wriggle out of the wrist binds, but my ankles were tightly strapped to the chair. Good thing Sabine had so courteously dropped the blade where I could reach it. I cut myself free, put the knife in my belt, and went to the door.

The tunnel was empty.

I backtracked by memory to the point where I'd regained consciousness on my trip down here. Daylight funneled in up ahead. I raced toward the opening, breached it, then almost wished Sabine had killed me below.

I stood on the highpoint of a hill, Beta spread out in the distance before me. Every word that Cutler had told Linc about the Amphitheater attack came back to me: *I better get rid of you or he'd blow up Beta with you in it.* Only I wasn't in it; Linc was.

Sky-wide mushroom clouds hung over the Territory. Predators cruised through them, dropping bombs I felt in my soul as if I were standing right in their path of destruction.

I fell to my knees, giving in to huge racking sobs. "Oh my God. Oh my God!" My hands stretched toward Beta. "LINC!"

I wept until there was nothing left but the need to get there, to find Linc, Cannon, Nate, and the others. I'd regained my feet when my shoulders were grabbed and I was spun about.

Denver's hands slid to my wrists, restraining me again.

"You sold us out!"

His black eyes bottomless and blank, he looked down at me. He showed no strain as I struggled to get free. His lips quirked. "Don't get hysterical, woman," he said, plucking my last weapon, Sabine's knife, from my belt and adding it to his arsenal.

"It's *Lieutenant*, and I don't get hysterical." Tears stained my face and my voice was hoarse from crying, but he wouldn't get inside my head.

That was a good thing to remember, because I was thrown over his shoulder—again, I assumed—and taken back below. He thrust me into the chair I'd escaped from. And a few moments later, CEO Cutler strolled into the room.

He stepped over Sabine's body without a second glance. "Take that away, Denver, before she starts to smell the place up."

Denver hefted Sabine into his arms and exited.

Cutler brought his hands together before him, watching me as I glared at him. "I'd thought Lieutenant Burr would be a worthy opponent against you. Clearly I was wrong." Cutler's gaze wasn't simply cold. It was empty of all humanity. It was as if he was missing the gene for feeling. That thought incited real fear in me as a small smile played over his lips.

Chapter Seventeen

It took all my restraint to keep from jumping on him. There had been so much loss in my life caused by him in one way or another. My dad and my mom. Judging by the inferno that was now Beta, it was a very real possibility I'd lost Linc too. His city, my friends, and now it looked like my life was gonna be the last thing Cutler would take from me.

"I'll wager you're wondering when I learned of Linc's and your defection."

"Actually, I'm wondering how it feels to know both your sons hate your rotten fucking guts." What the hell? I had nothing to lose.

Wearing his polished shoes and his immaculate suit, the CEO pressed templed fingertips to his lips over a smile.

I was suddenly thrilled I was here. If I got the chance to frag this monster in his own house, where he'd had my dad slaughtered, it'd be nothing short of poetic justice, and I needed a little poetry in my life.

"You could at least thank me for leaving you unbound this time. I thought it would be more sporting. Of course, if you continue to run your mouth in such a disrespectful manner, I might be forced to gag you."

"Like you put a gag order on my father?" I spat back at him.

He threw back his head with a laugh. "Excellent, Miss Grant. Yes. You *are* a spirited thing."

His amusement, his ingratiating compliment, made me feel like slicing and dicing through his solar plexus with a dull, rusty blade. Leaning forward, he said, "You see, a hard-liner girl like you, one who's been known to get her face punched in rather than double-cross on her friends, telling me she's going to hand them over all of a sudden? I smelled your treachery from a click away. You miscalculated, that and the fact Linc wouldn't raise his head to me."

"Took you long enough to wake up and smell the muck of your own making, didn't it?"

"Sabine did disappoint in that respect. I don't think she took her job keeping tabs on the two of you seriously enough. Thank you for cleaning up my dirty work." He had the audacity to wink at me.

"At the water tower, you really set it all up, didn't you?"

"Oh yes," he agreed. "And how did you find Leon to be?"

"Not right." My upper lip curled off my teeth in distaste.

"It seems Dr. Val was a little overzealous dispensing the pasithiatrics. You see, the fact your father came out of his conditioning after only eleven months almost ended her promising career."

My worst fears about Leon's time in Cutler's clutches—about his amnesia—confirmed. "Why did you want him?"

"Insurance policy, as Taft informed you."

"I don't buy it."

He snorted. "Good show, Grant. You shouldn't. I'll admit, some of the other Company backers and I got a little overenthusiastic, too, with the Pneumonic Plague back in fifty-eight, fifty-nine. A few otherwise staunch supporters even tried to pull out. Much to their surprise, they found themselves afflicted. Dead before they could talk. Quite like your mother, the lovely Peg. Dead before she could spill a word. But that wasn't my fault. She did it herself. No backbone to that one, not like you."

Ice ran through my veins, stealing into my heart.

Crazy fanatical Cutler couldn't look saner as he rolled out his insane reasoning for infecting multitudes of innocent civilians. "Your father and Dr. Val cooked up the Plague. A pair of geniuses, those two. Put them together, with me as their patron, the world could've been ours. It was the same deal I cut with Taft, but these prodigies are so susceptible to the artistic temperament. Which, you understand, is the original reason we outlawed the arts to begin with. Free thinking is far too dangerous to the Company credo." He paused to consider while I wrapped my brain around how deeply his depravity ran. "I'll have to get Val to invent an antidote to that as well, since my people keep growing consciences."

"It's all about uniformity, Lizbeth." My head snapped aside when he used the full name my dad had called me. "Homogeneity and heterosexuality are the founding principles of the InterNations government. Individuality, deviancy, differences destabilize communities. We can't have that, can we?" He was positively gleeful in his prejudice. "Purification of the genesis of our people was necessary after the Purge. We were trying to *purge* the population of their rebellious nature. It was as if the earth herself wanted it." He smiled dreamily.

Okay. He was only one lug nut loose, possibly two, from being totally unscrewed in the head.

"In order to remain strong forty years on from the Purge, we had to bring the people back to critical mass. We had to justify the RACE laws and get rid of all undesirables at the same time. Blaming it on a homosexually transmitted disease was the answer—if one contracted the so-called Gay Plague, that was proof you were guilty."

"Children died! Mothers, fathers, completely blameless citizens!" My arms knotted with tension, so ready to strike out.

"It got slightly out of control, and we shut it down."

"You make me sick."

Cutler squared his shoulders. "That won't happen this time. The Revolution will end soon, and I will be head of the InterNations."

"That doesn't explain what you wanted with Leon." If I could keep him talking, I could buy time. To file my fingernails, finger my empty holsters, count my dying breaths, it didn't matter.

"Monsieur Cheramie is a whore."

"Your people made him that way, paid scrip to keep him that way!"

"I didn't think you'd have a soft heart, Lieutenant. It almost seems as if you consider Leon an equal."

Leon was so far above my equal. I'd bleed for him the same way I'd give my last breath for Linc.

"Those DCICs, weren't they glorious?" he asked, unaffected by my outburst.

Taft choreographing his creatures had been unbelievable, unlike anything I'd ever seen. And I never wanted to see the likes of them again. "I'm glad they're destroyed."

"Philistine." He tutted.

Evil bastard.

"Leon was an impersonal mark. But very personal to *y'all*." He straightened the cuffs at his wrists. "I really just wanted to measure how much the boy meant to you all, especially that warrior Darke."

"And the DCICs?"

"Written off. I have a secondary delivery system in place, and no one will want to kill it. One thing I learned from losing Eden is never put all your eggs in one basket."

My nerves jangled with every soft warning he spoke. "Why am I here? I don't have anything you could possibly want."

"Well, you do have Lincoln." He paced around me, and I forced myself to stare straight ahead. "Such a fine, brave soldier. An excellent commander, my Linc. Unfortunately, it's likely his love for you will have gotten him killed."

I sucked in a breath, held it.

"You see, it's hard to love a woman, give her everything. It's harder when she takes your heart and runs away. I do know about that."

"Eden ran from you because you beat her."

"So you do know where she is. I thought you might. Of course we both know where Nathaniel is, too, probably sharing a rubbly grave with his twin and that *faggot* Cannon." He returned to face me, no remorse showing on his sharp features.

"Don't you even care about them? Aren't you the least bit sorry?"

A flicker of emotion passed over his face; then it was gone. "I regret I ever let Eden make a deal with me. I detest that Nathaniel decided he was queer, throwing away his career so he could fuck a man, knowing full well I would disown him and put a bounty on his head. What other choice did I have? I am the CEO, after all."

Unable to take any more of his shameless bullshit, I spit at him. It hit the fine fabric of his trousers, then his gleaming leather shoes. He merely chuckled and bent to wipe it away with a handkerchief.

"My, my, you do have a temper, don't you? I'll bet you're a feisty piece in bed. I can almost see how you managed to snag Linc. Trapping him with your wiles, capturing his devotion through your cunt. That's the way of a woman."

"What about Linc?" I bit through the words as if they were bullets.

"You've got quite a lot of tenacity, too. I'm sure that's done you well with the Corps." He tapped his lip, considering. "It does distress me that I had to employ such extreme measures with Lincoln. I'd hoped he would be beside me when I took my true place as the undeniable ruler of the InterNations government."

My mouth trembled and tightened. Tears threatened to fill my eyes, tears of anger, tears of anguish. If nothing else, I wanted to know Linc was alive before I died, but I wasn't stupid enough to think I'd ever see him again.

"I kept abreast of your dealings from the day your father joined the effort to rid the world of rebel factions." A fire leaped in his irises, hate the only feeling that fueled him. "I had to make sure you didn't know anything."

"All those years…" Spyware was one thing; it was expected, part of the daily routine. But the idea Cutler had kept tabs on me for a decade made my skin crawl.

"You joining the Corps worked in my favor, made my surveillance effortless. I know about your close friendship with Cannon. Your forays to the black market, your illegal purchases. All indiscretions I could excuse as curiosity because I decided I liked your vim." His eyes narrowed into hard blue points. "But when you turned up in Beta, started sticking your nose into Robie Grant's business, spreading your greedy legs and using my favored son to dig for information, I'm afraid you tested the last of my patience, my dear."

I shot to my feet. "What do you want from me?"

"The digi-diary, the one that belonged to your father."

A harsh laugh rose from my chest. "That old thing?"

"Do not toy with me, my dear." His hands swung out fast, curling around my upper arms. "I'm the lion; you're the gazelle. I'll tear you to pieces, making sure you're kept alive while I do it, until I get what I want."

"You got me all wrong." I drove my knee into his groin and yanked my arms free. "I'm a tigress."

Faster than I would've believed, he was fully upright again.

The patience I'd tested cracked. "I need the goddamn digi-diary so I can bury the information about the Plague once and for all. Tell me where it is."

"I don't have it. It's too late anyway." I dodged past him.

He grabbed my arm, whirled me around. A Glock already in hand, he pistol-whipped me across the face. Starbursts of light popped in my eyesight. A sunburst of pain spread from my cheek.

I lifted my hand to my face, looking down as my fingers came away bloodied. "Good. Now I've got bruises to match the ones Sabine gave me. I like to be symmetrical."

"You stupid bitch." He captured my chin in a tight grip. Jerking my face to the other side, he prepared for a second blow when the door slammed open.

Linc filled the doorway, breathing heavily, his face covered in a veil of ash, his uniform torn. In the split second it took him to draw his gun on his father, my heart exploded with wild hope.

Cutler turned to his son, his Glock trained on me, and smiled in greeting. "I had a feeling you'd survive. You've been instilled with my determination. Now the real fun begins."

"What the fuck did you do to her face, *Father?*"

"Let's just say my efforts at diplomacy failed." Cutler smirked. "She's got grit, your girl. Now, if you wouldn't mind, drop the gun, Lincoln."

The seething rage that rolled off Linc contorted his face into an animalistic snarl until he was a living mass of fury. When Linc's finger twitched on the trigger, Cutler swung the gun down and fired. *Sonuvabitch, that hurts.* He'd gouged a hole near the steel toecap of my boot.

Linc raised his gun, unloading into the ceiling before flinging it aside. "Do not touch Liz again." Directly in front of his father, his voice shook with a very thin thread of control. "I will rip your head from your body."

Linc's eyes scanned over me. He wasn't happy with what he saw. His jaw snapped, and his indigo irises crystallized with wrath.

Cutler backed me up to the chair and placed me in it. The gun muzzle remained pressed under my chin.

"I'm okay, Linc."

Fists tight by his sides, his chest pumped in and out as his gaze darted between his father and me. He didn't believe me, and I wouldn't have either. Rising welts on both sides of my face, a trickle of blood oozed from my boot. Sweat and grime covered me head to toe. I was pretty sure I looked like a pinup for a full-on D-P display of why messing with the CO was not a good idea.

"Isn't that sweet? She's trying to allay your worries. You've done her good, Linc; you softened up the shrew."

"So help me—"

Cutler cut him off. "I'm glad you showed up. I wouldn't want you to miss what I have to say next."

"What?" Linc's eyes sheared toward him.

"You remember that day you assassinated Liz's father?"

Linc paled. "She already knows. Any way you think you can twist this, you can't. It's done."

I concur whole-freakin'-heartedly with that sentiment.

"Perhaps." Cutler looked as magnanimous as a messiah in front of his disciples. "What you never knew, though, is that you didn't actually make the kill shot. I did."

"What?" My feet stamped to the floor so I could fly upward, but Cutler's hand planted on top of my head kept me chair-bound.

His wide grin took up all the airspace in front of me as he leaned over. "Linc couldn't carry through; he hesitated too long. His trajectory was off. He missed. But I fired at the same time. Made sure the deed was done. I killed your father."

Cutler pulled the gun away, and my head dropped. Tears I'd been fighting slid over my cheeks. Relief at Linc's innocence, the desperate desire to live, it all tumbled out of me.

The CEO pressed on, preying on both our emotions. "Keeping you in the dark all this time—letting your guilt fester—was an excellent means of control and motivation over you, son."

I wiped my face, needing to see Linc. He'd swallowed his own surprise, standing with arms crossed over his chest. His breath had slowed, his hot emotion cooled into a deadly demeanor.

The decade of shame and remorse Linc had endured, the worst of it coming when he met me, fell in love with me, convinced all that time he'd murdered my dad. "I'm so sorry, Linc," I whispered. *I'm sorry I ever doubted you.*

His hand lifted toward me, but Cutler cut between us, always with the gun on me.

"Sending you to inform Liz and Peg was punishment for your failure to be a man and commit to the plan of ridding us of our problem with Robie Grant. You had to prove your mettle some-how."

"He was only fourteen!" I screamed out.

"That extra-sick detail you ordered me to carry out? You are an

abomination, Father. Your mother should've killed you at birth."
Linc leveled lethal eyes on Cutler.

A flicker of astonishment flashed across Cutler's face before he
wiped it away. He spun toward me. "I guess it falls on me to finish
the job my son signed on for."

"Father, don't."

"What? You haven't told your little bed warmer here the
whole truth? I'm shocked. I thought there were no more secrets
between you."

Dread flooded my system.

Cutler advanced. "I'm sure he told you he was protecting you
by keeping you close, safeguarding you from me probably. But
why do you really think he let you reenlist? Why did he move you
in with him? Why has he been fucking you, *sweetheart*?"

If he was trying to rattle me, it worked, especially when Linc
shouted, "I said stop!" He drove forward, snapping his forearm
around his father's throat.

Cutler held his gun steady, point-blank on my face. The trigger
ticking back made Linc withdraw his arm.

"That's better." Cutler preened. "You come at me again, and
she's dead on the spot." Then he unleashed another tit twister on
me. "Linc was supposed to murder you. That's why he's been so
attentive to you, my dear."

"That's not true! In the beginning, I agreed to it, but I never
planned..."

"No, no, no," I muttered. The CEO had let his last little bit
of nasty out of the bag, playing us against each other. The only
way he could kill our love was if he shot me straight through the

heart…with a gun, not his wheedling words. Linc and I had already paid our dues.

I straightened my shoulders and stared him down. "Too bad for you he didn't do it, right?"

I took considerable pride in his blanch while he backpedaled. "You don't think the fact he considered it should perhaps be a slight demerit against him?"

In Linc's eyes, intense and raw, I saw the bitterest regret, more of the hated guilt.

"Nah." I shrugged. "He loves me; he didn't do it. He wouldn't have. Believe me. I gave him more than enough ammo on plenty of occasions. I can be quite a handful. Which is why I've got one thing to say to you." Absolute calm filtered through me, and I smiled. "Fuck you, Lysander Cutler."

In that moment, with my affirmation, I watched Linc try to absorb all the power my love gave him. Love that defeated all the deceit his father had brought down on him. Love, from Linc to me, which had delivered me from a lonely, hollow existence.

We were stronger together. We could still beat Cutler.

A gun would be handy, too.

Perhaps Cutler sensed imminent failure, because he suddenly did a one eighty, holstering his firearm.

"Come with me, my son. I offer clemency for you and your *lover.*" He swept a hard gaze over me. "If she vows allegiance to my cause. I extend the same to Nathaniel, of course. Where is he? Has he not come to see me off?"

Linc had swallowed more than enough of his father's crap for a lifetime. His voice throbbed in a growl. "Nathaniel's waiting to off you, maybe."

"Is that any way to speak to me?" Cutler asked.

Clearly, the mad motherfucker had a severe case of tunnel vision if he thought for one instant Linc was gonna fall back in line. It was so appalling, I found it amazing that he still hoped for a total Cutler dynasty.

"You are no longer my blood kin, Lysander Cutler." Linc's eyes carried a detached calm.

"We'll see about that. Speaking of blood relations, how is your mother? You know how much I miss her. Perhaps I should pay a visit to Chitamauga." He tried a new tactic.

The threat hung between the two men before Linc smiled. "I've never been gladder our momma got away from your sick, twisted facsimile of love."

Thrown off his step, Cutler started for me again, but Linc blocked his way, forming a wall of man and muscle and menace between his father and me. I watched from behind him while he faced Cutler down.

"You asked about Nathaniel? He's a little busy right now." Linc pulled out a D-P from his jacket. "You'll want to watch this, *Dad*."

Their attention turned to the D-P as Linc fired it up. I had just enough time to locate Linc's forgotten firearm, directly in front of me. Sticking to the cover Linc's body provided, I slid off the chair. I crouched low and picked the gun off the ground, tucking it into his waistband.

I heard Linc's D-P hum to life, and there was no way I was

gonna miss this. I didn't give a shit if Cutler shot me on the spot. *No way* was I gonna lose the chance to watch his prospects for Cutler's One World Order crumble before his very eyes.

When the broadcast started up, my throat constricted.

These are validated recordings of the digi-diary and documents that belonged to Robie Grant, First Class Medical Officer and Chief Geneticist. First of January, 2019 through Fourth of July, 2060.

Document: Pneumonic Plague: 30-March-2059

"The mutation is live, viable. Genetically altered plague will be ready to spread in three weeks, targeting the growing rebel subculture. Its toll will be devastating. The CEOs are pleased. I received a personal note of commendation from Alpha CEO Cutler himself."

Document: Live: 31-May-2059

"InterNations Plague Event has gone airborne. Subjects planted in all sixteen Territories have been reported infected, the surrounding area swiftly making black marks on the geo-maps."

This time I watched with thrilling wonder mixed with the choking horror I'd initially felt. Nate had spliced the memocasts and data files together to create a concise video of all the CO's wrongdoings and CEO Cutler's part in it.

Cutler tried to knock the D-P from Linc's hands, but Linc's grip was strong. "What the hell is this, Lincoln?"

"I believe it's Robie Grant's personal data and recordings. Remember? The ones you didn't want Liz to get her hands on."

The promo spot wasn't over. My favorite part was yet to come as I heard my dad's voice ringing true and clear.

26-June-2060

"I helped engineer the Pneumonic Plague, what the Company re-

named the Gay Plague, to use as an internal and deadly deterrent against all deviants. Only a year and a half ago."

Another short statement followed, the screen alive with my dad's confessions and accusations.

28-June-2060

"The death count keeps climbing. I have a responsibility to the citizens of the InterNations. I can't let this go without blame, without taking the blame myself."

For the first time, Cutler appeared visibly dazed. His lips compressed in a whitened line, fists tight at his sides.

29-June-2060

"I'm going to whistle blow. I won't have much time after the announcement."

Robie Grant, First Class Medical Officer and Chief Geneticist, murdered by the Company, 4th of July, 2060.

My father's face melted into a stark black background.

Cutler let loose a caustic laugh. "You think to bring me down with this?" His hand waved negligently toward the D-P. "A recording on your D-P? Give me some credit, son."

Credit was due a second later when giant red letters exploded onto the screen.

DON'T BELIEVE THE FEED! THE GAY PLAGUE WAS COMPANY CREATED AND DISTRIBUTED TO YOU: ITS CITIZENS. THE SECOND PLAGUE STRAIN IS ON THE HORIZON. WE CAN STOP IT TOGETHER. THE FIGHT STARTS NOW. JOIN THE REVOLUTION. LIVE IN FREEDOM, LOVE AT WILL!

I'd learned to ignore the daily D-P feeds, but this one, *this one,* was so out of place, so totally in your face, it couldn't be ignored or unseen.

"What...what is the meaning of that?" Cutler's white-lined lips barely moved. He ripped the D-P from Linc's hands, hurling it to the brick wall. It shattered to pieces. "What have you done?"

Linc and I stood together before him, tight in our hearts and our mission.

I spoke clearly, making every word count. "That was a live broadcast. It just went out on all the D-P channels, *InterNation-swide*, thanks to your other son, Nate."

Victory spread through me, overwhelming me. We'd fulfilled my father's last wish. To get the truth out to the besieged people of the InterNations Territories, *worldwide*.

Cutler dusted his palms on his trousers, yanked his cuffs. All the while, a measured breathing pattern forced its way in and out of his chest.

When he looked up, the calculation was back. "Think you're going to save the Revolution? You two and your army of Nomad dimwits and whatever Corps castoffs you can rummage up? You think this transmission will change what I have planned?"

Drawing the gun from his back, Linc said, "Yeah, that's exactly what I think."

Cutler's face turned into a macabre snarl as he watched the weapon lifted in his son's hand. "You couldn't kill her father. You certainly don't have it in you to kill your own. You've become as weak as your brother."

Steely of voice, Linc replied, "It's time to end this."

"Yes. Yes, it is."

Cutler swung so fast, I didn't see it coming. From one glorious second to the next not-so-glorious, the impact of the slug to my sternum flipped me off my feet. Breath wheezed in and out of my lungs. Cutler's words sliced through my shock. "I won't be stopped."

I blinked and he was gone, replaced by Linc.

"Easy there, sweetheart." Mortal terror warped his features. "Oh Christ!" He saw where the bullet hit the left side of my chest. Both his hands over mine, he lowered his head until glowing blue eyes filled my vision. "You keep breathing. Keep breathing for me, Liz!"

"You have to"—I curled up, a gasp cutting through my words—"go after him."

"Are you out of your fuckin' mind? I'm not going anywhere!" He looked deranged. "We've gotta stop the bleeding."

"It's okay. I'm fine…" I whispered.

Face torn apart with despair, he barely kept it together. He ripped my shirt open. "Oh God. Oh…"

I looked down to see his fingers slipping under the body-armor vest, between it and my breast. I'd been goddamn shot. Another bruise for my collection.

"You wore a vest."

"Not totally foolhardy; remember to tell Cannon."

Hoarse cries came out of him, and he clasped my face in both trembling hands. "Thank you. *Jesus Christ*, Liz, thank you."

"Told you I'm always coming home to you…"

Linc pulled me onto his lap, smoothed his hands all over my body, gentling his touch when he reached my injured foot. His voice was raspy. "Don't you ever, *ever*, get in the way of a bullet again; you hear me?"

I pressed my mouth to his throat, letting a sigh swell through me because I had him. He was here. We hadn't won, not by a long shot, but we'd made a direct hit to Cutler's supposedly bulletproof shield. Beta might've fallen, yet the two of us had weathered the biggest, ugliest storm.

I whispered through tears, "Still riding my ass, Commander?"

His laugh was forced. His heart boomed steadily against mine. "Can you just let me be grateful that you're safe for a moment before you give me any more lip, Lieutenant?"

I nodded, my hands wandering over him. I captured his gaze and then his lips.

It would've been nice to catch some downtime, but that was still one major dream we had to make come true. Despite the fact I'd been kidnapped, we'd both been strung up, and I'd been shot twice in the past six hours, returning to Beta to pick up the pieces probably outfactored our desire to sit in the bunker and canoodle for hours.

Although my legs were working as well as all my other ambulatory parts, Linc wouldn't let me walk out of the tunnels. I didn't bother putting up a fight because having his arms wrapped around me was the best thing I'd felt all damn day.

He knew every turn and tunnel, swiftly steering through the underground to topside. Outside, the air smelled smoky, a strong wind rustling from Beta. It had grown dusky—whether that was from the time of day or the leftovers from the Territory explosions, I couldn't tell.

What I did surmise, when we approached the Cruiser parked out front, was we weren't alone. A long, dark shadow leaned against the driver's side door. Denver. Placing me behind him, Linc pulled his weapon.

Denver approached, hands up in front of him. The scars on his angular face shimmered in the half-light. Black ponytail swinging to one side of his lean hips, he bowed his head in greeting. "*Konbanwa*, Linc. I'm supposed to kill you."

"Go ahead and do it, but don't you goddamn touch her."

A low chuckle rippled from Denver. "You don't think the both of you would be shaking hands with the reaper by now if I intended to follow through with orders?"

"You might die trying."

Denver staged closer. "You could say thank you."

"I could also take you out right now." Linc shoved right up against Cutler's personal-protection detail. "You played a part in my woman's capture. Think that sits well with me?"

"Hey, *bokuno tomodachi*, it would've gone worse for her if I wasn't there. I only walked her down, tied her up. I could tell she had body armor on."

"A vest wouldn't have stopped a bullet to the brain, you cocksucker."

Brushing past Denver, Linc deposited me in the vehicle. He tucked me gently inside before turning back. "I'm gonna get payback from you. You owe me now."

"Plenty of time for that." Denver dipped his head. "But how about this, for starters? The CEO is headed to Omega. With Dr. Val."

"That's enough to keep me from doing the deed right now."

"And what do these grant me?" From both inside pockets of his tunic, he palmed my Desert Eagles.

My breath skipped when he handed them over to Linc. The muscle along Linc's jaw ticked. "*Arigatou.* I'm still gonna collect."

With another bow, Denver departed, Linc watching all the way. After the man vanished from sight, Linc rounded the vehicle and slipped inside. He started the engine, then ran his arm around my shoulders to hold me near.

Tired beyond words, I slumped against him.

"You can sleep, sweetheart. I got you now."

I squeezed my eyes shut, hovering on the edge of hope.

Chapter Eighteen

June 5, 2071

Scrapes, scars, scares…I've had enough to last me one life-time and the next too. Sometimes the battle scars earn me respect; more often Cannon razzed my ass for being cocky and careless. That's okay, because we're all here, and the visible wounds—including the goddamn toe graze from Cutler—are much less substantial than the internal kind Linc helped heal.

Yeah, we're all here, and for the moment, it's all good. We decamped from Beta twelve days ago. Not in defeat, but in victory, one that had a ripple effect through the rest of the Continental Territories. The civil war is over, at least in the former United States of America.

The planes might've bombed the hell outta Beta, but we aren't about to write it off. Not like Cutler, who did a cut and run, heading abroad. Damn good thing he did too. The Corps surrendered. The Posse, too, cutting the CEO off from his army of diehards. The remaining higher-ups too stupid to have evac plans were rounded up, indicted, and jailed in the recommissioned RACE Tribunal. Their hearings for countless atrocities are on the docket.

I looked up from my book, a hardbound journal Linc had snuck into my duffel before we left Beta, along with the slinky gray dress he'd bought me...and the lingerie. I smiled, remembering his self-satisfied look when I rolled my eyes and unpacked the layers of girly shit he'd hidden among my ammo, leathers, weapons.

He had my number from day one. And the smug bastard knew it, too.

Cannon caught me caressing—fucking *caressing*—the leather cover of my journal from across the fire. He pretended to stroke one out, hand cupped to his crotch. I flipped him the finger. As if he had any room to make fun of me. He'd just finished showing Nate a picture of some rare bird he'd snapped with his D-P earlier in the day, a habit he'd taken up while escorting Nate to the Brier last autumn. So I didn't feel like such a schmuck about my writing, even though Cannon got a dig in whenever he could.

The Quad survived, most of S-1 and S-2 as well. Linc's own survival was a close call, one I don't dare inspect. My heart still drops when I think about him running onto the bridge to save Moxie and her troops.

We're traveling to Chitamauga Commune. Sebastian opted to join us; Farrow too. My lover and my ex in close quar-

ters…fun times for all. Ginger Johnson stayed behind. Leaving him in charge of Beta during our absence might be a mistake, but there isn't a whole lot left for him to mess up. Besides, rebuild is in the future—Linc and I won't leave the Territory to a fate of dust, rubble, and death.

Ginger's acting as Linc's proxy on the Governmental Convocation until Linc returns to his rightful place as one of the leaders of Beta, just not as his father had schemed. Vance is in charge of the Reformed Corps, and Moxie, once recovered, is tasked with working with the civilians to get the infrastructure back online. The plan for Beta and the other two Continental Territories, Gamma and Epsilon, is to follow the Alpha model. Representatives from the citizens, the Corps, the Freelanders, the Revos coming together.

I've informed everyone—three times over per Cannon, of course—about what the CEO divulged while he held me captive. We still have no idea what he plans for his secondary assault tactics.

Bookmarking my journal with a finger, I laid my head against the log propped behind me. Wood popped, sizzling in the fire at my feet, used to cook our evening vittles. Summery days had been our constant on the journey south. We'd commandeered three vehicles, taking them straight down Alpha-Beta Route 2. No hostiles, no hotspots; it was damn near peaceable out here.

A few days ago, we'd ditched the battered convoy, heading inland. No roads into the Wilderness, we hiked on foot for the last leg. But we were gonna change that, too. There'd be no more gates, walls, checkpoints. The communes speckled around the Wilderness wouldn't be orphans cut off from the Territories anymore.

Stretching out, I wiggled my feet and winced as the irritating bullet wound sent a sliver of pain up my calf.

"That booboo hurting you, Grant?"

I scowled across at Cannon. "Not as much as I'm gonna hurt you when I use your ugly mug for target practice."

He beckoned the fingers of both hands at me in challenge.

I raised one Eagle and blasted it into the night sky instead of at his grinning face. "Asshole."

"Pussy," he returned.

"I got one. You wanna see it?" I asked.

Linc appeared beside me. From far above, he glanced down with a formidable frown. "Yeah, I think you're done here."

I beamed up at him. "Am I, *sir*?"

"Liz." His mouth tightened over my name.

"*Mm?*"

He raked his hands through his hair, then ass-planted beside me, drilling a glare at his brother-in-law, for all intents and purposes.

I swept a quick kiss along his cheek. "I wasn't really gonna whip it out for him. Besides, Cannon's seen it before in the locker room, just like I've seen his johnson—"

"Do not need to hear any more of that." Linc's fingers hushed me. "You got me by the nut sack here; you know that?"

I chewed the corner of my mouth, swallowing my grin. *Damn right I got you, babe.*

*It's the night before we reach Chitamauga. Things are good be-
tween Linc and Nate, even better between Linc and me. It's
been near on twenty years since Linc had contact with Eden.
I'll never understand the sacrifice he gave for his brother, his
mother, at his own expense.*

I tucked my hand under Linc's biceps, feeling the hard flex of
his muscle at my touch.

His lips trailed to my ear. "Need you, Liz."

My desire for him became a hot coil of need. I closed the book,
shut my eyes, and nipped his strong jawline. The hoarse rumble
from his chest vibrated against my hand, and my eyes snapped
open.

Leon sat diagonally across the fire, Darke directly in his sights,
and he was watching the bigger man with his sleepy golden eyes.
Darke was no better, staring at his should-be lover, broad palms
running up and down his thighs.

The action clearly a turn-on to Leon, he licked his lips and a
breathy, "*Mon Dieu,*" rolled out of him.

They'd never been truly together before, and they certainly
weren't now. Leon still didn't know what had happened to him
at Doc Val's hands. Darke was all new to him and more off-limits
than ever before because Darke was using Leon's amnesia to keep
his distance.

That didn't do a damn thing to stop their attraction, though.

Fingertips coasted along my neck. Calloused, rough, warm. I
turned toward Linc as a shiver made its way down my spine from
his touch.

"Time to hit the sack, sweetheart."

I shut up shop quick because the glint in his eyes meant I was gonna get some. Not that I hadn't been getting it plenty all along the road. Every pit stop was a chance to *hit it hard,* and the best part was, there was no quitting Linc.

Farrow wound one fair curl around her fingertip. "I call her *sweet girl.*"

Cannon elbowed Nate in his ribs, watching us.

Damned woman. Even when she gets what she wants—Linc and me together—she's still a prissy little troublemaker.

On his feet, Linc held his palm out to me. "She is that, too."

"Maybe when she keeps that sassy lip zipped." Cannon tossed aside the stem of grass he'd been chewing.

Linc stroked his thumb across my *sassy* mouth. "She's usually too busy with this to do much talkin'."

Cannon laughed. Nate looked like he was gnawing the inside of his cheek to keep from smiling, and Linc was one word away from getting his thumb broken off...by me.

I squared off with Cannon. "Go ahead and laugh, lover boy. Just remember who had your back before *Blondie* got all up in there." I turned to Linc, fingers on my holsters. "And you? You best be rethinking talking trade secrets about me or you'll be shacking up with your *little bro* and his boy toy in their tent, maybe in the Love Hovel, too."

A teasing grin pressed the dimples into his cheeks. "Wasn't complaining about what you do with that sexy mouth of yours, babe."

"Good. Get your hot ass in the tent before I rip your clothes off right here." I swished ahead of him, swinging my rear.

He cleared his throat, said some kind of good night, and hustled after me.

As soon as we were inside the flaps, he seized my lips with his. His breath beat hot and fast against my mouth when he rasped, "Gonna rip my clothes off, Lieutenant?"

I curled a leg around his thigh, rubbing against his solid erection. "Yeah." I tore the buckle on his pants open and yanked the button and fly apart. Palms flat on his stomach, I traced the dense muscles up to his pectorals, taking his shirt with me.

His shirt tossed aside, I skimmed my fingers along the muscled slopes of his arms and around to his lats, lastly settling on the deep grooves of his pelvis, where his pants clung to lean hips. Linc's body clenched with each of my touches. He groaned and twisted when I explored his chest with my lips.

"Definitely not complaining about your mouth now." He grunted, thrusting his hips forward.

A dirty laugh escaped me. His cock was a thick bulge in his pants. I lazily cupped him in one hand, trailing my fingertips over his cloth-bound length. "What if I put my mouth down here?"

His neck arched, cords of muscle straining beneath tanned skin. "Fuck, yes."

I licked from the flat discs of his nipples to the line of hair leading to his groin, lapping the soft, springy curls. A wreath of hair widened at the base of his shaft, revealed by his opened pants.

I buried my nose in his thatch. "You smell so good."

Strong fingers convulsed on my shoulders.

Pressing my mouth inside the placket, I licked as much of his length as I could reach, teasing him with my tongue. "You taste hot, delicious, Linc."

His abs clenched as I worked his pants away from his wide shaft with my lips, my tongue, my teeth touching and kissing. The steel-hard bar of iron-hot cock slapped against his stomach once finally freed.

"*Ah*, yes, woman."

I immediately sucked him into my mouth. Shuddering when the flared head bumped the back of my throat, I took him even farther inside.

His groans thundered through me, sending wicked pleasure from my breasts to my sex. Wet, wild need swelled my pussy. I thrust my mouth back and forth on him and started to yank my fatigues open. I was desperate to sink my fingers into myself.

Linc withdrew from my mouth. I kneeled in front of him, gasping. His lips were red, cheeks bright, eyes dark. His cock stood against his belly, and he shivered from head to toe, watching me watching him.

I licked along the inside of his thigh, smiling when he slipped one hand through my hair, the other across my lips, which were wet and shiny from his use.

"Greedy woman."

"Linc." I gasped when his thumb pushed inside my mouth.

"You were gonna fuck your fingers?"

I nodded, biting the pad of his thumb.

"I got perfectly good hands, right here."

These hands are not just for death.

I sat back on my heels. "I need you."

Features stern, he said, "Get up."

I lifted my arms and undulated against him the same way I did when he sat in a chair with me on top of him, fucking him, bucking on him. "You want me to shut up, too? Because you'll have to put something back in my mouth to accomplish that, Commander."

He inhaled sharply, staring at my breasts pressing against my thin shirt. "Get. Up."

"Yes, sir." I complied, my belly full of upside-down daisies.

Taking my top in both hands, he tore it down the middle. I gasped and shivered. He gathered my naked torso to his, stilling me with a kiss and husky words in my ear. "Stay still."

"I can follow orders."

"Prove it."

In less than thirty seconds, my socks, panties, and pants were destroyed. My toes curled into the soft blanket beneath us, but otherwise I didn't move. Linc lowered me to my knees and planted my hands on the ground in front of me. Prodding my thighs as wide apart as they'd go, Linc covered my back from behind. His heat baked me. His thighs pressed against the back of mine. His cock sat hard at my entrance.

I arched against him, and he pinned my hands within one of his at the base of my spine. My hips writhed, my ass lifted to him. Linc rode his shaft along the seam of my sex, his cock butting my clit, scorching me with every blunt-headed pass.

"Ask me for it, Liz."

"For what?" I shot back.

One hand drove into my hair, and he drew my head back to

the harsh thrust of his tongue in my mouth. "For my cock, ask me."

I bit down on his forearm, trying not to moan.

"Beg me for it. Beg me for my cock, Liz. You're soaking, swollen. You want it." His lips hovered just out of reach of mine when I lifted my head.

"You should be begging me."

"You want this?" Dipping inside, the crown of his cock filled me, made me drop my head, raise my ass to take more inside.

A hand on my spine stopped me from moving. "I said ask."

"Take me, Linc, please."

"I'm not gonna take you. I'm gonna fuck you. Hard. But not until you make me." He drew back, tapping my pussy, entering a little bit, chuckling when I moaned.

He pulled out again.

"Jesus Christ, Linc, fuck me!"

One fast lunge filled me, stole my breath. Deep inside me, he stilled.

"Oh God. *Don't stop, Linc.*"

Arms traversing my belly, he drew me up against his chest. His thighs rubbed inside mine as he pumped into me fast. He assaulted my nipples with short twists of his fingers. I slipped a hand down to fondle his warm, damp sacs as he plunged in and out of me.

His lips slid across my neck on hot kisses. I clamped down on him as soon as he circled my clit with a finger, teasing an orgasm out of me. I thrashed in his arms, screaming with my release, wild as he continued his masterful onslaught.

"Yes, Liz." He held my hips, pulling me onto his cock over and over.

I didn't feel bad about being a moaner. I bet Cannon and Nate were going at it, too. This time it wouldn't be the Love Hovel shaking but the tent coming apart at the seams. As another orgasm burst through me, I laughed.

"This funny?" Linc pressed me onto the floor of the tent on my stomach and spread-eagled me. He prowled between my thighs and guided his cock back inside me.

"No." I gasped.

Every merciless thrust drove me along the blankets. His voice in my ear descended into harsh pants. Our feverish lovemaking became the elemental need to beat back the scary realities we'd endured.

"He almost killed you." Closing his fingers around my breast where my heart pounded, Linc growled, "My father almost fucking killed you, Liz."

"He didn't."

His deep groan against my neck tore through my heart. He pulled out long enough to roll me onto my back. Staring into my eyes, he guided himself back inside.

My hips rose up to meet him. "You have me. You can feel me. I'm right here." Wrapping my arms and legs around him, I held on through his powerful plundering. It felt like he wanted to crawl inside my skin, be inside my soul. But he already was. "I'm not going anywhere without you."

He slowed, giving me long, deep thrusts. Linc caressed my cheeks, and his fingers came away wet. He nuzzled my lips. "I'm stuck with you?"

"Yeah."

His eyes were so beautiful, the blue of the sky at the end of a pretty day. "Good."

When he came, stretched above me, splendidly male in his great, final strokes, he conjured another climax from me. This was the first time we'd made love without fear and terror chasing us, the only emotions between us trust and utter devotion.

Linc resituated the blankets and bedrolls, making a nest he placed me into. Slipping beside me, he traced my cheeks, my lips. "I'll never hurt you."

Breath left my lungs. I found his hand, linking our fingers over my heart. "I know."

He lifted my face up. "I'll never hurt you like that again, Liz."

My dad, my mom…their deaths, the war. False blame. Disaster had shadowed us, but it wasn't shading his eyes any longer.

"I love you, Linc."

His chin dipped to my neck. He shuddered around me. "Stay with me. Please."

"I'm here. Always. You don't have to ask."

* * *

The next afternoon, on a clear, sunny June day, we walked into Chitamauga. The scene was wildly different from when I'd left in February, when snow clung to the trees and meadow. There'd been no fanfare to see me off, just Nate and Cannon accompanying me on what I'd thought for certain would turn out to be a death mission.

Now the meadow exploded with bright wildflowers. The fields were in the full throes of cultivation. The center of the commune—from the mess hall to the meeting hall to the schoolhouse—was clogged with people. Communers shouted and congratulated us, passing us from hand to hand. They simply gathered us up in the tide and carried us along. It seemed like anything was cause for what these people called a *knees-up,* from a handfasting to a good harvest-*cum*-orgy to the homecoming of warriors who'd made it out of Beta Territory in one piece.

Separated from the others, I lost sight of Cannon and Nate, Darke and Leon, Sebastian and Farrow. I lost sight of Linc as we were propelled in opposite directions of the celebration.

The gray-furred mutt with the uncanny ability to track down a loner in any crowd bounded up to me, his owner not far behind. The old man sported the same wiry hair as his dog, and as usual, his words were gruff. "Welcome back," he said.

"Thank you."

"You lookin' for that tall young man, are ya?" He cleared his throat and spat into the dirt at his feet.

"No, I—"

Leaning down to slap his dog's rump, he squinted at me. "That there's Eden's other'n, one that got away?"

"Yes. Lincoln Cutler."

"Cutler, you say?" He scratched the dog's ears and then his own. "Nice-lookin' boys, Nathaniel and Lincoln. Sure 'nough the both of 'em took the pick of the litter, too, seems to me."

I shook my head and hid a smile, my face warming with his praise.

"Now, why you be lookin' at me like that? I'm too old for ya, missy. You bet yer britches I couldn't best that boy over there in a fight over ya. 'Specially not the way he's been starin' at ya ever since he searched the whole darn crowd for a little look-see."

Glancing behind me, I saw Linc. In his dark blues and wavy blond hair, his tall stance and huge shoulders, he stood out clearly. The sight of him intently watching me caught me in the heart and melted like hot liquid through my body.

"Well, watcha standin' here for?" Stomping away, he whistled. The dog followed his master, his tongue lolling to the side.

I turned just as Linc roamed up to me.

"I need to find my mom. Come with me?" he asked.

He navigated us through people who slapped our backs and grabbed hugs in welcome. Suddenly, the mood shifted, quieting down. Linc froze. In front of us, Eden flipped wispy hair from her eyes, Nate and Cannon on either side of her. Her hand flew to her mouth. Then she was running.

Linc met her with fast strides.

"Momma." His voice was ragged with emotion.

She rose on tiptoes, taking his face in both her hands. "Lincoln."

He wrapped her in his arms, lifting her off the ground. Laughter and murmurs passed between the pair as a mother and son who'd been estranged for too long finally reunited in front of everyone who mattered to them.

"I never forgot about you. I just couldn't let Dad use me to get to you." Linc's voice broke.

"Oh, baby boy." Leaning back, Eden stared at him as if to memorize every feature.

A grin cantered across his mouth, and his eyebrow arched. "Baby boy? You must mean Nathaniel, Momma."

Of course Nate had to get in on the action. "Linc, you only came out first because I was tired of sharin' my breathin' space with you."

"You keep telling yourself that, *baby bro*."

Such a glorious smile lit Eden's face I had to suck back my sniffles.

"You sure grew up. Now put me down." Her feet touching the ground, Eden went hands on hips, which would've been a serious moment except for the grin on her lips. "You ain't so big I can't give you what for."

The laugh that came from Linc made my heart squeeze and my tears run. Which meant, inevitably, Cannon found me exactly when I was having my weak moment.

"Hankie?"

"Fuck you," I returned.

"Reckon Linc wouldn't approve."

I snorted. "Because Nate would?"

Immediately, Cannon's gaze leaped to his man. Nate swiveled toward him. The two insatiable horn dogs started working their way toward each other, Cannon having forgotten all about teasing me. *Bingo. Mission accomplished.*

"Liz brought you home," I heard Eden say to Linc.

"Yeah, she did." He broke away from his mom, coming toward me.

He swept me into his arms. He kissed me, long and deep and passionately. Until my head spun and my knees buckled. Until all the regrets and worries, the knot inside my breastbone, loosened.

Aaaand whistles, claps, and catcalls called me back to the commune while we made out in front of everyone without a care in the world.

Linc finally put me down, and Eden gathered me into arms that trembled. "Thank you, Lizbeth."

I swallowed to soothe the ache in my throat, remembering her one desire to have Linc back and my fear I couldn't follow through.

I hadn't simply brought him back to her. I'd found him for myself.

* * *

During the subsequent weeks in the commune, Linc was beside me through combat talks, strategic planning, and nights of carnal fucking. And I had absolutely no complaints about that.

We were on standby until Cutler played his next move or until we preemptively figured out what that move was. Our time in Chitamauga was a reprieve, but as summer soldiered on, we knew it couldn't last. The quiet in the Continental Territories as regrowth and revitalization took root didn't drown out the news from abroad. Cutler was in Omega Territory, where the Revolutionaries were too sparsely placed to combat his Corps machine. He was set to topple one Territory after another unless we took him out first. "That doesn't look so pretty, darlin.'" Farrow eased onto the step below me outside Linc's and my caravan while I fingered a slightly battered daisy chain.

I'd preserved the purple flowery crown Linc had given to me in the Central. Even though it wasn't anything close to the luxury items Farrow owned, it was absolutely precious to me.

"Linc made it for me."

"That explains it." She winked at me.

We shared an easy grin, but as the silence stretched between us, it brought an undercurrent of unease. Farrow was my first female friend, my first and only *girlfriend*, and I didn't know if what we'd shared as lovers would mean I'd lose her closeness and confidence.

"Farrow…"

"Oh, hush up now, sweet girl. Ah know what you're thinkin'. We weren't evah gonna last anyhow. Why do you think Ah encouraged you to go for Linc?"

"Encouraged? You mean you threw me at him the first chance you got and practically pushed my pussy into his face." I narrowed my eyes.

"That's what Ah said." She leaned against the rickety wooden railing. "Ah might've hoped for more with you, but we're still gonna get along just fine."

When I reached for her hand, slim and somehow cool in the simmering heat, she grasped mine. Closure and peace passed between us there on the steps under the noonday sun.

"How's Sebastian holding up?"

Farrow straightened the flouncy skirt around her knees. "Taft's suicide did a number on him. He can be so damn naive, Lizbeth. Ah don't know whether to take a willow strip to his ass or give him a hug."

Hell, Taft's death had done a number on me and I hardly knew the guy. "I'd opt for a willow switch, but he might like that too much. You know, maybe we should hook him up with Leon after all."

"*Mm-hmm*. Imagine how that'd go over with Darke."

"'Bout as well as anything goes over with the man. What Darke needs is to get over his past so he can get on with his future."

Her voice dropped low. "How's Leon doin', then?"

"Eden and Evangeline have been working with him, trying to dispel the forced amnesia. Seems Leon's mother knows just as much as Eden about herbs and holistic healing, but they haven't broken through. I can't see something like leaves and natural shit making a dent in what Doc Val did to his head."

"She sounds like a right piece of work."

"Evil bitch with a death wish is what I call her," I bit out. "Evangeline asked Darke to help jog his memories. She sees how strong their connection is even now." Shaking my head, I said, "He won't do it. Darke's been avoiding Eden and Evangeline."

"Jesus Mary. You'd think he'd jump right to it. What's he got better to do?"

I glared at the treetops. "I suppose he doesn't want to hurt Leon any more. He doesn't want to get hurt himself. If Leon can't remember…" I shrugged.

"Always goes back to Wilde and Tammerick."

"Yeah."

Swinging toward me, Farrow looped her arms around her knees. I often forgot how young she was—how young we all were, making it or breaking apart trying in this war. The sun's rays glinted off her pale hair and pretty face. "You ready for tonight, sweet girl?"

I nodded, suddenly unable to get words out of my closed-in throat.

She slipped her fingers between mine once more. "Linc will be with you."

I squeezed her hand and let her go.

Chapter Nineteen

During a final trip to my parents' condo in Beta, I'd found my dad's earliest journals, handwritten in the manner I kept mine. A particular passage about my mom hit me straight through the heart.

"Can I read you something?" I asked Linc.

Across the small room of our caravan, he lifted his eyes from a map of Omega Territory he'd been inspecting. He rolled it up and placed it aside. "Is it yours?"

I shook my head. "My dad's."

He climbed onto the bed in front of me, giving me his full attention.

The paper crinkled in my hands when I flattened it over my legs. Brushing my thumb along Linc's jaw, I whispered, "I learned some terrible things about him in Beta, but I wanted to share this with you because this is what I'll remember."

A tear slid down my cheek, caught by Linc's fingertip.

"And because family means everything. They're gone now"—I linked our fingers together—"but you're not."

His Adam's apple worked up and down his throat slowly, and he leaned forward to press a sweet kiss to my lips before I started reading:

Peg Marcher said yes. Not because it's ordained or prescribed by the premiers in the Company. Our families don't even approve—I'm supposed to focus on my career, not take a wife and have offspring. I don't care. The minute I saw Peg, with her long legs and her black hair, those eyes so open, her smile so shy, I knew I was going to do everything to make her mine. The marriage council tried to put the kibosh on it. I told them to shove it. Career be damned. I'll run away to the Wilderness and make do if that's what it takes to have her by my side because she's already inside my heart forever. When I took her hand in mine to give her the ring, my palms were sweaty. She smiled, a smile I will wake up to every day now. Peg Marcher said yes! No one else knows, but she's already expecting. A husband, a father. I'll protect them both. I'll love them as no one else could. Peg Marcher said yes, and our family is just beginning.

I swiped my eyes, then Linc's, too.

He pulled me into his embrace. "Your father was a good man, Liz."

A harsh sob escaped me, but I didn't want to mourn anymore. It was time to let go. "I'd like to do something for my mom and dad. Come with me?"

"You lead."

I slid off the bed and winked back at him. "Really? Maybe we should switch places. I'll be the commander in charge, and you can be my lieutenant..."

His deep chuckle followed me out into the evening.

Linc kept up the lighthearted repartee as we meandered down to the commune's lake, his arm around my shoulders. The glassy lake surface came into view, reflecting the spiny treetop surrounds and the scattered white clouds offset by splashes of orange and red from the setting sun.

I hadn't told him my plan; only Farrow knew. He tilted his head when I bent to remove my boots and socks. The grass was warm beneath my bare feet from being sun-baked all day, and I watched him shuck his boots too.

There was a rustling from the water, followed by Linc's, "*Shh*." He towed me back to the tree line.

"Wha—"

His hand clamped over my mouth, and I followed the finger he pointed toward the lake.

Leon rose from the waist-high water in a partially hidden cove. His tawny skin shining wetly as the sun sank and the moon rose, he shook out his hair. There was a crack of branches off to the side of us. I peered through the growing darkness. Darke, hidden from the water by the trees, watched Leon emerge from the lake, water streaming down his body. Rubbing a hand over his eyes, then over his mouth, Darke looked as if he wanted join him. But in the end, he forced himself away, heading toward the village.

We waited until Leon had gathered his clothes and started in the same direction as Darke.

Taking my hand, Linc led me to the shore. "Your mom and dad?"

I nodded, a feeling of solemnity settling over me. With his fingers between mine, I walked to the edge of the lake, where glades of tall grasses swished in the breeze. I rolled up my pants and stepped in. Linc waded beside me, the water rippling around our legs.

I pulled out my mom's wedding ring. "I want to give them a send-off."

He grabbed my wrist. "Are you sure?"

"I want them together."

"What do you need me to do, sweetheart?" He rubbed his palm up my arm.

I passed him the ring, which he closed in his hand and held to his heart, just as I would've done. Pulling out the piece of paper from my dad's journal, I folded the edges to create a cradle.

"The ring goes here, my love." I pointed into the small vessel I'd made.

When Linc placed it gently inside, my hurt, my pain...all the blame dissolved. I moved further into the water, Linc right next to me, his hand closed firmly around mine.

"Peg Marcher, Robie Grant. Be together forever. I forgive you, Daddy. I love you both." Tears made my vision as watery as the lake and my fingers shook, but I lit the little paper-made boat with its beloved cargo.

I sent the small flaming boat into the water, a fiery devotion to my mom and dad as the evening's last light swooped into night's darkness. Their bodies were long gone, but their spirits, their love would inhabit me always.

Linc guided me to his lips. "What do you need from me, sweetheart?" he asked again.

The boat extinguished quickly, but fiery emotion leaped from my chest. I tangled my arms around him. "Just you."

He claimed my mouth. "That's all I need, too."

With predatory grace, he shucked my clothes and then his own, throwing them ashore. He lifted me into his arms, striding deeper and cleanly diving into the water. When we rose, his lips were on mine, my face carefully held between his hands.

My fingers wandered down the hard planes of his body, but before I could make it to his groin, he slid my palm back up to his heart. "Just want to take care of you tonight."

He turned me in his arms, and my breath juddered as his forearms crossed over my belly. "Come again?"

"Just wanna be with you."

Water slithering between us, we kissed and caressed. After we'd scooped water over each other to clean away the day's dust, Linc dried me off. He helped me dress and held my hand back to the caravan, wearing a grin full of pride.

An hour later, Linc and I lay together in bed. Candles burned low, their light burnishing his skin to a coppery glow. My breasts pressed against his chest, and my fingers traced up and down his arm. I quivered with every pass of his hand along my naked back.

"You didn't kill my dad." I breathed in his warm scent, nestled closer to his solid form.

"No, I didn't." His lips touched my earlobe.

"How does that feel?"

Leaning back, he hooked my chin between two fingers. "A lot less fucked up in my head. You?"

I nuzzled my nose into his springy chest hair. "Happy."

Arms tightening, he rolled me closer to him. "Happy." His timbre deepened to a slumberous tone, and Linc stretched and relaxed beneath me. "You make me happy."

* * *

I hoped the fool man had been as sleepless as me. *Happy*. How about horny? Keeping me up all night with his hot breath against my neck, his thigh between mine. I'd wiggle, and he'd clamp a hand to my hip to stop me moving. Annoying tease.

Linc woke early and cheerful, and I squirmed deeper under the covers.

"Meet me at the outskirts in an hour."

That sensual curve of his upper lip beckoned me when I puffed the sheet off my face. "Yessir."

One hour and two minutes later, Linc wielded a machete while I tromped beside him into the woods of the Wilderness. I didn't need Cannon to tell me a man with a machete, sweat tracking down his temples and coursing over his throat, was hotter than the midday sun.

"You taking me somewhere specific?"

He hacked through a scree of vines, angling his gaze toward me. "Yep."

I lifted my shirt to wipe my face. Linc's gaze strayed to the undercurves of my breasts, bare of a bra. "Gonna get there sometime today?"

He tore his eyes away and strode forward, grumbling, "We better before I throw you on the ground right here."

A couple hours of beating back bracken and branches, we entered a clearing. The remains of a rambling house stood in the center. The upper levels spiked up to the treetops in a rebellious show, the white paint on the wood curling back to reveal old, age-worn planks. Tree limbs laden with fragrant blooms overshadowed the verandah and flowered vines overtook the railings, climbed the walls, framed windows and doorway.

I recognized the porch. It was the house in the photo Linc had rescued alongside my journaling. The picture of his mom and granddad he'd kept for so many years the colors had faded. The Rice family homestead in front of me was beautiful, covered in nature's living homage.

"Your mom's home, Linc?" I found his hand and kissed his knuckles. "You goin' soft on me?"

"Not soft enough." He walked up the slanting steps. "Never been here. I didn't think it'd still be standing."

As he stood with his arms braced against a latticework choked by overgrowth, I knew Linc was thinking about Beta's destruction, about all the years he'd willfully lost from his mother and brother. About neglecting that which you were supposed to care for. I took the steps two at a time, and I embraced him around the waist, kissing the underside of his chin.

He grasped my face, taking my mouth in a kiss that burst into sparks exploding through my entire body.

Voice husky with emotion, Linc said, "I want to do right by you." He tilted his head to stare down at me. "I've been thinking a lot about family." His fingertips ran along my arm to my hand. "I've been thinking a lot about you, Liz."

He lifted my hand to his mouth. The dark fan of his lashes lowered. "Thinking about being able to make plans. I told you I wanted to make this a permanent assignment, you and me. I gave everything up until you came along, but not anymore. That night in the Central? I feel even more than I did then. I'm not going to give you up."

"You don't have to," I whispered.

"I'm not done yet." Clear, calm blue eyes traipsed to our laced hands and back to meet my gaze.

"This is you getting romantic on me."

"Yeah."

"Do I need to take my guns off?"

His lips twitched before settling into a firm line. "Maybe you could holster your mouth for a change instead."

My laughter died abruptly when he sank to one knee.

I inhaled sharply, exhaling a quiet, "Yes, Linc."

"Eager?" he asked in delight.

"Egotistical asshole," I scathed.

"Gorgeous woman." He kissed the heart of my palm, then placed it against the thundering beat in his chest. He pulled a ring from his pocket, balancing it in the middle of his free hand. "This was my grandmother Harmony's."

Tears sprang to my eyes, quickly overflowing. My bones went loose, and I thought I'd fall to the porch right in front of him, but his grip moved to my hip and squeezed.

"I need to you to keep standing for me, darlin', okay? I want to do this right."

I nodded, backhanding my cheeks.

Blue eyes, beautiful smile, the world beat inside my chest. The diamond ring captured the sun's rays as sure as Linc had captured my heart. "I want to be the man you come back to. I want to be the one, the only one for you, Liz. I want to be your family. Will you marry me, Lizbeth Grant?"

"Can I answer now?"

He nodded and winked.

I pressed my hand to his face, his damp lashes caressing my fingers. "Yes. Absolutely, Linc."

A smile burst across his mouth before it dimmed.

"What?" I asked.

Instead of placing the ring on my finger, he closed it in his hand. "I don't want you to feel obligated."

Just my luck. The man proposes and he's already trying to pull out? "Linc."

"I know we were thrown together because of the Revolution and you were forced to be with me." He rambled, nothing like the famous Beta Commander but a bashful young man asking the woman he loved to be his.

"Linc."

He stuttered but didn't stop. "I don't want you to think you owe me something, because you don't, Liz. If anyone owes something, it's me. I never would've had the courage to—"

"Lincoln goddamn Cutler."

He finally halted.

"Shut the hell up." I pointed at the ring. "I want this. I want you."

"Yeah?"

"Affirmative."

He stared up at me, a smile tugging his lips until I cleared my throat and pointed again. "The ring?"

When it slipped over my finger, the betrothal band hugged my skin, cool and snug and perfect. Pulling me to the porch in front of him, his mouth dropped over mine. His tongue teased out to guide mine through a sleek, hot dance. His breath rasping along my neck to my collarbone, Linc nudged my shirt aside with his lips. I grasped his hair, arching up to his touch.

He moved to the hem of my shirt, tickling underneath, making me desperate for the deeper touch of bare skin on skin. Deft fingers skimmed along the waistband of my cutoff camos…and I squirmed from under Linc.

His eyes cut to mine, hazy and hooded. Lips shining from our kisses, he snaked one hand up to cup my breast, sending wet arousal between my legs, but I shifted away.

He frowned. "What?"

"Well, look at me." I waved down my body.

He did, for a long, appreciative moment, wolfish grin gracing his lips. "And?"

"I'm not even wearing a dress. I don't even want to wear fricking dresses. I'd rather have guns than necklaces. I don't have a ring to give you or—"

"Stop."

"I have nothing to offer you." *Shit. Apparently, it's my turn to suffer from a case of the insecures.* "Look at me, Linc. Plain uniform, plain panties…Hell, I take better care of my weapons than my goddamn nails."

His mouth landing on the pulse point of my neck, Linc smoothly and surely silenced me. His tongue darted out, the warm, wet glide taking my respiration on a rapid ride. "Did I just ask you to marry me, handfast me, whatever you want?"

"Yes, but I—"

"And you said yes."

"Yeah, but—"

Linc tugged on my bottom lip with his teeth. "Plain clothes, a party dress. Shit, especially just in your panties. It doesn't matter. Liz, every time, *every time* I'm with you, I cannot believe you want me the way you do. Jesus, you love me?"

"Yes."

He nodded and moved up to draw my earlobe between his lips. "You gave me my pride back, Liz." His guttural avowal snatched the breath from my lungs. "Now shut up and kiss me, woman."

I scrambled onto his lap, latching onto his mouth. Hot and needy, our tongues stroked, coiled, and chased. Raging heat drove straight into my belly, lancing my desires open. Gyrating against the ridge of his cock, I gasped when he jerked his hips up.

He pulled his lips from mine. "We have to get back."

I licked a line up the taut tendon of his throat, parched for the salty taste of him. "Do we?"

He launched to his feet, taking me with him. "C'mon, missus."

My eyes opened wide. "You did not."

He roared with laughter.

Fingering my guns, I stabbed him with a glare. "Might I remind you these are loaded before you get any more cocky?"

He grabbed on to the full weight of his shaft through his pants, returning, "Might I remind you this cock is loaded and ready for you, later?"

* * *

The commune was bursting with festivities, a scene of such jubilation it matched the euphoria filling me. Time to let the demons go and embrace some dreams.

The meadow was ablaze with bonfires. Tables stood here and there, laden with food and heavy from casks of homebrew. Music crescendoed the closer we got, but it couldn't compete with the sound of people gabbing and laughing. It looked like the entire damn population of Chitamauga converged for the party, and Linc led me right to the middle of it.

The villagers quieted, watching us expectantly. My face flushed, and I searched for Cannon or Farrow, anyone to ground me while my heart pumped and thumped furiously in my chest.

It turned out it wasn't Cannon or Farrow I needed. It was Linc. And he anchored me with his hand on my waist, his kiss brushing my cheek before he faced the crowd and raised his voice. "She said yes!"

Beaming, he was beaming…with that pride he'd said I'd returned to him. I lifted onto my tiptoes and kissed the curve of his smile, peeking out at the sound of applause and whistles.

And shouts:

Kiss 'im harder!

Go get 'im, girl!

"Well, there goes anothah one." Farrow strolled up to us with a grin. She was only the first in line for a hug.

Nate congratulated his brother and turned to me. "Proud of you, Lizbeth."

Cannon loomed beside him. "Shit."

I wriggled from Nate's embrace and punched Cannon on the arm. Then I grabbed him into a hug, trying not to sniffle.

I leaned back. "So, we've got matching brothers now, huh?"

Laughter boomed from his belly. "Yeah, something like that."

When Linc took his place next to me, Cannon rubbed a hand across the back of his neck and squinted at the other man. "You're sure you don't mind hitching up to an older woman?"

That earned him a whack on the head from me, a hiss from Farrow, and a glare from Blondie. Linc sucked in his cheeks, and I could tell he was trying not to snicker.

"Don't you even think about laughing, Linc Cutler," I spit.

Hands up, he backed away, right into Miss Eden's warpath. She looked like she was about to yank both Cannon and Linc by the ears and probably trot them around the entire commune.

"Caspar, mind your manners," she scolded.

"Yes, ma'am." His cheeks turned pink.

I smirked at him.

"Lincoln Cutler, are you disrespecting your future intended?"

He stared glumly from me to his mother. "No, ma'am."

"*Hmmph.* Get on over here, Liz, and give me some sugar." I slid past the two upbraided men and into her arms. Warm, maternal, and a total hard-ass, Eden whispered, "I advise you keep him

from havin' his way with you tonight. Nothin' like cold comfort
in bed to keep a man in line."

Then she stepped back and smiled brightly. "Welcome to the
family!"

Nate took his cue from her and sent up a shrill whistle. "Let's
start this shindig, y'all!"

"See? Any excuse for a hoopla," I murmured to Linc.

Darke sidled up, eyes merry as they hadn't been since Leon's
abduction. "More like a hootenanny."

"Hootin' what?" Leon ambled over, tucking his thumbs into
the low rise of his jeans.

"Ah like to call this kind of soirée a hullabaloo. One that's well
deserved." Farrow linked her arm through Sebastian's.

"It's a hoedown, folks, so get dancin'!" Nate took Cannon's
hand, tugging him to the center of the meadow.

Linc ushered me after them and I called back, "But what if I'd
said no?"

"*Merde alors.* As if you'd do that." Leon chuckled.

The other dancers dispersed when Linc hooked his arms
around my hips, leaving me, him...and Smitty strumming his go-
dawful banjo. A few calls for *Eden and Nathaniel* caused the pair
to straddle two stools with their guitars, and their singing started.
Cannon stood to the side, his worshipful gaze never leaving his
man.

Alone, in the middle of it all, Linc and I danced. This time I
didn't mind being the center of attention. I didn't care about flying
above the radar. With Linc, his body pressed against mine, his lips
in my hair, and my hands curling around his shoulders, I soared.

Closing my eyes, I felt the slight weight of the ring on my finger, catching the diamond with my thumb. I'd come full circle the moment I'd stepped back into Chitamauga one month before, but that circle hadn't felt complete until now. Back where I started but with a full heart, a full future, and the man who'd brought it all together for me. *With me.*

I danced with Cannon and Nate, Hills and Leon. Farrow turned me around the clearing in the meadow while we passed Linc talking to Darke. The heavy-lidded blue of his eyes snapped to me, hitting me with a bellyful of longing.

There was a lot of hell headed our way. I knew it, but I'd take this night, my man, my friends, whatever I could get of the now, and rejoice in it.

Eventually, Big Man Cannon found Blondie, and the two set a path of fire with their slow moves against each other. Just like the night of their handfasting, they feasted on each other's eyes, lips, motions.

I expelled a sigh when large, rough hands circled me from behind to settle over my belly.

"They're in love," came Linc's gruff voice.

"So am I." I flattened my hands over his, feeling him smile against my neck.

He turned me in his arms and trailed his fingertips along my cheeks and down my neck. "Me too."

Music hummed in the background as we moved slowly together, never looking away from the other's eyes, carefully brushing our lips together until a wonderful, yearning—one I knew he'd ease—blossomed inside me.

Dancing together, we whispered quiet words about when we would have our handfasting and who would be present. I asked him if he wanted a ring, and he dipped his head, smiling, saying he wanted everyone to know he belonged to me.

My fingers slipped up into his hair from the nape of his neck. I drew him down for a longer kiss, enjoying these moments that brought our love out in the open. When we drew apart, the longing had intensified, darkening his eyes, speeding my pulse. My laugh came out low and quiet. I swiveled my hips in lazy circles against his, dragging my gaze around the other carousers. My recon stopped at Leon and Darke not too far away. Leon drew his hands into the shoulder-length waves of his hair and licked his lips. He slid one lean thigh between the bigger man's and drew it back slowly while Darke's chest billowed in and out. Then Darke shook his head and frowned.

Quickly disengaging, he vaulted over the fence and nearly tripped on his feet beating a hasty retreat. Leon looked on, hurt and bafflement washing over his features at being pushed away.

In a *big sister* moment, I decided to set Darke straight. I caught up with him after making my excuses to Linc. Our conversation was spoken through gritted teeth—Darke destined to break both his and Leon's hearts again, and I determined to give him a piece of my mind. When I left him, we were at loggerheads.

Maybe Darke was content to screw himself into a black hole of stupidity, but I sure wasn't. I made my way back to Linc. I wasn't going to waste another second of our time together.

I drew Linc into my arms. "Bed. Now."

Micah, who danced near us, hooted with laughter. The searing flash of Linc's eyes corroded every last ounce of social graces I possessed. And there weren't that many to begin with.

"Giving me orders, Lieutenant?"

"Damn right I am."

Speeding me from the celebration, he sent no good-byes, gave no apologies.

Ravenous desire ripped through me. The sultry night air clung to me, and Linc's words melted my body when he grunted, "I hope you're ready to get fucked hard, sweetheart."

In the caravan, I stood beside the bed, shaking inside my skin. Linc leaned over the washbasin, filling it with water.

Hurry up. Hurry up!

I detailed him from his shoulders to his amazing ass, to the solid girth of his thighs. "Take your shirt off."

Linc didn't look at me. With one hand, he reached behind to raise his shirt up over his head. Muscles fanned out, bunched, gathered and made me gasp. My fingernails curled into my palms, I wanted to touch him so much.

He didn't say a word, precisely shaving. Across his cheeks, down his throat, shaking the razor off.

"You gonna dawdle all night long?" I asked.

Toweling off his face, he swung his head toward me. Half naked, glistening, that extra curl to his upper lip on one side was so sexy, so Linc. I longed to pull it between my teeth.

"Come over here and find out. Take off your shirt first." He winked.

I discarded the top. His back tensed when the bundle audibly hit the floor. I made sure he heard my approach, too, with a mouthful of dirty words. "Can't wait to suck your cock."

He folded his fists around the basin, white-knuckling it.

"I'm so wet for you, Linc."

I slid against him, my nipples raking along his back. He hissed.

I kissed my way along his eagle tattoo, from one straining shoulder to the other. I put my hands in his back pockets and squeezed. "I like this."

"My ass?"

"That too. But being with you…knowing I'm going to be with you tomorrow, the next day, for all the years to come." Bringing my arms to his front, I moaned. The hard-packed muscles, the ripples of his stomach, the trail of hair to the thick roll of his cock inside his pants…

Curses fell from his lips when I opened his buckle. My fingertips brushed, tantalized, ached to close around his length, but I held off. Dragging the pants off, I cupped his balls, pendulums of heat and virility.

I spun him around and sank to my knees between his legs. I teased his sacs with my tongue. "Put them in my mouth."

Moaning around the luscious rounds of Linc's flesh as he fed it into my mouth, I rotated my hand up and down his cock, rubbing the head on each pass. His testicles dripped from my mouth, wet and drawn up. Only then did I lick the underside of his shaft before taking him in my mouth.

His hands grasped my hair; his animalistic panting filled my ears. From far above and deep inside my throat, Linc guided me slowly off the thick length of him. A string of precome joined my lips to his pulsing tip.

He pushed my shoulders until they met the floor, then crawled over me. He suckled both my nipples until my head pounded back, my hips tilted up. Linc ripped my pants off, lifting me onto his hips so he could carry me to the bed.

Parting my thighs, he groaned. I was wet from my slit to my upper thighs, totally his, and he knew it. He wasted no time, surging into me with his tongue, licking and nipping. He held my legs open, helpless, unable to escape the onslaught of his hunger.

Groaning, grunting, he lapped my tender flesh. His tongue thrust inside, and he sucked so hard I cried out. Every hot moment of him between my thighs made me blind with lust. He reached up and caught my hand, bringing it to his mouth. He kissed the ring he'd given me, made a circuit over it with his tongue, then dragged both our hands down my body. Across my breasts, rasping my nipples, along my belly, between my legs. Inside me, where his fingers and mine twisted together.

"Mine," Linc chanted as he fucked me down on both our hands.

Knees open, heels planted, I gasped. "Yes."

He rose above me, and I clasped his shoulders. I yelled when he entered me, pure power in every single one of his motions. He slipped a hand down my side and grabbed my bottom, pulling me up to meet the last of his length. His first full thrust sped me into a climax that drew my body like a bow shaft.

Rigid. Pulsing. Pushing in, drawing out.

Linc groaned into my neck. "Come like that, girl. Come on my cock again."

His angle changed, and my ongoing orgasm rippled through me again. "Linc!"

Four deep thrusts later, he came, holding our hands clenched between our hearts. After several more slow grinds, he lowered to his side and pulled me against him.

"*Libertas.*" I ran my fingers up over his shoulder to the tattoo on his back. "You freed me, Liz."

The funny thing was, Linc had liberated me in return.

Every threat, we'd met. All our secrets were out in the open. There was just me and Linc and a whole lot of happy swirling around inside me. Lifting to my elbows, I watched the glowing gold of the ring on my finger pressed against his chest.

His cheeks were flushed. His eyelashes fluttered and rose when he tilted his chin to look at me. Linc trailed his hand up my arm, along my neck, into my hair. "Hey, beautiful," he whispered.

I wanted to take him inside my body once more, to be filled by his essence as my heart was filled with his love. I smiled instead, and kissed his mouth, his chin, his throat. With our fingers laced together, he rubbed the ring over and over through each kiss as my breath halted and my heart restarted.

I surrendered completely to what I wanted, needed. To the love I'd always thought I could never have. "I'm living the dream with you, Linc."

The rumble of his voice came from deep within his chest, his hands trembling slightly as he tightened his embrace. "Me too, sweetheart."

Please see the next page
for a preview of *Under His Guard*

Chapter One

Music swelled from Eden's and Nate's guitars as they took over from Smitty's painfully out-of-tune banjo playing. Thank God. The meadow was a landscape of bonfires and boisterous revelers all celebrating Liz and Linc's betrothal announcement. The scene was one hundred eighty degrees different from the months spent in the urban Beta Territory, where bombs dropped and guns fired and the Revolution had almost been lost. Victory was ours in the end. As always, it was paid with a high price. My price for a similar rebel win in Alpha had been the lives of my two partners. This time it was Leon's memory of me and our time together. In all these instances, CEO Cutler was guilty, yet he'd managed to escape unscathed once again.

This wasn't the time for such dark thoughts. Perhaps that was why my mother had named me Darke and not because of my incredibly dark skin and inky eyes. Maybe I'd been a broody little bastard from birth. I nearly laughed at the thought, but I couldn't do that either. Not when the one person who knew how to lighten my mood danced in the middle of the meadow, as carefree and unbelievably sexy as always. That it was my fault he acted as if I didn't exist didn't do a goddamn thing to ease the stab of jealousy making my blood run hot and my eyes narrow when Leon gave the type of wicked smile he'd always reserved for me to some young buck named Jake or Jack or Jackal. *Hmm. Yeah, Jackal it is.* Fire was added to my envy as Leon twined his arms around the other man's neck and gyrated against his hips.

After giving my congratulations to Linc and Liz, I'd ambled away from the group I'd been with through the battles of Beta, mostly to get away from Leon. He was too much of a temptation, especially on a night like this, spent in celebration of new love, when I shouldn't be mourning love lost. I couldn't take my eyes off him. Finally, turning my back on him and the intoxicating movements of his ass, his chest and long hair, I mingled with the other villagers. I danced a fast-paced jig with Lyra, but declined a second dance when the music became slower and more sensual. I ended up drinking a couple tankards of ale with Micah as we laughed over his twins, Callie and Dauphine. They made their *uncles* Cannon and Nate squire them about the field, which meant Smitty was back on the banjo, much to the agony of everyone's ears.

"Your girls are gonna be heartbreakers, man." I knocked my mug against Micah's.

"Shit, Darke. You don't need to tell me that. Jesus. They take after their momma." He pushed a faded green cap off his brow and winked at me. "Kamber had my nuts twisted tighter than a blue-balled bull the first time I met her."

Swilling the dark alcohol in my cup, I grinned.

"Mind now, that'un over there's a heartbreaker, too, ain't he?"

I looked in the direction he pointed, letting loose a groan. Leon had switched partners. With the raunchy song filled with dirty lyrics sang by Smitty, he grinded his ass against a guy called Dixon. Or Dickhead, as I dubbed him.

"Yeah, he is." I gritted my teeth through a smile, pretending the shaft of pain wasn't burning a hole right through my heart. I hadn't made my peace with Leon. I'd made avoiding him my latest detail, going out of my way to eat at opposite sides of the mess hall, ensuring Cannon headed up any military training with him. Despite my efforts, I still knew where he was and what he was doing almost every second of every day.

An hour and three more teasing dances from Leon later, I'd grinded my teeth through. I couldn't hold back any longer. When I saw him leaning against the fence, his own mug of ale in hand, I stalked toward him. The moon had long since risen and was making its way across the other side of the sky. The glow from the cool white orb above outlined his striking features and his hair—damp with sweat and down to his shoulders—in silver. He was stunning. He stole my breath as well as some of the jealousy he'd stoked. He always played havoc with my emotions and jumbled my brain. Words that were usually brusque came out even gruffer with him because he was so damn beautiful, he made me nervous.

His golden gaze found mine as I approached. Leaning his head back, he dragged the hair away from his face, leaving me with a mouthwatering view of his clenched biceps and the cords of his neck.

I ran a finger down his neck, listening to him gasp. He lifted his head as I sucked my fingertip, licking off the clean, salty taste lingering there. "You about done making a spectacle of yourself out there with Jackal and Dickhead?"

"Who?" Leon's chest was shiny with perspiration, his shirt long gone. Copper-colored nipples sat on his tight pectorals. I wanted to kiss them, lap them until he cried out my name. His chest was smooth until a thin line of soft-looking dark brown hair ran from his navel to the top of his pants, nearly dripping off an Adonis belt of muscle.

My gaze rose from wandering all over the body he displayed. "Jack. Dixon. And that other one who was all over you."

Taking a long, lazy sip of his drink, he cleaned his lips off with a slow roll of his tongue. "What do you care? I know you won't help my momma and Miss Eden tap into my memories. I know you're hidin' somethin." He rubbed his stomach like a tiger preening itself, muscles rippling beneath his hand. "But guess what? The world don' revolve around you."

The words were eerily similar to something he'd said the night I'd tracked him down to Farrow's apartment in Beta. A weeklong journey that nearly made me lose the last of my sanity, wondering if he'd made it to the city unharmed. He'd been angrier than I'd ever seen him, downright pissed off at me for following him when he'd wanted only to get away from me. He didn't remember any of that now.

Leon was right. I used his amnesia to keep him at arm's length for all the goddamn good it did me. Fresh emotion boiled through me. Caging him against the fence with both my hands on the rail beside him, I bit out, "I care." I'd cared then, and I for damn sure cared now. My nostrils flared. My jaw jumped.

"You jealous, big guy?" Leon didn't shrink from my presence. Instead he arched into my body. A breath hissed from me as his chest came into contact with mine and the contours of his lean legs brushed my thighs.

I swallowed hard. "Yeah."

Winding his fingers through his sun-streaked hair, he licked his lips. They were red, and juicy, always plump, begging to be kissed. I couldn't look away. Sliding one long thigh between mine, he drew it back slowly. The ache in my groin exploded into a full-blown erection from that teasing stroke alone. "Then why don't you fuck me already?"

It was as if lightning struck my body, sizzling right down to my balls. Heat bloomed all over me, and for a second all I could get out were curses. My hands clenched the fence rail, but I wanted nothing more than to drive them inside the back of his pants, grasp his tight ass, pull him against me. Find some relief from this longing, this exquisitely raw seduction that had been building for six months whether he remembered or not.

I jerked away when his lips sought mine. A kiss, one kiss from this man and I'd be a goner. I couldn't, I just *couldn't* get involved with Leon. My chest billowed in and out with the effort to put a stop to this one more time. Words, harsh and low, fell from my mouth before I even considered them. "Because I don't fuck. I make love."

Leon's face crashed in an instant. "And you don't love me." He moved as far back from me as he could.

I frowned at him. There was no answer to that. None I was ready to give. Turning away from his pain, I vaulted over the fence. I almost tripped over my feet to beat a hasty retreat, but I couldn't move fast enough to outrun the guilt and desire that battered me. Leon always flew too close to my emotions. I couldn't let him in enough to hurt me.

From behind, I heard Liz shout, "Hey!"

My shoulders drooped; my sprinting stopped. She'd been looking out for Leon since he'd arrived in Beta. She hadn't stopped just because we were back in Chitamauga. Liz was as much a woman as a soldier, and I had a sinking feeling she was about to kick my ass and then give me love advice.

"What the hell are you playing at?" She grabbed my arm, tugging me around.

So it was to be the ass-kicking first. At least she was predictable. She stood a good seven inches shorter than me but was formidable nonetheless, even without her usual pair of weapons holstered at her hips, and her mouth knew no bounds.

"I'm not playing anything. This isn't a game you can tactically decide from the sidelines, so back the fuck off." My shitty night capped off by a dressing-down from Liz, I let manners take a backseat.

"Not gonna happen. Why don't you tell me why you're running away from Leon, again? What was all that shit you spouted when Taft brought him back to you?"

I folded my arms across my chest. "Ignorance, arrogance, and blind stupidity."

"You know what? All that blindsided fucked-up emotion? That was the first honest feeling you've shown toward Leon." Her finger pointed at me, and if she'd had one of her guns, it probably would've gone off right then.

"You don't know me." When faced with a woman going all mama bear, it was best to play dumb. It was just too bad Liz had had a front-row seat to most of my and Leon's not-so-romance.

"Maybe not, but I got eyes in my head. I know what I see. It just so happens I saw you last night, Darke, at the lake, watching Leon."

Ah fuck. "You saw me?" I hadn't known anyone else was there. I hadn't intentionally followed Leon, but I'd heard him, whistling. Then playing in the water. I'd kept to the tree line, shaking with need. Leon swam, and his sleek body teased me from the lake—a flash of his perfect ass rising above the waves, the splash of water running down his chest. It'd taken all my restraint to keep from joining him, to walk away.

I glared at Liz. "Wait. You saw him naked?"

"Easy there, *big guy*. I got a man of my own, and you could, too, if you pulled your head out of your ass. So why don't you tell me what the hell is going on?"

Fingers clamped into my hair, I pulled hard. A rumbling groan grew from my chest in sheer despair. "I don't know."

"Are you shitting me? Do you remember sobbing over him when he was gone? I do. Because I was right there with you."

"Maybe the amnesia thing is better for him, a clean break…" My lips twisted over the excuse for not getting my heart broken one more time.

"I'm gonna clean break your neck." She got right in my space, shoving her finger in my face. "Look. Did you see what he was doing out there? He made you jealous, and it worked because you're about one step away from devouring him on the spot every time you see him. He wants you. So it doesn't matter what the hell he does or doesn't remember, Darke. He's into you. He is yours. Still."

"Not my problem anymore." I dodged Liz's eyes, squared my shoulders, firmly setting myself on the path of probable personal destruction.

"Wrong. He is always gonna be your problem and your man. You need to grow a pair already."

She looked thoroughly disgusted with me when she pivoted on her heel and took off for the meadow. It didn't matter. No one could be more ashamed of myself than me.

* * *

I trudged back to my caravan. I had to stop before going up the steps. As always, I shut my eyes for a moment to prepare myself for the scene inside. Closing the door gently behind me, I bent to unlace my boots and place them aside. I tried not to look around too much. Tam and Wilde's belongings—their books, clothes, weapons, and trinkets—were how they'd left them. I hadn't moved or removed a single thing. I couldn't bear to touch them. I couldn't bear to part with them. Though Wilde and I had spent one summer clobbering two caravans together and the place was bigger than most others, it suffocated me with memories.

Their ghosts still lingered.

There was no room for Leon here. I'd made the right decision regarding him, but even so, he'd filled the hole in my chest for a little while, back in the winter. Now it simply gaped open.

Broody bastard? I'm downright maudlin. I sniffed out a smile. Lighting a few candles, I undressed and washed quickly. The big, empty bed was another torment, but instead of memories of old, it filled me with fresh, increasingly hot fantasies. No, it wasn't Tam or Wilde I thought about. It wasn't either of them who kept me up night after lonely night, awake and so aroused I had to relieve the physical ache with fingers I pretended were long and slim and tanned. A hand I wet with my tongue so when I wrapped it around my jutting cock, I could imagine I was being sucked and teased and blown by the poutiest, reddest pair of lips beneath two heavy-lidded gold-flecked eyes. Even coming so hard I had to bite back a holler and mop away strands of milky liquid all the way up my chest, I was left unsatisfied. The emotional turmoil I perpetuated never disappeared.

Tonight was no different. I thrashed around the bed, sleep chased away by images of Leon—laughing, dancing, flirting—the scent of him that was earthy, his guttural accent spoken in a soft, low voice. Hunger for Leon never waned. It became harder with each passing day to maintain distance. I hoped like hell he'd gone to bed alone and not with Jackass or Dickface or any number randy males he could pick from.

It felt like my eyes had only just shut when my Data-Pak went off over and over, showing no signs of stopping its piercing alert. Snatching the handheld comms device from the floor beside the bed, I checked the incoming. *Linc Cutler.*

Wiping an arm across my bleary eyes, I barked into the thing, "Thought I said congrats earlier, man. It's too fucking late for you to be on the horn on your betrothal night."

"I've just gotten word from Denver. This is strictly on a need-to-know basis, so I'm not gonna spread it over the D-P. Be in the town hall in ten minutes." The tension in Linc's voice sounded clearly through the airwaves.

Instantly, all weariness fled. I flung the D-P onto the bed. Yanking on the clothes I'd taken off only a couple hours before, I slammed outside. I didn't even bother with my bootlaces.

The town hall became a tunnel through which I saw only Liz and Linc at the end, looking grim. Linc stood behind the table, Liz at his side. Hatch, Nate, and Cannon hurried in after me. Both Linc and Liz nodded at them, but they bypassed me. The way their gestures were already exact mirrors of the other would've been funny, but there was no levity in this situation. My frayed nerves unraveled even more.

"What the hell's going on that this couldn't wait until the morning?" My boots resounded on the wood floors as I marched up to Linc. When he didn't answer and still wouldn't meet my gaze, dread funneled through me. "Give it to me straight, right now."

"Denver came through with some intel."

Patience wearing thin, I shoved my face into his. "You already said that."

Liz placed a hand on my arm, her touch not soothing me at all when she said, "It's bad, Darke."

I swung my gaze to her, then back at Linc. He'd lost his healthy tan. His eyes looked bleaker than I'd ever seen them, and seeing as we'd been through hell ten times over in Beta, I wasn't sure if I wanted to hear Denver's info.

Linc passed a hand over his face. "Leon's a human time bomb."

His words hit me like a blow to the stomach. "What?" Sweat trickled down my back, as cold as the fear slicing through me. My hands started to shake, and I clamped them around the edge of the table until my knuckles turned as white as Liz's ghostly face.

"This is what our *father* meant when he told Liz he had a second wave planned. It's why he didn't really give a shit when Taft blew up the DCICs. The asshole masterminded a human delivery system. Leon's infected with the new Plague." Linc's fist clenched as he exchanged bitter looks with his twin brother, Nathaniel. "I should've killed that fucking bastard when I had the chance."

I gasped for breath, my legs almost collapsing out from under me. My body, my brain, my heart all shutting down.

"To kill the Plague, we'd have to kill Leon—his body is a Trojan horse we won't be able to destroy, because…because…" Words failing her, Liz swiped across her eyes.

Bile rose in my throat. I swallowed it back. "Because he's ours." *He's mine.* "That's why no one else showed at the water tower. He's a plant."

"The virus is implanted in Leon, but it's dormant." Hatch scanned through the message that had been sent to Linc via Denver, CEO Cutler's bodyguard.

"His body's a weapon for the Company." Numb, I could barely raise my eyes to the others.

Nathaniel pushed up beside me. His hand was heavy on my shoulder. "Father let Leon go because he knew we'd take him in."

An incendiary blaze of hate for CEO Cutler, Linc and Nate's hated and estranged father, fired inside me. "I'd still take Leon in, no matter what."

Cannon stepped up, pounding a fist to the table. "Imagine how many others he's infected."

"When?" All the life was leeched from me in an instant.

"When what?" Linc asked.

"WHEN DOES IT GO LIVE?" I bellowed.

"End of August." Linc grabbed Liz's hand.

"There has to be an antidote, a cure, something!" I spun around, halting when I saw Leon just inside the door. Shock and fear, worry and concern all clashed within me. And want, foremost.

I could never get enough of him. I never would. No matter how hard I tried to push him away, I always pulled him back. His sun-bright eyes looked almost kohl black and suddenly too big for his face. His hair was wild, tangled, down around his shoulders. I tensed, reaching for him. I just wanted to feel Leon against me. I didn't want him to know. *I* didn't want to fucking know. Leon walked toward me with his loose-legged swagger. The half tilt of his lips hit every erogenous zone in my body, as if his world hadn't just been turned upside down one more time.

My heart pounded. My mouth went dry.

He ambled closer, and everyone moved away from us. They fell silent, became nonexistent.

"Thought I heard a commotion." He stopped in front of me.

"Leon." *Angel*. "How much did you hear?" My hands clenched beside me. I was desperate to touch him.

His slight smile was tremulous around the edges. "Jus' a little of this, a little of that. Somethin' 'bout me bein' an incubator for the new plague and set to infect." He clicked his tongue against the roof of his mouth. "*Mais*, I always wanted to be famous."

"Leon." I struggled to breathe, a watery sheen of tears threatening my eyes.

"Guess we know what that Dr. Val did to me now, yeah?"

I was torn between punching my fist through a wall and hauling him against me.

"Darke." He ran his hand along my jaw. "I wanna know who you are, what you mean to me before I die, 'cause I can feel it," he whispered.

Leon closed his eyes when I groaned at his touch. There was no one else. Never. Not like this. Guilt wormed its way into my gut when thoughts about Tam and Wilde warred within me. But I wouldn't deny this passion. I couldn't. Not anymore. Not if Leon was going to die as a pawn in the InterNations war.

"*Cher*," he whispered against my neck.

A great gasping sob broke through my lips as I crushed him to me. He hadn't called me *cher* since his abduction. He'd forgotten me, what we'd started, what I wouldn't let myself have.

Now it was too late.

He pulled back. Courage fought with sadness in his eyes as if he was looking at a man who would never be his. I felt the same, and it made me clasp the back of his neck, bringing him against me once more.

"There might not be a cure." His hoarse whisper was warm on my skin, but it instilled coldness in my heart. And sheer resolve.

"You do not say that. You do not *think* that." I lifted him against me. "You are not going to fucking die, Leon."

Nuzzling his hair, running my hands over his body just to feel his warmth, I barely noticed when the others departed. Filled with aroused torment, I slid him down and stepped back. I was barely holding on by a thread. To fuck him and make him mine once and for all. To lash out and kill something, someone. My hands shook at my sides. "Go wait for me at my place. I won't be long."

My abdomen tightened when Leon brought his hands to my face. He kissed me sweetly, just a brush of lush lips. "You know there's only life or death between us now."

Or love.

I groaned against his lips, tasting mint and scotch. "I need you in my bed."

"*Mais*, you din't want me earlier." Leon stepped away. His chin shot up. Despite his recent, intimate words, he stood defiantly in front of me. It was my fault. I'd spent the past two months denying what we'd both always wanted; each other.

I'd forgotten about his fire, the bright flame that had first surprised me and then enthralled me. I grabbed his arm as he spun away. "Yeah, I did."

He wrenched free. "Just 'cause there's a death warrant hangin' over my head don't mean you have any rights to me." When I advanced, he slammed a palm to my chest. "Pull me one way, push me another." He flicked his hair back, his eyes going from soft and sultry to flat and flinty. "I'll be fine without you."

I wouldn't be. I'd never be fine again if something happened to him. Convincing words failed me as I watched him sweep out into the night. Muscles straining, I barely contained myself from running after him, dragging him home with me. My emotions were at boiling-over point. If I went after him right now, I'd have him bent over and screaming for my cock. Just to own him. To be inside him where nobody and nothing—not the Revolution, not fucking Cutler, not my ghosts—could touch us.

After he left, I waited as long as I could until the rush of rage overwhelmed me. Overturning the table, I roared to the rafters, "NOT HIM!" Tears ran down my cheeks unchecked. "Not Leon, not now. Please. If there's any God at all. Don't. Don't take him too."

I hunched over as pain gripped me from the inside out. "I've already lost everything once…"

It could've been days later when I reined in the dry, racking sobs coursing through my body. It felt like a lifetime had come and gone during the past hour. I looked around the room. The town hall had seen some of the best moments of my life. My handfasting with Tammerick and Wilde. My nomination as the head of the Chitamauga militia. The night Cannon and Nathaniel had promised themselves to each other and Leon had caught my eye. He'd stayed by my side the entire time, talking to me and teasing me until he'd coaxed that first smile from me, and I thought he might be someone worth living for again.

Now the town hall was the scene of one of the most horrific moments I could ever have imagined. I had to leave. Outside, the village was quiet at this late hour. Only the loud blaring crickets sounded as agitated as I felt. The humid July heat hit me and clung to me as I headed down to the forge, figuring it would be empty. Smitty always closed shop early to hit the home brew, and it was well past midnight.

As I entered the barn where he did his ironwork, the smell of hot coal and metal stung my eyes. I made my way to a pallet covered with a ratty blanket, a mirage of all the different sides of Leon swimming around me. Defiant, confused, hurt, protective, playful...sexy as hell. My cock stiffened at the mere thought of his stubborn streak. I shifted on the planks of wood, easing my dick inside my pants.

The pallet creaked and the red haze of the never-ending fire in Smitty's cavern reminded me of the last time I'd been in here with Leon. Before he'd run away from me in the dead of winter to Beta and straight into harm's way. I'd asked him to tattoo me with Tammerick and Wilde's names.

I tore off my shirt and tossed it aside. Stretched on the pallet on my stomach, I felt the heat of the fire beside us blaze across my body. Leon sat back on his heels, sweat forming in the hollow of his throat. He shrugged off his shirt. In the orange and yellow and red light, his skin glowed. Tight pecs, a dusting of caramel-colored hair thinned from his belly button to his pants.

Sweat started to glisten on his chest. His smell was mouthwatering, and I swallowed through the need to suck his damp nipples into my mouth, teasing the tan peaks until he cried out for me. Rocking my hips, I lay my head on my arms.

"Do it. Mark me."

He found his pouch and perched beside me, cleaning the sharp bone awl that would pierce me. A vial of black dye was set beside my head. I arched and hissed when he touched me, not with a tool but with his hand. I had to lift my head and watch him. His paler fingers stroking down the center of my back were pronounced against the deep black of my skin. He swept under the waist of my pants, and my ass clenched hard. My muscles tensed, and I threw my head back, on the brink of coming from one little touch from this gorgeous man who had marked my heart with his spirit as indelibly as he was about to mark my skin.

"Mais, I don't wanna hurt you, Darke." The white shard of his tool quivered above my skin.

"Been hurt through a lifetime; a little tattoo won't kill me." I rolled over and caught his wrists, bringing him across my body. "Do me, my angel, my devil. Make it so I'll never forget my lovers."

Prodding me onto my belly, Leon cursed quietly. I moaned when the bone cut my skin. Leon groaned through every needle tap that pushed ink into my skin.

For Tammerick and Wilde.

Guilt festered, and I burrowed my face deeper into my arms.

He took his time, but the pain didn't affect me. It was his touch that had me on tenterhooks for hours. His breath washed across my shoulders when he leaned close to fill in the lines. My cock was so aching hard I bit into my arm to muffle a moan when his moist lips roamed up my spine with soft kisses, the tools set aside.

No one had touched me like this since they'd died, and now their names were etched into my skin by his hand.

Leon's forehead rested against my neck. His hot tears splashed against the warm blood. "I want my name on you too, cher."

As soon as he cleaned me up, with a kiss to my shoulder, he left. The agony I felt wasn't just of the flesh. It was of the heart. But it didn't stop me from sliding my pants to my thighs and gripping my cock. My hand came away with slick precome, as sticky as the blood that had dripped from my back, the same blood that was on my soul. My shaft throbbed thickly with veins, and my head craned back. Three strong strokes and the sting of the tattoo was all it took. Come splashed my sweaty chest and slid to my groin. It was the first time I'd let myself orgasm since Tam and Wilde had died.

They weren't the ones I thought about when I came.

Ah, Christ! What had I done to Leon? He would have agreed to anything. He'd done everything for me, and I'd made him pour his heart out just so I could have a memento of my dead lovers on my skin? My only reprieve was that he didn't remember any of it.

I growled into the dark room. This was no good. Every place held memories of the two of us when what I really needed was to be with him. Kicking myself into gear, I almost made it to the door when Old Tommy and his mutt shuffled in.

Old Tommy, he was the town crier. Knew just about every-thing about everyone, but he tended to keep it to himself unless he thought he could impart some kind of wisdom. It came as no surprise he and his dog—the shaggy gray mongrel Tommy simply called Gal—were up and about at this otherwise deserted hour, or that he already seemed to know what had gone down earlier.

Instead of laying on the pity, he looked me over with his fierce bushy brows pulled low over his eyes. "Is hidin' in the dark any way for a warrior to behave?"

"I was just heading home."

"Shoot. You ain't goin' nowhere." Taking my spot on the pallet, he motioned Gal to one side of him and me to the other.

I grumbled but took a seat anyway and he started right in.

"Lemme see if I got this straight. Now, remember, Old Tommy here ain't the sharpest tool in the shed." He grinned at me with a mouth missing most of his teeth. Summer teeth he called them.

I fought the urge to tell him to mind his own business, but the nosy old son of a bitch wouldn't pay me any attention anyway.

"So your boy—"

"He's a man."

"I'm happy to hear you say that, the way you coddle him like he's still in a romper one minute, then run from him like he's gonna jump them big bones of yours the next." He plugged a wad of raw tobacco inside his lower gum so his speech slurred even more. "Your young man got taken from you up in Beta and you went off your rocker. And when he came back, he din't remember you."

My jaw clenched when I was hit by everything I didn't want to relive. The crazed worry when I discovered Leon had hightailed it to Beta to join Liz and Farrow. Feeling like my heart was ripped right out of my chest when CEO Cutler abducted him. Leon returned from that slick bastard's clutches, wild and unsure. The way he'd pulled away from me, claiming not to recognize me after the medically induced amnesia the Company scientist had used to wipe the last few months of his memories.

The sheer agony of driving away the man I wanted because I was a damn coward.

"But y'all decided after a fashion there was a good way to play that mind scrub thing of Leon's, yessir. Keep that son of gun at arm's distance 'cause you're too damn scaredy-cat to get close to anyone again." At the mention of cat, the dog's ears perked up, and her long, wet tongue rolled out. "Ain't no cat here, Gal. Jest me and Darke settin' things straight."

"Where's this going, Tommy?"

He spat a line of brown juice onto the rough wooden floor and scrubbed it in with his boot. "See now, I don't rightly know. You were fixin' on lettin' Leon go all this time. In fact, ya never did claim him as yer own. But you ain't cut him loose yet. I know this 'cause I see the way you watch him, and so does ever'one else with eyes in their head."

I exhaled a frustrated expletive. Tommy the goddamn gossipmonger was good for nothing but telling me my fucked-up love life was the talk of the town. "I should probably be on my way. Make sure he's all right."

Locking his wiry hand onto my thigh, he made me stay put. "I reckon you ain't ready to face that demon yet, son. Leon's got that sickness now, and you fell apart as soon as nobody was watchin'. Ain't no good for him if he sees you like that."

"Dammit, Tommy! Have you got the whole fucking commune

wired or something? Yeah, I lost it." I shoved his hand away and jumped to my feet. "He's gonna die. Do you get that, you interfering old busybody?"

He didn't blink in the face of my outburst even though I towered over him, angry, pumped up, more than capable of doing some damage. Gal growled at me but put her head back down on her paws when he petted her. "Cool them heels and sit down. Won't do if Gal takes a bite out of you. We don't need to add rabies to the list of ailments."

Dropping beside him, I rested my head in my hands.

"Do you want that boy to remember you? Because it sure do look like he loved you before and he's fixing to get that way again."

"That doesn't really matter now." My hands curled around my head, but there was no use blocking Tommy out, not when he was hitting me with the bare-knuckled truth.

"Never thought I'd see the great warrior Darke defeated."

I lifted my head and glared at him. "Fuck you, old man. I'm not defeated."

Leaning over to spit again, he wiped his mouth on his sleeve. "And I never thought I'd see you get attached again. After Tam and Wilde. That was some love right there between the three of you. Don't imagine I've ever seen the likes of it before; nor will I again. That don't mean there's not enough room in that big ol' chest of yours for someone like your boy to be given some space. I seem to think he might deserve it, and you're just a stubborn jackass."

"I'm not attached." I clashed my teeth together.

Tommy went right on ignoring me. "Don't know what's happenin', all this love in the air."

"I'm not in love." Seconds later I went from defiant to defeated. "Leon scares the shit out of me."

"*Mm-hmm.* There's some truth right there." His gnarled hand finally let up on my leg and moved to my shoulder. He squeezed and then patted me, like I was his dog. "What're ya gonna do about this plague business?"

"Save him. Fight for him." Steely determination pulled me upright. I'd used Leon's amnesia to guard myself, trying and failing to cut and run before shit got too heavy. Now all bets were off.

"Don't this seem like a damn fool place to spend the night? Me and the old girl are gonna hit the hay." Tommy made a big show of cracking his back and wincing, trying to make me feel sorry for him.

The old coot wasn't getting any sympathy from me. "You're the damn fool."

"Hey, now. My place it right next to Nathaniel and Cannon. Them boys are screamers. I gotta wait until they pass out from fucking before I can get any shut-eye. Oughtta be old enough to be deaf already." He slapped his scrawny thigh and whistled. "C'mon, Gal."

Left alone once more, I stood. I walked to the door and looked out. Up and down the lane, lights were off in the mess hall, the schoolhouse, the trade hall. In the distance, beyond a sentinel of trees, a glow showed from the neighborhood of caravans with their lanterns shining outside.

I squared my shoulders and walked down the road, alone but

resolved. Leon might try to put me off, but I wasn't going anywhere without him by my side. He might not remember what we could've had, but I was gonna make goddamn good and sure he knew we had a future together.

No one was gonna take him from me. Not Cutler, not the Revolution, and certainly not another fucking round of the Plague.

About the Author

A Yankee transplant via the UK and other wild journeys, Rie happily landed in Charleston, South Carolina, with her English artisan husband and their two small daughters—one an aspiring diva, the other a future punk rocker. They've put down roots in the beautiful area, raising children who meld the southern *y'all* with a British accent, claiming it's a comical combination.

After earning her degree in fine arts, Rie promptly gave up paintbrushes and canvas for paper and pen (because she decided being a writer was equally as good an idea as being an artist; of course it was). That was fifteen years ago that her writing career began. With a manuscript of superepic proportions! Safely stored under a lace doily in a filing cabinet. Possibly in England…

Since then she's done this and that, here and there, usually in the nonprofit arena, until she returned to her dream of being a writer. Even though Rie basks in the glorious southern sunshine as often as she can, she's mostly a nocturnal creature adjourning to her writer's atelier (spare bedroom) in search of her next devious plot twist or delicious, passionate tryst.

No matter what genre or gender pairing she's writing, she combines a sexy southern edge with humor and heart—and a taste of darkness. Enjoy!

www.riewarren.com

Twitter: @RieWrites

Facebook: https://www.facebook.com/RieWarrenRomance